STARS and SWIPES

Sophie Gravia is a Scottish author, former nurse, and podcast host known for her humorous and candid novels about modern dating. Her debut novel, *A Glasgow Kiss*, shot straight to number one in the erotic charts and has been a word-of-mouth sensation ever since, leading to a series of bestselling sequels, including *What Happens in Dubai, Meet Me in Milan* and *Hot Girl Summer*. Her books have collectively sold hundreds of thousands of copies, with *The Dicktionary Club* becoming a number one Scottish bestseller. Her success has also led to a collaboration with BBC Studios to adapt *A Glasgow Kiss* into a television series.

ZAFFRE

First published in the UK in 2026 by
ZAFFRE
An imprint of Bonnier Books UK
A Bonnier Books UK Company
5th Floor, HYLO, 105 Bunhill Row,
London, EC1Y 8LZ

A CIP catalogue record for this book is
available from the British Library.

ISBN: 978-1-78512-760-1

Also available as an ebook and an audiobook

1 3 5 7 9 10 8 6 4 2

Typeset by IDSUK (Data Connection) Ltd
Printed and bound in Great Britain by CPI (UK) Ltd, Croydon CR0 4YY

The authorised representative in the EEA is Bonnier Books
UK (Ireland) Limited.
Registered office address: Block B, The Crescent Building, Northwood, Santry,
Dublin 9, D09 C6X8
compliance@bonnierbooks.ie
www.bonnierbooks.co.uk

This book is written for all of the daydreamers who believe that true love really does exist. Keep searching, keep believing and enjoy the adventure.

To Joyce, for introducing my girls and me to the magic of New York. We will never forget you and the incredible things you did for us x

Chapter One

Ella

Three fucking days stood between us and New York. This was a city I'd fantasised about since my teenage years, when I was convinced that one day, I too would strut through Manhattan like Carrie Bradshaw in my designer heels, balancing love, career and friendship with a group of rich, overly moisturised men chasing me around with a classy cocktail in hand. In reality, my teen era was a long way from cosmopolitan chic. I mostly spent it wrapped in a hand-me-down Berghaus, courtesy of my cousin Andrew, clutching a bottle of Merrydown at the graveyard with the local neds, and the only people chasing me were the polis every other weekend. Carrie had couture, and I had cheap cider and a jacket that seriously stank of wet dog and Mayfair. (The cigarettes, not the classy London borough.) But now, finally, twenty years on, my fantasy was becoming a reality.

The Big Apple, the city where dreams come true, wallets go missing and everyone pretends not to notice the rats, was to host our most important meeting yet. Zola, Katy, and I had been summoned to Flirtify's headquarters in Times Square to pitch The Dicktionary Club website to the board of one of America's biggest tech companies. Some people go to New York to find themselves, but we were going to flog a website full of dicks, or rather, the dickish men who were ruining the dating scene. But, with only a few days left until we jetted off, we were stuck, confused and completely distracted.

I sighed again, aimlessly scanning through notes I'd written but I couldn't seem to take anything in; the scent of burnt espresso and the aroma of restless ambition clung to the air around us. My laptop glowed beside the clatter of empty lipstick-stained cups and my thoughts were in a total shambles, my heart pounding with each anxious beat.

'Have you mentioned anything to Philip yet?' Zola asked, slurping her matcha and gazing at me over our Starbucks litter. That was the real secret that pressed against my chest. Not the pitch. Truthfully, I hadn't given the pitch as much focus or attention as I knew it deserved.

'Yeah, Ella, how did he take it? He must have been to New York a thousand times with his work,' Katy added, scrolling through her phone.

'I . . . er . . . I haven't mentioned it to him yet. He's been so busy, it hasn't come up.' I shrugged, knowing my friends could sense my apprehension.

'Jesus Christ, Ella! What the fuck are you waiting for?' Zola blurted.

What was I waiting for? Honestly, I wasn't sure. The only thing The Dicktionary Club had brought into my life up until now was chaos, and, OK, enough money to pack in my job, start up our own PR company, and pay my mortgage for a good few months. But still, I couldn't understand why I felt so anxious about telling Philip about the New York trip, but something had been stopping me. Maybe I was just trying my hardest to enjoy how nice things were between us before I dropped a giant fucking grenade in our path. I wasn't sure how Philip would react. Things had been perfect since he forgave me for creating the alleged man-hating website that had nearly ended our relationship before it properly began – not to mention getting him plastered over a double-page spread in the *Daily Record*, slandering him as a self-centred womanising shagger, all thanks to me. Now that everything was settled between us again, I didn't imagine Philip would be thrilled with me working on something tied to a project that had almost ruined his reputation, his career and our relationship. I couldn't really be blamed for trying to keep the peace for as long as possible, could I?

'I just know how much he hated The Dicktionary Club site to begin with, and I promised him it would never be part of our lives again. I know he disagrees with everything it stands for, and honestly, it doesn't sit well with me either after everything that happened.'

When my words were met with silence, I glanced up from my laptop at the faces of my two friends and saw them trying hard not to smirk.

'Guys, seriously? It's not funny!' I insisted, playfully slapping both their arms. 'I can't believe you're laughing!'

Zola burst into giggles. 'You know, it is a tiny bit funny. We caused so much turmoil.'

Katy finally put down her phone and joined in. 'And drama! I live for the drama!'

I shook my head. 'Exactly, it was awful! And we lost our jobs because of it.'

Zola paused, then let out a deep, evil cackle.

'Zola!' I gasped, but her laughter was infectious and I joined in, still feeling a weight of guilt in my chest.

'Come on, losing that shitty job was the best thing to ever happen to us,' Zola said, 'but let's face it – we need money right now. Finding PR jobs on our own is tough! I have seriously been considering googling the market for farting in jars. But if this meeting goes well, I won't have to! We could make an absolute fortune. Plus, it's New fucking York, Ella!' she squealed.

'Oh my God, I wonder what Tinder's like over there!' Katy's eyes lit up. 'I bet it's full of fit blond guys with rock-hard abs!'

Zola shook her head. 'Somehow, I doubt we'd be invited to pitch The Dicktionary Club if it were. I think the Americans have the same problem as we do . . . The Yanks' dating scene is full of wanks.'

'That's actually a catchy name for the new US website if we have to rebrand,' I added. 'Wanks versus Yanks!'

'Or the Yankee Wank Tank?' Katy suggested.

'Wankee Doodle Dandy,' added Zola.

We laughed together, then went back to looking over our notes, making an effort to take our business seriously.

'How did Curtis take the news about New York?' I asked Zola, knowing things had been rocky with her and her fiancé since she was finger-blasted down Ashton Lane by a Spanish hottie she'd met through The Dicktionary Club.

Zola paused, then shrugged. 'I didn't give him the opportunity to have an opinion. I told him I was going to New York with the girls, and he grunted.'

Katy smiled sarcastically. 'You guys really make relationships seem so worthwhile. I seriously can't wait to meet the one.'

'Oh, come on! There's no such thing!' Zola shook her head. 'But, El, we need you to be fully committed to this. It's a life-changing opportunity, and we fucking deserve this, OK? When we created that website, something told me to copyright it for a reason! And yes, shit went down in our personal lives, but clearly it's more than a good idea if the Americans want to use it! We have to revisit this, give it our all, then really run with the idea. Get your head in the game!' She flicked her long braids. 'Come on, seriously, what happened to that big ball-buster, taking-no-shit-from-any-man-ever Ella? You've changed, girl. Tell Philip you're going to New York and be done with it.'

I sighed, 'I have not! I'm still the same. Maybe I'm just a bit more conscious about not pissing off my man! Look, I am going to tell him, and I'm sure he'll be fine.' I shrugged it off, but inside my stomach churned with dread.

We finished off our emails, and I headed home, Zola's words echoing in my mind. Deep down, I knew she was right, even if I would never admit it out loud. But over the past few months, I had changed. I'd become a softer, more sensitive version of myself. But isn't that what people do when they fall in love?

Philip was caring and kind. And he had a dick more powerful than the Elder Wand. Still, I did find myself prioritising his preferences over my own, sometimes without even realising it. He never seemed to ask me questions about my work or how my business was going, either, yet we'd spend half the day chatting about the vital decisions he has to make in his. Granted, since we started our own company, the PR work had been slow, and most of my days were filled with sprucing up local businesses' social media accounts and charging a one-off flat fee. There wasn't anything exciting going on in my work life compared to the hospitality sector he was taking over. But I did make sure to prioritise him, and his needs. All of a sudden, I was happy to watch football most nights, instead of my usual *Gossip Girl* reruns. And, I mean, just the other day in the supermarket, I automatically picked up an overpriced loaf of shitty sourdough instead of my usual Warburtons toastie loaf because I knew Philip preferred it.

Shit. I walked up the stairwell to my West End flat slowly. My mind raced, as I started to wonder if I had lost myself a little more than I was aware of. If relationships were about making compromises, then surely Philip would understand why I had to try and revisit The Dicktionary Club. *Why did I care so much what he thought?* New York should be the most exciting thing to ever happen to me. I should be singing about it from the rooftops. Fuck, I should be working on this pitch day and night to make sure I nailed it. So why wasn't I? Instead, I was lying in bed at night, wondering how to tell Philip – worrying about his opinion. Would he be angry? Mad? Or would he even dump me? He was the first guy I'd opened up to in years; the thought of not having him, or of starting all over again in my mid-thirties felt like an unbearable gut-crushing ache. Philip loved me, and when I was with him, I really felt the intensity of that love. He would bring me flowers and compliment me a hundred times a day. I didn't feel insecure or worried that he would run off with someone else. He was reassuring, steady and understanding. Maybe I had built this whole thing into some giant problem when it didn't have to be.

I reached the door of my flat and pushed it open, hearing something fall on the other side. Philip's jacket had fallen off the peg. I picked it up and clutched it close to my chest, inhaling his fanny-fluttering scent that I loved so much. Why was I so worried about this? I shook my head and let out a small laugh, making my way over to the sofa and stretching out.

I wanted to go to New York. I'd always dreamed of the sightseeing, the shopping, the incredible people, of tucking into those huge American portions of smoked-salmon bagels and Little Italy pizzas, guilt-free. Not to mention the work side of things – the bustle of the city and walking down sidewalks lined with glorious skyscrapers. As I envisioned it all, I felt butterflies flutter in my stomach for the first time in a long while. This opportunity was huge for us, and Philip was a businessman; he would understand that. It suddenly wasn't just about a life-changing meeting – it was about doing something for myself again, pursuing the kind of career I'd always wanted, and proving I could still be the bold badass I was before Philip Khan. My head had been distracted, focused on how to be the perfect girlfriend, and my career had taken a kick to the side. *But why can't I be both?* I wondered.

I could feel anger simmering inside me – not at him, but at myself for building this into something much bigger than it had to be. I realised all this anxiety and worry was on me – I didn't want to lose him. I thought about Philip, his kind eyes, his warm body and how he also prioritised things for me. How he scheduled date nights in his calendar: he'd drive to Glasgow from meetings in Edinburgh just to see me, then head back. Fuck, the other day he emptied out one of his gym's stock of salted caramel protein powder because he knew I was running low.

Philip was the perfect boyfriend; he'd not even question my trip to New York. Perhaps it was just as Zola said, trauma from The Dicktionary Club launch had made me apprehensive. But we'd come so far since then, fuck, that part of our lives was well and truly in the past.

I felt a tiny glint of optimism spark inside me. Tonight, I'd tell him, and we'd celebrate this opportunity together. What the hell was I so worried about?

Chapter Two

Ella

As I got ready for dinner that evening, I went through the conversation I'd planned with Philip in my head, over and over. He'd ask about my day, and I'd say, '*Well*, actually, it was amazing. We've just had an unbelievable last-minute invite to go to New York! What the fuck!' Then I'd smile incredulously, pretending it hadn't been in the works for months. And after he was done congratulating me, he'd ask what the invite was for, and I'd massively play down The Dicktionary Club part and say it was a tech company thing. Everything would be fine.

I took a deep breath, flicked out the layers of my hair, then slipped on a long silk skirt with a sizeable split up the side and a cropped black top. I added a touch of Mac lipstick and gloss. Sophisticated and sexy – yes.

Just after six, I heard a toot outside and headed down the stairwell. I could see him smiling at me through the window and my nerves settled.

I opened the passenger door and Philip leaned forward and kissed me on the cheek. He looked as fresh and handsome as always – his deep musky scent engulfed me in a second. His toned, tanned arms on the steering wheel – fuck me, he was gorgeous.

'Hi, how are—' I began, but he raised his hand and pointed to the speaker. He mouthed 'Sorry'. Then I realised he was still on a work call. Great.

He chatted aimlessly to one of his bar designers as we drove through the city, occasionally mentioning actual work, but mostly making inside jokes about interior fails. At the same time, I gazed out of the window. It was approaching September, and the autumn leaves were beginning to appear on the trees. We continued through Glasgow's rush-hour traffic, eventually reaching Mini Grill, our favourite spot for steak. But as Philip parked up, he continued his call. I stared out of the window, watching crowds of glammed-up women enter the King's Theatre across the street, ready to enjoy their night. I eventually turned, watching him laugh and crack jokes, not even aware I was death staring him by now.

'OK, mate. I have to go. I have a night of making up to do with Ella. She has listened to far too much of this renovation chat.'

He finally cut off the call and faced me, bringing both his hands to my cheeks and pulling me in for a kiss. I began to laugh as he kissed my lips and moaned, muffling 'I'm sorry' over and over. Eventually, I batted him off me, wiped my Mac 'Locked Kiss' (not as kissproof as the price point would have you believe) off his face, and shook my head. 'Let's go, I'm hungry!'

We headed inside and were seated by the friendly staff at a small table by the window.

'I'm sorry about that, but duty calls! There are big developments with the bar opening in Leith,' he said as he picked up the menu.

'Oh, that's good,' I replied, trying to sound interested. But inside, I felt nervous, wanting to get this New York weight off my chest as soon as possible.

Philip raised a brow. 'Are you OK?'

The waitress approached, smiling widely. 'Mr Khan, what would you like to drink?'

Philip's eyes lit up. 'The house red for you?' he suggested, looking my way. 'Coke for me. I'm driving.'

I shook my head. 'Actually, I'm more in the mood for champagne. We're celebrating!'

'Oh, sure!' the waitress replied and headed back.

'Wow, champagne?' Philip looked surprised, placing his menu down. 'What's going on? Are we getting blotto? I can park up for the night, so we can get a taxi home?'

I started to laugh. 'I thought we could celebrate some work news that I have for a change!' I sat back and smiled, although nerves twisted under my skin.

'Go on . . .' Philip began, then his phone started ringing once more. 'Aghh, shit. I'm sorry.' He hesitated, glancing between the phone and me. 'Duty calls.' My face fell at that stupid fucking catchphrase yet again. He stood up and walked to the restaurant door. I watched him through the glass wall as he giggled and gestured at the other end of the call.

'Champagne?' the waitress announced, returning with two glasses and popping the cork.

I forced a grin, but familiar disappointment settled in.

I gulped down my glass and the waitress refilled it, watching Philip chat and chat on the phone. He'd occasionally glance towards me, then his attention was pulled back to whoever had called. I was halfway through the second glass when he finally came back in.

'Right. Tell me your news?' His dark eyes fixed on me playfully – his way of apologising, no doubt sensing I was annoyed at the continuous interruptions.

'Do you have to take calls when we're out for dinner?' I asked, sitting up a little too straight. 'Surely they can wait until you're home?'

Philip's lips twisted. 'Yes, they probably could, but I like my employees to know they can reach me at any time. It shows I care. Look, I'm sorry!' He stuck out his bottom lip jokingly.

I eventually smiled.

The waitress approached with her notepad. 'What are you guys having then?'

'Could we have the Chateaubriand? Medium-rare? You're good with that, yeah?'

I handed back my menu. 'Sure, thank you.'

'So, come on! No more interruptions. The news. Tell me!' Philip sipped on his Coke, ignoring the flute of champagne.

'Well, I'm going to New York in three days to pitch to a huge tech company with the girls!' I gabbled quickly, taking another gulp from my glass.

There. It was out. It was done.

I watched Philip tilt his head, looking unsure.

'What?' I asked.

'No, nothing. Wow! It's a shock, I suppose. I thought you were focusing on social media? Making business pages more aesthetic? That type of thing.'

Great start. I felt like he had taken a massive dump over my news, squeezing it directly into my champagne flute.

'No,' I said with a laugh that was starting to sound a little forced. 'That's basically all the work we can get at the moment, but I was running major events for massive companies before, remember? So, I have to think bigger than Instagram reels. And now we've been offered this pitch in New York and . . .'

Philip sipped his drink, seeming more convinced. 'What's the company? One I know?'

I felt my breath turn shaky, then cleared my throat. 'Erm, the company is called Flirtify, and they've asked the girls and me to pitch to them.'

Philip smiled, his eyebrows raised in shock. 'Owned by Jimmy Link? Wow. Now that is impressive! Why did they ask you girls? Did you send an application to pitch something specifically?'

I took a swig of champagne and slowly shook my head. 'No, actually, they read an article about The Dicktionary Club and wanted ideas for setting up something similar in the Big Apple. Cool, eh?' I took another gulp, finishing the glass and immediately reaching for a refill, not waiting for the waitress.

I noticed the silence between us and eventually gazed up at Philip, who looked like he had been smacked in the face with an eight-ounce steak by one of the kitchen's beefiest chefs.

'An article about me?' he asked, and I managed a tight smile back. There were so many articles when the shit hit the fan with The Dicktionary Club, but almost all of them did mention his name. 'OK. News really does travel, eh?' He paused briefly, then continued. 'I thought you hated that website, Ella. I thought you hated everything it stands for.' He set his glass down with a small thump that made me jump.

Shit, he's *ragin'*.

'Well, I hated what it did to you, to us, yes. But obviously there's a market for it if these guys are reaching out. It's an amazing opportunity that we need to explore. If we don't, then someone else will.'

Stone-cold silence surrounded us. I began wishing his phone would ring again to help ease the tension.

Eventually, I got the balls to look up from the table and into his eyes. Philip was leaning back in his chair, his dark eyes glazed over, staring straight through me.

'What? Why are you acting so weird? I don't really think this is a big deal.' I started to giggle in a pathetic attempt to restore the mood between us.

'Maybe not for you, Ella. But I don't think you should go and pitch that horrendous club to anyone else. You and your friends went on dates to review and ridicule men purely for your own entertainment. And I was included in that, in case you've forgotten. How do you think it made me feel? And just when I thought we'd moved on from it, you tell me you're taking the idea to one of the biggest cities in the world?' Philip shook his head, disgusted with me.

Before I could muster the courage to say anything else, the waitress appeared with our steak.

'OK, guys, we have the Chateaubriand. Would you like anything else?' she asked, setting our plates down.

'No, thanks,' I answered for both of us, then lifted my cutlery as she disappeared, knowing that not even my steak knife was sharp enough to cut through the tension between us right now. I felt like I had been booted in the stomach. Eating was the last thing I wanted to do.

Eventually, Philip spoke again. 'I'm so surprised you would say yes to this without even consulting me. I feel disappointed, if I'm being one hundred per cent honest. How long have you known about this, Ella?'

My jaw dropped and I felt dizzy – maybe from the champagne, or maybe from adrenaline pulsing through my veins. I didn't know whether to scream, apologise, or cry. Truthfully, I'd known for months that Flirtify wanted us over to pitch, but I hadn't wanted to rock the boat with Philip when it wasn't absolutely set in stone that it would happen.

'You're disappointed? Wow. So, when was the last time you asked me about how my business was going?' My head tilted. 'Hmm? When have you ever actually asked, Philip? Do you know what I'm working on? Or how empty our bank account is?'

He smirked as if I'd swung a low blow. 'If you wanted to talk about it, then I would have assumed you would! But I'd expect you'd at least speak to me before deciding to jet off to New York. And as for continuing The Dicktionary Club, I'm baffled, to be honest. I thought we had moved past that. I thought you had changed, Ella. I guess I was wrong.'

I could feel my hands shaking. I watched him move his food around the plate.

'You know, maybe that's the problem. The past few months have been great, but honestly, the more I think about us, the more I realise how much I've changed to suit you.'

Philip pulled a face, laughing under his breath, immediately disregarding what I was saying. I could feel myself shake with anger. How dare he act like this?

'I used to be this hard-working marketing bitch when we met, but recently I've put all my focus and energy on us as a couple. I need to get back to myself and my career. I have goals and dreams I want to accomplish too.' I said it all so quickly, trying to keep my voice low, but I knew, regardless, we were making a scene.

'What? Oh, come on!' Philip's voice was rough and angry now, and it made me sit back, placing my cutlery down, abandoning my pretence to tackle the steak. 'Don't blame me for this. Don't use me as an excuse because you know you're making the wrong decision.'

I let out a slight laugh, bitter with frustration. 'Wrong decision? What's wrong with it? It's an amazing opportunity to even be asked to pitch to this company. I'm self-employed now, Philip. I don't have a huge fucking empire like you and I definitely can't turn down jobs because my boyfriend doesn't approve of them. But let's face it, I have changed. Admit it.'

I waited for him to say something, but he remained silent.

'I feel like I give and give just to make you happy, but I don't get the same back. You can't go five minutes without picking up your fucking phone when we're together. And even when we stay in and watch the telly, you put on football, football highlights, or a football podcast. I fucking hate football, by the way! When have you ever stuck on *Gossip Girl* or *Emily in Paris* because you know I like it? Eh?' With each word, my anger rose, spilling out into the open in a torrent of confrontation.

Philip's face reddened as if he was about to chemically combust.

'You expect me to watch *Gossip Girl* after a hard day's work?' he questioned.

I shook my head, knowing that who was the boss of the remote wasn't what the argument was about.

'Well, I do it for you. I do things I know make you happy. I come to your openings, I cook your meals for work, which have to be prepped and weighed out and take half the fucking day to sort, I cancel meetings if we have plans, I play fucking tennis so much that I'm basically signed up for a loyalty card with the fucking physio because my knee is constantly throbbing!'

Silence hung between us.

'Look,' I said, calming my voice. 'This opportunity fills me with happiness and excitement, and I would appreciate your support. TV choices aside, you're a great person, and I love our relationship, but I need to do this.'

He rubbed his face in frustration, then sighed.

'I'm sorry you feel that way, Ella. About us. I thought I treated you well. I have set aside so much of my time to make sure I take you on dates a few times a week, I include you in my hobbies with my friends and staff, I pay for all of our meals. I treat you with the greatest respect, Ella. But I can't support you going to New York and pitching something that almost ruined me.'

My chest was thumping. I could hear my pulse rattle in my eardrums.

Philip stood up. The chair screeching across the floorboards made several heads turn.

I pulled a face. Was this self-righteous *cunt* leaving me here?

'I hope you enjoy New York, and best of luck with your pitch.' His dark eyes, usually full of mischief, hardened. He was furious. Suddenly, his phone rang, making us both jump a little.

A laugh fell out of me. I shook my head at him. 'Yeah, yeah. You'd better get that. I know. Duty calls – once more. See you, Philip.' I turned back towards the huge steak in front of me. I could feel him pause briefly behind me, then I heard his footsteps leave the restaurant.

Stunned, I lifted my champagne glass, hand shaking as I brought it to my mouth.

Was this it? Would he come back to apologise? Had I done the right thing?

I pushed my plate away, sick to my core. I felt tears escape my eyelids as I palmed them off to the side, thinking about everything he'd said. He did always include me in his plans, he made a fuss every week about going on nice dates, he was respectful and caring. My stomach churned. Had I just fucked all of this up for nothing?

After thirty minutes of replaying our conversation on a hideous loop, I realised Philip wasn't coming back.

That was one meal I'd have to pay for, I guess.

Chapter Three

Ella

It was the morning of our trip to New York, and I walked into Glasgow airport feeling exhausted and drained. I hadn't spoken to my friends about what had happened, just in case he calmed down, came back and was hit with the prick status forever. However, Philip had been silent since he'd walked out of Mini Grill, and since then I'd experienced a wave of emotions. One minute, I was excited about New York; the next, I wanted to cancel, admit he was right, beg for his forgiveness, explaining that the whole concept was a terrible idea in the first place. I had cried in the bath, eaten shitloads of pizza and jumped at the sound of footsteps in the outside hallway just in case it was him coming to sort this mess out. But it was radio silence – no calls, texts or emails. And as much as I wanted to reach out, I hadn't. After all, he was the one who left me alone in the restaurant with a bill so monumental I'd considered asking for Klarna to pay for it. Still, a couple of days on, I couldn't help but wonder if this was really it.

As I approached the check-in desk, I immediately spotted Zola's colourful braids, now finished with fluorescent pink beads at the bottom. She was standing beside the queue, dressed in low-rise jeans and an oversized denim jacket, exuding her usual trendy energy. Next to her, Katy stood yawning, her sleep mask pushed up onto her forehead and her neck pillow already in place, clearly prepared for a Transatlantic nap in her comfortable grey Adidas tracksuit. I felt a genuine smile form when I saw my friends, and they both began jumping in excitement as I walked over to join them.

'How crazy is this, Ella!' Katy hugged me, making me laugh.

'Yeah, it's wild! Are we organised?' I asked, trying to hype up our New York vibe, despite feeling numb inside.

'Shit, I was ready when we got that email. I can't believe it's actually happening, though. Go check in, girl. We need to talk business!' Zola pointed towards the check-in desk. I nodded and started wheeling my neatly packed case over, handed my passport to the attendant and received my boarding pass before returning to where my friends waited.

After security, we wandered through the duty-free area, where Zola and Katy seemed to try on every pair of overpriced sunglasses, taking selfies happily. Meanwhile, I pretended to browse the shelves of travel-sized toiletries while actually checking my phone nonstop, wondering if Philip would text. A simple *Don't go, Ella* message would be better than this. Even an angry text would be something. I couldn't help but wonder if I'd made this whole situation worse, if I'd massively overreacted with my 'I've changed' patter that I was mouthing off with. Had I pushed away someone I loved because of this opportunity? Would it be worth it? What if we'd got so carried away with a free holiday that I'd lost the first man I cared about in years on a complete whim?

'OK, I can't anymore. Spill,' Zola said as we headed towards the bar.

'And don't say it's nothing, Ella. Your face has been like a smacked arse since we saw you, and you've barely been on the chat in days,' Katy chimed in.

I blinked fast as tears stung my eyes, scrubbing at them before they could fall. Not here, not now.

'Well . . .' Zola held her hands up. 'What's going on?'

'Me and Philip had a massive fight at the Mini Grill about this whole New York thing and how he doesn't support it because of everything that happened with The Dicktionary Club in the past. Basically, he walked out and left me. We haven't spoken since.' Immediately, I watched my friends' faces fall in shock.

'So, he's jealous?' Zola asked.

I shook my head. 'I don't think so.'

'Controlling,' Katy said.

'Honestly, I don't think it's that either,' I sighed. I looked at both of them as we made our way to a booth and slid into the velvety seats. 'I also told him that I had to do this for me, because I haven't felt like myself recently and . . .' I hesitated, glancing down at my hands. 'So, lately, I feel like I've changed. And I don't think he's changed me, but I just keep prioritising everything he wants – watching his shows, going to his events, having dinners only when he's free. Philip is such a great boyfriend, but I've put so much effort into our relationship that I feel like I've let my career slip. So, I told him that.'

'Ouch, I bet he loved that.' Zola bit her lip nervously. I sighed again, acknowledging that she was right.

'So, wait, does that mean you're single now, Ella? For New York?' Katy asked.

I side-eyed my friend. American boaby was the last thing I wanted to think about right now.

Katy stood. 'I'll get drinks. You need something strong, Ells.' She went to the bar.

'I can't believe he just got up and left you in the restaurant like that.' Zola put her arm around me and pulled me in towards her. 'You should have told us before now. We could have helped, you know.'

I smiled at her kind, worried face. 'I didn't want to be a buzz kill. You both were so hyped.'

Zola shook her head.

'He made such a scene in the restaurant, too, walking out with food still on our plates. And I had to pay the bastarding bill!'

Zola's face fell in disbelief.

'Yep. And, we'd had steak and a bottle of champagne! You can imagine the fucking price of those bad boys, Zo!'

Zola giggled, covering her mouth at his audacity. 'The cheek of that man! What did you do?'

I felt my jaw tighten just as Katy rejoined us, balancing a tray of drinks. 'I may have put it on the business account. Sorry, girls!' I admitted, reaching for my glass of prosecco and taking a quick swig. My two friends burst out laughing at this confession.

'Well, Ella, you better do the best pitch of your life tomorrow then, because we fucking need funds,' Zola concluded. 'Badly!'

'OK, guys, I just downloaded American Tinder – oh my God!' Katy scrolled, Zola and I smirking at her expression.

'Whatever happened to the Irish guy? I thought he was still hanging about?' Zola asked.

'Yeah, Sean. He is, but it's casual. He comes over, we shag, then I don't hear from him for weeks.' She shrugged.

'Wait, and you're OK with that?' I asked, knowing my friend had real attachment issues and thrived on male attention, especially post penetration.

'I mean, I'm not going to lie and say I haven't jumped on Rightmove at times and priced houses in Ireland, but at the same time, he kind of annoys me.' Her voice was soft and carefree. In the decade I'd known Katy, I'd never seen her so relaxed about a man she was pumping.

'He annoys you?' Zola nudged me.

'Yeah, in what way?' I probed.

Katy let out a huge sigh and set down her phone. 'Well, when we're having sex, OK? I am giving him sookie after sookie, my jaw practically locked at times. He's always like, "*You* want to kiss *him*, don't you?" in that fucking accent. But now I'm like, no, I actually don't. My mouth is throbbing. I can't be arsed, especially since he doesn't do anything for me. He sticks a finger in if I'm lucky, then we're having your bog standard missionary sex.'

'So selfish,' Zola tutted.

'Yes, so selfish,' Katy replied. 'And at the start I didn't mind, because – well, that voice – but now I think, I'm not sucking *him* without you pleasuring me, pal.'

She sounded so angry that both Zola and I burst out laughing.

'You're quite right, babe. Know your worth!' Zola smiled, her beautiful set of white teeth on display, and I agreed.

'To Katy and her quest for New York dudes who actually put out!' I raised my glass in the air for a cheers, and together we clinked.

We sat in the bar for another hour, chatting and sipping our drinks, before gathering our bags and heading to the gate. When our flight was called, we walked side by side onto the plane, following the line of passengers.

As we boarded, I scanned my boarding pass again and showed it to the flight attendant. She grinned pleasantly and held her hand out to the right.

'Business class is this way, ladies.'

I turned to my friends. Their jaws were on the floor.

'Business class?' Katy bellowed. 'Shut the fuck up!'

Zola nudged her, and together we followed the flight attendant through to the far fancier part of the plane. Leather seats, extra leg room, and menus on tables. I grabbed my friends' arms.

'Get this on our TikTok, Zo!' Katy shouted, but Zola's phone was already out, recording the entire experience.

We reached our assigned seats and sat down, each of us placing our bags either on our laps or under the seats in front of us. I took my seat by the window.

'There's a cocktail menu!' Katy exclaimed.

'And a goodie bag with eye masks and socks and a tiny toothpaste,' Zola said. 'Plus, the seats tip back flat!'

I grinned at their excited faces, settling in for what promised to be a comfortable flight.

'This is insane,' Zola said, grabbing my hand.

I squeezed her fingers for a second then pulled back as I opened my phone again. The screen lit up. Still nothing from Philip – no *Safe flight*, no *Good luck*. My chest tightened at the emptiness, the feeling of abandonment. Zola saw the flicker of disappointment on my face.

'This is going to be amazing, Ella. I've got a feeling our entire lives are about to change here. Don't let some fucking guy you've known for a few months take this opportunity away from you, OK? If Philip is the right man for you, he'll come back; they always do.'

I nodded at her encouragement, and she gently pressed my shoulder before turning to rejoin Katy. They rummaged through the business-class goodie bags left on their seats, exclaiming at the contents.

I gazed out at the slick grey tarmac and let my breath out slowly. Zola was right. We'd got lucky, yes, but I'd also put years of work into this, and now was my moment. Philip's doubts weren't going to decide for me; I wanted to prove to him that The Dicktionary Club could change for the better, too. Squaring my shoulders, I reached into my cabin bag for my laptop. Seven hours. I was about to pour everything I had into this pitch.

Chapter Four

Ella

As the plane touched down at Newark just after 5 p.m., I closed my laptop. I had spent the journey creating and fine-tuning a presentation on The Dicktionary Club and how it would benefit American women by giving them an exclusive app to help safeguard them against the multiple pitfalls of online dating. I'd included how the app could be easily modified to accommodate same-sex relationships. The only thing left to do was debrief and practise the pitch with my two friends, who had spent most of their journey sleeping, binge-watching TV and sampling the cocktail menu.

'I need off this flight,' Zola said, squeezing her hands together in anticipation.

I laughed. 'Me too! Do we have the email with the details about where we're staying? It's somewhere near the Hudson, One Hudson Yards, I'm sure.'

'Aw, who cares! Just get me off this plane and let me explore!' Katy said, adding in her best Italian-American accent, 'I need pizza!'

'OK, ladies. Thank you for travelling with American Airlines. You will be first to disembark the flight today,' a smiling air hostess said, as both my friends stormed past her towards the door.

'Thanks,' I said, laughing. 'First time in New York.' I nudged my head at them as they scrambled to get out the door, and she laughed back.

We headed through passport control, collected our luggage, made two trips to the overcrowded bathrooms and then we were finally ready to leave Newark airport.

'The taxi rank is out this way.' I pointed towards a sign above the busy terminal door.

Zola was already fanning her face as we tried to figure out the airport signposts; the September heat in New York was blazing compared to the drizzly Scottish weather we'd left behind.

'Guys, look!' Katy bellowed. 'It's our names!'

I glanced across to where she was pointing at a tall man in a black suit holding a sign that read: Miss Ella, Miss Zola and Miss Katy.

'Oh my God!' I screeched as we headed over to the driver. 'Hi!'

'Hey, girls. Need a ride to Hudson Yards?' His smooth American accent made my stomach flip in excitement.

'Yes, please! But tell me you have air conditioning in your car?' Zola asked.

'Why of course, ma'am. Let me take your case. I'm Leroy.'

Leroy took hold of Zola's bright leopard-print case and headed out the door. We followed behind him, dodging between the chaos of travellers coming to and from the airport. After a few minutes, he stopped at a sleek black limousine.

'This is us. You girls get settled and I'll sort your bags.'

'Thanks, Leroy,' I replied, opening the car door.

'You're the best!' Katy added, following behind me.

When Zola shut the door, we silent-screamed together in the back of the car. I'd never been in a limo – well, apart from my eighteenth bitch bus, but it wasn't like this. This exuded class, with its mini fridge, dimmed lighting, plush black leather seats and tinted glass windows. I couldn't help but wonder how we'd gotten so lucky to be here, with all our expenses paid in such style.

Finally, Leroy took a seat behind the wheel and turned to us. 'Y'all ready?'

'We were born ready, Leroy!' Katy replied cheesily, making my toes curl, and Leroy set off.

'You always have to take it too far,' Zola teased. 'We were born ready!' She mimicked Katy's voice, and together we laughed hard in the back of the limo.

The journey continued, and as my friends experimented with every electrical device in the car, I rested my head against the window, enjoying the views as we passed through New Jersey's industrial side, with its giant shipping containers and oil tankers. I was working out the time difference back home and wondering what Philip would be up to. It felt strange to have this vast exciting opportunity and not to be able to share it with him.

'Guys, look!' Katy gasped.

The road had curved, and suddenly out of nowhere the skyline appeared. It was like something out of a dream – glass buildings so tall they were disappearing into the clouds. The view grew sharper as we drove towards it, and the girls pointed and squealed at every iconic building they spotted. It felt less like we were approaching a city and more like it was drawing us in. Into the city, the chaos, the hustle, the opportunities. Then darkness swallowed us as we glided through a long tunnel. I clutched my friends' hands as we huddled together, waiting for what was next. And then the light appeared again – and the skyscrapers were everywhere, soaring above us. People hurrying along the streets heading to work, tourists snapping photos of every street sign, lamp post and traffic light.

'Wow,' Zola whispered.

We drove along in awe as the sights of New York surrounded us. I was here, in America, with my two best friends. I felt a surge of emotion – maybe because of the jet lag, maybe because of Philip, or maybe because the energy of New York had immediately stolen my heart.

Leroy eventually pulled over at the front of an apartment block and turned around to us. 'One Hudson Yards. Ladies,' he said with a wink. 'Signed, sealed and delivered.'

My jaw almost scraped the ground. We were at a mountain of glass teetering into the sky.

'Our apartment is here?' I asked. 'In this building?'

Leroy laughed. 'Yes, ma'am. Mr Jimmy owns the building. He likes his guests to travel and live comfortably.'

'Jesus Christ,' Zola snorted, scrambling to get out of the car for a better look.

'Is Mr Jimmy single?' Katy joked under her breath, taking it all in.

'You girls get yourselves to the reception, and I'll have the concierge bring up your bags,' Leroy said, sensing our impatience.

'Thanks, Leroy,' Katy said.

Together, we headed into the apartment block, the doors opening for us as two men dressed in maroon suits stood by.

'Welcome to Hudson Yards,' they greeted us.

'I will *never* get over how cool the accent is,' Zola whispered as we approached the reception desk.

'Zola, Katy and Ella, I'm guessing?' the bubbly young receptionist said, handing us a small envelope. 'You're on the thirty-first floor. Here are your key cards. Someone will be on the desk twenty-four-seven if you need anything.'

'Amazing, thank you,' I replied.

'Your elevator is just on the right,' she added.

I turned to see Zola and Katy bumping into one another as they bolted towards it. I followed, stepping inside and pressing the button for the thirty-first floor. The doors closed over, and we all stared at one another in anticipation. My stomach swooped as the elevator rose, climbing higher and higher. I'd never been in a building with so many floors before.

'How is this happening to us?' I asked, completely at a loss for any other words.

'Because we are badass bitches who deserve it?' Zola tutted.

'Yep, so we better be badass business bitches,' I said. 'I tweaked the pitch on the plane, and revamped the slideshow, so we have to go over everything tonight. Make sure it's perfect for tomorrow.'

The lift pinged and Katy ran out as soon as the doors parted enough to let her through. I was expecting to step out into a corridor of identical doors; instead, our feet met the floor of a huge, immaculate apartment.

'Wait, this lift is literally inside an apartment,' Katy said. 'Does that mean . . .'

'This is our fucking gaff!' I screeched.

Vast walls of white and gold marble filled the space. An open-plan kitchen and living room stretched across the floor, and light flooded in through the floor-to-ceiling windows, showcasing a stunning view of the Hudson River.

'What the fuck!' Zola's jaw was still hanging wide.

'I bags this as my room!' Katy's voice echoed as I followed her happy yelps of delight and found her bouncing on a huge bed. I turned the corner to find two more bedrooms.

'I'll take this one,' I said, smiling as I took in the view of the skyline. Everything seemed so perfect, almost like we were in a film. I took out my phone and snapped a picture, then felt a stabbing pain of sadness, realising I couldn't share this moment with the one person I wanted to. I wondered if Philip had thought about reaching out, if he missed me.

Zola suddenly yelled out. 'I got a walk-in wardrobe, bitches!' she boasted, and we ran in to see.

Flabbergasted and exhausted but ecstatic, we slumped down on the floor of Zola's pristine walk-in wardrobe.

'Should we order in food and load up the PowerPoint for tomorrow?' I suggested.

Zola nodded. 'If we nail this pitch, God knows how many times we'll get to come back to this place.'

Katy's phone pinged from her back pocket and she lifted it out, smiling at the screen.

'You guys don't really need me for prep work, do you?' Her voice was quiet and sweet, as if she was up to something.

'We actually do, babe,' Zola replied. 'Why?'

'Of course we do, Katy. We have a full pitch to get down,' I added. 'It's lock-in time.'

'Because I've kinda got a date. But, I mean, it would only be for a couple of hours. I swear I'll be back and ready to do whatever work you want me to do tonight!'

Katy grinned widely, as Zola pushed her playfully.

'We haven't even got our luggage yet, and you're seriously already thinking about your hole!' I replied, giggling.

'Look, I promise I'll be back by eleven, ten even, but I'll definitely be back with more than enough time to go over everything. Deal?'

Zola looked at me, trying hard not to smirk.

'Ugh, fine!' I moaned. 'But seriously, don't fuck up, Katy. This is such a big deal!'

'Urgh, as if!' She tutted. 'But I can't promise I won't get fucked, because I'm young, free and single! And I'm in New York City, baby!' She lifted her top, flashing us her small, neat tits and jiggling them about till we were laughing and squealing so much we were soon hysterical in Zola's luxurious walk-in wardrobe.

Chapter Five

Katy

Katy left the apartment around eight that night, freshly showered and wearing a strapless navy minidress. Her hair was down, puffier than usual from the heat of the hairdryer and the humidity of the new city. She was meeting Mason for a drink at the Please Don't Tell bar, so she hopped in a classic yellow taxi for the fifteen-minute journey to the East Village to meet him. As the car took her through the streets, she admired the city. She passed by the massive buildings with butterflies raging in her stomach, desperate to explore. Part of her didn't even care about the pitch; she just wanted to spend time in New York with her friends, scoping out the American men and this crazy city they lived in.

As the car pulled up outside a hot dog shop, Katy got out, feeling confused. She took out her phone and texted Mason.

Katy: *I'm at the address, but can't find the bar? Maybe I told the driver wrong? X*

She glanced along the bustling street, squinting her eyes. Fuck, lost in New York was not what she had hoped for.

> **Mason:** *Go down into the Crif Dogs, turn left at the phone booth and dial 1. I promise I'm not luring you to your death x*

She had been messaging Mason for only a day since she'd updated her Tinder location settings to New York. He was American, but was in the city for work tonight, so this was the only chance they had to spend together. Mason was cute and kind, immediately commenting on how pretty and natural she was in her photos. Even if she had Snapchat-filtered the life out of herself, she took the compliment. To Katy, it felt like a movie plot: how they'd meet up once and have a perfect night together, only to go their separate ways, always wondering what could have happened if they weren't ordinarily separated by the Atlantic Ocean. Realistically, deep down, she knew Mason was probably after a quick pump in a hotel room while he was travelling, but who knew? He could be the one. She liked his cute, shy demeanour combined with his endless flow of compliments. He asked lots of questions about her, not like the usual Scottish men who spent half their conversations boasting about how much they could lift at the gym or how big their dick was. Mason seemed respectful and genuinely interested in everything Katy had to say. She liked him, and she hadn't even met him yet.

She turned towards the Crif Dogs hot dog shop and walked down the steps to enter. Slight hesitation clouded over her as she wondered if she was about to be trafficked by a New York street gang and live off hot dogs for the rest of her life. Even if the second part of that option felt slightly appealing, she didn't fancy the first. The shop was busy with a small queue of people waiting for food. She walked a few more steps inside and spotted a large vintage wooden phone booth, just as Mason had described. It looked more like decoration than anything else. Was this a prank? Get the Scottish dafty to enter a phone box, dial a number, so that anyone watching could have a good laugh at her expense? Katy started to feel anxious.

Mason: *Are you there? Dial 1. Excited to see you x*

She took a breath. *Katy, you have one life. Get a grip.* She entered the phone box and dialled '1' on the antique red phone, cautiously glancing around to make sure no one was watching.

Suddenly, one of the walls of the booth opened, revealing a secret passage, inside which a petite, smiling waitress was waiting to greet her.

'Welcome to Please Don't Tell. Come on in,' she said, leading Katy into a chilled-out cocktail bar.

Katy grinned from ear to ear, hearing inexplicably cool jazz music surround her. She took a few more steps inside and allowed her eyes to adjust to the dim lighting. Wow.

'Hey there.' A blond man with dark brown eyes approached her. He was about six foot tall, wearing a white Ralph Lauren shirt, belt and combat-style trousers.

He looked exactly like his Tinder pictures, or even slightly better.

'Hi, Mason,' Katy said, grinning. 'This place is amazing!' She was still taking it all in. The only secret parties she had ever attended were in her teenage years, when she would hide out in gaffs, often ending up in someone's gran's dusty old cupboard, waiting for the police to disappear.

'Wow, your accent is so cute.' Mason held his chest, then leaned in to kiss Katy on the cheek. 'And you!' he said, stepping back, his dark eyes scanning her body. 'You look even better in real life,' he added, with a devilish faux-swoon.

Katy blushed, feeling grateful.

'So do you!' She returned the compliment. 'I can't believe this place is inside a hot dog shop!' She laughed. 'I thought I was about to get trafficked.'

'Trafficked?' Mason beamed, leading her to a cosy booth. 'No, I usually wait till the roofies kick in before I traffic my women. Makes them a lot more cooperative.'

Katy gasped, laughing hard. 'Wow, you're a sicko! I love that!'

'I ordered you a drink. It's minty. I know you like a mojito!' Mason pushed a cold cocktail glass towards Katy and lifted his own bottle of beer.

'How did you know I liked them? And thank you.' She smiled, immediately raising the delicious cocktail to her lips.

'Agh, you got me!' He blushed, taking a sip of his drink. 'Is it bad if I say I've spent most of my day looking at your photographs?'

Katy shook her head. 'Not bad. Slightly creepy, but not bad.'

They shared a laugh, then continued drinking and making small talk for a few more rounds. She found the time slipping away as his easy demeanour and generous personality shone through. There was something about him that made him so captivating. Katy wasn't sure if it was his accent, his confidence or his masculine appearance, but she knew one thing for sure – there weren't men like Mason kicking about the Barras.

'So, where are you from anyway?' Katy asked, enjoying another cocktail from the menu.

'Pennsylvania, born and bred. Have you been?'

'No! This is my first time in America, but I think Pennsylvania looks amazing. It must be cool at Halloween.'

Mason tilted his head. 'Halloween?'

'Do you not get a lot of tourists? With the whole Dracula side of it?'

Mason just about spat his drink across the table, making Katy jump in surprise.

'What?'

Mason was regaining composure. 'Sorry. Wrong continent. You're thinking of Transylvania, but fuck living there – far too spooky!'

Katy blushed, feeling hideously embarrassed.

'Pennsylvania isn't too far from New York, but I only have to commute to HQ once a month, so I don't spend a lot of time here. Have you always lived in Scotland?' Mason asked, still chuckling.

Katy nodded. 'Yeah, Glasgow. Have you ever been?'

'I've been to St Andrews for a golf tournament but didn't get to go to Glasgow.' Mason smiled. 'I loved St Andrews, though. The people and the views – it was a beautiful place.'

Katy agreed, smiling as she remembered the last time she visited St Andrews. She'd been thrown out of the caravan park for pissing against someone's van after a crazy night out with Zola and Ella. No golf was involved.

'And what do you think of New York?' Mason asked, sipping his beer.

'Honestly, I haven't seen it yet. We arrived, went to the apartment, then I got ready to meet you. This is the first place I've come.'

'Oh, you have got to be joking! How long are you visiting?' he asked.

'A few days, well, it depends on how our work goes out here. I don't want to bore you with work chat, but we sort of have an interview tomorrow. We don't really know what to expect, but they said we'd be here for at least a few days.'

Mason paused, deep in thought, biting his lip.

'What? What have I said now?' Katy laughed.

'Fuck it, let's go!' He stood up, lifted his beer, began chugging it down.

Katy stood too, wondering what was going on, giggling with him. 'What! What are we doing?'

Mason shook his head. 'Katy, you have a couple of days in New York, and I'm honoured – truly honoured – that you're spending your first night with me. But, in good faith, I can't let you miss out on the greatest city in the world because of me. So, grab your purse, and let's go sightseeing!'

Katy burst out laughing as Mason threw a pile of notes down on the table and grabbed her hand.

'Come on, I'm serious, baby!' He marched her back out of the bar, through the secret passage and into Lower Manhattan.

The street had turned dark, and flickers of lights surrounded them from the street signs above. Mason stood closer as her giggles subsided.

'You are so beautiful,' he said. 'You deserve to see this city in style.'

Katy's heart pounded as she felt his breath hit her face; she could feel her clit pulse between her legs as they stared at one another. Was he about to hail a taxi to start cruising them through New York?

Suddenly, Mason turned and let out a loud, high-pitched whistle, making Katy flinch and cover her ears. Just like magic, a young man cycling a rickshaw emerged out of the traffic and came zooming towards them.

'After you, please.' Mason gestured for Katy to step onto the tiny vehicle, which had bright, fluffy pink seats and a glittery roof.

'You're serious?'

'Deadly!' He held his hand out for her to step in.

Katy paused and grinned. 'Where are we going?' she asked.

'Central Park, please, buddy. And you can take the scenic route,' Mason instructed the driver, then sat back, pressed tightly against Katy.

'Welcome to New York, Katy,' he said and pressed his soft lips to hers. Their first kiss was just a slow peck, but Katy could feel the passion sizzle between them. The chemistry, the undeniable connection. Mason had captivated every bit of her mind, body and soul, and knowing she would only get to spend this one night with him made it all the more special.

The rickshaw took off, and the two jolted forward in fits of laughter as the driver wove in and out of traffic, scuffing by cars and trucks and the occasional bus, squeezing in between them all. Katy gazed out, mesmerised by the sights. She pointed and gasped as she spotted the Empire State Building glowing in the distance, while at every turn, a new dazzling sight came into view.

'I love watching you take it all in,' Mason said, his dark brown eyes observing every expression on her face.

'I just can't get over this. I mean, I've obviously seen New York in movies, but not like this. I love everything about it,' Katy admitted. 'Thank you,' she added, squeezing his hands in excitement.

'No, thank *you*,' Mason returned. 'You're the bright light I needed tonight.'

Katy tilted her head and they stared at one another, taking in every inch of the other's face. She had just met him, yet there was a sense of comfort and trust between them she rarely felt. It was like she'd known him for years. Then suddenly a loud banging burst out of the rickshaw, as Estelle's 'American Boy' began playing loudly for all of New York to hear. The driver turned, giving the widest grin, while Katy erupted into song, singing at the top of her lungs.

After twenty minutes and a cheesy tourist playlist, they finally reached Central Park. Mason paid the cyclist, and they hopped off. Adrenaline was pulsing through Katy; she was wide-eyed and relishing her night, no sign of jet lag yet. The park was quieter than the bustle of the city streets. A cluster of horse-drawn carriages were parked up on the road, their drivers calling them over to take a ride.

'We're better on foot,' Mason explained as he gently guided Katy by the waist into the park. Small lanterns glowed magnificently, lighting the winding paths, and couples leaned close together on benches, whispering in the night. Ancient trees and dark ponds surrounded by quaint rowing boats sat proudly against the backdrop of skyscrapers and glass towers. Katy took it all in.

'Oh my God! This is where they come in *Home Alone 2!*' she screeched, spotting the exact bridge that the pigeon lady frequented.

Mason laughed hard. 'It is! So many movies have been filmed here. I suppose I take it for granted. I like it best down here.' Mason grabbed hold of Katy's hand, steering her down a set of grand stairs.

At the bottom, he paused and turned to her.

'I can't believe I only get you for one night,' he admitted.

Katy let out a puff of defeat. 'Tell me about it. This is the best date I've ever had! We can keep in touch, though. I mean, Glasgow isn't too far away.' She rolled her eyes.

'Will you be coming back to New York if your meeting goes well?' he asked.

Katy shrugged. 'Honestly, we have no idea. I have my own PR agency with my friends, and we were randomly invited out here because of an article the press back home wrote about us. We don't have any details of what will happen next. It all depends on how tomorrow goes.'

Mason nodded. 'You must be pretty good at your job for the press to do a piece on you.'

Katy blushed, not wanting to go into the details of how they'd created a website to facilitate women getting revenge on men, inspired by the fact that a man had dumped her while he was still inside her.

'And . . . er . . . what about your work?' she asked, keen to swerve the line of questioning.

'Boring. Finance.'

She tilted her head, happy to hear more, but then suddenly realised they were standing under a grand arched underpass.

'Wow,' Katy whispered, hearing her own voice echo back. Beyond that, she could hear the ripple of distant water as she wandered through the ancient tunnel, her fingers tracing the walls in delight.

'This is Bethesda Terrace,' Mason informed her, but his dark eyes remained on Katy. 'The fountain is through here. It's my favourite part of the city, especially at night.'

'We have underpasses in Glasgow, but they stink of piss and have nasty graffiti covering the walls,' she said, laughing. 'I may have contributed to some of them in my younger days, too. But this? This is magical!' She almost jumped towards Mason, wrapping her arms around him tightly.

He picked her up and spun her around. 'We have them too, but I have to admit after "underpass", I have no idea what you just said.'

When Mason put her down, their eyes remained on one another.

'You're unbelievable, Katy,' he breathed, his voice soft and genuine.

Katy grinned. 'So are you, Mason.'

He leaned forward and they began kissing, more passionately this time. Mason pressed her against the beautiful golden wall, skimming his hands up and down her breasts.

'Jesus, Katy,' he panted.

Katy's heart was pounding. She had never felt so sexy, so empowered. She ran her fingers through his hair while wrapping her tongue around his. The kissing became rougher, and Katy took a glance around, finding them entirely alone. She slid her hand down his trousers and felt his dick.

'Fuck,' she said. Knowing there was no way she could resist an eight-incher, she wondered if Zola and Ella would take the huff if she arrived a few hours later than expected. I mean, it wasn't every day you met a man like this. Surely the girls would understand? After all, she was on her holidays.

Katy moved her hand up and down his dick, while Mason kissed and bit her neck.

He was panting as he slid his hand up her dress, tugging her thong to the side and pushing a finger inside her.

'Mmmm . . . I've made you wet,' he whispered.

Katy nodded, feeling goosebumps travel from her neck to her nipples, making them rock hard. 'From the minute I saw you,' she replied.

His eyes had become alive, fire blazing behind them. 'We need to go back to my hotel room, Katy. I have to fuck you – now.' Mason slipped his hand from between her thighs and dragged her back up the marble steps.

'I promised I'd go back to the apartment to prep for this meeting!' She giggled, knowing that nothing was further from her mind.

'Come on!' He grinned as she followed behind. 'I'll get you home safely when we're done.'

For the next ten minutes, the pair walked, kissed and panted as the passion grew between them. Finally, they reached the park entrance, where Mason popped out his hand to flag down a yellow cab.

'The Carlyle,' he said to the driver, then placed his hand on Katy's face. 'I never want this night to end.'

And truthfully, neither did she.

Chapter Six

Ella

It was the morning of the pitch. I woke at 5 a.m., bright-eyed and alert, sunlight streaming through my bedroom window – I'd been too tired to close the blinds the night before. Zola and I had spent the entire evening perfecting our pitch together, munching on pizza and cookies as we cut slides and tinkered with the presentation until well past nine, when jet lag had finally claimed us both. Katy, despite promising otherwise, hadn't reappeared from her date with her American fling. But it was OK – neither Zola nor I had really expected her to. As long as she turned up and wasn't hungover, it would be fine.

I got up and dressed in my gym gear, planning to run along the Hudson before waking the others. Then we'd rehearse one final time, walk Katy through her part and head to our meeting fully prepared. At 10 a.m., we'd strut in there and smash it. I felt calm and in control as I brushed my hair into a neat ponytail, adding a navy bow to complement my lululemon set.

Reluctantly, I glanced at my phone – nothing from Philip.

An ache settled heavy in my chest every time I thought about him. It felt strange not to wake up beside him and not to receive my usual good-morning messages. But I couldn't stop thinking about the way he'd stormed out of the restaurant, the disappointment in his eyes when I'd told him I was coming to New York. Had I taken it too far? Had I gone into full-on defensive mode because I knew he'd be angry? Bringing up ridiculous things like his shitty sports obsession? My eyes began to fill with tears, but I brushed them away immediately. *Not today, Ella. Today is about the pitch, not Philip fucking Khan.*

I took my key card and headed down to the lobby. A doorman stood there.

'Hey there, you're one of the girls on floor thirty-one, right?' His smooth accent and wide grin made me smile.

'That's right. I'm Ella, lovely to meet you,' I said, holding out my hand.

He shook it proudly. 'Call me Otis. I was wondering when you'd come out of your room. Did jet lag beat you three last night?' He laughed, pulling open the door.

'Yes! Well, one of my friends, Katy, went out and she hasn't surfaced yet. She was probably eating dollar pizza slices and telling you all about her man problems at two in the morning last night.' I giggled, picturing how much Katy would love a chatty doorman to vent to.

'No, ma'am, she didn't pass through here last night. I know every person who comes in and out of this building,' Otis replied.

I paused, my hand hovering over my Apple watch.

'You must have missed her. Maybe you were on a break?' I offered.

'No, ma'am. I don't take no break,' he said, tilting his head.

I was just about to ask how he went for a piss when the implication of his words hit me: *What if Katy hadn't come back?*

'I'm sorry, Otis, I have to go back up and check something,' I said, a bolt of panic drumming through me.

'Sure thing, Miss Ella,' he said, still holding the door open as I ran towards the elevator.

It counted upwards slowly while my mind raced. *Where was she? What about the pitch? Was she OK? Had she got drunk and passed out? Got lost? Or worse. Why the hell had I let her go out with a complete stranger?*

The lift pinged open and I bolted towards Katy's bedroom, flinging the door wide open. Her bed was untouched, her suitcase still lying on top of it.

'ZOLA!' I screamed at the top of my lungs. I pulled out my phone and called Katy – no answer. 'Zola!' I screamed again.

Zola staggered out of her bedroom moments later, wearing a black T-shirt and her pink silk bonnet. 'What's up? It's still the middle of the fucking night, El,' she said, her voice cracking with sleep.

'Katy isn't home yet. It's quarter to six, Zo. She's not answering her phone. Have you heard from her?' I texted frantically as I spoke.

'For fuck's sake.' Zola shook her head. 'Why does she do this? She'll be fine. She probably hooked up with some loser and lost track of time.'

My hands shook. 'What about the meeting? She knows how important this is! She wouldn't miss this, Zo. We don't know where she is or who she's with. We don't have his name or anything. What will we do?' Every possible scenario flooded my mind in quick, relentless succession.

'OK, whoa. Calm down.' Zola wrapped her arms around my shoulders. 'We'll pitch just as planned. We know it inside out. Katy will be back by then, and we can tell her to smile and nod, OK? Let's get ready as planned, yeah?'

I nodded, trying Katy again, but the phone just rang out.

'Come on, let's grab a coffee. We've got this,' Zola said with a smile, ushering me through to the living room.

Chapter Seven

Katy

Katy woke to the feel of luxurious cotton sheets against her skin. She sat up, a weight moving in her head.

'Ow,' she moaned, turning to see a naked Mason sound asleep beside her.

She ran her hand up his muscular back, admiring every inch of his skin. They'd been up most of the night, bent into positions she hadn't thought possible. Her mind flashed back to him pounding on top of her, as she scraped her nails into his skin. She traced the pinkish claw marks with her fingers, a small smile crossing her face.

Mason stirred and opened his eyes.

'Mmmm . . .' he murmured, turning his handsome face around to face her. 'Hey, beautiful, you good?'

Katy nodded, suddenly aware of how stark bollock naked she was. 'I am good,' she said, smiling shyly. 'A bit sore, though,' she admitted.

'Sore? Oh no. Down below?' Mason asked, his brows raised with curiosity as he propped himself up on an elbow.

Katy blushed, nodding slightly. She felt as if her fanny had just birthed a hedgehog.

'Yeah, sore head and sore . . .' She wondered what the American translation of fud was.

Mason's eyes widened cheekily as he edged closer. 'Would you like me to kiss it better?'

Katy laughed, knowing she'd love nothing more, but also realising she desperately needed a quick bird bath in the sink first to take away the stink from a serious night of shagging. She kissed Mason's soft lips and stood up.

'Let me nip to the toilet first, then I'm all yours!' she promised, grabbing her bag and shuffling into the pristine bathroom.

She unzipped her clutch and pulled out her phone. Twenty-six missed calls. Her heart sank. She scrolled through streams of messages from Ella and Zola, then checked the time: 09:09.

Oh no.

Fuck.

Oh fucking no.

She bolted back into the bedroom, bumping into the furniture.

'Hey, hey, what's up?' Mason asked.

'Mason, it's ten past nine! I have my meeting. I'm going to be late,' she said, panic rising.

He glanced at his watch. 'Shit, fuck! No! Me too!'

Katy sat down on the bed, her hands shaking almost too much to text the girls back.

Katy: *Guys, I'm sorry. I'm OK, just overslept. Send me the address and I'll meet you there before ten xxx*

Katy: *I'm so so sorry xx*

She stood up, pulled on her tiny boob-tube dress, then made her way back to the bathroom to wash last night's makeup and semen off her face. She glanced at her reflection in disappointment. Fuck. Mason approached from behind.

'Hey, hey, you're gonna be fine, yeah?' His voice was gentle as he noticed how stressed she seemed.

'Look at me, Mason.' Katy sighed. 'I'm going to have to go into this meeting looking like a hooker. I can't get changed; I have no makeup. This is the biggest opportunity of my career and I've blown it.' She felt her shoulders drop. 'I think I'm going to tell Zola and Ella to go without me. They'll make a better impression without me showing up like this.' She looked down at her almost non-existent dress and shook her head.

'Whoa, whoa. That's not true. Stop it. Hey, how about . . .' Mason stepped back into the bedroom and lifted his white Ralph Lauren shirt from the floor. 'What about this?' Coming back to her, he touched her face thoughtfully. 'Wear it, and it'll remind you of me and the amazing night we had.' He shrugged, his eyes playful.

Katy found her face breaking into a soft smile. 'I don't think I could forget last night if I tried,' she replied, gazing into his kind face. 'What will you wear?'

'I have a clean shirt in my case. Besides, you'll look better in that than I ever did.' Mason draped the shirt around her shoulders and winked.

'Thank you.' She grinned, tying the material at the front to make it look more stylish. 'I really do have to go, though.'

'You do, and hey, I know you'll crush it,' he said, flashing her an encouraging smile. 'I've got to rush out too – I'm going to be late for my appointment.'

Katy pressed her forehead against his. 'I don't want to leave and never see you again,' she admitted.

He nodded. 'Let's stay in touch and see what we can manage. Transylvania isn't too far from here, remember?'

Katy laughed.

'Seriously, though, I can't remember the last time I had a night like that,' he said.

She pressed her lips against his. 'Me too.'

Her phone began vibrating against the sink, making her jump.

'OK, I really do have to go,' she said. 'My friends might disown me at this rate.'

'Good luck.' Mason kissed her once more. She pushed past him, grabbed her shoes and bag, then made her way down to the lobby of The Carlyle to catch a cab.

Chapter Eight

Ella

Zola and I were standing outside the Flirtify headquarters on Times Square at nine forty-five, waiting for Katy's arrival. I had never seen anything like this place – from the endless bustle to the lights to the giant advertisements featuring celebrity endorsements, it was all on such a grand scale that it was almost overwhelming. I knew that on any other day I would be taking it all in, but today Katy had well and truly shat all over my New York buzz. I couldn't believe she had stayed out the night before the biggest deal of our lives. But I knew I was prepared; I wasn't going to let her ruin it for us all.

Around ten to ten, a taxi pulled up and Katy staggered out, still in the same clothes from the night before with the added bonus of what looked like a man's shirt tied around her waist. Her face was chalk-white, and her hair looked like it had been brushed with a fucking toffee apple. Great.

'I'm so sorry. Honestly, I'm so, so sorry,' she said, rushing towards us.

'It's fine, but we need to sort you out. Here.' I rummaged through my bag, pulling out my favourite Chanel bronzer and Mac lipstick. I began applying it to her face, trying my hardest to spruce her up a little. Everyone in this city was polished to perfection and my so-called business colleague seemed to have slept under a bridge.

'What about the hair?' Zola asked, touching the ends.

'I'd be careful, Zo. Last night was pretty wild.' Katy side-eyed Zola, who immediately pulled back.

'Lovely,' Zola said, exhaling a deep breath.

'Should I wear the shirt or not? Mason gave it to me,' Katy said proudly.

I was in the zone, too busy concentrating to ask about Mason at all. 'Wear it. It covers you up a bit, makes you look slightly more professional.' I took a step back and shook my head. 'It's the hair.' I pulled out my neat bun, feeling my hair flow down my back, as I passed the bobble and scrunchie to Katy. 'I have a brush in here somewhere.' I dipped my hand into my bag again.

'Thanks, Ella.' She smiled gratefully and brushed her hair firmly as we headed into the grand building.

Flirtify was situated right in the heart of the city. I couldn't help but wonder how much a building like this would cost to rent. After being greeted by the doorman, we joined the security queue, which seemed more rigorous than what you might expect at the White House. Katy was still brushing the crusty tugs from her hair, which was getting bigger and fluffier the more she carried on.

'Guys, I think I'm in love,' she said.

Zola and I shared a glance. I could tell she was struggling not to smirk.

'I had the best fucking night of my life last night!' Katy continued.

'Next here. ID?'

I passed over my passport.

'Look straight to the camera, miss.'

I did as I was told, and an ID badge with my photo was printed. I stood at the other side of the line, watching the storm of people enter the building behind us.

Eventually, Katy and Zola joined me.

'OK, we've to wait at the reception on level four.'

I edged towards the elevator, where we squeezed in. Zola leaned forward to press the button.

'I went to Central Park! And on one of the wee bike rickshaws,' Katy whispered, not managing to keep her excitement in.

I felt my face squirm as she spoke. 'Katy, what's that smell?' I asked quietly.

'Jesus, yip.' Zola covered her nose and mouth. 'It's strong, girl.'

Katy's face reddened. 'Is it me? Is it the . . . you know?'

'You didn't grab a shower?' Zola rolled her eyes dramatically. 'Jeez Louise.'

'I didn't have time! I came straight here, remember!'

'Shh. It's fine, we'll go to the bathroom,' I muttered under my breath, nudging them both, feeling butterflies turning to dread in my stomach. I was trying to go over the pitch in my head, but with Katy's disappearance and reappearance in full-on tramp mode, I seemed to be forgetting all of my major points.

We stepped out of the lift on the fourth floor and headed to the reception, where we introduced ourselves and were shown to the waiting area. I pointed to the bathroom, and the three of us scrambled inside.

'It's not that bad, is it?' Katy panicked, pulling her knickers down at the sink.

'Babe, it smells like BV!' Zola gagged. 'Bacteria in that vag is nasty.'

Katy started splashing water up over the sink and under her dress in panic.

'Fuck. I'm so sorry, guys. Is it away yet? Maybe I should wait here. Let you two pitch?' Katy's eyes were watering and I wasn't sure if it was the realisation of being so underprepared, the hefty hangover she was experiencing, or the smell that had been accumulating between her legs.

'Katy, look, it's fine. You stayed out late, you're safe,' I said. 'Zola and I know the pitch inside out. You can stand there and nod that bushy head of yours, OK?' I said, gently touching her hair, then – remembering what it contained – pulling back.

'Are you sure?'

'Yes! Come on!' Zola pleaded, glancing at her watch. 'It's five past ten now.'

'I'd better fix this.' Katy gasped, looking at her reflection in the mirror and noticing the full glory of her hair.

Zola nodded. 'Yes.'

Katy pulled up her knickers and combed water through her hair, tying it into a small, respectable bun at the back of her head.

'You good?' I asked, hearing my foot tap nervously off the floor.

'Yeah, but I can't wait to tell you all about Mason,' she gushed.

Zola and I burst out laughing as we headed back to the waiting area.

'After the pitch, of course, but honestly, I think American guys might be different! I'm starting to think that maybe I was born on the wrong continent!'

We'd barely sat down when a petite woman in a pinstriped suit appeared.

'Ella, Zola and Katy?' she asked. 'I'm Harper. Mr Link is ready for you now. Follow me.'

I glanced at my two friends and gulped down my saliva. This was it. This was our big chance.

'Oh God!' Katy murmured nervously under her breath.

Zola stood, smiling widely at the woman. 'Just smile and nod, Katy. We have the pitch. We're going to be just fine.'

Chapter Nine

Ella

We followed Harper down a corridor and into a vast conference room. Tall windows opened out onto Times Square, overlooking the endlessly bustling streets. A handsome man sat at the head of the circular oak table, chatting with a pretty young woman with a short, bobbed hairstyle.

'Your ten o'clock, Mr Link,' Harper said, widening the door and allowing us to step inside.

My palms were drenched in sweat, and I could tell by the looks on my friends' faces that they felt the same way I did. Terrified.

Jimmy Link's eyes fell on me as a broad smile appeared on his face. 'Finally, I got you three to America!' He approached us, holding out his hand in a gesture of pure confidence.

'Nice to meet you. I'm Katy,' she said, giving his hand a shake.

'And I'm Zola.'

He turned to me, his head tilting slightly. 'Which means you must be Ella.'

Jimmy Link was not only handsome, he was jaw-droppingly handsome. He looked like he might be Michael B. Jordan's brother, with his smooth dark skin and crystal-white teeth. He held an immediate presence in the room; I could feel his energy and charisma bouncing off the walls.

'Yes, I'm Ella. It's so good to meet you finally in person,' I replied, quickly skimming my sticky palm off my dress before shaking his hand.

'Please, come in. This is my sister, Fee.' He nodded to the young woman beside him. 'Come right on up here.' Jimmy walked back to his seat, ushering us to follow him. 'Sit up here, with us. This damn boardroom is too big. I hate how everyone spreads out.' His informal vibe immediately made me feel more at ease.

'Thank you.' I grinned, pulling out a chair and taking a seat beside Fee and Jimmy, my two friends doing the same.

'So, the floor is all yours, ladies. Why don't you give me and Fee the lowdown on The Dicktionary Club and how it would benefit the American people. I gotta say, when I read that article, I was blown away by the concept. How did it all come about?' Jimmy leaned in, seeming excited already.

My two friends looked at me, and Zola nodded her head for me to begin.

'Well, it actually began because of Katy here.' I giggled, smiling towards my friend. 'She hadn't had the best luck on the dating scene, and the men she was meeting on apps were just awful and getting worse. We thought:

why do we leave reviews for everyday products we buy, for tradespeople and restaurants, but we can't leave reviews for the men we've dated? The good, the bad and the ugly, you know?' I glanced at Fee and saw encouragement and amusement in her brown eyes. 'So, we developed The Dicktionary Club, a women-only website designed to review the men we encountered on apps and leave honest, reliable feedback – pretty much like Trustpilot – so other women can check out who they might be dating and what you should expect. And, naturally, who to avoid like the plague.'

Jimmy and his sister laughed together and nodded, keen to hear more.

'It's genius!' Jimmy said. 'Have you considered turning the website into an app before?'

I glanced at Zola, our IT expert, but she was already focused and ready to begin. 'Yeah, absolutely. I mean, that is the natural next stage, and of course the site is easily transferred with the correct programming skills. Obviously, there are so many apps out there, and we wanted to do it exactly right. We know that if we collaborated with your Flirtify company, Mr Link, creating this type of app would offer unbelievable potential for all of us. We have created a slide deck on everything, if you have time. It runs through all our ideas and the scope, the benefits, the development offer of The Dicktionary Club.' She sounded confident, totally on it, like I knew she would be. Zola was the actual brains behind the business, understanding how to code and program to create the sleekest, most user-friendly and professional-looking product possible. Without her, we could never have pulled off The Dicktionary Club in the first place. We'd still be stuck at the concept stage.

'Hell, yeah, for sure we have time.' Jimmy glanced at Fee, who smiled back.

'I should probably say, my husband, Travis, will be joining us in due course,' she said. 'He's head of finance here, but he's just landed from Florida, and he's stuck in traffic. Don't let him scare you girls off if he enters mid-pitch now.'

We stood up, shuffling our way towards the back of the room. Like magic, a white screen began slowly sliding down the back wall and the blinds tilted shut, allowing our slide deck to take centre stage in the boardroom.

I took a breath, nodded to my two friends, and began the pitch I had rehearsed a million times – going through the importance of websites like this from a personal safety point of view, delving into Clare's Law, and speaking about an equivalent for Americans. I finished up by showcasing some reviews from the website. They laughed at the examples I highlighted, from the excessive wanker to the hat-fisher. At that point, Zola took over and explained in detail how she was able to tap into Tinder and the mainstream dating networks, downloading their pool of clients, which allowed us to create our own search engine for women. Jimmy clapped enthusiastically as we continued the pitch, while Katy did her best to smile and nod just like she was told to.

Zola was finishing off her part of the presentation when the door of the conference room opened. She paused briefly as a tall, immaculately dressed man entered. I felt Katy grip my hand, and I smiled.

'It's fine. It's going well,' I whispered.

'Ahhh, finally my husband returns. Ladies, this is Travis. Travis, the Scottish girls who Jimmy brought over to pitch the new dating app, Ella, Zola and Katy.'

'It's very good to meet you all. I'm Travis Mason.' He paused for a second, and I wasn't sure if he was about to shake our hands or head back out of the room. After a few lingering seconds, he headed up to the back and sat beside his wife.

'How was your trip?' she murmured, straightening out his collar.

Katy whispered, 'Oh my God,' to Zola and me. We nudged her to keep quiet.

'Please, continue,' Jimmy said.

'That was good timing. As we have pretty much wrapped up our Dicktionary Club presentation,' I replied with a smile. 'Thank you so much for your attention.'

The blinds opened again, letting the city light flood in, as the screen rose back into the ceiling.

Jimmy clapped once more, and I felt myself blush at his appreciation for our work.

'Come on back up here. Good work.'

I felt a wave of relief pass through me, knowing at least that part was over, and turned to Katy, who had gone translucent.

'Are you OK?' I spoke through my smile, trying hard not to make it obvious.

'No,' she hissed back.

We all sat back at the table, and Jimmy turned to his sister and brother-in-law. 'Questions?'

'Yes, I have one. You ladies obviously know the Scottish dating scene very well,' Fee began. 'But what experience do you have of American men? How much crossover can we anticipate? I mean, different countries, perhaps different dating cultures . . .'

Katy tutted. 'The same problems, I'm afraid, Fee.'

I laughed, nudging my friend to keep quiet.

'But with respect, how would you know?' Fee questioned. 'If we were to invest in this idea – which I think has significant traction, by the way – we'd be investing millions. We need to do extensive data analysis, to ensure the problems women face in Glasgow are in fact the same on this side of the Atlantic.'

I felt my heart sink. Shit. She was right. We hadn't spent enough time exploring the dating scene in America. I mean, I had watched movies, TV shows, insta reels and seen similar issues, but I didn't have hardcore evidence that the fuck boy epidemic was worldwide.

'I understand,' I agreed, feeling a wave of defeat.

'Oh, it's the same as Glasgow,' Katy piped up. 'If not worse.'

Jesus Christ, what was wrong with her? I wasn't sure if the jet lag had got out of control or if her hangover dehydration was causing some weird psychosis.

Zola laughed in a faux-cheery way, trying her best to cover up for our friend.

'And how is that? Where is the evidence?' Fee questioned.

'I am the evidence!' Katy called out, rising to her feet. 'Me!'

I stared at Zola, who looked as freaked out as I was.

'Hahaha, *sit down*,' Zola warned.

But Katy began pacing. 'Last night I arrived in this gorgeous, mind-blowing city and went on my first Tinder date.' Her voice trembled. If she was about to confess her love for the American guy she met less than twenty-four hours ago, she'd ruin the entire pitch. We were trying to expose the flaws of dating apps, not present a perfect NYC love story.

'Uh-huh?' Fee replied, completely engrossed.

'We went for cocktails, and he decided to take me on a whistlestop tour of New York since I'd only just arrived. One thing led to another . . .'

I edged forward, eyeballing Zola. What the fuck was Katy doing?

'And before I knew it, I was back at his high-end hotel room – taking part in the devil's tango, if you get me, Fee?'

Sitting beside Fee, Travis let out an enormous cough. Jesus, I felt for him. This poor guy must be wondering what the hell he'd walked into.

Zola stood up. 'Babe, come on. Fun as it sounds, these lovely people do not want to hear about your sex life.'

'Devil's tango!' Fee shook her head and for a hot moment I was genuinely afraid we were about to be deported. Then she leaned back in her chair and grinned. 'Oh, girl, we do! Trust me, we seriously live for the drama. What happened next?'

Zola slowly sat back in her chair, covering her face with her hand.

'Well, we did the tangoing, no messing. Nine times, if we're collecting data here.' Katy let out a puff, as if she'd run a marathon. 'And I really had high hopes he could be the one, you know. But as I left the hotel room, I . . . I . . .'

Zola and I exchanged confused looks. Before she'd stepped into this meeting, Katy had been happier than Donald Trump at a Miss Universe beauty pageant with this guy.

'I saw a message pop up on his phone. From . . . from his wife! He was working away and obviously thought he'd dip his dick in a dippy Scottish tourist who didn't know better.' Her eyes were filling with tears.

Jesus H. Christ, give this girl an Oscar, I thought.

'Wow, honey.' Fee let out a low whistle of disbelief. 'You don't deserve a douche like that.'

I agreed as sympathetically as I could.

'So, you see? It's a global problem,' Zola concluded, holding up her hands. 'A default option for sleazes the world over.'

'Jesus, it makes me glad I skipped the apps,' Fee admitted.

'Tell me about it.' Katy's lip was quivering. 'I mean, it toughens a girl up, but no one should have to be so god-damn resilient. It's time, let's face it, for a reckoning—'

'OK, OK, let's break up for a few hours,' Jimmy interjected. 'Travis will review the numbers, then we'll reconvene to discuss. How does meeting back here at two sound?'

I grinned, beyond grateful for an out.

'Perfect for us,' I said, standing up and almost scrambling to the door. 'Thank you all for making us so welcome.'

As we left the conference room, Zola and I turned to Katy, who was now as white as a ghost.

'What the fuck was that?' Zola asked, hissing under her breath. 'We told you to stay quiet!'

I pressed my hand against Katy's forehead, making sure she wasn't about to die on us. No, she wasn't running a fever.

'That was him.' She was zoned out, completely dumbstruck. 'And I've got his Ralph freaking Lauren shirt tied round my waist.'

'What?' Zola probed as the lift hurtled back to the mayhem of a New York lunchtime. 'What are you talking about, gal?'

'That was my date. Last night.' Katy glanced up at us, tears falling down her adorable wee face. 'Fee's husband, Travis Mason. He's the one whose spunk we were brushing out of my hair earlier.'

Chapter Ten

Ella

The three of us found ourselves sitting in Raising Cane's, a fast-food restaurant Katy had demanded we visit based on her TikTok recommendations. Fried chicken and crinkle-cut fries were piled high on the table as Zola and I munched, interrogating Katy.

'So, he didn't actually say he wasn't married, right?' Zola questioned.

'No,' Katy answered quietly. I could see the cogs in her brain in overdrive as she replayed her entire night.

'But he didn't say he was either. He was on a dating app, for fuck's sake, Zo!' I protested. 'He's the one in the wrong here, not you, Katy. He obviously thought he was going to get away with this and didn't expect to be caught.'

'I feel like such a bitch,' Katy mumbled. 'Fee is gorgeous.'

'And so are you, duh?' Zola held up her greasy hands. 'He's clearly a fucking scumbag, but he's got damn fine taste in women.'

'Look, the question isn't who's prettier out of the two of you. That's what men want us to do – they play us women off against one another. Stop with the pick-me dance already, Katy! Look, you slept with a Tinder hook-up, so what? You had no idea he was married. You haven't done anything wrong. But we need to figure out what we do about *him*.' I dipped another fry into a little paper cup of sauce and sat back.

'I am in shock, though. Last night was the best night of my life, I was on such a high.' Katy was trembling, her food untouched.

I pulled her head into my shoulder. 'Come here.'

'He took me to a secret bar. It was so cool – you had to enter through a phone box, and suddenly a wall opened up and there was, like, a hidden passage. I felt like I was in Hogwarts.'

Zola scoffed. 'A secret bar? Seriously. What was its name?'

'Emmm . . . *Please Don't Tell*, I think. Have you heard of it?' Katy asked innocently.

'No, I haven't, babe. But a secret bar, Katy! For fuck's sake, gal. There were signs!' Zola seemed frustrated with our friend for being so gullible once more.

'Hey, not her fault,' I reiterated, pointing a finger in Zola's face. 'So, back to business, before Travis turned up, how do you think the pitch went?' I changed the subject, keen to get Katy out of the hot seat.

'Good.' Zola nodded. 'I could tell they liked us. I suppose it'll come down to working out if the money adds up for them.'

'I didn't realise launching an app like that would be so expensive. Fee mentioned investing millions.' Katy sat back up.

'Yeah, think of the PR they'd have to pull off to keep up with competitors, never mind the development side of things. The dating game is big business!' Zola replied.

'What are you thinking, Katy? How do you want to play this?' I asked when she looked more settled, her hangover hunger finally driving her to dig into some fried chicken.

'I don't know. I don't want to ruin this opportunity for us, but I have to be honest. Fee deserves the truth.' She took a deep, steadying breath. 'No one's husband should be out fingering tourists in Central Park, let alone shagging them senseless in a fancy hotel room.'

I laughed at her bluntness. Finally, she had some anger behind her voice.

'Am I wrong?' Katy challenged.

'No, you're one hundred per cent right. But, if you are honest, we need to be realistic that a working relationship with them would be next to impossible once you spill the tea.' I shrugged.

'This is such a great opportunity for us, Katy,' Zola reminded her.

'I've been majorly fucked over, Zo!' she snapped back.

Both Zola and I agreed that our friend was in an impossible situation. Part of me hoped Katy could just forget the night with Travis had ever happened, so we could take whatever opportunity came with Flirtify, but another part tugged at the injustice. My friend had been played by exactly the type of man we'd created the website to avoid – the kind of man who deserved to deal with the consequences of his actions. The kind of man who belonged in a dicktionary. Mr Travis Mason needed to learn that he couldn't go around hurting women like this.

'OK,' I said after a long silence. 'If you want to tell Fee and clear the air, we've got you. This isn't your fault, Katy, and you shouldn't be penalised for him not being able to keep his dick in his pants. But . . .' I paused. 'If you want my honest opinion, I'm still not sure that I would. I mean, we're skint, Katy, and fuck knows how much a deal like this would mean for us financially. That's if Travis doesn't insist on pulling the deal, of course. And even if we forgot about the money for a second, working with Flirtify would look fucking amazing on our CVs when we're pitching to potential clients back home.'

Katy's face saddened. I knew she felt like she needed revenge, but I wondered if taking the cash and being in constant display around Travis's wife and family would unsettle him enough to constitute her own unconventional form of payback. Plus, I knew I had taken a massive gamble on coming here. I didn't want to return a few days later, even more penniless than before, for this trip to be all for nothing.

'Yeah, I mean, I do see your point, Katy.' Zola huffed. 'But there is no way they will take us on if you reveal what Fee's hubby was up to, so it's one or the other. We will do whatever you think is right, babe.'

'Thank you.' Katy nodded, looking slightly more relieved. 'Just let me have a wee think about it.' She was always the most caring person and I knew she wouldn't be able to live with herself if she kept this a secret. She would never treat anyone the way Travis had treated her, and his wife.

'But if I tell her, I want to do it in style.' Katy preened. 'I need to get out of this dress. I feel like Julia Roberts in *Pretty Woman*.'

I laughed. 'Why don't we go shopping?' I suggested, 'Clear your head?'

'Ooh! Sephora's just around the corner, too. We could get our makeup done?' Zola said, wide-eyed.

'Yes! Come on then! Let's shop.'

I stood up, tugging on Katy's arm. She finally managed a laugh as we made our way towards the shops, planning and plotting how she could confront Travis and spill all the beans on the night's events to his wife.

*

It was ten to two when we walked back into the Flirtify headquarters, bags in hand. Katy had bought coconut-scented face wipes to scrub her noon in a McDonald's bathroom, then changed into a burgundy midi dress with a cool slashed boat neck. She also bought huge new shades after having her makeup done pristinely by a lovely girl at Sephora, with whom she had overshared her whole first-night-in-New-York ordeal in full-on detail. She exuded confidence as she strutted in, looking like an entirely new person, but I knew her well enough to know that, internally, she was in turmoil. Katy didn't do well with rejection and she seemed to really think she and Travis had something.

For the second time that day, we headed through security and handed in our passes.

'Sorry, wait one moment, ma'am.' The security officer held out his arm, blocking Katy from entering the building.

'What? What is it?' She pulled her shades down.

'I have to check something.' He began typing and peered closely at his computer screen.

'This is because of him, isn't it?' Katy snapped. She was talking to Zola and me, but her voice was so loud it echoed across the lobby. 'He's blocked access in case his truth is revealed to the world. I'm not having this, Ella.' Her voice was angry, but I could hear flickers of more vulnerable emotions tremble around the edges of it.

'Calm down, Katy,' I said quietly.

'Look what he's done.' She held her hand up, and I glanced around at the queue forming behind us. 'This is supposedly the home of free speech. He's taking away my First Amendment rights. I have the right to free speech, mister!'

'Jesus, calm down, Martin Luther King Jr.' Zola tittered. 'Is there a problem here, sir? We have a meeting in five minutes. We really do have to get up there.'

The broad security guard huffed, turning his computer screen around. Spread across it was a photograph of Katy taken that morning with huge hair and pale, crusty-looking skin.

'I'm working out if you are who you say you are, ma'am,' he said.

I began to giggle looking at the photo. It really was a shocker. 'She is. She just had a bad . . . well, a terrible hair start to the day. But come on, you can see it's the same person, no?'

The noise in the lobby was increasing as we held up the entrance, as the guard continued to squint between the photograph of Katy and the glamorous version of her standing before him.

'OK, on you go, ma'am. Next time, get that hair under control. Next!'

Katy's jaw was gaping as Zola and I laughed, pushing her towards the lifts.

'What a cheeky cunt!' she practically screeched as she pressed the buttons.

We stepped into the lift and the doors slid closed.

'Babe, no offence but you actually looked like Justin Bieber's mugshot in that picture.' Zola exploded as the lift shot us up to the fourth floor.

The doors popped open to the lobby, and once more we headed to the waiting room. As we neared it, Katy grasped my hand.

'What will I say, Ella? I think I should tell her,' Katy said quietly. The realisation of what she was about to do seemed to overwhelm her.

'What do you want to say?' I replied.

Katy glanced up to the sky, her eyes watering in thought. 'The truth? She deserves to know.'

I smiled, although selfish disappointment weighed down on my shoulders. 'Well, you could tell them who it was last night. But, Katy, it might be kinder pulling Fee to the side.'

She gulped. 'Can you do it for me?'

I shook my head. 'I think something this big needs to come from you, babe. It could end a marriage. We don't know if they have kids . . . or . . .'

Katy paused, looking as if the wind had been knocked straight out of her.

'Hey, guys,' Harper said, appearing in the waiting area to greet us. 'Good to see you again. Follow me.'

She led us back into the conference room, where Jimmy, Fee and Travis were sitting, this time surrounded by a whole load more people.

'Come on in, ladies. Take a seat,' Jimmy began, gesturing to the few empty seats left at the table. My eyes immediately darted to Travis, who seemed twitchy. He avoided eye contact with any of us as we entered. 'I know it's a little busier than this morning, but I wanted you to meet a few people.' Jimmy sounded almost exuberant.

I glanced at Zola, whose face was lighting up. She was smiling widely at the guests.

What the fuck was going on? They must be making us an offer.

I turned to Katy, but her gaze was fixed on Fee and Travis, observing every interaction between the pair. It wasn't much – he had his eyes stuck on a few loose papers, continuing to avoid eye contact at all costs.

When we were seated comfortably, the room fell into silence.

'Let's start with the good news: we loved your pitch. We loved your idea and, most importantly, we loved you!' Jimmy began. 'We thought The Dicktionary Club was such a genuinely unique take on the dating world, and as Katy described, an absolute necessity to protect yourself in this dating culture we find ourselves in nowadays. Whether we're in Glasgow or the Big Apple itself!'

Katy was nodding her head aggressively, agreeing so hard I worried it was about to come off its hinges. I felt my stomach twist, knowing we were about to land a fantastic opportunity, while I wasn't sure when or how Katy would execute the destruction of it all. I felt my breathing become shallow and I sat up, hoping for it to pass.

'We believe The Dicktionary Club is definitely something we could use stateside, and we'd love to make you an offer.' Jimmy winked towards me, and I felt myself blush.

'Thank you!' Zola laughed. 'Amazing!'

'Subject to a few minor clauses . . .'

I felt my stomach fall out of my arse. We could be about to sign up to receive a seriously life-changing amount of cash. I mean, a measly twenty grand could keep the three of us going for a few months. But I felt nervous about the clauses, not knowing what they had in store for us.

'Minor clauses?' Fee grinned widely. 'Pretty major ones, Jimmy!' She tilted her head, almost giggling. 'Look, the most salient point here is that we loved you girls as much as your idea. And buying the rights to The Dicktionary Club – or whatever we decide to call it over here – is a tremendous idea, but ultimately we'd be looking to make you three the face of dating in America!'

I glanced at my friends, whose faces were as shocked as I felt.

'We want the three of you to be our relatable Scottish girlies who have landed over here to rid us of the self-obsessed, entitled assholes who are ruining the dating game.' Fee's voice was full of energy, alive and excited.

'But you will have to live here until the app is ready. We'll sponsor your visas, set you up in an apartment, give you an office at the headquarters and all the time work with you to design an app that we'll push all over the States,' Jimmy added. 'We'll pay for your living expenses – we can go into detail over the finance aspect with Travis, but basically, our offer is for you to stay here for the next eight weeks, working with our developers to make the best goddamn dating app this country has ever seen! And, of course, you will each receive a signing-on fee,' he concluded.

I knew my jaw was hanging open in a so-not-cool way. Unsure if I was dreaming or not, I turned to my equally dumbstruck friends.

'So, what do you say?' Jimmy asked, holding his arms out towards us in a gesture of welcome.

I looked at Zola, who seemed as if she couldn't hold her bubbling excitement together a second longer, then at Katy, who looked as if she had been hit by a yellow cab.

'Please take your time deciding. This is a huge commitment. We know your lives are back home in Glasgow,' Fee said, her voice full of understanding.

I felt a sudden pang in my chest, knowing that there wasn't much left for me in Scotland anymore, not now Philip had pulled a ghostly Houdini.

'I'm in,' Zola said decisively.

'Katy?' I said quietly. 'Is there anything you want to say? Maybe have a chat with anyone in private about the clause?' I raised my brows high and kept them there as she paused.

'No. Thank you for this opportunity. I'm in,' she replied. 'Subject to reading the contract, of course.'

A strange wave of relief ran through me. I knew Katy was passionate about the truth, and I wanted Travis to pay for his shabby behaviour, but we'd worked so hard for this opportunity. We deserved the chance to prove ourselves and take our business to the next level; well, actually, the top fucking level. I didn't want a ridiculous one-night stand of continuous shagging to ruin it for us all.

'Well, I'm in,' I said. 'Once the contracts are checked. But it sounds like an extraordinary opportunity. We'd be honoured to work with you and the Flirtify team!'

There was a cheer in the conference room, followed by a great round of applause.

'Welcome to the family. Come, stand up, I want you to meet everyone.'

Jimmy ushered us round the table as champagne was brought in to toast our deal. One by one, we met app designers, IT specialists, graphic designers, assistants, personal assistants, data analysts and marketing and PR specialists. This company had everything, and we were about to be part of it.

After thirty minutes of introducing us to our new work colleagues, Jimmy led us to the door.

'Come, I'll show you to your office.' He nudged his head, and Katy, Zola and I followed him.

We walked around the open-plan office, which had a great vibe – welcoming, edgy, techy – featuring areas with giant screens, huge shiny plants and beanbag chairs throughout.

'I've put you girls in one of the big offices, next to mine. It means you have room in there for three desks, but if you prefer individual working spaces, we can take care of that, no problem.' Jimmy headed round the corner to a row of glass-boxed offices. 'This is Fee's, and Travis has the corner office, then mine, of course, and the one opposite is yours.'

My eyes widened, trying to take it all in without looking like a totally unsophisticated rookie. We had the biggest on the whole floor, bigger than Jimmy's.

'Wow!' I grinned.

Zola skipped towards the space, with Katy following behind.

'Did you expect this?' Jimmy asked when it was just the two of us.

I shook my head, still admiring the bright modern space right at the heart of New York.

'I think we'll make a wonderful partnership, Ella.' His smile was warm, a little shyer than the hardcore businessman we had seen leading the meeting earlier.

'I do too.'

'Will it be a pain to rearrange life back home and live here for a while?' he asked.

I laughed. 'Absolutely not!'

'So, no one special . . . a husband or a boyfriend you have to break the news to?'

I turned to Jimmy. His eyes were dark, mysterious, almost. I wondered what he was thinking. Was he trying to get to know a new colleague a little more? Or maybe he was being kind? Although this was a fantastic opportunity, it was a lot to ask of someone – to move to the other side of the world.

'No one worth mentioning,' I answered quietly.

There was a moment between us, his eyes scanning my face.

'You have got to see this view, Ella!' Zola called from inside our new office.

'She's right, you know. It's the best view in the house,' Jimmy said. 'I have another meeting to get to, but I'll make sure someone brings your contracts around Hudson Yards tonight,' he said, hands casually resting in the trouser pockets of his expensive suit. 'In the meantime, have a look around, get to know the place.'

'Thank you,' I replied. 'We won't let you down.'

I headed into the office to meet my two friends and when I turned back, Jimmy was gone.

'What the fuck!' Zola was bouncing up and down, too hyped to stand at peace.

I laughed, walking over to the window and admiring the unbelievable view of the Empire State Building and midtown Manhattan spread out around us.

'Look at the desks!' Zola continued. 'And he said we'll have our own assistants if we want. I picked that up, right? Plus, coffees on tap!'

'We have to really read the contracts in depth, maybe get a lawyer to look over it all,' I said, knowing there might be some hidden clause we'd have to be careful of. 'These extras are great, but—'

'Ella, now is the time to be excited. Look at our fucking office!' Zola continued, skipping about like a toddler after too much birthday cake.

'Are you OK with all of this, Katy?' I asked my friend, who was quietly swirling in a plush leather chair.

Eventually, she nodded. 'Yeah. I am.' She paused and looked up. 'Fee seems lovely.'

I couldn't disagree – she seemed genuine and warm-hearted.

'I wish I had the balls to tell her, but I didn't want to upset her. I didn't want all of this to go away either. Does that make me a horrible, selfish person?'

I walked over to Katy, placing my hand on her shoulder. 'No, it makes you human, babe. I don't think I could have told her,' I assured her, honestly.

'I mean, if you're dead set on outing him . . .' Zola trailed off. 'You did meet him on Tinder, right?'

Katy agreed, her face lifting as she caught onto Zola's plan.

'We could always expose him on the app . . .'

I turned to my friends, knowing how toxic that had been for me.

'Guys . . .' I interjected.

'Not straight away. Bide your time. Even do it when we're back in Glasgow. But there are ways and means. Think about it,' Zola continued. 'There would be a certain poetic justice in that man being taken down by the very app his wife's company invested in.'

My heart picked up pace again, knowing I didn't want to relive the chaos The Dicktionary Club had caused in the past.

'I'll think about it.' Katy grinned widely, finally realising she had the upper hand.

'But, until then,' I said, 'please don't go anywhere near Travis Mason!'

Chapter Eleven

Ella

We walked through the streets of Manhattan after leaving Flirtify, having declined a lift from Jimmy's driver so we could soak in New York in all its glory. The streets were alive with tourists and New Yorkers going about their everyday lives. I couldn't believe that was about to be us – three Glaswegian girls calling the Big Apple home for the next couple of months. I felt excited, but agitation swirled about the opportunity; it felt too good to be true and I couldn't wait for the contracts to arrive so I could study them in depth. None of it would feel like it was really happening to us until I saw it in writing.

Zola was chewing on some strawberry laces to keep her energy levels up when we finally spotted our apartment in the distance, while Katy staggered slightly behind. I knew she was rereading old messages from Travis, making sure she hadn't missed any clues indicating a wife or the prospect of infidelity.

'Babe, can you put that away in case you end up calling him by mistake?' Zola tutted, noticing Katy still analysing the texts.

'I'm not a complete idiot, Zo,' she snapped back. 'I'm entitled to read my messages!'

Zola offered me an eyeroll and I simply smirked.

'Have you spoken to Curtis about all of this?' I asked my friend, noticing how quiet she'd been about her own love life, hardly using her phone or mentioning him since we landed.

Zola sighed. 'Nope!'

I bit my lip. This could be awkward. 'How do you think he'll take it?'

Zola paused briefly, then continued chewing. 'Honestly, I don't think he'll be arsed either way. We're not like most couples anymore; we're not together all the time. I do my thing and he does his. I'm not even sure he'll notice that I'm gone.'

Katy had found her second wind and caught up to us. 'But I thought you guys were trying to sort things out after the Spanish guy?'

Zola sighed, no doubt remembering her encounter with the stunningly handsome Alvero. 'So did I, but after a few weeks, it just went back to normal. He stopped looking for jobs or courses, and I started focusing more on work again. We have been together for over a decade now. Maybe it always ends up like this, I don't know. I love him, I mean sort of more like he's my brother or something, but I do love him, and I care about him.'

Katy's confused expression matched my own. 'So, you don't fancy him or have sex?' she asked.

'Ugh! Babe, I've just said he's like my brother. Who wants to shag their brother? Ew!'

I laughed as we headed into our apartment building. A doorman held the door open for us as we traipsed through the lobby, grateful for the cool air conditioning blasting down on us.

'Maybe the spark will come back,' I said, walking to the lift.

Zola shrugged. 'Maybe.'

The lift ejected us into the apartment, and a deluge of bright light shone through the glass as we walked through to the lounge.

'This shit gives me my spark right now,' Zola concluded, mesmerised all over again at the view.

I couldn't disagree. Thirty-one storeys high, looking out to the Hudson River with the sun beaming – this place was unbelievable.

'What are the plans for tonight?' Katy asked, heading to her bedroom, which she had hardly set foot in since arriving.

'Well, the contracts are coming and I'd like to go through them properly. We could grab a bite to eat and head back here. We'll need to go through the plans for the app as well. Think about names and— '

'Ella,' Zola interrupted. 'We are in New York and we've landed a shit-hot, once-in-a-lifetime deal. Let's celebrate!'

I smiled, slightly unnerved. I was so grateful for this incredible opportunity that I didn't want to risk blowing it with a night on the town, and truthfully, after the whole Philip fiasco, I wasn't in the mood to party.

'I mean, I'd be up for a toast, but I was thinking today in that meeting – we don't actually know very much at all about the American dating scene, Zo. And they did kinda call us out on that, so we should take it seriously. Let's spend some time researching it and getting to know the problems the women face here. We need to be prepared.'

Katy giggled suspiciously. 'Well, I have an idea that might kill two birds with one rock or whatever.'

'Stone, but carry on, babe,' Zola said with a laugh.

'Well, the app I've been using keeps sending me notifications about singles nights in the city, and there's a really popular one for twenty-fives to thirty-fives tonight!' Katy looked around at us and grinned; that girl really was irresistible when she wanted to be. 'We can go out, celebrate – and research the single men over here.'

'Fuck, I'm up for that, gal!' Zola clapped with delight.

'You're engaged, Zola!' I huffed back. 'And I'm . . . well . . . fuck knows what my status is.'

'It's only speed-dating strictly for research purposes, babe. C'mon, it'll be fun. We can come back afterwards and read over that precious contract of yours.'

I looked at both my friends and felt my head sink to my chest in defeat. 'Fine!'

Chapter Twelve

Zola

Zola let herself enjoy getting ready that evening, mulling over the day's events as she stood beneath the luxurious spray of her walk-in shower. She picked out a cute baby-pink strappy dress and paired it with white Converse. Her makeup was minimal and her braids sat effortlessly, the pink beads at the ends adding a bright splash of colour. She walked past the other girls' rooms, who were still both getting ready, then flopped down on the couch. Remorse weighed down on her as she replayed in her head the earlier conversation about Curtis. Although she knew it was the truth, she still felt riddled with guilt admitting out loud that their relationship was more platonic than anything else nowadays.

She pulled out her phone to FaceTime Curtis. He answered, then placed the phone on the coffee table. She was staring at the ceiling of their living room.

'S'up?' he said, gunshots in the background echoing down the line.

'Hey, I'm just checking in,' Zola replied, already regretting the call. He seemed so uninterested to hear from her.

'Cool. How is it?' Curtis asked, distracted entirely. She could hear the frantic tapping of the PlayStation handset. Could he not even pause his game for five minutes?

'Curtis, I have news. Can you please stop that fucking game?' she snapped. 'I haven't spoken to you all day.'

He sighed a little at the inconvenience, then picked up the phone. Zola saw his face finally. His beard was growing in, bushier than she liked. He had his hood up, and he was rubbing at his face.

'What's up?' his deep voice asked.

'I had my meeting today,' she began.

'Uh-huh . . .'

'And it went really well.' She smiled happily, feeling proud to share her news. She had been working so hard on software and code before she left, researching the best ways to develop The Dicktionary Club for Flirtify.

'That's good, babe,' he replied, letting out a large yawn. 'Hey, have you seen my gym bag? I can't find it anywhere.'

'No, I haven't, Curtis. Did you listen to anything I just said?'

'Yeah, you got the deal?' he said, like it must have been the easiest thing in the world to do.

'Yeah, and they've asked us to stay out here and work on the new app design. They want me and the girls to be part of it all – the design, the testing, the PR – and they want our faces to launch it all over America.' Zola grinned widely. 'We're just waiting on the contracts getting delivered.'

'Cool. That's cool.'

She wondered if he was in any way interested in a word she'd said, but carried on regardless, keen to share her news. 'This place is so great, Curtis. You have to see the apartment we're living in, the view and—'

'When you home, Zo?' He cut her off, completely indifferent.

'Ehh . . . Well, that I'm not sure about, they were talking like eight weeks or so.' She felt her nerves fill her stomach as she waited for his reaction.

'Eight? And you realise that I'm not moving out there, yeah?' He sounded pissed.

Zola screwed up her face. 'What? I never asked you . . .'

'But that's what you do, Zo! You get this big opportunity and need to move, and I have to pack up and come too. That's what happened before, and look, I'm still sitting in Glasgow and now you're in New York!'

'What are you even talking about? You followed me to Glasgow because you wanted to.'

Curtis sighed, shaking his head. 'I ain't following you to New York. I'm saying that now.'

Zola laughed, confused. 'Do you know, I was wondering what you'd say. I was thinking it would be something muggy, but I hoped that maybe, just maybe, I'd get a "well done for landing the deal, Zola. I'm so proud of you," but obviously not.'

'I can't keep up with your deals and pitches, woman,' he snapped back. 'Every day you're working on something else. How am I meant to know what you need congratulating for?'

'Maybe you can't keep up because you're not fucking interested, Curtis!' she replied, feeling her voice echo through the apartment. 'And for the record, I don't want you to come live out here, and for fuck's sake, if you're so unhappy in Glasgow, then just go home, Curtis. Don't hold the way your life has turned out against me.'

Curtis was shaking his head, slightly off camera. 'Whatever, Zola. I got to run,' he said.

'Seriously?'

'Seriously, I'm busy.' Curtis placed the phone back on the coffee table and the view of the ceiling returned.

'Yeah, keep on building your criminal underworld online, you fucking sad act of a man!'

'Sweet!' he sniggered.

The ceiling disappeared: he'd ended the call.

Zola glared at her phone. Her blood was boiling. How dare he hang up on her? The man lacked class, that was for sure.

'Are we ready to go?' Katy shouted out from her bedroom.

Zola flicked back her braids, suddenly needing to gently dab the tears sneaking out from the sides of her eyes. She stood up, clearing her throat.

'I'm ready when you are, babe!'

Chapter Thirteen

Ella

We headed to Flute Champagne, the bar where Katy had booked our singles night. I honestly couldn't be arsed with speaking to anyone, let alone a man who wanted to test his cheesy chat-up lines on me. However, I was intrigued by the New York dating scene. I was sure there would be similarities to the one in Glasgow, but I also knew there would be some differences. If this app was going to succeed, I had to be aware of all of them.

The Flute was a relatively small bar, so we followed the signs and headed upstairs to the event space. The dim lighting, red velvet sofas and private booths made me feel like I had entered some seedy gentlemen's club. We approached the woman who seemed to be the organiser; she was directing the men to a separate room of the bar and, when she was free, we introduced ourselves. She handed us our name tags and explained that we would each have three minutes with each date, then a bell would ding and we'd get up and move on to the following available table. We'd mark each man using a traffic light system, and if he also gave you a green light, you'd be sent his number at the end of the night.

I glanced at Katy, who seemed genuinely excited about the prospect of meeting multiple single men, then at Zola, who was still a bit zoned out from her call with Curtis. I popped my hand on her shoulder and pulled her in tightly.

'You OK?' I asked. 'We could go home, if you'd prefer? I know the research is vital, but I'm more than up for any excuse to leave.'

She giggled bravely, shaking her head. 'I'm good, babe. I need a distraction.'

Katy squeezed in between us. 'And I need a dick-straction. Today was traumatic!'

'OK, ladies! The men are about to take their seats,' the woman called out, 'and you will be free to mingle. Remember, use your time wisely!'

And then the door opened.

A pack of men who had been held in another room came busting in, aiming for the more secluded booth spots. As soon as they were all sat down, the bell rang.

'Here we go!' Zola mumbled, as we headed towards the available tables.

I sat down opposite a tall, slim man and smiled awkwardly. It felt strange, and I hadn't thought of a script or prepared how I would interrogate the daters.

'Hey . . . Bill.' I pointed to his name badge. 'I'm Ella.'

'Sorry, can you repeat that?' he asked, turning his head to show me his ear.

'I'm Ella,' I said a little slower.

'Once more, please, it's the accent.' Bill smiled, slightly squinting.

I pointed to my badge and mouthed as slowly as I could. 'ELLA.'

'Agh, Ella. Sorry. It's great to meet you.' He chuckled. 'How are things?'

I felt my pulse settle as I took him in. He was handsome in a geeky kinda way, with small, round glasses, but I couldn't help but notice the red woollen jumper he had on, even though it was thirty degrees outside.

'Yeah, I'm good, thanks. How are you?' I watched him scrunch up his face as if I was speaking another language entirely, but he was clearly too polite to ask me to repeat myself yet again. Great fucking start, I thought.

I glanced over to my friends, who seemed lost in conversations at their tables, and I suddenly wished I were back at Hudson Yards with my pyjamas on and top knot in. I hated the idea of dating again, even if tonight was purely for Katy's benefit. I hated putting myself out there. Something inside of me just almost cried at the thought of Philip and how I missed our everyday life. Fuck, right now I'd jump at the chance to be curled up on the sofa watching a Man City game.

'So, how about I start?' Bill jumped in. 'My name is Bill, obviously. I work for a Wall Street trading investment firm, boring data analysis, that sort of thing.' He laughed loudly, snorting a little. I wasn't sure if he was nervous or just plain dorky, but his awkward friendliness made me warm to him.

'My uhh . . . my last relationship was about two years ago.' He pushed his glasses further up on his nose, seeming tense. 'I've intentionally stayed single since then. I put myself right into therapy to work on improving myself and learning how to become a better partner, a better . . . man, I suppose. That accounts for the lapse in my dating life, but now – now I'm ready to go again.' He sipped his water and held his hand out for me to take my turn to speak. I watched a bead of sweat glide down his forehead, and my heart felt heavy in an instant. His honesty was refreshing, admirable even. That admission couldn't have been easy, never mind executing it with a red fucking turtleneck on.

'OK, I'll go slow. I'm Ella. I'm from Scotland.' I grinned, knowing it explained the communication issue. 'I work in PR and marketing, but I'm currently developing an app over here at a tech company. I've been single for . . .'

Fuck, not even a week. That's if I am even single? I wasn't actually sure. Do I admit that I'm in a sort of relationship limbo stage ? I felt my heart beating loudly in my chest. Bill had been so honest with me, but I knew I had no intention of meeting up with anyone after tonight. 'Well . . . for . . . a while, and I suppose I would like to start dating again.' I shrugged innocently. I couldn't be honest. I felt terrible, but I wasn't ready to talk about my Philip ordeal with my best friends, never mind a complete stranger. I wondered if a therapist might be the answer. 'Do you mind me asking, Bill, what was it exactly that you thought you had to change? Like, what behaviour did you have to work through with your therapist? I love how open you are about it. Do you recommend it?' I wondered if he was maybe too quiet or suffered as an overthinker in relationships.

He nodded. 'Not at all. I rave about therapy to everyone! Speaking about it helps, actually.'

Wow. I wondered how Bill and Katy would get along. This was the type of man she needed. He seemed genuine and open, and he was clearly self-aware enough to seek help for his issues. His honesty was charming and he made an effort to engage in our conversation – when I spoke slowly enough. I started to wonder if maybe these New York men were different, better even, than the tracksuit-wearing neds we had back in Glasgow, whose only therapy appointment would be a mandatory background check for their latest court appearance.

'Well, basically, Ella, if I can be honest with you, for a while, I'd fuck anything that moved. White, Black, man, woman. If they had a hole, goddamn it, I'd find it.' He tittered. My jaw dropped open. He almost sounded *proud*. He must have spotted my smile evaporate because he hastily added, 'Hey, all above legal age and all consenting, of course.'

I was still speechless.

He stared at me for a reply, and it took me a few seconds to find my voice. 'What? Wow. I'm sorry. I . . . I didn't expect that.' My mind was racing. How could I get someone so wrong? 'And you don't do that now?' I asked, trying to end our time on something that might resemble a positive note.

'Sorry, Ella, what?' He leaned in.

'You don't do that now? You're, ahem, celibate?' I asked louder, noticing a few heads turning.

'I mean, I can fight my sexual urges now. And if the right woman came along, I believe I could try to abstain. But, momentarily, I'm single.' He looked me in the eye and I found I couldn't look away as he delivered his killer line. 'And if Little Billy wants to mingle, trust me, he does.'

Ping.

Saved by the fucking bell. I stood up and shook Bill's hand.

'Great to meet you, Ella. I'm not supposed to say this, but I'll give you the green light on my card. You can hit me up anytime.' His eyes widened behind his glasses, which were slightly fogged with condensation from the heat and, no doubt, his knitwear.

'Aww, that's so sweet of you. Thanks,' I replied, shuffling my way to the following table. I briefly made eye contact with Zola, trying to warn her that Big Billy was an absolute beast.

'Nice to meet you, I'm Ella,' I said, sliding into a chair opposite a young man with dark hair. My eyes skimmed his badge: Adrian.

'Lovely accent you have, Scottish or Irish?' he said.

'Scottish,' I said, still gobsmacked by Bill and his sex addiction admission.

'I love the Scottish accent.' His voice was smooth and deep. 'I have family over there, not that I've met them or anything.'

'That's nice,' I replied, still settling in.

'So, have you done this before?' Adrian asked. 'Because the last time I came to one of these events, that was when I first met my ex-girlfriend, and I really thought she was the one, so this is bringing up some unresolved trauma for me.'

Oh, here we fucking go, I thought. Not another therapy session. Jesus sweet Christ. Was I doomed to a night of talking to the rejected guests of fucking Jerry Springer?

'In the last few months of our relationship, she would always tell me she was working late and I started to have my suspicions that something was going on . . .'

'God, I'm so sorry!' I tutted in sympathy at his sob story, completely uninterested.

'No, no, there wasn't anything going on, she *was* working. But I started to follow her to and from work, for my own peace of mind,' he said with a self-righteous huff. 'Until she spotted me.'

I sat for the next couple of minutes, hearing all about how his ex-girlfriend brought stalking charges against him, how he was currently fighting for custody of their dog, Hillary, as he believed he could give the pooch a better life than his overtime-addicted ex could.

Ping.

Halle-fuckin'-lujah.

Next, I sat opposite Chad, a head tennis coach who had relocated from Washington, DC to New York. He worked at one of the city's most prestigious sporting clubs, catering to the wealthy so as to give them the competitive backhand edge.

'So, you must have met some really famous people?' I asked, impressed, as he divulged his career.

Chad nodded with the utmost sincerity, like he was breaking some form of confidentiality clause just mentioning it.

'Like who?' I probed. 'Come on, spill.'

His white teeth gleamed as he grinned. 'OK, OK, I've met Beyoncé, Jay-Z, Kanye.' He leaned in and whispered, 'Trump. But I'd better keep that on the downlow. We Americans take our politics very seriously.'

I smiled, observing the handsome, laid-back, athletic man I was chatting with. He seemed completely normal so far.

'Honestly, Ella, I've made it sound way cooler than it is. Most of the time I'm teaching tennis to businessmen who are far too used to everything going their own way so can't understand why I can't turn them into Novak Djokovic on ninety minutes a week.'

'Well, I am impressed. Even if I hate tennis. My ex used to make me play a couple of times a week.' I winced at the memory. 'It killed my knees.'

Chad seemed confused. 'Why didn't you say no?'

I paused, thinking back to that time. Why didn't I say no? I wondered. Why did I always try to accommodate everything Philip liked?

'I'm a pussy!' I shrugged. 'What can I say?'

He blushed slightly, opening his mouth, then stopping himself and shaking his head.

'What?' I asked suspiciously.

'No, it was stupid.' Chad smiled, his icy blue eyes still bright in the dim lighting.

'Tell me!'

He ran a hand through his wavy blond hair. 'I was about to say . . . OK . . . Here goes – if you need help with your ball skills, or a massage for that dodgy knee, then I could always help?' He paused, looking slightly embarrassed, then we both burst out laughing.

'I knew that line wouldn't land – not with you?'

'You would be right,' I admitted.

'Damn!' He shook his head. 'Have I turned you off? I've lost you now, haven't I?' he asked, looking panicked.

'I knew as soon as you sat down, you were different, that you'd be more difficult to hit on.'

I couldn't help but smile. 'To be honest, I broke up with my boyfriend last week and I only came here tonight because my friend Katy has had this crazy bit of guy drama since arriving in New York. She wanted to do this to cheer her up. So, I was never going to give a green light to anyone.'

Chad paused, then leaned in. 'You only got here yesterday? And she's already having man troubles? Which one is she? C'mon, you got to point her out!' He was turning his neck, stretching to see over the booths.

I burst out laughing. 'Stop!'

Ping.

'Oh, no!' Chad replied, hearing the bell. 'This was the first conversation I've had tonight that's not fake or corny.'

I agreed, standing up, before I added, 'You did try and make it a little corny!'

'Yes, yes, I did. And I apologise. I guess this is it then, since you have no intention of matching any of us.'

I shrugged. 'I guess so . . . unless.' I turned back around to face Chad. 'How about I forgive your cheesy chat-up line, and I green light you, but only if you promise to tell me some celebrity secrets?'

'Oh, that is extortion,' Chad called out as I moved to the following table. 'Which means it's definitely a deal!'

I giggled my way to the next table and found myself opposite a grey-haired gentleman named Leo.

'Hi, I'm Ella,' I said, shaking his hand. I wondered if he'd come on the wrong evening, as Katy had said it was a twenties to thirties thing.

'Lovely to meet you, darlin'. I'm Leo.' He was dressed in a cream cowboy-style shirt with a matching hat.

'Oh, are you from Texas?' I asked, noting his southern drawl.

'Yes, ma'am, that's right,' he replied. 'I'm in the oil business, you see, pays real good.' He raised his eyebrows, and I watched his forehead scrunch up. I wasn't quite sure if he wanted me to deliver him some form of standing ovation for having a well-paid career. 'I wind up in New York a fair bit, so I thought I'd mosey on into one of these nights, see what's what.' Leo leaned forward, making me pull back automatically. 'Thought, well, you never know, I might stumble across some pretty little gals lookin' for some company from down south.'

I tried to keep a straight face, but I couldn't help but twist it in utter revulsion.

'Cool! And what age are you, Leo, if you don't mind me asking? I noticed they had different age groups on different nights of the week. They seem to cater for everyone here.'

'I'm sixty-five, miss.' He rested his hands proudly on his substantial stomach.

'Aww, OK, that's good,' I said, wondering if he was going to take my not-so-subtle hint that he didn't meet the criteria for tonight's event.

'Y'see, sugar, I much prefer the younger ladies. These darn knees are in bad shape now.'

Fuck, I know that feeling, I thought. Me and Leo, we have so much in common.

'And I suppose I've realised as time's gone on that I like my women how I like my mares: young, fit, lean . . .'

He winked, or at least that's what I thought it was . . . 'and always ready for riding.'

I wanted to die inside. I honestly felt violated as he gazed across the table at me. I shuffled in my seat. How fucking long was left? Mares? This was a fucking mare all right. I was ready to kill Katy.

'Right. OK. And have you attended one of these events before?' I continued, trying to appear relaxed as I glanced over my shoulder. I wanted to catch Zola's attention, but she was in fits of laughter with Chad.

'Yes, ma'am,' Leo grunted.

'And do you have any luck?' I questioned, wondering who in the world would fall for this piss-poor patter.

Leo grunted again, his stomach bouncing upward at the question. 'I did say I was in the oil business, didn't I?'

His eyes skimmed up and down my body and, very slowly, he licked his lips. I felt a shiver run down my spine. Maybe I should excuse myself to go to the bathroom?

'And let me tell you, darlin', you look like you'd taste as sweet as a fresh Sunday pie. Mmmm . . . Hell, I could eat you right up this second.' He grinned widely, his lips still shining from where he'd licked them.

I glanced behind me, hoping, praying for the bell to ring.

'Oh, my God. OK . . . Thanks. Yeah. So, do you have any questions for me?' I asked, not knowing if I should go along with his blatant misogyny or insult the Texas tycoon. But I had seen enough of *Yellowstone* to realise there was no way I was starting beef with a cowboy.

'No, ma'am. I am a man of few words.'

Could have fooled me; the cunt hadn't stopped talking since I sat down.

'I'm more about big old gestures,' he almost snarled as his crinkly eyes peered down to his groin.

I really didn't want them to, but my eyes automatically followed his and – dear Jesus – his bulge *was* gigantic. Leo had his own Empire State Building poking at the stitching of his cream trousers, striving to get out. Yip, Grandpa had a rip-roaring rager. No wonder his knees had gone, lugging that weapon around.

Ping.

I stood up, eyes still popping as I struggled to shake off the image of the cowboy and the extra-long lasso coiled up in his pants.

Eventually, it was over, and Zola, Katy and I sought refuge in a pizza slice shop opposite the bar to analyse our dates. We sat around a table, giggling over our evening, with a selection of slices scattered across it.

'Well, I greenlit quite a few,' Katy concluded.

Zola and I stared at one another in complete disbelief.

'Katy, *who*? There was one, maybe two max, guys in there that I could secure any form of normal chat with,' Zola said.

'What!' Katy looked shocked, pizza slice halfway to her mouth. 'Well, there was Chad, he was cute, Rory, Bill, Adrian, and Leo was so sweet!'

'Leo! Leo was a dirty old trouser snake pervert! And Adrian was a fucking stalker!' I laughed, wondering if she was joking with us.

'A convicted stalker at that,' Zola added. 'Honestly, I know Curtis is hard work, but at least he's not a certified psycho! I'll give you Chad, though, he was well cute.'

'When do we find out who's matched us?' I asked Katy. I hadn't greenlit any of the sad fuckers, but still, it would be nice to know who liked me.

'Eleven,' Katy announced. 'We'll get a text. But we only get told the ones who have liked us if we've liked them too.'

Zola huffed and sat back in her chair. 'So, that was pointless then.' She also hadn't given anyone the green light.

There was a brief silence between us, then Katy said, 'I was thinking maybe I should text Mason and clear the air.'

'NO!' Zola and I shouted across the table in unison. It was like a reflex. The few other people in the pizza shop turned to us with puzzled looks.

'Katy, no! There is no point,' I said in a quieter voice, leaning across the table towards her.

'But if we're going to be working together . . . I just thought . . .'

Zola grabbed Katy's hand. 'He doesn't deserve a conversation. It will confuse you more. Don't let him mess with your head. It was one night, babe. Let's forget it happened, yeah?'

Katy attempted a smile, but I could see how much she was hurting inside. 'You're right.'

We sat for another twenty minutes, trying our best to cheer Katy up by re-enacting all the speed dates we had just encountered. Eventually, I stood up and pulled my friends from their seats.

'Let's go back to the apartment and look over this contract, eh? I'm exhausted,' I admitted, feeling the effects of jet lag, a new job, a temporarily missing friend and being sexually harassed all evening weighing heavily on me.

'Sure, but I'm staying up until eleven,' Katy warned us. 'I'm waiting to see my matches!'

I nodded slowly, wondering if this girl would ever learn her fucking lesson.

Chapter Fourteen

Ella

We entered the apartment just after nine, and my eyes immediately darted to a large brown envelope sitting on the sofa with a note attached. Curious, I sprinted towards it.

I turned to my friends, grasping the envelope high in the air. 'Our contracts are here, and there's a note!'

Let me know if you have any questions. Jimmy x

'You don't think Jimmy was actually in here, do you?' I asked, suddenly conscious of the leftover pizza and Crumbl Cookie boxes piled up in the kitchen.

Zola smirked. 'You like him, don't you?'

I pulled a face. 'Eh, I do not,' I said, shaking my head wildly as I tore open the envelope.

'I don't blame you if you do. Those fucking eyes,' Zola grunted in a deviant, sexy growl.

'And his shoulders,' Katy added. 'C'mon, you must have noticed his shoulders. They're like swimmers' shoulders. Big hold-on and fuck-me shoulders.'

I burst out laughing. 'I can't say I've noticed, no.' I felt my face warming as they joked around me.

'Hmmm . . .' Zola side-eyed me, watching as I skimmed through the contract. 'So, what's it saying?'

'Blah, blah, blah.' I paused, a number jumping out from all the legalese jargon. 'Oh my God!' I bellowed.

'What?' Katy asked.

I ran my eyes up and down the section detailing our proposed fee again.

'What the fuck!'

'*Ella!*' Zola warned me impatiently.

I looked up at them, my heart thumping. 'We will each receive one hundred thousand dollars just for allowing Flirtify to use our idea.'

My friends gasped, then roared nearly as loudly as I had.

'Shhh!' I warned them, feeling my pulse bounce through my body as I continued reading. 'And we'll earn a salary – five thousand per week that we're here working on it.' I turned to my friends, who were clasping each other now. 'Plus, all our expenses are paid. We'll each have a company credit card for food and drinks.' I laughed like a loon as I read the words, hardly able to take them in.

'Show me the fucking plastic!' Katy cheered. 'We're rich! We're fucking rich, Zo!'

'What's the catch? There must be some sort of catch.' Zola shook her head, not ready to fully believe it yet.

I shrugged. 'I'm not sure there is one. He wants to work with us, for us to create and sell a new way of dating to the American people. We will get paid the day the app launches.' But truthfully, I didn't know what to think. I felt overwhelmed. I was so absurdly grateful for the opportunity, but at the same time, something inside me felt like maybe pushing The Dicktionary Club out to another country was morally wrong. Maybe I was still full of trauma from the last stint with Philip. I had to try to think beyond that. I mean, they were offering us an *insane* amount of money. It could cover a significant portion of my mortgage and allow us to invest in our company and really grow it.

'And what if we can't?' Katy asked.

'Can't?' Zola questioned. 'Can't what?'

'What if we can't sell a new way of dating to the Americans? I mean, we aren't American. We don't know anyone here. What if the app flops?'

I ran my eyes down the contract again.

'Then we go home.' I shrugged. 'With our hundred grand *each*, and they own the rights to The Dicktionary Club for eighteen months. As long as the app launches, then we're paid.'

Zola snatched the contract from my hands and started to read it over herself. Katy and I waited anxiously for her take. Eventually, she looked up.

'It has to be ready to launch for the night before Thanksgiving. That's tight, but we have a team of really good people in that company.' She paused, letting it all sink in. 'I guess we have nothing to lose.'

But an ache pressed on my stomach, knowing I'd probably already lost Philip because of this deal. Even if I could go home now and try to fix it, maybe there would be a slight chance we would be salvageable, but

I'd be in New York for eight weeks! That's a long ass time to be away from my boyfriend. As I glanced at Zola, quietly taking it all in, I wondered if she felt the same way about Curtis.

*

That night, after washing and drying my hair, I settled into the king-sized bed in my room, my head bouncing with ideas. How would the Americans take to an app criticising their dates? It was the land of the free, but if you so much as farted in the direction of the wrong person in this country, they could file a lawsuit. How would the legal side work? Who could I ask about that? And what would I wear going into the office? What was Philip doing? Was he missing me or was he glad of the peace?

Then, just as my head was going into overdrive, my phone pinged from the bedside table.

> *Hey, Ella, I brought over the contracts today, but you gals were out. Hope everything is satisfactory. I will be available tomorrow morning if you need to review anything. I have arranged a car to pick you up at 9:40 a.m. to take you all to the office. Sleep tight, J*

J? It must be Jimmy. I suddenly felt a surge of warmth flood over me, causing me to kick the covers off. Should I reply? *Sleep tight* seemed very informal, intimate even. Was he flirting? Was this just how Americans were? I felt knots gather in my stomach. I clicked off WhatsApp and googled Jimmy Link. Before I knew it, I'd read three articles on his wealth and how he'd risen from poverty to riches. Then I searched for images – most seemed to be of him strutting on the red carpet at award shows, along with some media photos from charity events. I was halfway through the Getty haul when I spotted photos of him sunning himself on a yacht in Cannes and gasped. Katy was right. Those shoulders. His chiselled chest looked like he'd been PTed by Terry Crews.

I was suddenly aware of a throbbing pulse between my legs. I put my phone down, reached over and turned off the night light, then slid deep beneath the covers to sleep. That was enough for one night. I couldn't start looking at our *investor* like that. I tossed and turned, trying hard to get the image of those wet, shiny abs out of my head. But it was no use. I sat back up, glancing at my phone screen again, then slipped my fingers down inside my PJ shorts. I kept my eyes glued to my phone, to Jimmy. Then I slowly began circling my clit, feeling every sensitive touch and panting gently into the night air. I stopped. *What was I doing?* I felt shame and guilt creep up on me, then took my phone and shuffled through pictures of Philip. Eventually, I relaxed back into bed, a soft smile on my face, focusing on his eyes, his lips, remembering what it was like to have them kiss me. He was perfect, gorgeous. I wanted his hand to be touching me, Philip's, to be squeezing my breasts and strumming my clit. I fantasised about him coming to me in my new office when no one was around, stripping me slowly, bending me over the desk, telling me how sorry he was about our fight, until I climaxed, hard and wet. My legs were shaking as I pulled my hand out.

Immediately, I locked my phone and placed it down. What the hell was that? I turned over in bed, squeezing my eyes tightly shut. Fucking hell. I was so incredibly horny, I must be ovulating; or maybe I was just spending too much time with Katy?

I took a long, deep breath, feeling sleepy now that I'd come. OK, I thought. Jimmy Link and Philip Khan's abs, shoulders, dicks were now well and truly out of my system. *Let's refocus on work, Ella*, I told myself. After all, I had a nation to conquer.

Chapter Fifteen

Ella

The next day, I got up and went for an early morning run along the Hudson. It was a gorgeous, sunny New York day, with light bouncing off the water and other runners out in their own sweat-drenched, heart-pumping worlds. I felt full of optimism, eager for our first day in the office. I returned to our apartment building just after eight, did some stretches outside, reluctant for this magical part of the day to end, then, as I walked to the elevator, I heard someone clear their throat behind me. I turned to see Travis Mason standing there in his suit, looking almost as stunned as me.

'Good morning,' he said, slightly lowering his head.

'Morning,' I returned. 'Are you OK? Do you live here too?'

Travis held up his hands. 'No, no, don't worry. I um . . . I was hoping to catch up with your friend Katy, before . . . uh . . .'

'Got it,' I replied, stepping into the lift.

'Should I . . .' Travis hovered, clearly not knowing what to do. God, he was not smooth at all, I thought.

How was this man managing to run his very own fuck boy empire?

'Yeah, well, I think you're probably best catching up with Katy inside the apartment rather than in the lobby for everyone to hear, don't you?'

'Yeah, absolutely.' Travis stepped in beside me, and the doors closed.

We remained silent as the lift propelled us to the thirty-first floor. I wondered what he would say. I hoped Katy had at least started to get ready. I didn't want her all bed head and barking breath as he turned up doing a passable impression of Christian 'Fifty Shades' Grey.

When the lift stopped, Travis allowed me to step out first.

'You should wait here,' I said, forcing half a smile towards him while practically skipping to Katy's bedroom.

As I opened the door, nowhere near as cautiously as I should have, I was confronted by the sight of her as naked as the day she was born, mouth wide open. I readjusted my eyes, noticing the number of limbs on display. Oh fuck no. Lying entangled with her was Bill, the geeky shagger from speed dating. Proud owner of Little Billy, who I really didn't need an eyeful of. *You have got to be kidding me!*

'Is it the morning?' Katy croaked, her voice muffled.

'Katy! Get the hell up!' I hissed, trying not to wake her date.

'Sorry, have I slept in?' She yawned, attempting to sit up.

'Katy.' I crouched down to her face, nerves filling my stomach. 'Travis Mason is in the fucking living room, and he wants to talk to you!'

Katy's eyes pinged wide open. She turned to Billy Big Balls beside her, looking horrified. 'No, no, Ella. No! What if he sees . . .'

'Ssshh!' I warned. 'You have to go out and see what he wants. I'll make sure Banjo Bill stays here,' I whispered.

'Ella, look at me!' Her hair had yet again quadrupled in size from the humidity, not to mention the ball sports she was obviously participating in last night. The girl really needed a gallon or two of Frizz Ease out here.

'You're fine. Shove on a dressing gown and brush your teeth!' I said, but I was panicked, having no real idea how to handle the situation.

'Katy! Can we talk?' a deep manly voice called out from the hallway. Katy and I froze. Bill began rustling amid the covers.

'Go, go!' I pointed to the door. 'You don't want him walking in on this!'

Katy stumbled to her feet, hauling a leopard print silky dressing gown from her case, before heading into the lounge.

I tiptoed behind her, closing her bedroom door quietly and standing guard to make sure the Billy Boy cunt didn't try and leave.

'What's going on?' Zola appeared at my side with a towel wrapped around her. 'I heard voices.'

I nudged my head towards the living room and whispered, 'Travis Mason has turned up to speak to Katy!'

She gasped, covering her mouth.

'And look who's lying in her bed.' I opened the door a smidge, letting Zola witness Bill out cold with his little tadger on full display.

'Girl, I know! I heard them at it all night. Didn't you? She was like Moaning Myrtle in there!'

I blushed, immediately flashing back to my own climax under the sheets. *Why did I do that?* I thought, then dismissed it. *Why shouldn't I?*

Zola nudged me. 'Can you hear anything?' she whispered.

I shook my head, then took a few steps towards the lounge. I peered around the corner and saw Katy sitting on the sofa, looking seriously uncomfortable, fidgeting from side to side, flushed and stressed, with Travis opposite her.

'I didn't mean to hurt you,' he said softly. 'I . . . I . . . never for one minute expected to see you again.'

Katy huffed. 'Well, thanks.' For a second, I wasn't sure if she'd break down and cry – she was always the softer one of us all.

'No, not in that way. I meant you were the last person I expected to see in that boardroom, Katy. Fuck, I assumed you were over here to pitch to a PR firm.'

'And I assumed you didn't have a wife, so it was a bit of a shock for both of us, Travis,' Katy retorted.

Good girl, I thought.

'Yeah. I know,' he hummed. 'I'm sorry.'

'Sorry?' Katy replied, with a confused twang in her voice. 'Sorry, you're married? Or sorry you got caught?' She stood up, then sat back down, looking so fidgety it was almost unbearable to watch her.

Wow, I thought. An unanswerable question. She was killing it, though.

'Honestly, I'm not sure. Things in my marriage are tricky right now, but that's no excuse for dragging you into them.'

Katy stood up again. 'Look, let's not do this. I have to get ready. We can work together without needing to interact. I'm not going to tell anyone your dirty little secret, so if that's why you're here, don't worry.'

He paused, looking sombre.

'OK. If that's what you want.' Travis stood up and headed back towards the elevator. Katy sat back down on the sofa, her body swaying from side to side in agitation.

Just before Travis entered the elevator, he turned to Katy. 'For what it's worth, I had a wonderful evening. The best.' His words echoed through the apartment.

I gasped, covering my mouth, knowing this was the sort of sentimental bullshit Katy fell for. I watched her shoulders drop. *Please don't run to him*, I thought. *Don't fall for his crap*.

'I'll see you around,' he added.

'Yip. See you, Travis.'

Katy remained still. I heard the elevator door open, then close, and I rushed over to her.

'What the fuck was that!' I laughed nervously at the drama. 'I wasn't sure if you were going to run into his arms all over again at one point at the end there.'

'I wanted to . . .' She was quiet, and I watched her eyes fill with tears. 'But I couldn't.' She took in a sharp inhale.

'You couldn't, Katy, not after . . .'

'No, I, like, physically couldn't, Ella. Look.' Katy peered down at the floor, opened her legs and relaxed. There was a slight thud on the floor, and I watched as a small silver object dropped into a pile of fluid.

'What the fuck is that?' I asked Katy, who was crouching a little to examine it.

'A butt plug.' She shrugged. 'Bill shoved it up me last night and I must have fallen asleep with it in. I didn't realise until I sat on the couch there and felt like I had a poker up my arse.' Katy sighed, her eyes staring at the metallic object as the light hit it, casting a colourful rainbow across the room.

'Jesus!' I said, feeling my arse clench at the thought. 'Was it fun? Like enjoyable?'

'Yeah, I suppose.' Katy shrugged again. 'I don't even know,' she sighed, standing to her feet. 'I'm such a mess just now, Ella.' Her bottom lip was trembling, with what I imagined was regret over her mad shagging antics the past few days.

'Katy McIntyre, you are crazy, but never a mess.' I hugged my friend. 'Maybe you needed an intervention, a wake-up call. This is it.'

'I really like him, Ella. We had such a gorgeous time together; it felt different, genuine. I was so embarrassed walking into that meeting yesterday.' She began to sob, covering her face.

I nodded, pulling my friend in for a hug, careful of my foot placement. 'I know.' I allowed a few quiet moments to pass, holding her. 'But right now, we have to get to work and prove to every man who ever hurt us that we are badasses who are capable of anything. We – and that includes Zola and me, by the way – can't keep letting men affect our lives like this. Look at the opportunity we have, Katy. Let's use the anger and the hurt to really show them. I promise you that we are going to let Travis Mason know he's messed with the wrong girl, OK?'

Katy sighed. I could feel her pulse race against my skin.

'First, can you help me get rid of the speed dater?' she asked. 'Butt Plug Billy has to go.'

I laughed. 'Yes! Gladly!'

'And Ella?'

'Hmm?' I replied, still patting my friend's back.

'What about this? Do I give it back to him?' Katy asked. 'I'm unsure about the single-to-multiple-use policy on a butt plug.'

'Zola!' I called out.

'Yeah!' she shouted back, still guarding Katy's bedroom like a rottweiler.

'Before we totally bottom out here, we need your expert opinion on something!'

Chapter Sixteen

Ella

Later that morning, we sat around the boardroom signing contracts with Flirtify's legal department. A wave of pride radiated from the three of us. Here we were in New York City, about to earn a life-changing amount of money from an offbeat idea we had concocted together. It felt bizarre, extraordinary, incredible.

I couldn't help wanting to reach out to Philip, to tell him. I wanted him to be proud of the businesswoman I was becoming. I wanted to share with him my cheesy photo signing the contract. But I still hadn't heard a thing since he left me, and I was too stubborn to make the first move, even if deep down I missed him. Though I couldn't specifically say *why*. I didn't know if I missed having someone around most days – someone to message and talk to, someone who paid me compliments and made me feel good. In reality, maybe I just missed someone who ate me alive most nights like Hannibal Lecter, someone who knew exactly how to please me. Or perhaps it was a combination of everything.

After the legalities were settled, Katy, Zola and I headed to our office. There we found a small group of people hovering around the door.

'Hey,' I said, smiling at them.

A few raised their heads in acknowledgement. Then I heard a loud voice behind us.

'Good morning! Did y'all sleep well?' Jimmy asked as he swept over to us.

I felt myself blush immediately, remembering how the orgasm I had to his face and abs had me out like a light.

'Yes, we did, thanks,' Katy answered.

'Yeah, we all had a nice quiet night in,' Zola said, smirking in Katy's direction.

'Wonderful.' He grinned broadly, and my body tingled nearly as hard as it had last night. 'I thought it would be a good time to meet your teams. I don't know how you ladies prefer to work, but we've got a whole team of specialists to help you. Though be sure to tell me to back off if I'm overstepping.'

I glanced at my friends, who seemed as intrigued as I was.

'So, Katy, I picked up that you were more of a market researcher kind of girl, right?' Jimmy continued.

Katy gulped, nodding. 'I suppose you could say that, *yes*.'

Fuck, I thought. Market research was all she'd been doing since she hit New York. I wondered who the lucky guy would be tonight.

'Well, I've teamed you up with Tanya. She's the best we have at Flirtify – she delves into all the latest social media trends and fads. I thought you two would work great together on delivering the key features of the app and finding out what women really want to know when they're reviewing men.'

Katy turned to Tanya, who had bright orange curly hair and equally colourful clothing.

'It's great to meet you,' Katy said.

Tanya hugged her tightly. 'I'm so excited about this one!'

'And Zola, the whizz kid. I've paired you up with Darren and Ethan. The brains behind almost all of my operations. But Darren is heading off on paternity leave soon, so it will be Ethan, our head IT specialist, who's mostly working on this.'

Zola nodded, utterly impressed. She turned to the pair on her left: one was an older gentleman wearing brown cords and a grey cardigan, the other a young, handsome guy in an Illuminati T-shirt and Japanese denim jeans.

'Nice to meet you both,' she said politely and smiled.

'Likewise.' The older of the two stuck out his hand and shook Zola's. She turned to the younger one and he bowed his head quietly.

'Which leaves Ella,' Jimmy said, turning to me. 'I've teamed you up with Britney, head of our PR and marketing team, and Fee, who you've already met. Fee helps develop apps and is our go-to for her great creative ideas. She's in a meeting right now, but will check in with you today.'

I waved over to Britney, an older woman dressed in a wide-legged pinstriped suit. She was writing notes and didn't lift her head.

'We've also scheduled you a media interview tomorrow with a journalist we know pretty well; she will run a piece on Apple News about the three women aiming to rid America of its toxic dating culture. There'll be photos and a chat, so be prepared. We don't want any of the app's features to be revealed until it launches, so for the interview we'll focus more on safety and how the dating world has changed, mostly for the worse, in recent years. Got it?'

I gulped. Jesus, this was such a big deal. I suddenly felt more than a little sick.

'Everyone happy?' Jimmy asked the group.

There was a scattering of 'Yep' and 'Sure thing' as everyone acknowledged his introductions.

'OK, let's get to work then, people!' Jimmy clapped, making me jump.

This deal was enormous. Huge. Worldwide. Apple News? I could feel my pulse in my hands throb so hard like the blood was trying to escape my body. Then I felt Zola and Katy at my side.

'This is insane!' Zola laughed.

'This is overwhelming, no?' I replied, keeping my voice low. 'We haven't even discussed what we're doing. What type of app are we making? What's its name? What are its functions?'

'Whoa, calm down, Ella,' Zola murmured.

'Calm down? Zola, we literally have a team of people relying on us here!'

'Babe, you're panicking. We're recreating The Dicktionary Club, just like we pitched, remember?'

'But even better!' Katy grinned.

Neither of my friends seemed in any way fazed, but I felt a wave of anxiety rush through me, remembering how awfully that turned out the last time for me. I mean, sure it was a massive hit with the women of Glasgow, but it basically ruined my life, my career, and my relationship. What if this went the same way, but on a much larger scale? What if we pissed off the wrong guy on our new app? A politician, or a sports star? A musician, or some hotshot lawyer? We could be extradited from the USA, couldn't we?

'Look, we got this. We know what we're doing. Just stick to our teams, we'll all do our own little bit, then we can reconvene.' Zola rubbed my shoulder, calming me down slightly.

I spotted Katy glaring at Travis as he passed through the corridor opposite with his head low. 'American women need this app, Ella,' she said as soon as Travis was out of sight. We're basically like Batman – well, Batwoman, I guess – a group of hardcore vigilantes, coming to save their love lives from imminent disaster!'

There was a quiet moment between us. Zola and I stared at Katy, who eventually turned to us when she noticed we hadn't responded.

'What?' Katy asked.

'Too far again, babe. Always too bloody far!' Zola shook her head.

'Ella, shall we head to my office? I have a group of staff there waiting to begin,' Britney said, piping up beside me. Her face was deadpan. I couldn't tell whether she was resting-bitch-face dour or if she hated me already.

'Sure.' I smiled at my friends as they scattered off to their own teams.

'So, how long have you worked at Flirtify?' I asked as I jogged behind her to keep up.

'Quite some time, now.' Britney sounded completely indifferent to my efforts to chat.

Great, I thought. *I've landed an Ice Queen*. We continued in silence until we reached her spacious office. The door was slightly ajar and I spotted a cluster of people gathered around a desk.

'OK, Ella, this is the PR and marketing team,' Britney informed me as we entered.

I examined the young, sharply dressed team in front of me.

'Nice to meet you all,' I said, spotting an empty chair and steering towards it.

Britney tittered, and it wasn't a friendly sound. 'Can you lead, Ella? This is your pitch, after all. Tell us about this app and what you need from us.'

Shit, she definitely hates me, I thought.

'Sure,' I replied, deciding it was not the time for a seat.

What do I even say? I felt totally unprepared. I headed up to the front of the table, where the group were glancing between me and their notebooks.

'Well, hello, everyone. I'm Ella. And I've been asked to come over to the States to redesign, relaunch, a website my frie – my colleagues and I developed back home in Glasgow. We called it The Dicktionary Club and—'

'You realise that name won't stick here?' Britney interrupted.

Nods of agreement from the group in front of me.

'Do you understand?' Britney asked.

I hovered, not knowing if she was addressing her minions or me.

'Yeah, totally. It's too long,' one of them stated, with an unimpressed glint in her eye.

'Oh, OK,' I said, my tone as understanding as I could make it.

'Way too vulgar,' another added.

'We could take it to a control group, but it's giving gossip column,' one concluded.

'OK, well . . . we called it that in the first instance, and the principle of the website was always to—'

Britney raised her hand.

'We can't continue without a name at this stage. We need something we can launch in the press statement tomorrow, Ella. I'm afraid the concept of the app will have to wait until we have a market-ready working title.' She attempted a polite smile, but I'm pretty sure there was venom behind those teeth.

What a fucking bitch, I thought.

'OK, right. Got you. Should we . . .' My mind was racing. 'I mean, we could always brainstorm?' I suggested, knowing how much a group imaginative session would help ideas come to life at my old work.

'My team work better researching what names are already on the market. Perhaps we should reconvene at twelve?' Britney suggested, staring at her watch.

'Yeah, OK, that's fine.' I was still standing, facing the group. There was an impassive wall of silence glaring back at me. 'Will I just . . . go then?' I asked, not knowing my place or value at this company.

Britney glanced at me with an undisguised look of disapproval. 'For now, I think that would be useful.'

'Cool, see you all at twelve then.' I headed towards the door, hearing what seemed to be a brainstorming session ignite behind me.

What the fuck was her problem?

I shook my head and stormed back to the office, hoping Zola and Katy would be there to vent to. Unfortunately, the room was empty. The vast glass walls gave a clear view out to the bustling office, full of work and focus and creativity. I slumped down in my chair, not having a clue what to do.

'Agggghhhh!' I groaned, punching my fists off the desk in exasperation and fury.

'Well, I can see your first day is going to plan,' a deep voice said.

I lifted my head and spotted Jimmy leaning against the door frame.

'Y'all having fun?' he asked, looking somewhat entertained at my lashing out.

'Sorry.' I immediately sat up and sorted myself.

'Hey, don't apologise, carry on, that's what offices are for. But here's a quick tip . . .' He stepped in and closed the door, taking a few steps towards me. 'If you don't mind.' Jimmy leaned over the desk, his neck and chest sweeping by me. His warm, fanny-tingling scent engulfed my senses. Then I noticed we were in darkness. The glass had tinted over, making the world beyond disappear. No more office, no more New York skyline. It was just us.

'The switch for privacy is right here.' His voice was soft as he showed me, his finger lingering over the button just under the lip of my desk.

I cleared my throat, allowing my eyes to adjust. I was hyperaware of his muscular silhouette leaning beside me.

'Thank you,' I managed, clearing my throat.

I thought I could feel an obvious tension in the room, but was I making it up? Was it because I'd masturbated to him last night? Well, only for a second, technically, so it doesn't count if it was Philip who made me cum, right? *Nonsense*, I told myself. *For the love of God, stop thinking about it, Ella.*

I pressed the button, allowing the sunlight and the office bustle to reappear magically beyond the glass.

'So, what's the problem, Ella?' Jimmy asked, casually resting his thigh on my desk.

My eyes skimmed over his physique again. Jesus Christ, his quads looked like they could crack open a watermelon at any given time.

'Nothing.' I forced a grin, not wanting to seem weak. This guy had just taken a massive gamble on our idea, and I didn't want him to think I wasn't capable of delivering.

'Well, when nothing bothers me, I like to take a walk. Would you care to join me?' he asked, standing again.

'I have to get back here at twelve for Britney,' I explained.

'Noted. Come on.' He nodded towards the door and started walking. 'Don't leave me hanging.' His voice sailed back to me as he exited my office and eventually I smiled, getting to my feet.

'Oh! There she goes!' Jimmy laughed as I joined him, and together we headed out of Flirtify's headquarters to stroll the hectic streets of midtown Manhattan.

Chapter Seventeen

Zola

Zola had just explained to Darren and Ethan in microscopic detail how she'd set up The Dicktionary Club website using data from mainstream dating apps, and how she hoped to do something similar with the American app they were creating.

Darren had agreed throughout, encouraging Zola to continue her speech while Ethan listened, fidgeting in his seat, looking bored and uncomfortable.

'Any questions?' Zola asked as she finished up and turned to the two men.

'All good with me. We own a percentage of most dating apps here, so it should be easy enough to transfer data,' Darren replied.

'Amazing!' Zola smiled. 'And Ethan, anything you would like to add?'

Ethan's handsome face and chiselled jaw lowered. 'I was curious about where you went to school?'

'Ethan . . .' Darren warned him.

Zola swung her head between both men, unaware of any underlying issue that Ethan might be aiming at.

'Or specifically, what your IQ is?' he continued.

'Ethan, please, stop already,' Darren warned more sternly this time.

'What? I like to know who I'm working with, Darren!'

'Why? We work for Jimmy, and Jimmy has brought Zola on,' Darren said in a huff. 'That should be enough of an endorsement for you.'

'No, no, hey, it's fine,' Zola interjected. 'I went to a school in London, uni in London too. Then I worked in Glasgow for the past few years. I can send you my certificates if you like?' Zola grinned, slightly teasing, but also proud, knowing she'd graduated with top grades.

'And your IQ?' Ethan asked again.

'Err . . . Honestly, I have no idea.' Zola held her hands up, baffled. 'I'm happy to find out if it makes working with me any easier?'

'I will email you a regulatory test tonight,' Ethan said, totally deadpan.

'OK. Sure! Can we get to work now?' Zola asked.

'I'd love to.' Darren shuffled his chair up towards Zola, while Ethan sat across the room and popped on industrial-looking ear-defender headphones.

Zola let out a small sigh as the room fell silent.

'I'm sorry about him,' Darren said softly. 'He is . . . unique.'

Zola smiled. 'That's a polite way of saying rude.'

Darren smirked, pushing a notepad of passwords towards Zola to help her log in to the server. 'Look, Ethan is a complete genius but can come across as a bit of an ass, especially with new people. He likes routine, which means if anyone new comes into this office, he freaks. Not even Jimmy sets foot in here. This is a big change for him. Me going off on paternity is a big change too. I guess what I'm saying is to be patient. Ethan knows what he's doing and is honestly the best in the city at this stuff.'

'Got it.' Zola lifted the notebook, ready to get to work, then peered back at Ethan. He was already wholly captivated by his computer, fingers flowing over the keyboard, his bright green eyes focused on the screen. She brought out her phone, thinking of Curtis and really feeling for the first time that she missed home.

Zola: *Morning! Or whatever time you're on back home. Sorry I was cranky yesterday, think I am homesick already! You OK? Xx*

Chapter Eighteen

Ella

Jimmy and I chatted aimlessly, and before I knew it, we were headed down Fifth Avenue, chatting about the weather and life back home in Scotland. The conversation felt effortless; he seemed genuinely interested in getting to know me. The air was muggy, with clouds scattered across the sky. I wasn't sure if it would rain or burst into sunshine at any given moment, but my cute pinafore dress was sticking more firmly to my underarms with each step in this swelteringly warm city.

'So, Britney. She's a hard nut to crack,' Jimmy said, then laughed, acknowledging some passers-by who recognised him in the street.

'She seems it.' I grinned. 'But my old boss was much worse than her. I honestly think Hitler himself would have been terrified of Andrea.'

Jimmy gasped, then laughed. 'I never understood people like that. Surely, it's better if everyone gets along, then you can bounce ideas and concerns off one another.'

I agreed, stepping in sync with him between the crowds of tourists.

'I learned that in the system, you know, at an early age. The foster homes where you weren't afraid always helped me progress much further at school or with my development.'

I turned to Jimmy, not realising he'd grown up in care. Fuck, my late-night rabbit hole search hadn't mentioned a single thing about this.

'I didn't realise. I'm sorry.' I studied his face, but he seemed happy, easy-going.

'It's all right. I was a crazy kid, so at least some of it was my own fault. I got back to my mom and my sister when I was sixteen and honestly, now, I realise it was the best thing that ever happened. It brought us closer. And I vowed to stay out of trouble and not to let anyone separate me from my sister. Yeah, I cleaned up my act and brought her in when this whole company started.'

My heart felt heavy for all his earlier troubles, and my mind was full of questions. But I knew it was none of my business, unless he chose to share more. Ultimately, his success was even more earned and deserved, given the obstacles he'd had to deal with at such a young age.

'It's lovely how close you are,' I replied. 'I have that with Zola and Katy.' A grin immediately appeared on my face, thinking of my two friends.

'Exactly like I said. When you work with people who have the same mindset, who aren't afraid to take risks and can air their troubles freely, great things happen. You girls really impressed me with your idea. I read it and, my

God, I nearly busted a rib laughing.' As though to prove it, he started to laugh now, making me laugh too.

'It wasn't fun at the time, trust me,' I admitted.

'Tell me about it,' Jimmy said.

Up ahead of us, a spectacular, ostentatious building caught my eye, with its bronze-tinted glass and gold writing – Trump Tower. I giggled, pointing. 'Is that Donald Trump's?'

Jimmy turned, noticing the building. 'Urgh. Sure is. There are condos up top and coffee shops, bistros and food on the lower ground level. The public can go in; it's a nice enough building. But I don't set foot in it.'

I peered behind the security guards at the door and noticed an enormous American flag hanging proudly in the lobby.

'It sounds a bit stupid to say it,' I admitted, 'but everything is so Americanised over here.' It was true – every shop, taxicab and hoarding seemed to declare, *You are in America*.

'It's our stars and stripes, baby, and we're proud of them!' Jimmy grinned, looking pleased that I was soaking in the atmosphere.

'Stars and stripes,' I repeated, with a snigger.

I glanced back at the giant flag, repeating in my mind: *Stars and stripes.*

Then I turned to Jimmy with a gasp. 'I've got to get back to the office.'

My cheeks were flushed – maybe from the heat, maybe from the handsome man I had been hanging out with, but I was sure the flush was actually with focus.

I had the name in the bag, and I really wanted to present it professionally to Britney and the team.

'Already? We haven't been out all that long.' Jimmy watched me curiously. 'We are still in time to catch your curfew, Cinderella!'

'It's about a twenty-minute walk back,' I laughed. 'You carry on without me. But I have to go. I think I've figured out a name.' I clutched his arm excitedly, feeling the warm muscles flex underneath his shirt. 'Thanks for this,' I added, then began backtracking towards Times Square, weaving in and out of the crowds of people, trying to keep pace with the speed-walking New Yorkers rather than the ambling tourists.

'Ella! Hey, Ella!' Jimmy called out behind me.

I turned to see Jimmy waving at me in bemusement. 'The walks do good, yeah?' he called out.

I nodded and grinned. 'Yeah!' Then I turned back, hurrying towards Flirtify HQ.

*

As soon as I was back in my office, I hammered out an email to Zola and Katy with a plan. Zola was quick to reply, sending template ideas and creating backgrounds and logos. I laughed as she joked that her day was going about as well as mine with her new team.

Until I realised my time was up.

I clutched my laptop under my arm and returned to the PR office, where Britney was already stationed with her team around her.

'OK, Ella, take a seat,' she ushered me.

I crossed the room and sat down, setting my laptop on the table.

'We've been researching and brainstorming and we have our top three names. First off is "The Audit",' Britney said, indicating to a young dark-haired woman to take over.

'So, yeah, I personally loved this one. It sounds official, easy to remember, and it's funny, right? It's also exactly what the app will be about, essentially,' she said, and the people around her nodded in unison.

'I like it.' I smiled. 'I've also got a suggestion . . .'

'And we have Rate Club. I believe Texas suggested that one.' Britney gestured towards another vivacious young woman.

'Yes!' Texas swooped in. 'Tag line – think *Fight Club*, but with opinions. We thought the word "club" would be a cute way to connect it to the original name, make it feel like an inclusive space or a secret organisation.'

I nodded, wondering when or how to introduce my idea.

'And finally, we have The Ex-Files. But I'm not sure about that one, given that our primary purpose is for people to date, not attack their ex-boyfriends.' Britney turned to me. 'Well?'

'I like them all. Thanks, guys,' I said. 'Really snappy and of the moment.'

'I recommend a focus group this afternoon,' Britney carried on.

'Sorry, I wasn't finished, Britney. I'd like to add another suggestion to the mix, if you don't mind?' I opened up my laptop and clicked on the image that Zola had created in a matter of minutes, based on the brief I'd given her. 'I was thinking . . . I mean, you guys love an American flag over here, you're so proud of your culture and your country, and that's really just so inspiring. So, what if we leaned into that a little bit more? I was playing around with a design idea and was thinking of this.' I turned my laptop around to the group. On the screen was a giant American flag, but in place of the fifty stars were fifty shiny purple aubergines. 'Stars and Swipes!'

A few giggles filled the room, but Britney gasped in horror.

'Our flag,' she muttered.

'It's bold.' Texas laughed, then tilted her head. 'I like it. It's giving Gen Z.'

'You have insulted the Founding Fathers!' Britney shook her head.

OK, calm down, Hamilton, I thought.

'No. It's memorable, Britney,' I said, trying to be diplomatic. 'And there's a long tradition of playful reimagining around this image; just think of Andy Warhol and Keith Haring.' I felt a little smug, I admit, at my easy pop-art references. 'Look, the American flag represents unity between the states, right? One way we could spin this is for unity between women. Think about it!'

Britney opened her mouth to say something, but a knock at the door cut her short. Fee entered, looking as bright and bubbly as ever.

'Sorry, I missed the morning meeting, everyone. How y'all getting on?'

'Well . . . Ella has devised a new name for the app,' Britney replied, her tone dripping with disdain, 'and she was just showing us a mock-up logo, which, quite frankly, is outrageous!'

I glanced at the girls who'd seemed to like my idea for backup, but they lowered their heads, clearly too afraid to speak out.

'Outrageous! I love it already. Let's hear it, girl?' Fee beamed, dispelling the negativity Britney had conjured with her put-down.

'Stars and Swipes.' I shrugged, turning the laptop of cute rows of shiny aubergines around.

Fee covered her face, threw her head back and clapped her hands. 'Oh my God, I love it! Don't you, guys?'

The other girls eventually laughed, and I watched their shoulders drop as Fee's laughter and enthusiasm instantly made the atmosphere in the room feel so much lighter.

'Great work, Ella. What a start!' She winked at me. 'Should we let these guys try out some taglines and sketch out a fun way to release this to the media while we catch up?'

I glanced at the group, who seemed to bite their lips in amusement, knowing how Britney would react when we left.

'We should trial the name with a focus group?' Britney said. 'That would be best practice.'

Fee turned to the laptop again, then back to Britney. 'No need. I love it.' She grinned widely. 'Can I have the taglines and media approach on my desk for three?'

Britney fumed. 'Sure.'

'Come on, Ella.' Fee walked towards the door, holding it open for me to follow.

Once out in the hallway, I turned to her and laughed.

'That was amazing, thank you.' I paused, not sure how much solidarity I could assume. 'But I thought Britney was about to combust!'

Fee tilted her head at me. 'She knows all too well not to rattle me! She'll calm down and come to my office kissing ass by the end of the day. Stars and Swipes, eh? I love it. How did you come up with that?'

I felt my cheeks heat up and immediately lowered my head. 'It was something Jimmy said.'

Fee kept her eyes on me. 'Interesting!'

We headed down to her office and spent the rest of the afternoon preparing for tomorrow's interview, deciding on the perfect outfits for our photo shoot and brainstorming strategies for making sure Stars and Swipes would soon be trending.

Chapter Nineteen

Katy

Katy was having the perfect first day with her new pal Tanya. She immediately fell in love with Tanya's warm, bubbly nature, which was just as happily infectious as her own.

In the morning, the pair had spoken in depth about the essentials women needed to know when dating someone, from manners and values to job prospects and education. They then targeted more superficial elements, such as general attractiveness, height and various generic pros and cons. They even considered penis size, which prompted Katy to overshare her disappointing micro-penis experience after her ex had promised her Big Foot's dick.

Together, the women created a list and headed out to the city's gyms and cafés, asking the public what they would like to know when considering a potential partner. At around one o'clock, they had just entered a small coffee shop uptown for a rest and to regroup.

As Tanya headed to the counter to order them both a drink, Katy pulled out her phone. A message appeared on her screen.

Unknown: *I know what you did!*

Immediately, Katy's heart began pounding. She glanced at the people around her. Everyone seemed to be going about their business, drinking overpriced coffee and chatting, or working on laptops. What the fuck? She quickly took a screenshot of the text and forwarded it to the group chat.

Katy: *I have just got this from an unknown number??*
Zola typing . . .
Ella: *What did you do? X*
Zola: *It will be a scam, babe. Don't stress xx*
Katy: *You serious, Ella???*
Zola: *It will be a scam. No one knows about the other thing. Don't worry fs xx*

Tanya returned to the table and sat down with a matcha for Katy and a ginger shot for herself.

'We did great work today.' She grinned.

'Yeah! Everyone was so forthcoming! I feel like we got loads of really useful information out of them.' Katy sipped on her matcha, still feeling unsettled.

'Aren't they in Glasgow?' Tanya asked.

'Hmm? What? I'm sorry.' Katy was caught up rereading the strange message.

'Aren't people forthcoming in Glasgow? When you stop them in the street for info?'

Katy rolled her eyes, shaking her head. 'Oh my God, no! Not on the street anyway. We have to target them at gyms or at clubs. On the street they usually ignore us, or creepy guys want to try out their dodgy pick-up lines, or they tell us to bolt!'

Tanya burst out laughing, causing her bright orange hair to bounce up and down. 'Bolt! That's hilarious.'

Katy grinned, thinking about home – the patter, the fresh cool air – and for the first time, she began to miss it.

'So, let's discuss today's findings.' Tanya pulled her notebook out. 'Religion is one of the front-runners we didn't anticipate.'

'Yeah, it makes sense. In Glasgow, you're usually Celtic or Rangers, but over here, my God, I hadn't heard of half of their religious inclinations.'

'That's so weird. I haven't heard of your Scottish ones! But I do think that religion should be included. There's no point in dating someone if you would never consider them as a long-term prospect. We want our American girls to find the one!'

Katy sat up, refreshing her phone – no new messages. Thank fuck.

'I agree! OK, what else should we include?' Katy asked, feeling her emotions settle down a little.

'Well, by way of contrast, penis size wasn't mentioned.' Tanya side-eyed Katy. 'I think we should leave it out.'

'No way!' Katy groaned. 'It's *so* important!'

Tanya took a sip of her shot in thought. 'OK, hear me out. Yes, it's important, but isn't it a nice surprise too? You get to look forward to it. All that messaging, flirting, anticipation, then bam! The wiener is out!'

'Wiener!' Katy giggled. 'But when it's small, it's really not a small disappointment.'

Tanya hummed. 'Honestly, I disagree. I've always found the men with ones on the smaller side are better in other ways.' She winked. 'They sure know how to make up for it.'

Katy blushed, then agreed reluctantly. 'Fine, maybe penis size is too rude for Americans.'

Tanya's jaw dropped. 'Girl, we are not scared to talk about sex. But if a counter app launches and it decides to rate us women by our vaginas, then I'm screwed!'

Katy's face squirmed. 'Fuck, me too!' She giggled. 'Can you imagine, though? There would be outrage! I have way too much meat-to-skin ratio!'

'Exactly, right? Let's keep this new app in the headlines for all the right reasons. It's informative, safe, easy to use – and it's saving us a lot of freaking time by stopping us making bad mistakes,' Tanya said.

'Yep, I sure wish it was available before I came to New York,' Katy muttered under her breath.

'Oh, spill! Bad Tinder date? Or hook-up?' Tanya sat up, eyes widening.

Katy shook her head. 'Just a total time-waster. OK, so, where are we headed next?'

Tanya picked up her phone and scanned down the list. 'Times Square! Just outside the office. There's a huge footfall, especially at lunch.'

'Great!'

Katy and Tanya finished their drinks and headed back towards the office. They'd spend the rest of their day interviewing women about what was important to them in online dating.

*

That evening, Katy arrived home to find Ella and Zola sprawled out on the sofa, chatting while rewatching another episode of *Gossip Girl*.

'Hey! You've been working hard!' Zola called out as Katy's tired face appeared.

'How was your day?' Ella asked, turning down the TV.

'Yeah, it was fine. Tanya's lovely,' Katy replied, sitting beside her friends.

'No more messages?' Zola asked, noticing Katy's usually bright light was dimmed.

Katy shook her head. 'What if someone does know?' Even voicing the possibility out loud made her panic.

'No one knows, Katy. You're being a paranoid android.' Zola shoved Katy to loosen up.

'I've had a million similar emails, Katy. I have a few saying they've caught me watching hardcore porn, and if I don't pay immediately, then they'll send my family the weird genre I watch! It's crazy. Because we all know I don't watch that shit.' Ella flicked back her hair. 'It's a stupid scam, babe,' she reiterated, trying her hardest to make her friend feel better.

'But they didn't ask for money. It literally just said "I know what you did!"'

Zola shook her head. 'Babe, you've done *a lot* of things. You don't know if it has anything to do with Travis. Look, we have a big shoot tomorrow. Ella's picked up our outfits. Let's have a chill night, then go and smash the interview and put that two-timing prick behind us. You're overthinking!'

Katy huffed, leaning into Ella for a hug.

'How was your day with Fee?' she asked eventually.

Ella pushed back Katy's hair. 'Honestly, she's lovely. She's kind of impossible not to like, and she really stuck up for me with Britney, who is a complete bitch, by the way.'

Katy sat up. 'How come?'

Zola rolled her eyes. 'Wait till you hear this!'

Ella darted up. 'Grab the laptop! I want to show her the finished logo too!'

For the next few hours, the girls sat around, recounting their days to one another. Surrounded by takeout pasta and cookies, with the breathtaking view of the city's lights beyond the apartment's huge windows, they gossiped and vented, enjoying a chill night in New York.

Chapter Twenty

Zola

Zola woke to three missed calls from Curtis.

She squinted at the screen, trying to work out what time it had been back home when he called and whether it was an emergency. She sat up, rubbing her eyes. It was 6 a.m. in New York, which meant it was 11 a.m. in Glasgow. She called him on WhatsApp, and he answered immediately.

'Hey, how are you?' she asked. 'I have missed calls. The day's only just started here, remember?'

'Zola.' His voice was low and croaky. 'I've done something.'

'What? Are you OK?' Panic flared as she swung her legs out of bed.

'I'm OK. I just . . . Last night after the gym, I met up with some lads I train with and . . . there were some girls there too . . .'

Immediately, Zola's stomach dropped. She closed her eyes, bracing for what he was about to say.

'And I got really drunk, and I've been missing you, Zo.' She could hear the shake in his voice.

'Uh huh?' Zola felt her hands tremble. She pulled the phone away from her ear and took a long, deep breath, trying to stay calm till he continued.

'With one of the girls, one thing led to another, and I . . . I slept with her, Zo.'

Silence down the phone line.

Zola was speechless. She knew she and Curtis weren't in the best place, but he'd always been someone she could trust. They had been teenagers when they first met and had grown up together. Despite their differences, she thought he'd always be there.

'I'm so fucking sorry, Zo,' he blubbered. 'I hate myself.'

She tried to speak, but felt sickness scorch her throat.

'Zola. Are you there?' Curtis called out in panic.

Zola cleared her throat. 'I'm here. I – I just don't know what to say.'

'Look, I know. But it's not like you haven't done this to me. You met up with that guy last year, and I know two wrongs don't make a right, but . . .'

A rush of anger catapulted through Zola. 'I didn't sleep with him, just to be clear. And I took some time out. I thought we worked through it, Curtis. We were trying. I was trying! I put so much effort into fixing us, and slowly, but surely, you simply went back to the way you were!'

'I fucking tried too! How do you think it made me feel, Zo? You humiliated me!' he yelled.

'And now you have done it back! I know exactly how you fucking felt, Curtis!'

There was a deafening silence between them. Zola could hear the sound of herself trying to catch a breath.

'Look, I'm sorry, babe. I'm so sorry, but it's hard. I've been here alone. You speak to me like shit when you call. And . . .'

Zola shook her head. 'I haven't even been away a full week! And you don't want to speak to me when I fucking call!' she exploded. 'I'm here trying to earn us money for a nice fucking life, while you play video games, hang out training at the gym and now fuck random girls!'

'I know!' He broke down.

Zola held the phone away from her face again, still working out how she should deal with this.

'You know, at least I've told you straight away. As soon as she left, I knew it was wrong. I knew I had to tell you. I'm not like that fucking Philip, parading some girl around town just to cause a scene.'

Zola paused. 'What are you talking about? What about Philip?' She stood up, feeling her legs tremble.

'I saw him in the paper the other day with some new girl he's dating. Apparently her dad's some rich footballer. You didn't know?'

'No,' she replied softly, glancing towards the door.

'Look, how do I fix this, Zo? Tell me, I'll do anything,' he continued.

Zola sighed, exasperated. 'I don't think there's anything to fix. I'm done with this. I need space. I need to concentrate on this deal. I'm over here to work and I can't handle this right now.'

Curtis began stammering. 'No, no. I'll come to you then. I'll find you, we can talk. I need to sort this.'

'Come to me?' She laughed. 'You don't fucking listen enough to know where I am to find me, Curtis. And even if you did, you're not welcome.'

'Zola, we need to talk face-to-face. I have to see you.' There was a ripple of anger edging through his tone.

'I'll be in touch to sort out the house,' she snapped. 'But I can't talk to you right now. I can't believe you've done this,' she admitted, feeling the reality beginning to sink in.

'Is that it? Surely you have something more to say? Zola, I will do anything.'

'Thank you for being honest with me. I appreciate it.' A shaky breath departed her body. She felt a stab in her heart and bent over in pain.

'No, no, Zola!'

She cut off the call. Tears streamed down her face as she lowered herself into a ball on the floor, where she found she couldn't stop weeping.

*

Zola lay there on her bedroom floor, crying and shaking for what seemed like an eternity. Then she heard one of the apartment's doors shut, making her sit up. She stumbled to her feet and peered into the hall, then she heard the lift door close. She looked at her watch: seven thirty. Ella must be heading out on her run, she thought.

She headed into the kitchen, put the kettle on and made a coffee. Her head was pounding from all the crying, and she felt sick and empty. She sat on one of the breakfast bar stools, her mind racing with questions she wished she'd asked Curtis. *Who was this girl? How long had he known her? Was she a total random? Did she know about Zola?* Each time she wanted to call, something inside stopped her. She knew this was unfixable. She knew the damage had been done.

Zola headed over to the window and gazed out. Far below, she spotted Ella running along the Hudson River, only recognisable from that height by her cute lululemon bow. She felt a soft smile spread across her face as she watched her friend's peaceful momentum through the city.

Then she remembered Curtis bringing up Philip. 'Fuck.' A stab of anxiety sent her diving towards the laptop on the coffee table. She typed into Google: *Philip Khan's new girlfriend*. The screen quickly filled with paparazzi photos from the past few days. The girl's name was Erin Cook, and she was a twenty-three-year-old influencer. One picture showed them totally glammed up at the Pride of Britain Awards dinner; another was of them cosying up for a movie night, which seemed to have been taken from her Instagram. Zola shook her head in disgust. Philip had always been private about Ella, keeping her out of the limelight, but only a few days after she was gone, Erin was taking pride of place on his arm in every newspaper and gossip site in the country.

Zola bit her nails. The girls didn't keep secrets, but she knew how important today was for them. And she didn't want to hurt Ella, who was handling the Philip breakup remarkably well. Zola closed the laptop and went into Katy's bedroom, stepping over the clutter of discarded clothes and toiletries.

'The mess,' Zola muttered under her breath.

'Urgh. Have I slept in again?' Katy mumbled, attempting to sit up with a makeup-stained eye mask tilted across one eye.

In spite of the emotions crashing down on her, Zola giggled at the sight of her friend. 'No,' she whispered.

'Are you OK?' Katy asked, clearly sensing something was off.

Zola paused, then shook her head. 'No,' she whispered again, then started sniffling, feeling herself break down.

Katy sat up properly now. 'What's up? Come here!' She shimmied along the bed, giving Zola some room.

Zola sat down and recounted the whole conversation she'd had with Curtis. Katy hugged her tightly, cursing Curtis and promising Zola she was better off without his sorry cheating ass in her life.

'I just don't know what to say to Ella,' Zola explained. 'She's not brought up Philip in a few days, and she's gone out jogging this morning. She seems good.'

Katy shrugged. 'I'm not sure. I mean, she could easily Google him and find out. I suppose the question is – are we better off telling her before she finds out elsewhere?'

Zola covered her face, already exhausted by the day's onslaught of traumas. 'OK, but after the interview. Let's focus on that, then we can sit Ella down.'

The door of Katy's room squeaked open and Ella stood there, her face flushed and bright. 'Good, you're both up,' she panted, pulling out her earphones. 'Are you OK?'

Zola screwed up her face. 'Curtis cheated on me last night. He called to tell me.'

'Are you fucking serious? Oh my God, Zola!' Ella rushed over to the bed and wrapped her arms around her friend. 'What are you going to do? I'm sure I can speak to Fee and rearrange this interview.' She looked panicked.

'No!' Zola grabbed her hands. 'I can do this. I think I'm probably better off getting out of this apartment and doing something.'

Ella seemed reluctant.

'Ella, I'm fine,' Zola assured her. 'Things haven't been great for a long time. It was just a shock.'

Katy flopped back down onto her bed and let out a growl. 'I fucking hate men!' she shouted.

'Ditto!' Zola high-fived her. 'When do we have to start getting ready?'

Ella glanced at her watch, then back to the girls. 'Now. But if you . . .'

'Ella, I'm fine. I will be fine. It takes me a while to process, but when I get over this initial shock, I will have both of you with me. I know I'll be fine.'

'You will be,' Ella repeated, rubbing Zola's back. 'You're a superstar.' She grinned. 'Now who's for one of my special matcha smoothies?'

Chapter Twenty-One

Ella

By eleven, the three of us were sat in front of journalist Tia Smalls, dressed to the nines in similar sexy office-style outfits. Despite our outward poise, my mind kept drifting back to the morning's chaos. Curtis's early morning confession of infidelity seemed unbelievable. I kept glancing at Zola, who, surprisingly, remained composed, focused and radiant. Usually, she wore hardly any makeup – her skin glowed naturally – but today, with a full face, she looked every bit the supermodel.

Was it possible she felt relieved by Curtis's betrayal? I wondered. They had been together for years. I'd never known Zola in her single days. Zola without Curtis was sort of like an Ant without Dec, Richard without Judy. Joe Exotic without Carole Baskin, even. But quietly, I'd always wondered if he held her back. Without him, I could only imagine the things she might accomplish.

'OK, ladies, I'll record this for my notes,' Tia said, putting her phone on the table. 'So, Ella, Zola, Katy?' she began, looking at each of us in turn.

'Yes,' I confirmed, smiling at my friends.

'Perfect. Let's start with finding out why you three are here in New York,' Tia said, eyeing Katy, who was eager to reply.

'Well, we were invited, Tia, by the lovely Mr Jimmy Link of Flirtify to fly across the Atlantic and help rid the American dating scene of toxic men!'

Tia laughed. 'That's quite the statement! So, you're creating an app for women. Can you tell us about it?' She turned to Zola.

'Sure,' Zola said, immediately switching to an assertive tone. 'We are creating something totally new and exciting here at Flirtify, a handy app to help women research men before they date them. There is so much easy access to dating so many different people nowadays, and while finding love is important – and fun, – there are also many safety issues to consider. We want to advise women on who – and what – to look out for.'

Tia leaned in. 'How are you doing that?' She glanced at me while jotting down notes.

'That's what you will have to wait to find out!' I smiled, remembering Jimmy's instructions not to give too much away.

She smirked. 'Why you three, though? Because of The Dicktionary Club project you have at home? Or have our American men broken your hearts already?'

The three of us glanced at one another, and Katy piped up. 'Unfortunately, yes, I have had my heart broken by one American so far. And what I will say is, men are men – Scottish or American. They're all liars and cheats!'

Tia looked surprised. I nudged Katy to rein it in.

'We're making this app because we believe good guys do exist, and . . .' I trailed off.

'Do we?' Zola shot back, almost drawing the eyes off me for attempting that sentence.

I laughed, batting her remark off as a joke while darting her a shut-your-face kind of look.

'Sorry to be outspoken, but I'm not sure there are so many good – single – men out there anymore! I prefer sticking to the safety aspect of the campaign,' she snapped.

'And that's a really great element to mention too.' I forced a grin, feeling panicked with how badly this was going.

Tia blinked. 'So, you're Zola?' She glanced at me. 'You're engaged?'

I shook my head. My heart ached for Zola.

'That's me.' Zola flicked her hair. 'And yeah, I stick by it. I'm not sure good men exist.'

There was a moment of awkwardly heavy silence at the table.

'But like I said, that's what we aim to find out!' I added, sticking up my thumb in a corny bid for positivity.

'Yeah, sure. OK then,' Tia agreed, still slightly unnerved. 'I know you have made The Dicktionary Club website in the UK. Do you have a new name for the app? Or are you sticking with The D Club?' she asked, giggling a little nervously at the name.

'Stars and Swipes,' we said in unison. At least we agreed on something, I thought.

'Great! Stars and Swipes hits on Thanksgiving eve. I'll check it out!' Tia grinned, though I had my doubts.

She reached for her phone and pressed to stop recording.

'Thank you, ladies. If you all smile, Jeff will take some publicity shots for the article.'

We leaned in together, smiling and laughing as bright camera flashes flickered in the office. I wondered if Philip would see the article and if he'd reach out. In anticipation of his eyes on me, I sat up straight and gave my best smile.

'What the hell was that?' I mumbled through my teeth, still posing.

Zola grinned back. 'Pure and utter honesty.'

*

Later that day, I was reading the findings from Katy's street-survey trip with Tanya. The notes showed that American women cared much more about a man's salary and ambition than Scottish women, as well as about religion and emotional intelligence. The drug-dealing, Turkey-toothed man-child racing down Strathy Park in a souped-up Golf didn't seem to have the same appeal as he did back home, interestingly enough.

Zola and Katy stumbled into the office around five and slumped down at their desks.

'I need a drink,' Zola stated.

'Me too,' Katy agreed. Both of them immediately glanced at me to agree.

I smiled. 'How's it going?'

'Urgh, Ethan still hates me, so he doesn't talk, and now Darren's off to have a stupid baby, so it's been a long few hours!' Zola groaned.

'Well, I've had a great afternoon. We rounded up some students and we're paying them to write reviews on men.' Katy grinned. 'Hey, have you heard anything more from Curtis?' He had been the elephant in the room since we arrived at Flirtify that morning, but there were too many people around to delve into the situation without risking a total breakdown, given how fired up Zola was during the publicity interview.

Zola rubbed her face. 'I archived him. I had screeds of apology messages pouring in all afternoon, and Ethan doesn't like noise, so I put him into a folder so I wouldn't get distracted.'

I gulped. 'That's probably a good idea.'

'Have you heard from Philip, Ella?' Katy asked softly.

'Nope, not a thing.' I hummed. I still wondered if he was waiting for me to reach out. After all, I was the one who caused the fight, resurrecting The Dicktionary Club after swearing to him it was gone. But in the past couple of days, I'd begun thinking that the time apart would do us a favour, and maybe he'd actually be proud of the work and friendships I was making over here.

'Look, Ella, I have to tell you something Curtis said on the phone today.'

Zola sounded serious. I felt nervous at her tone and sat up. 'Yeah . . .'

'He mentioned that Philip has a new girlfriend and that he's parading about town with her. I was so caught up in what he had just told me about himself that I didn't really take it in. But I've checked it out, and there are lots of pictures online of the two of them just in the past few days.'

I felt acid rise up my throat. I was numb. I wanted to talk, to ask questions, but I felt static. I didn't want to believe a word she was telling me.

Why would Philip do this to me? Who was she, and what did she have that I didn't? I hadn't seen him in eight days. How, I wondered, can he possibly move on in eight fucking days?

'I didn't want to say before the interview,' Zola continued, sounding remorseful.

'But we didn't want you to find out online either,' Katy said.

'You knew too?' I felt a stab of bitter resentment. Why had they both been discussing this and not told me?

'Only because Zola didn't know when to tell you or if you should know,' Katy said, babbling as she defended herself.

'Or *if* I should know?' I repeated, completely gobsmacked that they had considered keeping this huge, life-changing secret from me.

Zola shook her head. 'We didn't know what to do! You've been coping really well with the breakup. You're out running, you're focused on work. I didn't want to upset you.'

I huffed in indignation, holding my head, feeling a headache immediately crush into my temples. 'Why do you think that is, Zo?'

A silence fell between us.

'I keep busy constantly, so I don't start to think that I've made a horrible mistake coming here in the first place. Philip was the first guy I finally let in after what

I'd been through. He helped me with Andrea, he was kind and . . .'

'And controlling!' Zola blurted. 'If he loved you properly, he would have supported this project. But he only cares about himself, Ella, like them all. They're all genetically engineered to be selfish fuckers!'

I was shaking. I was angry, fuming at everyone. Zola, Katy and Philip. I shouldn't ever have left, I thought.

'At least you know now, Ella. And you know you made the right choice coming here,' Katy said so quietly I almost didn't hear.

'Did I?' I replied just as softly, trying to take this in. I felt broken, humiliated. 'You two go and get food or whatever. I'll stay on in the office.' I shook myself, feeling isolated and vulnerable. 'I need time to think.'

'Ella . . .' Zola dropped her shoulders in defeat. 'C'mon, let's go home. We can watch a movie, get cosy and cuddle in if you don't fancy a drink.'

I shook my head, feeling my bottom lip tremble. I bit it and cleared my throat. 'I'm fine. I just don't like secrets. And I didn't expect this from Philip.' I felt my lungs exhale a deep breath. 'Are you one hundred per cent sure?' I asked, feeling as if something malignant was crawling under my skin.

'We're sure,' Zola replied. 'And yeah, no more secrets, OK? We honestly just thought it was for the best.'

I nodded, but I was zoning out. I couldn't make any sense of this new reality. Why had he done this?

'We shouldn't be arguing with each other, you know. It's Philip and Curtis who have caused this, and look at us, bickering for no reason,' Katy stated.

Even as I recognised Katy's point, I still felt that poisonous sting of betrayal – my friends had kept something from me, and I couldn't shake the feeling of being on the outside.

'See you at home?' Zola replied.

I managed a smile, knowing Zola's pain matched my own more than she would ever let on.

'Yeah, see you in a wee while. And please, unpack your case, Katy,' I added. 'It's giving me the boke how you're living!'

'What?' She grinned, backing out the door. 'Can't hear you!' she called down the corridor, singing *La, la, la* until I heard the lift door shut.

*

Once they left, I slumped forward, forehead on the desk, letting exhaustion and pain wash over me. As the office grew quiet, my thoughts spiralled. Was he with someone else before I left? Maybe that was why it was so easy for him to walk away? Was this new girlfriend who he was on those constant calls with? But surely he wouldn't be so shameless? My head was spinning with unanswered questions until a loud knock on the door broke me from my thoughts.

'Normally I'm the last man standing.' Jimmy hovered in the doorway, his jacket draped casually over his arm.

'Not tonight,' I snapped back, reluctantly raising my head.

'Are you all right?' His voice sounded concerned, and I couldn't help but cringe at what he must have thought of me. First, I screamed in the office and now I was face-planting my desk. Great.

'Hmm?' I questioned. 'Oh, yeah. This is how I think my best thoughts.' I shrugged my dramatic behaviour off casually, knowing how ridiculous I must have looked.

'Right.' He grinned. 'Because you have a Post-it stuck to your forehead.'

I rubbed my throbbing head, making the bright yellow sticky note fall to the desk. 'Why are you so late?' I asked, keen to change the subject.

He let out a puff like he couldn't be bothered to even discuss it. 'I was going over some numbers with Travis. And . . . I got the email about your article with Tia. It was very . . . insightful,' he concluded tactfully.

'Really? Which part?' I questioned, holding my head up high.

Jimmy's face twisted. He took another step further into my office and whispered, 'Do you really think all men are cheats and liars? Or is that a PR angle?' He seemed genuinely interested in my opinion.

'That was Zola that said that.' I smirked, remembering how bolshy she'd been.

'And what do you think? Honestly.'

'Honestly?' I paused. 'Then . . . yeah. I think Zola's right. Men are all selfish, blood-sucking bastards who take and take, then when something better comes along, they vanish.'

Jimmy's eyes widened as if I had just dropped a fat brown one in the middle of the office floor.

'Wow, Ella! Don't hold back.' He laughed. 'But you don't think that, not really? Not *all* men?'

I thought back to all the men I knew – Curtis, Philip, my ex, Joshua. Fuck, even my own father messed about in his heyday.

'I'm serious. Unfortunately, I do,' I admitted.

'Wow, I'm sorry you feel like that,' he said. 'But in my defence, I have met a few truly crazy women in my time.'

'And that is precisely the kind of gaslighting statement a man would make, Mr Link,' I shot back.

'Ouch!' He raised a brow.

I held my hands up. 'Toxic masculinity. It's probably not your fault. I'm thinking that it's the way men are encouraged to behave these days.'

Jimmy shook his head, looking disappointed. 'I guess you've experienced some truly sketchy men, Ella. And I can see you don't trust easily. For what it's worth, I'd like to apologise on behalf of us all.' He patted the door frame in an awkward attempt to say goodbye and stepped out of the office.

'Wait. Jimmy!' I called out after him. He turned back. 'How bad was the article?' I asked, knowing how fired up my friends were.

Jimmy gave me a look that I couldn't quite get the measure of. 'It will make . . . an interesting read.'

I threw my head back and sighed. What a shitty day.

'I mean, look, it wasn't what I imagined, but it will get people talking, put it that way. And I'm sure Britney will be kept busy with PR calls.'

'And you're not annoyed?' I asked, knowing my old boss Andrea would have had us lined up with our drawers at our ankles, ready for a severe arse-whipping if we pulled a stunt like that under her.

'I trust you guys, Ella. I know you know what you're doing,' he said, a soft smile appearing on his handsome face. 'Night.'

When he was out of sight, I inhaled a sharp breath, slowly realising that whatever Mr Link might say, the truth was I had no fucking idea what I was doing. I had no real idea if I should have come to the States in the first place.

Chapter Twenty-Two

Ella

The next morning, the three of us were far more subdued than usual in the car that picked us up to take us to Flirtify. While Zola and Katy were recovering from a night out exploring the local bars, I had spent mine researching Philip's new girlfriend through her visible socials. She seemed flawless – beautiful, charitable, always posting about her good deeds at the cat and dog home, at the soup kitchen. I envied her life, her immaculate appearance, her sunny nature and most of all, her relationship with him. I noticed she first posted with him only a couple of days after Philip and I had that horrible row, and they looked cosy, contented and comfortable even. I wondered how he knew her. If they'd met before and always kept in touch, or if it had been a whirlwind romance. I spent hours trying to remember his smile, his touch, the last time we kissed. It wasn't long ago, yet I was forgetting it all. So much had happened in such a short time, and I wanted, more than anything, to have the chance to go back and do things differently with him.

We were driving slowly through the crazy New York traffic when Katy's phone pinged. Katy reached into her pocket to check it and then gasped, her hand flying to her mouth in shock.

'Guys.' Her voice shook.

'What now?' Zola tutted, squinting over to the screen. 'Shut the fuck up!'

I was craning my neck, trying to look. 'What is it? Show me!'

Katy turned the screen around so Zola and I could see clearly. It was a message from an unknown number with an image attached from yesterday's photo shoot. In the photo, which had clearly been shamelessly edited, Katy had a humongous pink dick coming out of her mouth, Zola had wild red devil horns and a tooth scrubbed out, and I had a huge black cross over my face with the letters 'irrelevant hoe' scrawled across it in angry capitals. We scrolled to the bottom of the message together.

> **Unknown:** *Time's up TARTan trolls. The Big Apple's allergic to haggis!*

My mouth was gaping open, and I felt Katy clutch my arm tightly.

'What the actual hell is this?' I asked, looking at the photo again.

'A threat!' Zola gulped.

'Someone really doesn't want us here,' Katy whimpered.

'Someone who doesn't know I'm English!' Zola shook her head. 'Who would do something like this?'

I suddenly became aware of our surroundings in the car. Our driver, who was completely silent, seemed to sense the chaos we'd sparked since flying over here.

Was anyone watching or listening? Maybe he was spying on us.

'And haggis? So stereotypical! I haven't even tried it!' I tried to laugh, but it came out as a weird titter.

'Really?' Katy seemed surprised. 'The wee haggis bonbons from the Smokin' Fox on Waterloo Street are genuinely banging!'

'Really?' I said, though I'd never been.

'Guys, seriously?' Zola hissed. 'Think!'

'What about Travis?' I whispered. 'I mean, he's clearly the one who has a motive to get rid of us. That wee bastard doesn't want his dirty cheating secret out!'

'Yeah, but he doesn't seem stupid. He's risking a total backlash when he's already tried to clear the air.' Zola was lost in thought for a few more seconds. 'I know the tech guys weren't thrilled I've joined the team, but I don't think they resent me to quite this extent. Plus, who am I kidding? They would be able to make that grim pink cock much more realistic.'

My eyes re-examined Katy's innocent face with the monstrous boaby sticking out. Jesus.

'Or Britney,' I hummed. 'She's snippy as hell – and obviously has an issue with me being there. I've no idea why. Maybe she has a crush on Travis? Or feels threatened by our PR background and Jimmy's enthusiasm for us?'

Katy covered her face.

'Could she have seen you two together?' I added, thinking of any possibility here.

Zola laughed. 'Babe, she was getting finger-blasted in Central Park – I'm surprised she didn't make the national news!'

'Yeah, where were the Central Park rangers when you needed them?' I giggled.

Katy ignored the question. 'Maybe we should go to the police. This is scary!' Her breathing quickened.

I rubbed Katy's back to calm her and glanced towards Zola, trying to gauge her reaction. 'Zo?' I asked. 'What do you think?'

'I think we should figure out who it is by ourselves.' I could see the cogs working in her brain. I'd always admired how clever she was, constantly thinking ahead.

'We have brought so much drama to the office in only a few days. We don't want the polis interviewing all Jimmy's staff on top of everything else. He will think he's employed a bunch of absolute zoomers!'

'So, do I ignore this, Ella?' Katy questioned. 'And live in complete fear?'

'Fear?' Zola laughed. 'Of what? A giant pink penis coming to attack you? You'd normally gobble that up!'

Katy looked unimpressed. 'Of someone wanting rid of us. This is blackmail, Zola.'

'I know, I'm sorry.' Zola hugged her. 'It's just so childish! Look, not a word of this to anyone, not yet anyway. We'll figure it out, OK?'

'OK,' I agreed, feeling jangled and out of sorts.

Why would someone want us gone so badly? Why would they go to this kind of bizarre extreme? Jesus, I loved *Gossip Girl*, but this kind of drama was way more intense when you didn't have a house on the Upper East Side and a friend-slash-evil-mastermind like Blair Waldorf in your corner.

Eventually, the car pulled up outside Flirtify and we all got out, heading into work together, where we were determined to keep our heads down and our eyes and ears open for any glimmers of who had it in for us.

Chapter Twenty-Three

Ella

A few more days passed, and Katy didn't receive any new messages. Yet she remained in constant panic, suspecting anyone who smiled her way in the Flirtify office spaces or asked her anything work- or life-related. In the group chat, she speculated about who might be the secret texter with the terrible photo editing skills. Zola, meanwhile, had stayed relatively quiet about her own suspect list, her mind preoccupied with Curtis. She hadn't mentioned him much, except for the odd 'wanker' remark, but I'd heard her bawling down the phone a couple of nights ago. I didn't know how to make her feel better, because I was going through the same shit with Philip. Every night, I watched his new girlfriend's stories on her socials and read the thousands of comments saying how happy they looked, what an adorable couple they made. And they weren't wrong. Philip seemed relaxed, carefree. I wondered if he even gave me a second thought.

The app was progressing well, despite our drama-packed days. The disastrous interview went live on Apple News, and a few American TikTokers shared highlights, seemingly excited and onboard for the launch. Over a lunch of the most generously filled smoked salmon bagels I've ever seen, Zola had informed us that the male data was almost all downloaded; now we just needed to add the right tabs and info for each. In Glasgow, we reviewed men ourselves; in New York, Fee and Jimmy had hired two thousand students, paying them each fifty dollars to review as many men as they liked. With over a month until Thanksgiving, everything was on track for launch.

I headed to the office with my coffee and sat at my desk. My friends were already at their stations. Britney preferred working with the PR girls and coming to me with a brisk update at the end of the day. That arrangement worked better. She didn't have to see me, and I didn't have to look at her miserable mug. Since the nasty text on Katy's phone, I'd been careful around her, keeping a low profile to avoid sharing any information she could use against us.

It was just after three when Fee knocked on my door, smiling with a small box in her hands. 'I brought you this, they're homemade,' she said, blushing. 'Blueberry muffins.'

'Oh, thank you!' I grinned, pushing my chair out from the desk. 'I didn't know you baked.'

'Oh, it's just a hobby. Helps me de-stress. I boxed one up for Zola and Katy, too.' I felt instant guilt at the thought of Fee baking her husband's one-night-stand muffins and lowered my head. She wandered into the room and glanced about. 'You really need to make this office more welcoming!' She laughed at the bare walls and pristine furniture. 'Do you have anything cheerful you could bring? Some photos, maybe?'

I shrugged. 'We're not staying long enough, so I guess it didn't occur to me,' I said before delving into the cake box.

'You may find that you like it here, you know. The land of the free and all.' She smiled warmly. 'What's in Glasgow for you?'

I paused. 'Well, I have my flat,' I said, then laughed.

'No hot Scottish man to come home to in that flat?' She tilted her head curiously.

'Not anymore.' I wondered whether her brother had talked to her about me; after all, they were asking very similar questions.

Fee sat on the corner of my desk. 'Girl, they ain't all that.'

I agreed, finally picking up one of the muffins, which was still slightly warm. 'Have you and Travis been together a long time?' I asked, nibbling the sides.

'YES!' She rolled her eyes. 'Since college. It's been an age! Jimmy was his best friend, you see, even back then, and he was thrilled when we started dating, of course.' She giggled. 'There was always something special about Travis. He calmed me; he really saw me. And I'd never had that before.'

I looked at her, wondering why Travis would cheat on such a beautiful, genuine woman. Even if her muffins were a wee bit dry, she seemed perfect.

'What? Too corny?' she asked, noticing my silence.

I shook my head. 'No – just the right amount of genuine emotion. Is it weird I'm jealous, though? I don't think I've ever felt entirely myself with any man. Probably not even with my parents. Yeah, I guess I've only felt my true self with Zola and Katy actually,' I admitted.

'Well, now *I'm* jealous!' She smiled, small dimples appearing on her cheeks. 'I don't have many girlfriends. Not enough time. I'm either with Travis, at work, or baking.'

'Wooo! Do I smell blueberry muffins?' Jimmy's warm voice echoed down the corridor.

'I swear that man has an FBI-level nose!' Fee laughed, standing up from my desk to go and greet her brother.

I heard their voices grow fainter, leaving me to wash my muffin down with a slug of coffee just as my phone pinged.

Katy: *SOS!*
Katy: *They have sent another message!!*
Katy: Forwarded message from
Unknown: *Oh hey, miss me? Or just the drama? I'm SO close to telling his wife everything. Pack your bags, SKANK – that monster Nessie's wanting her sister back!*
Zola: *WTAF!*
Katy: *This is it. We need to go to the police!*

My heart pounded. I spat out the last crumbs of the over-dry muffin.

Ella: *So, they deffo know about you and Travis. Can we eliminate him?*
Zola: *Unless it's a double bluff?*
Katy: *What??*
Zola: *Tell me one of you bitches watch Traitors??*
Ella: *I have watched nothing but the Champions League for the past four months, Zo!*

Katy: *I don't think Travis would do this.*
Zola: *You didn't think he had a wife either? Bet she doesn't think he would do what he did to you?*

I became aware of a weird rattling sensation and realised my leg was shaking from nerves against my desk. Gazing out over the office floor, I caught myself thinking, it must be one of the people in this building. But why? And who?

Ella: *I don't think Travis is that calculated. He's a dick – yes. But he's not vindictive. He nearly passed out when he saw you in the boardroom x*
Zola: *No one is off limits x*
Katy: *I think I want to go home now x*

I put my phone down and began pacing the office floor, restless and angry. And more than a little freaked out. I couldn't stop questioning who might gain from us leaving or from Travis and Katy's secret being exposed.

Around six, Britney's usual workload update arrived in my inbox. I scanned her launch party ideas.

Pre-launch party: Investors, journalists and influencers event the week before the launch date.
Theme: Mean Girls.
Description: We will create a 'Burn Book' and insert short summaries of what an ex did to us. Jimmy will welcome guests, with Fee and Travis on stage. Canapés with feminist slogan designs will be handed out. Zola, Katy and Ella will do a snappy

fifteen-minute presentation on the app and how to use it.
Dress code: 'On Wednesdays, we wear pink.'

I cringed at the basic plan and scrolled to the next attachment.

Launch Party: Ticketed event.
Theme: Feminist Thanksgiving.
Description: Fun goodie bags full of an Urban Dicktionary of Dating (Ella to design), lipstick and sanitary products. A three-course meal, viral walls with bar codes for maximum social media impact, live music, plus an app demonstration from Zola, Katy and Ella. Jimmy, Fee and Travis will join them.
Dress code: Female-inspired.

I felt my head flop back, as I stared at the ceiling, my chest tightening. What had we done? Guilt simmered in my gut. This was The Dicktionary Club, amplified by a million. I shut my eyes, rethinking all Britney's plans in a desperate attempt to tame them. There was no mention of women's safety or offering the hope of finding true love. The app was literally being marketed as a burn book – and we were willingly feeding that narrative to the press. Part of me thought it would do well initially, but it would eventually create such a hostile, bitchy culture. Deep inside, another part ached to be proud of what I'd created. I knew an app solely focused on slating men, no matter their past treatment of me, couldn't be the answer.

It was after six by now, and the office was dark except for my screen. I remained there, focused on researching similar apps and their PR strategies. Zola and Katy had gone home earlier; Zola said she would sleep with Katy tonight to help ease her stalker worries – as long as she promised to change the sheets.

A knock startled me from my work.

'Hey.' Jimmy's voice sounded tired. 'What's up?'

'Hey.' I looked up from my screen, my eyes blurry.

'Don't you ever sleep?' he asked with a slight smile. 'Or explore?'

I pulled a face. 'Explore? That's not my idea of fun.'

Jimmy stepped forward. 'You're in a new city, the best city in the world, I might add, but you never seem to leave this place.'

Raw panic suddenly seized me. 'How do you know I never go out?' I blurted, the words tumbling out before I could catch my breath. *Was he watching me? Could he be the weird texting stalker?* Paranoia prickled across my skin, growing more intense with every possibility that crossed my mind – had he seen too much? Did he regret hiring us?

Jimmy chuckled. 'I get reports on my desk every morning, who signs in and out, and you've been the last one to leave this building since you started.'

My shoulders relaxed. 'Aww, right. Well, I like to work,' I said, realising I sounded defensive.

'Come on, Ella. Didn't you have one thing on your New York bucket-list?' he pressed.

'OK,' I hummed. 'I have, and I will do it before I leave. Happy?'

'What is it?' Jimmy leaned closer. 'The Knicks? I can get you courtside seats.'

I laughed, shaking my head. 'I've seen enough sport to last a lifetime.'

'Come on, no judgement,' he said, now standing over me, brown eyes tired but mischievous.

'Fine. The Empire State Building,' I admitted. 'Cliché, I know!'

'Oh, so you're into skyscrapers?' He bit his lip. 'OK, got it.'

I laughed. 'Not like that! I just watch a lot of movies. And I find heights peaceful, quiet even. Plus, come on, it's the most iconic building in the world.'

Jimmy agreed, then rubbed the stubble on his chin. 'Have you heard of Summit One?'

I shook my head. I remembered it vaguely from one of Katy's TikTok reposts, but I hadn't paid much attention.

'It's cool. If you're up for it, I'd show you around.' He said it so casually I almost asked him to repeat himself.

'Emm . . . Sure. Maybe.' I felt my arsehole clench and was suddenly conscious of the plush leather seat sticking to my thighs. 'When I finish all this and . . .'

'Great.' He grinned. 'I'll pick you up at Hudson Yards tomorrow night at seven.'

'What?' Shit. I should've been clearer. Jimmy was hot, but also my boss, and I was fresh out of a breakup. Was this a date, or just friendly? 'Jimmy, I didn't know you meant tomorrow. I have . . .'

'I'm not listening now.' He laughed, covered his ears, then left.

When he was out of sight, I paused. A strange, giddy, excitable feeling tickled my stomach. I immediately brushed it off, knowing I should make up an excuse to bail. Then I thought of Philip and how carefree he was back home in Scotland with his new six-foot twig of a model to entertain. Still, I couldn't go, could I? How the fuck was I going to get out of this?

Chapter Twenty-Four

Ella

I waited until the girls and I were walking out to the car the next day to casually slip in my after-work plans. Alone time with Jimmy made me uncertain; I didn't know what it might mean or whether things might get messy. Yet part of me recognised that it offered the lift I needed. I longed to feel good again. Maybe a night out – escaping my thoughts about Philip, the endless work on the app design, Zola's sadness, Katy's casual sex noises – would do me good.

I turned to my friends and mumbled, 'Last night Jimmy asked me to go out with him, like tonight.'

I watched Zola almost give herself whiplash as she turned to me in shock. She cleared her throat. 'Sorry, *what*?'

Katy clapped happily as she skipped on the spot. 'And you said yes?' she gasped.

I lowered my head, almost feeling guilty. 'I mean, I tried not to, but he told me to be ready at seven. He's going to pick me up. He didn't let me make any excuses.'

Zola's face lifted in the first genuine smile I'd seen from her in days. 'Good for you, babe. You need this. Where is he taking you?'

The driver waited with the door open as we stepped in. I shrugged. 'A skyscraper – kind of what I said I wanted most to do while I was here.'

Katy had a dreamy expression, admiring the bold choice. 'Jimmy seems so sweet, Ella.'

Zola closed the door, sealing us in. 'Aren't they all in the beginning? Bloody lovebombers!'

I couldn't help but agree with her. She'd nailed it. Philip had pursued me relentlessly and then dropped me without a second thought. Maybe I should have trusted my gut and called him out as a player. Why did I ignore the warning signs? I didn't know Jimmy well enough to see any obvious red flags. But as with all men, I knew there would be some.

Zola brought me back from my thoughts. 'You seem pretty chill about it? For you?'

I puffed out a breath. 'He's hot, he seems kind, genuine. Why shouldn't I have a bit of fun while I'm here? Philip certainly is back home.' I glanced out the window, feeling a stabbing pain in my chest at the thought of my ex.

'Have you been stalking Erin again?' Katy asked. 'She's definitely on the Mounjaro, Ella. You look healthy. That girl is way too thin.'

'Thanks, babe.' I laughed slightly at the compliment. 'But I ended up blocking her last night – at one in the morning. I was spending way too much time analysing her videos, then those of her friends, even her dad's content. Bleugh.'

Zola reached over, grasping my hand in support. If anyone knew how I was feeling right now, it was her.

'Really, you haven't seen the one from today? She was working out in the teeniest pair of hot pants. I think it was one of Philip's gyms, too. Look!' Katy said, pulling out her phone. Her face fell immediately, and I knew it was at the sight of Erin's sculpted bod.

Zola noticed Katy's reaction. 'Another one?' she asked.

Katy nodded slowly in response, her eyes peering down at the screen.

'What does it say?' I asked, leaning over to glance at the screen as Katy clicked the message from the unknown number.

> **Unknown:** *I hate to judge, sweetheart. But next time you and Trav decide to poke around in Central Park, make sure there's no CCTV evidence. Buy yourself a plane ticket, or I'll send the X-rated vid to his wife and his beloved best friend.*

Katy went sickly white and mumbled, 'They know.'

Zola squeezed my hand tighter; it was the first time I'd seen her lost for words.

I held my finger up to my mouth and whispered, 'We need to be quiet. We don't know who this is.' I nudged my head towards the driver.

'CCTV!' Katy exclaimed as tears began to fall down her face. 'Poke around!'

Zola reached over and pulled Katy in for a hug. 'If they had the evidence,' she whispered, 'they would've sent a copy. Look, someone wants us gone. But why?'

'If it's not Travis, then who else would go to such lengths? We have to make a list of potential suspects.

But something's telling me this is bigger than us. Maybe someone out there doesn't want the app going live?' Zola was brilliant, I thought again – a natural problem solver who knew how to keep a clear head.

'Or someone who doesn't want the app to be a success?' I suggested, immediately thinking of the shitty PR efforts Britney sent over last night; a twelve-year-old could have put together a more original plan for their Bat Mitzvah.

Katy nodded. 'I don't want to ruin this opportunity for us. I'll go home if it makes life easier. Obviously, I'll still take my cut, but this is really scaring me, guys,' she said, trembling between the cascade of tears.

'No!' I warned her. 'You're going nowhere.'

'This is much bigger than Pocahontas in the park, Katy. We need to dig in and find out what they don't want us discovering. We need to make allies and track down as much information as possible,' Zola concluded. 'And maybe we have to start by telling Travis.'

I turned to Zola, surprised. 'Really? Isn't that throwing ammunition to the enemy?'

'He's high up; he'll know any beef that's clouding this company. And tonight, you'll have to rule Jimmy out. He'll be a great ally, plus he'll know if any competitors are really invested in wanting this app to fail,' Zola said.

'I can't tell him without admitting what happened with Katy and Travis, though.'

'Don't tell him that, for fuck's sake. Just ask the right questions. Gather intel,' Zola said, speaking quietly despite her indignation, so that the driver couldn't overhear us.

I swallowed, feeling unexpectedly energised, ready for a mission. Is this what Tom Cruise felt like in the 1990s before a job?

'Right. OK,' I agreed.

As Katy let out another wail, I squeezed her hand.

'We're in this together, Katy,' I told her. 'And no one gets away with blackmailing my friends!'

Chapter Twenty-Five

Ella

I finished work and left at a reasonable hour to prepare for my evening with Jimmy. On the way home, I picked up a new highlighter and instant tan at Sephora – the sun definitely wasn't as intense lately, and my sickly tiger-bread-style skin was on full show. After a long, exfoliating shower, I shaved and plucked my body until it was smooth, then dried and styled my hair. I was excited to go out – even though TikTok showed Summit One as crowded, the views seemed incredible. The only downside was that my trip there was with Jimmy. He was a lovely guy, but I knew I didn't want to rush into anything. I wasn't ready to date. Fuck, I wasn't even sure what had gone wrong with Philip; one slight inconvenience and he managed to move on to his next burd before my tea had turned cold.

They were swirling in my head, but I tried to push thoughts of Philip and his new girlfriend aside. When he flashed into my mind again, I forced myself to take a few steady breaths and move on. Like Zola had done with Curtis, I archived his WhatsApp, making sure I wasn't analysing when he was active, wondering who he was messaging. Maybe I needed this? A simple night out, feeling fresh and sexy again. Someone to harmlessly flirt with and distract me from Philip, even if it was just for a few hours.

Katy and Zola helped me pick an outfit, and eventually we settled on a classic black satin dress, a blazer and low pumps. I wanted to look polished but didn't fancy walking the streets in stilettos. At five minutes to seven, I was dressed and gazing at my reflection in the living room mirror. I looked good. My long blonde hair was slicked into a tight ponytail, allowing my new highlighter to emphasise my cheekbones. But I still felt subdued, and I knew I was overthinking the entire night. My stomach was in knots, and I wasn't sure if it was nerves or if I'd overloaded myself with coffee and actually just needed to go to the bathroom for my third poo of the day.

Katy and Zola, in contrast, were hyper, jumping around the apartment, arguing over Spotify tunes and playing the 'imagine if this happened' game.

'Imagine he just whips it clean out in the car and goes,' Katy slipped her voice into an exaggerated American accent, '"Wrap those mighty fine lips around this mighty fine hot dog, Ella."'

Zola was giggling and clapping her hands at the thought.

'What would you even say?' Katy asked, insistent.

I huffed, feeling a bit too nervous for this ridiculous game, just in case he came up to the apartment and overheard this entire conversation.

'I'd obviously tell him to bolt!' I replied, half-smiling as I glanced over at the elevator door as if he might walk through it.

'You wouldn't give him a hand job, then?' Zola managed between giggles. 'Not even if he asked nicely?'

'In the car?' I shot them a look as they both dissolved into fits of laughter. I smirked. 'OK – fine. Maybe just a couple of strokes.'

Zola's eyes widened. 'How big do you think? If you actually sleep with him, I'll die. Literally die.'

'Seriously, it's not like that. He asked me out because I always work late. He wants me to see the city a bit more. This is strictly platonic,' I insisted, though I kept wondering myself what his intentions were.

'Yeah, and don't forget we need to know if he has any beef with anyone, in or out of that company,' Zola added. 'If you forget to be *platonic* and sleep with him in between, then . . . enjoy it.'

I glanced at my watch and felt my nerves descend. 'It's almost seven, I'm going to wait downstairs. You two are far too unpredictable for him to come up here.'

'Aw, don't! Ella!' Katy moaned. 'I want to see his outfit.'

'I want to see his bulge!' Zola burst out laughing, and Katy joined in again.

'Bye!' I tittered, heading towards the elevator and making my way down to the lobby.

As I reached the foyer, the doorman, Otis, was standing as smart as always with a broad smile.

'Well, Miss Ella. You look fantastic, girl,' he said as he held out his hand for mine, and as I took it, he spun me around, admiring my dress.

'Thank you,' I said with a grin, blushing slightly.

'What's on tonight? Hot date? Business dinner?'

I hesitated, unsure how to classify my plans. 'No, my boss is taking me out because I never seem to leave the office in time to enjoy the evening,' I said.

'Mr Jimmy?' The doorman's eyebrows shot up.

I blushed again, by way of confirming.

'Well, ain't that interesting,' he concluded with a slight hum to his voice. We stood shoulder to shoulder, awaiting Jimmy's arrival for a few more seconds. 'He's a good man, Mr Jimmy,' Otis eventually replied.

I grinned. 'Yeah, he seems like it.'

There was a flash of headlights as a sleek car drove into the car park and I took a step forward. *Here we go*, I thought.

Otis grinned, voice teasing as he said, 'Don't stay out too late now, Miss Ella.'

'I'll see you soon,' I warned.

I walked over to the black sports car as Jimmy opened his door and stepped out to greet me. He looked good, dressed in a dark shirt and trousers. He grinned as he approached me.

'Damn, you look great, Ella,' he said, pulling me into a quick hug. I patted his back, a bit awkwardly, then he opened the back door of the car.

'Thanks,' I replied.

'No problem,' Jimmy said, his eyes still on me. He shut the door.

Fuck. What was I doing? He had his own driver who seemed oblivious I had even entered the car. I felt unsettled – overheating, nervous. Talking to Jimmy at work was easy, but this felt different. Bigger. Plus, I really needed to shit.

I watched him wave to Otis, and a few seconds later, he was sitting beside me, buckling up.

'How are you?' Jimmy asked, as his driver pulled away from Hudson Yards.

I gulped. 'Yeah. Good, thanks. How are you?'

He laughed. 'I'll be real – I was nervous as hell on the drive over,' he said, showing me his sweaty palms. 'See this?'

'I felt fine until I got into your car, then I felt really nervous too,' I admitted, laughing slightly.

'I'm glad I'm not the only one,' he said. His easy-going nature and admission made me instantly less anxious. I sat back and managed to feel my breath and stomach settle.

'So, you left the office on time today?' He raised a brow as he darted me a look.

'I did. I'll have to make up for it tomorrow now,' I replied. 'My boss can be a bit of a dick with that kind of stuff,' I joked.

Jimmy's face dropped and he swung round. 'Ella!' He sounded shocked. 'Wow!'

'You also leave pretty late, too, you know. Is there something happening, or is that normal for you?' I added, as casually as I could, hoping to gain intel to catch our stalker as early into the night as possible.

Jimmy exhaled. 'There's always something going on, trust me. I won't bore you with the details.' He shrugged it off.

'I'm a good listener,' I replied, smiling back at him.

Jimmy paused, glancing over at me. His dark eyes locked onto mine. Then I felt his hand pat my thigh.

'I bet you are, Ella,' he said, grazing his thumb ever so gently against my dress.

My heart raced, and I felt as if I were glued to the seat. Then, he lifted his hand, returning it to his lap. I peered out of the window, watching the buildings fly past us and listening to the purr of the engine.

But what was that? I wondered. Part of me wanted to remind Jimmy that touching my leg was inappropriate, but another part wanted his hand back there again. Was he just one of those touchy-feely people who think physical contact like that is perfectly normal? I wondered. Fuck, maybe it is in America. I'll have to ChatGPT that later, I thought, placing a mental note to myself.

'It's the investors, you see,' Jimmy said, noticing the quiet. 'They deal with financing everything. So, if we ask them for money and the project doesn't land, then I have to delve into it with Trav.' He turned to me again, noticing my silence. Jesus, I was still trying to get over that thigh touch. 'See, I told you it was boring!'

'It's interesting.' I smiled.

The car pulled onto a busy street.

'Is this us?' I glanced around, 'Are we here?'

'Sure are, it's that building just there.' Jimmy leaned closer. His scent was deep, musky, like Tom Ford and Prada had had a baby. Jesus, he smelled unbelievable.

My eyes skimmed the tall, slender building; it looked more striking than the others rising above Grand Central Station. It was a sleek glass design that seemed to catch the city's lights, illuminating the structure.

'I saw on TikTok we enter through Grand Central,' I replied.

'Normally you do,' Jimmy replied softly. 'But we can enter through that door tonight,' he leaned closer, pointing to a set of black doors, 'And I thought you'd enjoy it more if it was just the two of us.'

I turned to him in shock. He lowered his head, looking almost embarrassed at this grand gesture. I was lost for words, yet full of questions. Like, how much money and power did this man have if he could shut an entire tourist attraction just for me?

'Come on, let me show you around,' Jimmy said. His driver had hopped out without me even noticing and opened his car door.

I opened my door, not wanting to wait for any more Princess treatment. Instantly, I felt the thick, muggy air surround me. Jimmy jogged around the side of the car, holding the door for me to get out properly. Then we headed into Summit One together, surrounded by commuters racing to the train station, taxi horns honking and the generalised chaos of the city.

As we entered, silence returned. A young woman stationed behind the reception desk immediately walked around to greet us.

'Mr Link.' She beamed. 'It's wonderful to have you here. If you'd like to follow me, I'll escort you to the elevator.'

I followed behind, taking in the extensive winding queue system that was entirely empty. We passed through a huge foyer and headed straight towards a bank of elevators. The young woman pressed a button, and one of the elevator doors slid open. A man was standing by the controls.

'Welcome to Summit One Vanderbilt, please come in,' he said, inviting us into the mirrored elevator.

I stepped in and turned to Jimmy with a massive grin on my face. He seemed amused by my excitement.

'How many floors do we go up?' I asked.

'We're about to go over a thousand feet, ma'am. The observatory decks are floors ninety-one through to ninety-three,' the young man replied.

Jimmy stepped in and joined me. 'Are you ready, Ella?' He nudged me jokingly.

'Eh, yes! Let's go!' I laughed, completely bowled over, as the doors shut.

The elevator lights dimmed into darkness, and I turned to Jimmy, who smiled back at me. I felt pressure all over me as we soared into the sky. Brightly lit special effects played around the elevator walls as if we were flying through space. I grabbed hold of Jimmy's arm, feeling my ears pop on the way up.

Then, within only a few seconds, the lift came to a gentle stop.

'Enjoy your evening,' the elevator man said.

The doors parted and bursts of orange and pink immediately greeted us. I stepped out to find that the floor was entirely wrapped in glass, with floor-to-ceiling windows overlooking the city. The sun was setting, sending streaks of deep colour across the sky. It seemed like the city went on forever.

I suddenly realised I was still grasping Jimmy's arm and let go.

'Remarkable, huh?' He held back, allowing me to wander up to the enormous glass walls.

'This is absolutely unbelievable.' I laughed, feeling a whole intensity of emotions creep up on me. It was beautiful, calm and quiet. It was the first time I wasn't hearing background noise ploughing through my brain since leaving Glasgow.

'Wait. Is that the Empire State Building?' I pointed over to a tower so tall that its needle point seemed to pierce the sky.

I felt Jimmy's body press against me, peering over my shoulder. 'Sure is, and the Chrysler Building is just there.' He pointed to the beautiful, layered Art Deco spire, almost at eye level with us. 'And Central Park, of course, is just over there.'

I laughed incredulously and took out my phone, snapping videos of the iconic skyline. I wanted to capture exactly how the city looked in this instant, because it was breathtaking. We had this entire building to ourselves. How was that even possible? I felt so free. I slipped off my shoes and felt the cool glass floor on my feet. A childlike joy bubbled up in me and I turned to run around the vast space.

'This is so amazing, Jimmy!' I called out. 'Thank you!'

He stood laughing, arms folded, in complete agreement as I explored. I soaked up every inch of this incredible space, picking out as many landmarks as I could through the windows.

'Are you brave enough for the complete experience?' Jimmy said eventually, as my initial zoomies settled.

Oh God. Maybe he did have the wrong idea. My carefree happiness was being brought back down to reality. The complete experience? Did he want to finish this off with a shag against the glass of one of the tallest buildings in New York?

'What do you mean?' I asked, sounding sceptical.

Jimmy burst out laughing. 'Damn,' he blurted. 'Don't worry, it's just a fancy glass box, Ella.'

He grinned, heading towards the far end of the room. I followed behind like a puppy, then noticed the entirely glass cube that stuck out of the side of the building, suspended impossibly high above the street below, with nothing in between.

'When you look down, it's completely glass; it can be daunting,' Jimmy warned. 'Scary even.'

I gulped. 'Will you do it with me?' I asked.

'Of course.' Jimmy stepped forward, taking my hand. 'Ready?' His voice was cool and calm, betraying no hint of fear.

He made me feel more confident. I smiled and stepped into the box, my hand squeezing his.

'Look down,' he whispered. 'You're safe, Ella.'

I slowly began to glance down as we levitated above the bustling street at over a thousand feet.

Wow.

I felt my heart skip a thousand beats. Like I was flying. My stomach twisted, but I felt alive, like I'd completely escaped the everyday drama that always seemed to surround me. It all seemed so insignificant from way up here.

I walked to the edge of the box, still holding his hand with a firm grip, and peered over. 'Everyone seems so small,' I said, watching the people rushing around Madison Avenue far below.

'Problems seem small up here, too,' Jimmy replied, as engrossed in the view as I was. It was like he had read my mind.

I turned back to him. 'I don't want to leave,' I admitted. 'Ever!'

Jimmy grinned. 'Here in particular, or New York in general?'

I thought about that question for a few seconds. New York was unbelievable, almost certainly the best place I'd ever been, and I'd barely scratched its surface. And now Philip and I had split, it really felt like there was too much baggage back home. Maybe I needed a fresh start, a new adventure. Maybe I needed this.

'Well, right now – here. I could stay up here forever.' I pressed my head against the glass, feeling less nervous about taking in the view while being suspended in space than I had a few moments ago.

I brought my phone out of my bag again, dropping his hand, wanting to capture this moment for the girls to see. I turned to Jimmy just as he stepped back, allowing me to snap a few photos. 'Come back.' I smiled. 'Enjoy it with me.' I held out my hand, and he stepped back into the glass box as we pointed and giggled at the world going by us.

Eventually, Jimmy ushered me back to the main observation deck. The bright sunset had faded and the night sky seemed to envelop us. The city's bright lights took over our view, and everything glittered. I peered out at Manhattan, New Jersey, as far as I could, taking it all in.

Then I noticed Jimmy sitting at a small round table, which I could've sworn wasn't there when we arrived.

'Hungry?' he asked, standing up and offering me a seat.

'Is it a restaurant too?' I asked, looking around curiously.

Jimmy shook his head. 'No, not normally, but I've pulled some strings. What would you like to eat?'

I could feel my face scrunching up, completely bewildered at the lengths this man had gone to. It was unbelievably sweet yet didn't feel cheesy. It felt kind and genuine, like I was enjoying my time with a friend – a very good-looking and extraordinarily wealthy friend.

'What are the options?' I asked. 'Is there a menu?'

Jimmy let out a laugh. 'Just pick your favourite and I'll order it for you.' He smiled, looking like he was enjoying my confusion.

'What do you fancy?' I asked, feeling the task of choosing from the endless food dishes of the world to be far too great.

'It's your choice. What do you feel like eating?' He sat in the seat so elegantly, one leg crossed over the other. I couldn't remember the last time Philip let me pick our meal; he always chose. He acted like he knew the best dish on every menu at every restaurant, and I was happy to go along. At least, I'd thought I was.

'C'mon, Ella. What do you like?' Jimmy grinned. 'You don't have to pick small to be polite. Be outrageous!' His eyes twinkled, as if it were a challenge.

'Honestly, if I were being that outrageous, I'd pick a Big Mac and fries. I've been dying to try it over here. The portions seem humongous!' I laughed. 'Basic, I know!'

'A McDonald's!' he blurted, laughing hard, then rummaged through his pocket and brought out his phone. 'What drink?'

'Are you Just Eating this?' I giggled.

Jimmy peered up from his phone. 'No, I'm messaging one of my staff your order, and she'll go collect it and bring it here.'

'Are you having one?' I smiled, wondering if his personal trainer would allow him a night off.

'Hell, yes I am!' Jimmy replied, placing his phone back in his pocket. 'Extra-extra-large and all the cheese!'

Chapter Twenty-Six

Ella

Twenty minutes later, Jimmy and I were tucking into American-sized McDonald's burgers and fries, and sipping on Cokes. The burgers tasted infinitely better than back home, where they always seemed to forget half the order or the sauce.

Jimmy was halfway through his when he turned to me. 'Damn, I forgot how good these are,' he almost grunted.

I agreed and stuffed more fries into my mouth. 'So, so good!' I said between bites, then gestured with a fry towards Jimmy. 'You should start a McDonald's Friday at work – every Friday, order this in.' I smiled, feeling my cheeks push out as I took another big bite.

Jimmy's shoulders bobbed as he fought not to laugh with his mouth full. He covered his mouth with one hand and, after swallowing, turned to me. 'How are you liking New York so far?'

'It's good, everything is very cool,' I said. 'I feel like I'm existing in a movie set.'

Jimmy huffed. 'I'm glad. I wasn't sure if you were enjoying it because you never seem to leave your desk!'

I paused, a knot tightening in my stomach. Lately, nothing brought me real joy; the weight of the app, combined with Katy's stalker drama and the way Philip had ended things, all pressed down on me, sometimes making it hard to breathe.

'I've been a bit stressed, I must admit.' I tried to pull my lips into a shaky smile, attempting an eye roll to lighten the mood.

Jimmy's face remained serious, concern etched plainly in his eyes.

'Talk to me about it.' He set down the last piece of his burger, wiped his hand on a napkin, then leaned in slightly, waiting for me to continue.

'Honestly, I'm one of those people who stress and overthink anyway. Often about nothing.' I smiled. 'It's been a lifelong problem.'

Jimmy wasn't convinced. He sipped his Coke and sat back. 'Ella, have you ever heard the phrase "a problem shared is a problem halved"?'

I grinned, placing down my food too. 'I have, but the problem is, it's not one problem . . .'

Jimmy tilted his chin, looking for more.

'Well, my boyfriend broke up with me for coming out here. He didn't want me to pitch The Dicktionary Club; he disagrees with the concept, sees it as just malicious gossiping about men, which he kind of thinks is immoral. He's this huge entrepreneur back in Scotland, and I really wanted to make this project work, so I came anyway. Then, I found out after a few days that he's been papped with a twenty-three-year-old influencer, and they're an item.' I pushed my burger away, suddenly losing my appetite, thinking of Philip's glossy twig of a girlfriend.

'Well, that is a whole lot of stress,' Jimmy said.

'Yeah,' I agreed, my voice barely above a whisper. 'But the worst part is, I think he's right.' I spoke quietly, shame prickling along my skin like a confession I could barely contain.

'How do you mean?' Jimmy leaned in closer.

'I think The Dicktionary Club is sort of immoral. The concept is good, but it has so many ways to turn dark. Women can say anything, make terrible shit up, and it will be out there. I wanted to come over here and create something amazing. Something I would be proud of. I wanted to make a real impact on the dating game. But I'm not convinced this is it.'

Jimmy shrugged like I had told him about the easiest problem in the world to sort. 'Change it then. It's your project.'

I blew out a breath. 'If only it was that easy.'

'Ella, it is.' He looked confused. 'By the sounds of it, you think it's potentially unfair, immoral, right?'

I nodded.

'What would make it fairer?' Jimmy asked.

'Probably allowing men to rate women too?' I admitted. 'Instead of posting individual reviews, we could summarise what more than one person thinks about someone.'

Jimmy grinned. 'See?'

I laughed, feeling lighter just from sitting here problem-solving with him.

Jimmy was still grinning. 'There you go, Ella,' he said softly. 'How are you finding Britney's PR plan?'

I scoffed. 'Honestly? I think it's poor. I imagined the launch being at the Met or somewhere amazing, iconic even, but her plan is pretty basic.'

'The Met!' Jimmy laughed. 'Aim high, girl!'

'Somewhere like that. Like a fairytale. It's silly, I know.' I shrugged, a little embarrassed.

Jimmy reached out. 'It's not silly, Ella. Girl, if you want the Met, let's do it!'

'What?' I laughed. 'Do we have time for these kind of dramatic changes? We'd have to recalibrate the whole campaign. Thanksgiving is in, like, five weeks or something.'

'Anything can be done if you put your mind to it.' He smiled. 'We could call the team in and get them to meet us back at the office?'

I sat up, a beat of pure excitement running through me. 'What? Now?'

'Absolutely, if you're up for a late night?' I sensed him watching me closely, as if he was understanding how I worked. For a moment, I felt truly seen.

'Yes!' I stood up. 'Let's go!' Suddenly, I had a spring in my step. Everything felt lighter, one thousand feet in the air – even my knottiest problems.

Jimmy joined me on his feet. 'Let's do it.'

I skipped over to retrieve my shoes, glancing around the vast observation deck, sparkling with the reflections of millions of lights in the night sky, realising this was probably the best, most insanely memorable night of my life. I turned to Jimmy. 'Thank you.' I smiled.

He walked slowly towards me, stopping just in front of where I stood. Unsure if he meant to hug me, I didn't move away. Despite my uncertainty, his closeness felt welcome. I felt grateful for a wonderful night, for him listening to me, helping me.

Around us, complete silence settled. He slowly slid his hand up my arm, his fingers tracing my skin. Goosebumps rose all over me as his touch lingered. Then he leaned forward and rested his forehead gently against mine.

His voice was just a whisper. 'You are beautiful, intelligent and funny, Ella. Your ex has no idea what he's lost.' I felt his sigh on my face. He clenched his fists, looking as torn by the moment as I was. 'Let's make the best app out there, something that makes you burst with pride. I love when you glow.'

I shivered as desire pulsed through me, both exciting and grounding. The world narrowed to this perfect moment – Jimmy, the city lights, the mirrored surfaces, even the McDonald's wrappers littering the table.

Jimmy's hand slid down my arm, his fingers briefly brushing over my breast, making me instinctively lean closer. He interlaced his fingers with mine and gently pulled me towards the elevator.

As we descended, I felt butterflies and lust take over every inch of my body. He kept hold of my hand, a firm touch, and I imagined what it would be like for him to be squeezing my thighs, teasing my clit. I felt my underwear dampen at the thought.

Then the elevator stopped, and we stepped back out into the energy of the city, making our way to the Flirtify headquarters.

Chapter Twenty-Seven

Ella

On the drive over to Flirtify, Jimmy was busy on the phone, gathering the troops for an immediate revamp of Stars and Swipes. It was strange. Although he wasn't talking to me, I didn't feel neglected the way I did with Philip's calls; I felt involved. Jimmy didn't specify what we needed the troops for, only that all department heads were required to attend.

The elevator dropped to the car park, and Jimmy and I stepped in. As soon as the doors closed, he turned to me.

'I had a great time tonight, thank you,' he said, slipping a stray hair behind my ear.

I stepped closer towards him. 'I should be the one thanking you. It was the coolest, most memorable, outrageous moment of my life being up there with just you!' I admitted, a broad smile spreading over my face.

We looked at each other, faces lit by elevator light. I caught the tiny lines creasing at the side of his mouth and the stubble edging his jaw. He seemed lost in thought before I slowly raised my hand to the back of his neck, leaning closer.

'Jimmy?'

'Mmmm,' he hummed, still unable to take his eyes off mine.

'You can kiss me now,' I whispered.

Jimmy's eyes widened, surprise mixing with desire, then he instantly pulled me close and kissed me. Our lips met desperately, breaths harsh in the confined space as his hands roamed over my dress, pushing me into the elevator's corner. I hooked my leg around his hip, drawing him in. Then I felt it. His dick, pressing into me thick and long like a tree trunk trapped in a tailored suit. The heat and urgency between us intensified as we pressed together.

'Fuck, Ella,' Jimmy panted, moving his hand up my dress, sweeping my thigh, following it around the back to squeeze my arse.

The lift came to a halt and we reluctantly pulled apart as reality crept back in. The door slid open, revealing the semi-lit office.

'Some of the team must have arrived already,' he said with a grin.

I felt myself blush, not quite knowing what had just come over me.

'Hey,' Jimmy added, straightening out my blazer and gently wiping lip gloss from my chin. 'Let's make something remarkable, yeah? You got this, Ella. I believe in you, one hundred per cent.' He reached forward and kissed my forehead, not seeming to care who walked by the elevator.

'Yeah.' I grinned back, letting out a breath of intense sexual frustration and nerves. 'We got this,' I agreed.

Making our way further into the office, the dim light from a few scattered computer monitors lit the room, but we could see brightness coming from the large conference room, along with some chatter. I took out my phone and messaged the group chat.

Ella: *Are you guys here? X*
Zola: *Yeah. Where are you? X*
Katy: *What's going on, Ella??? Did you tell J about the stalker? X*

With a deep breath, switching myself into professional mode, I followed Jimmy into the conference room, spotting Katy and offering her a reassuring smile. The romantic energy that I could feel wrapped around me shifted immediately as I observed Travis at the back of the room, dressed in a tracksuit and sipping water, and Britney seated with a notepad, her hair in a tight bun. Zola and Katy were pacing at the side, and as I moved towards my friends, a voice from behind interrupted.

'We don't do on-call.' I turned and noticed Ethan, the IT specialist. Great, he too seemed pissed.

'Hey, Ethan,' Jimmy said coolly as he headed to greet him. 'I realise that, but this is important.' He pointed to a chair, but Ethan still seemed flustered, glancing around the packed room.

'OK, I think we have everyone.' Jimmy spoke loudly and authoritatively enough that the room took to their seats and the whispers between staff subsided. 'Firstly, I want to thank y'all for coming in at this unexpected time. I realise it's almost eleven p.m. and you've already had a busy day in the office. However, Ella shared some concerns about the app we're all creating, and I thought now would be the perfect time to brainstorm ways to address them.'

Zola and Katy's side glances felt like stabs of accusation. I hated that it looked like I was sidelining them; this project belonged to all of us. I should have talked to them first. Why didn't I? Guilt crawled in, tightening my throat.

Instead, I headed to the front of the table, standing beside Jimmy. 'Yes, and I firstly want to say I haven't even had a minute to discuss with my two co-founders, so Katy and Zola, please speak up if you disagree on what I'm about to say.'

Zola bobbed her head, while Katy offered a smile in my direction.

'I have concerns that Stars and Swipes is turning into an app for women, which may have negative *Tattle Life*-type connotations,' I began, feeling my sense of purpose and confidence grow. 'When we initially developed this idea, we wanted to do it in order to warn women about men who perhaps slept around, or were married, abusive or dangerous even . . .'

I watched Katy flick her gaze to Travis momentarily.

'It was created with absolute good intentions; however, what about the women who trick men, who cheat on their husbands, who perhaps catfish or exploit with their pictures?' The room was silent, and I suddenly felt slightly exhausted. 'Look, I think we're missing a whole market by targeting only women. We're excluding half of the population by creating this in its original form.'

Zola popped her hand up. 'But we're pitching it as a secret girls' club type thing? That is literally the point, isn't it?'

I grinned. 'But what if we weren't?' I felt a rush of adrenaline imagining the opportunities that lay ahead. 'What if we're pitching the future of dating for men *and* women? What if we ask the apps to partner with us on promoting safety features? Let's make an app designed to create genuine, safe connections in the search for love.'

Katy seemed pleased at the new concept, smiling as I spoke.

'And we still get people to write reviews? Like a Rate My Date type thing?' Zola questioned, wrapping her head around my idea.

'Yes, but instead of anyone being able to go on and write up anyone else, we give both parties forty-eight hours from meeting to complete a short questionnaire, which avoids scorned exes blasting someone's reputation. We get them to write a short paragraph, perhaps based on a questionnaire and . . .'

Ethan puffed, as if I was going too slow for him. 'We insert an AI tool which will generate an overall summary of the key elements people generally leave in their reviews of that person.'

Zola smirked. 'Cool, so if one hundred women call him an ass and two call him a god, he'll be described as an ass?'

'Precisely. AI filters the probability of the keywords used by the daters' questionnaire and creates an accurate overall review,' Ethan concluded.

'And I feel really strongly about pushing the safety aspect of the app,' I said. 'It's also great PR. We can add features to the app about safety and advice for meeting strangers. Maybe make users take a tutorial of safe dating tips when a first date is being arranged?'

Britney cleared her throat. 'I'm sorry, Ella, but this is such a U-turn from the app we thought we were creating. We've already planned the PR strategy around your initial women-only app. I don't think we'll have time to re-plan a whole PR campaign if we expect the app to launch by Thanksgiving.'

My heart dropped. I should have voiced my doubts earlier, but they'd somehow become all tangled up with Katy and Philip – too much background noise, and I'd kept quiet. Now, though, everything was sharp, crystal clear. This had to be the version we put into the world. I needed to stand behind something I believed in.

'I understand that time is a factor, Britney,' I began.

'Not just a factor, Ella. It's practically impossible to carry out all this work in a five-week time frame, I'm sorry!' She placed her pen down and stared towards Jimmy for some form of understanding.

'Oh, please.' Katy laughed loudly.

Zola swung her head round, facing her, making her braids rattle off the chair.

'That's not true!' Katy continued. 'Zola, Ella, and I have managed PR for projects this size and completed them in less than a fortnight. You're being so defeatist, Britney. You have a whole team of people.'

I bit my lip, trying not to laugh. But my friend was right. I had no real idea whether the app's technical side could be ready, but I did know the PR side inside out, and I knew it was doable, especially with the entire team of minions that negative cunt had.

'Jimmy!' Britney squeaked.

Jimmy remained quiet for a few moments, then turned his attention to Ethan, who was staring at his hands.

'Ethan, could the app be ready for download with all of the new features we've discussed?'

Zola threw back her head, assuming another issue was about to arise. She knew he didn't like working with her as it was.

'It will be ready, Jimmy. I can start tonight, which will give us a head start in the morning. We'd have to pull some pretty hardcore late nights, but it is possible.'

I grinned widely, turning to Zola and Katy.

'I can help with PR. Britney, remember that is my background,' I added reassuringly, but authoritatively.

'We can only try.' She puffed and pouted, keeping her stare fixed on Jimmy.

'OK, I think we're done then. I'll email everyone an up-to-date list of the features required. Please speak up if you think of anything else that will enhance our offer. I have a really great feeling about this,' I added, looking round at everyone to include them in my smile. After all, I really did need them on side.

'All right.' Jimmy clapped his hands, and the boardroom – minus Britney – joined in applauding my speech. I felt myself blush, turning to Jimmy and grinning.

Finally, I felt like I could do this.

Chapter Twenty-Eight

Katy

As the meeting ended, Zola and Katy made their way over to Ella, who seemed nervous. As they approached, she held up her hands.

'I'm sorry, I was at Summit One, and Jimmy was asking why I was worried about the app, and all of this change came to me so quickly. I should have run it past you both, but Jimmy suggested calling the troops in and . . .' She sounded so genuinely apologetic, stuttering over her words, that Katy leapt forward and hugged her tightly.

'I think it sounds like an excellent idea, Ells,' she said, meaning it.

'Good work,' Zola added with a wink. 'And I take it the date went well?' She bit her nail and swivelled around, looking Jimmy up and down while he spoke to Travis about investors a few metres behind them.

Ella blushed. 'Yeah, it was really nice, actually.'

'Uh-huh.' Zola smirked.

'What?' Ella nudged her shoulder, face reddening.

'Babe, your makeup is completely off around your mouth, and I'm guessing that's because Jimmy's wearing it.' Zola giggled loudly, clapping her hands.

'Fuck!' Ella lowered her head. 'I'd better go sort this.' She covered her face slightly, feeling suddenly self-conscious, and took a few steps back. 'I'm going to stay for a bit and write the new plan. Do you want to help?'

Zola turned to Katy, then spotted Ethan leaving the room. 'I think I might head to the tech suite and see what genius plans Ethan's got going. Not that he'll tell me, but I can always observe.'

Katy grinned. 'I'm going to get a coffee. To be honest, I'm fucked.'

The other two girls smiled and headed their separate ways. Katy walked down the dimly lit corridor to the kitchenette and grabbed a mug, setting it under the coffee machine. She began pressing buttons, but nothing happened. She hit the side of the machine.

'Come on,' she muttered. 'This is a caffeine emergency.'

'Hey, need some help?' Travis stood, arms crossed, amused at her conversation with the appliance.

'It's broke,' Katy declared. 'I'll just grab a can.' She turned to the fridge, avoiding eye contact with Travis for as long as she possibly could.

He took a few steps forward and plugged something in; the coffee machine lit up immediately. 'The cleaner switches it off at night,' he explained.

Katy sighed as she turned to face him.

'Right. Em . . . Thanks,' she replied, feeling embarrassed.

Travis's blue eyes remained on her, a soft smile on his face. 'How are you settling in?' he asked. It was the first time they'd been alone since him turning up to their place.

She nodded, reaching over to press some buttons. 'Mm . . . Fine, yeah.'

'You girls seem right at home,' he continued. 'New York suits you, Katy.'

For a moment, she remembered the stalker. Travis always seemed kind and respectful on the surface, but there had to be something darker lurking for him to treat his wife like that. Yet, somehow, he didn't seem capable. Yes, he was a cheat, but he was quiet and considerate and did try to sort the mess out like an adult. And although things had turned out terribly, he was always gentle with her, loving almost.

'Travis,' she said. 'I have to tell you something.'

He pressed his hand against the worktop. 'Me too,' he said.

Katy felt her heart skip a beat. Was he about to admit he was involved in all of this? Maybe this would be the moment he'd try to blackmail her. Fuck. She didn't get her share of the money from Jimmy until the app was complete and she was skint.

He began just as Katy opened her mouth. 'I haven't stopped thinking about—'

'Someone knows about us,' Katy spoke over him.

Both of them realised what the other was saying, and they stood looking at each other in shock.

'What do you mean? Who?' Travis hissed under his breath, stepping forward. 'Who have you told?'

Katy took a step back, feeling a little intimidated. 'I don't know who it is, they've been sending me creepy text messages telling me to go home or they'll expose us. And I haven't told anyone! Who have you fucking told?' She knew Zola and Ella were, of course, exempt from her list, but explaining girl code was not on the cards right now.

'Creepy messages?' Travis rubbed his temple. 'That doesn't make any sense!'

Katy rolled her eyes. 'Yeah, well, think how I've been feeling! I've been wondering if it was you,' she whispered. Nearby, she heard voices.

'Me?' Travis seemed surprised. 'I would never do that, Katy. Not to you, not to anyone.' He blew out a puff of breath. 'OK, so what did the messages say exactly?'

Katy pulled her phone from her back pocket, opened up the messages from the unknown number, then passed it to Travis, with a sudden lurch that she might be playing her hand too soon. He glanced over his shoulder, then walked into the little kitchen storeroom, ushering Katy to follow. The door closed behind her and she found herself in a tiny cupboard, surrounded by cookies, protein bars, cartons of oat milk and bags of coffee beans. Travis was concentrating on her phone, reading and then rereading the messages. She watched his eyes travel as he read, examining his handsome face. She could smell his warm, sweet aftershave, which immediately gave her flashbacks of him moving, naked, on top of her. She relished his body, his smell.

'This is horrible.' Travis looked pale.

'What is? Aw yeah, I know,' Katy agreed, shaking off her thoughts.

'You must be so frightened,' Travis said, rubbing her shoulder. 'I'm so sorry, Katy, for getting you involved in this.'

She gulped. 'Involved in what, though? Do you know anyone who would do this, Travis? Anyone who has a vendetta, or maybe someone who doesn't want the app to launch?'

Travis thought hard, but he seemed to still be in shock, shaking his head. 'I don't know anyone. I mean, Britney didn't look exactly pleased about the extra work, but she wouldn't do this.'

A brief moment of silence fell between them.

Katy's phone pinged again.

> **Unknown:** *So, we're doing late-night meetings now? Cute. But still no booked-flight email. Should I forward Mr Link your Central Park performance?*

Katy turned to Travis and watched his jaw drop. She glanced around the room, making sure no cameras were in sight. She could feel her breathing quicken as her hand trembled, still holding the phone.

'Someone is watching me, Travis,' she whispered, feeling her bottom lip quiver. 'And I really don't like it.'

Travis wrapped his arms around her tightly. 'Shh. Come on, we can figure this out. You're safe, do you hear me?' He brought his hand to her chin, turning her face to look up at him. 'I won't ever let anything bad happen to you.'

Katy was staring into at his kind eyes, getting lost in them. 'Maybe I should go back to Glasgow?'

'Hey, this is my fault. You're not going anywhere,' he replied sternly, although his gaze was full of an unmistakable fear.

The pair stared at one another for a few moments before Travis lowered his head and kissed Katy softly. He pulled back and paused, then leaned forward for another. Katy immediately folded, kissing him back, passionately. She felt his hand grab her arse and squeeze it.

'Mmm . . . Jesus! I've thought about fucking you every moment since I left you, Katy,' Travis grunted, growing rougher with his kisses.

Katy panted, knowing she felt the same. She was overcome with emotion – the stalker, Travis, the mountain of work ahead, everything seemed heightened – and she needed a release. She ran her hand down Travis's jeans, feeling his dick harden. She slipped her hand into his boxers, rubbing it up and down. Jesus, she had goosebumps all over her at the thought of his pulsing cock. This was what she wanted. Ever since she'd first met him, he was the guy she wanted.

He turned her around, lifting her floaty dress up to her waist and tugging her pants to the side. 'Bend over,' he panted. 'Come on, we have to!'

She automatically did what she was told, grabbing onto a shelf stacked with kitchen supplies for support.

Then she felt him push inside. No foreplay, no warm-up. Both of them had been craving this. She let out a moan and he pulled back her hair, covering her mouth. She could taste herself on his hand, and she panted some more. He was thrusting in and out, trying hard to be quiet, but little grunts flew out of his mouth.

'Jesus, oh, God, Katy,' he murmured.

Katy pressed hard on the shelf for stability, but she could feel it rattle. Suddenly, boxes of cereal tumbled off and landed on the floor. She gasped, turning to him as grains littered the sky, falling like biscuity dust on top of her. She spat out a few. But Travis was locked in, utterly oblivious to the chaotic mess they were creating.

She could feel his legs trembling from behind until finally he pulled her in. His arms slipped from Katy's face and mouth to her breasts, and he grabbed hold of them. He paused momentarily, letting out a few more quivering grunts, then released her. It was over in a matter of minutes, but Katy didn't care. She wondered what this meant. She wondered if he'd admit it to Fee and tell her how unhappy in their marriage he clearly was.

Katy fixed her knickers, pulled down her dress, and shook off the cereal crumbs from her clothes like a wet dog. She turned to Travis with a grin she couldn't suppress.

'I'm sorry,' he said, looking disappointed in himself.

'No, I was dying for you too . . .'

'No, Katy. Shit, I need to be more careful. It's just every time I see you, I want this. But I'm fucking married . . .' He lowered his head.

Katy felt a ripple of anger prickle down her spine. 'Are you joking me right now?' she asked.

Travis lifted his head, not knowing what had pissed her off.

'I'm literally standing here with your fucking jizz running down my leg and you're telling me you regret that it's happened?' She was shaking with pure rage. 'Look at the position you've put me in. I'm getting stalked because you can't keep that dick of yours away from me! And now that I've done this again, fuck knows what will happen when the weirdo stalker finds out!'

She shook her head, seething.

Travis's shoulders dropped. 'That's not what I meant, Katy. We can fix all of this,' he said, his tone more understanding now, reaching out to touch her hair.

She swatted his hand away and stood back, shaking her head.

'No, I've got it, Travis. Just stay away from me, OK?' She opened the door, 'You better tidy this shit up. No doubt your wife will start to ask questions!' Tears filling her eyes, she slammed the door shut behind her, leaving Travis surrounded by mess.

Katy stormed out of the kitchenette and headed straight to the toilets to get rid of any evidence that Travis had just pumped her in the snack closet. She sat in a toilet cubicle, running her hands through her hair, making sure all traces of the cereal were gone.

Who could the stalker be? And why the fuck did I do that?

She felt water drip onto her knees and sat up, realising she was crying. As she spotted the tears, she also noticed a white snail trail of semen resting gloopily on her thigh.

'Ewww,' she moaned, scooping it up with her finger. She let out a puff of defeat, tugging at some toilet paper to wipe it off.

She heard the bathroom door open and remained rigid in case Travis had decided to follow her in and make a scene. Though she felt sure, he didn't have the balls to do that.

'Those fucking girls are taking over, I swear to God.' It was someone speaking on the phone in the bathroom. Katy's head tilted, her ears pricking up.

'Oh, yeah. They want to totally change the PR plan, and now they've clicked their little Scottish fingers, everyone is running. And their idea is *good*.' The voice sounded worried, like a solid PR plan wouldn't benefit everyone at the company. 'You assured me they wouldn't pull through. You told me they'd fuck up!'

Katy very slowly and carefully stood up from the toilet, pulling up her knickers as quietly as possible. She turned to the toilet pan and delicately hobbled onto it, peering up over the stall.

'I'm so sick of it. You have leverage, and we had an agreement.'

Katy, spotting Britney's pale face, clutching her phone to her ear, covered her mouth to stifle a gasp.

'Well, you know I don't have shit on them. The blonde one is so far up Jimmy's ass,' Britney tittered. 'Yeah, well, whatever your plan is, do it quicker! You promised me this would work.'

Katy could taste the salty residue of the cum wipe, her face squirming at the thought. Spitting out the taste, she ducked as Britney turned, as if hearing a noise.

'I gotta go. I'll call you tomorrow.'

Several long seconds of silence passed. Katy remained crouched on top of the toilet. She wondered if Britney was going to boot the cubicle door in, or would she stick her head under the weirdly huge space between the door and the floor.

Finally, she heard the door open and then slam shut.

'What the fuck!' she hissed in the quiet of the empty bathroom.

She lowered herself back down to the ground, full of questions. So, Britney was in on it, but with whom?

She allowed a few more minutes to pass before leaving the cubicle in case Britney was lurking outside. Then she washed her hands and power-walked to the tech department to fill Zola in on the crazy fifteen minutes she'd just had.

The technical department was a whole suite filled with giant screens, monitors and partially dismantled computers, which Ethan would occasionally mess around with between projects. Katy walked up to the coding room, where Ethan and Zola sat in silence at their desks.

'Zola!' Katy called out from the door.

Ethan pushed his chair back from his desk.

Zola watched his uncomfortable reaction, then turned her gaze to Katy. 'Babe, you shouldn't be here. Ethan doesn't like visitors.' She cut a look over to Ethan, who was pressing his back against the wall.

'It's not that I don't like visitors, Zola. I don't like change,' Ethan replied.

Katy smiled understandingly. 'Oh, yeah. Sorry, Ethan. I find change annoying too.'

He relaxed his shoulders and sighed, slowly returning to his station.

'I'll meet you outside in five?' Zola said.

'Stay.' Ethan hummed. 'It must be important. Her eyes are red, and her skin is blotchier than usual.'

Katy glanced down at her pale arms, noticing the red blotches seeping through.

Zola paused, turning to Ethan. She waited until he was fully engrossed in his computer, then spoke. 'Did you get another message?' she mumbled under her breath.

Katy nodded, stepped forward, and handed Zola her phone. 'And, when I was in the toilet, I heard Britney on the phone talking about us. She was moaning to someone about the PR strategy changing and talking about leverage and going on about the fact they had an agreement!'

Zola seemed shocked. 'An agreement about *what*?'

Katy shrugged. 'I have no idea who she was on the phone with, but it was something about this.' She nudged her head towards her own phone.

Ethan stood up. 'Perhaps I'll let you two talk privately,' he said, making his way out of the room. As he passed Katy, he attempted a smile.

When the door was closed, Katy divulged her last half-hour sexcapade, her toilet jizz accident, then what she'd heard of Britney's phone call. Zola paced the room like she'd been listening to an episode of *Jeremy Kyle*, but Katy knew that even Jeremy and his aftercare team would not be able to sort this shit out.

Zola bit her nails, then turned to Katy. 'What the fuck? What the actual fuck?'

Katy moaned, shaking. 'I know, Zola. He was just there, and we were in this wee romantic cupboard and—'

'Romantic *cupboard*? Did the Pop Tarts turn you on, babe?' Zola interrupted, letting out a slow exhale. 'OK, right. So, we know it's not Travis. He was there when the text came through, right?'

Katy nodded. 'Right.'

'And we know it's not Jimmy if Britney said on the phone that Ella's up his arse? Right?'

'Uh-huh, and we also know it's not us,' Katy concluded.

Zola rolled her eyes. 'No shit, Miss Marple.' She began pacing again, trying to piece everything together. 'This is bigger than us creating this app. There's some seriously shady shit going down in this company, and whoever it is doing the texting wants us to leave it alone. They're watching us, and not afraid to let us know that.'

Katy seemed startled at the idea. 'What if they hurt us? What if we don't leave and they hurt us, Zo?' Katy's bottom lip trembled in fear as she whispered, 'They have guns here!'

Zola wrapped her arms around her. 'And we have us, working as a team. We need to get one step ahead, like really start digging. We know Britney is involved, and that's actually good for us. I'll try to find a way to hack her emails, see what turns up.'

'We need to tell Ella.' Katy nodded, her chin on Zola's shoulder. 'Let's go, Zo.'

The two friends headed out of the door and noticed Ethan sitting on a desk outside. Zola jumped, still on edge.

'Sorry, I thought you'd gone to grab a coffee or something,' Zola replied, attempting a smile and trying as hard as she could not to seem startled.

Ethan stood up, his eyes on Katy. 'I only drink coffee at eight a.m.'

'Right. Well, thanks for giving us the room,' Zola said, stepping away.

'How are you doing?' Ethan asked Katy.

She smiled at him. 'I'll be fine, thank you.'

He paused, looking unsure of what to say next.

'I'll see you tomorrow, Ethan,' Zola said, attempting to end the awkward encounter. She tugged on Katy's arm, dragging her back towards the main office.

Katy swivelled her head back for a second look. 'He's cute.'

'That's the most he's ever spoken to me,' Zola admitted, a confused look on her face. 'Now let's fill Ella in on everything.'

'He seems nice,' Katy replied, still getting dragged along behind a storming Zola.

Chapter Twenty-Nine

Ella

I woke up the next morning, sprawled out over the small sofa in my office, to the sounds of honking horns and passing sirens. After Zola and Katy caught me up on Katy's fanny-packed evening, we'd had a brainstorming session about who might want us out and why. Around 2 a.m., we realised we didn't have a fucking clue. Despite something pretty freaking hot starting with Jimmy, I knew he was my best bet for information, but I didn't want to betray him like that. I'd had the most fun in months – if not ever – at Summit One, and I didn't want to snoop around his business like fucking Isa in the background. But something inside me wondered: what if our investigations helped him too? Someone obviously had it in for him. Someone wanted the app to fail. Maybe if I dug a little deeper, I'd unearth the answers we all needed.

It was just after 5 a.m. as I sat up, feeling achy from only a few hours' sleep on a not-exactly-comfortable couch. I turned to see Zola and Katy sound asleep on the floor beside me. They'd pulled a mountain of bean-bags together and created a double mattress. I smiled as I watched them, snoring softly and entirely dead to the world, then stood up. I was still in the dress from my evening with Jimmy, and I knew the office would start getting busy in only a few hours, so I grabbed my bag and shoes to head home for a quick shower and outfit refresh.

The office was quiet. Eerily quiet. If I had half a clue what I was looking for, this would be the perfect time to go snooping – but I didn't. As I headed through the corridor, I spotted a dim light coming from Jimmy's office. He'd messaged me at gone midnight to say goodnight and that he was going home.

I stopped in my tracks. What if this was the stalker, scoping out trade secrets or digging for dirt?

I took a step closer, hearing rustling coming from behind his office door.

Fuck, I could feel my pulse pick up. Maybe it was just the cleaner?

I took a few more small steps, panic surging through my veins. I was just outside the door – I only had to peer my head round to see who it was, but the glass walls meant whoever was inside would see me too. *Fuck*. I stopped, took a deep breath, then walked straight out in front of the glass.

'Jimmy?' I said, noticing him sitting at his desk, raiding through his drawer. I stepped into the room and he lifted his head, looking just as surprised as I was. Relief began to settle through me.

'Ella?' He smiled, warmth in his eyes. 'Now tell me you haven't stayed here all night?' Jimmy was wearing a pale grey tracksuit, sweat visible on his chest like he'd run a marathon to get here.

'I did,' I admitted. 'I slept on the wee couch thing in my office. What are you doing here so early?'

Jimmy laughed, shaking his head, then continued to rummage. 'I took a cab home last night – I was too tired to drive. And I always pop round to my mom's in the morning, but I forgot the keys were in here.' He paused, finally raising a set of keys in the air.

'That's nice of you.' I felt my shoulders relax. A man who visits his mum to check in? Jesus, could this sexy cunt get any better?

'I'm not a mama's boy either, if that's what you're thinking,' he said, holding his hands up in defence.

I grinned, stepping closer to his desk. 'Are you sure about that?' I teased. I stepped around him and shimmied my bum on top of the desk, facing him in his chair. I lifted a framed photo of him, his mum and Fee, smiling together at a family BBQ.

Jimmy burst out laughing. 'Busted! So maybe I am. She doesn't keep well, so I like to stay close.'

I glanced up at him, placing the photo down. He sat directly facing me, his forehead still damp from his early morning jog.

'Tell me, did you have fun last night?' he asked, his voice as confident and smooth as ever.

I bowed my head. 'A lot of fun! That place was perfect,' I said, thinking back to the multicoloured sunset lighting up the sky, then the city glittering like a sea of stars in the darkness. 'Next time, I'll take you to the Empire State Building or the observation deck at Edge. I can't promise it will be only the two of us, but we'll have one hell of a view.' I grinned, part of me hoping for reassurance that Jimmy wanted to do it all again.

'Absolutely,' he said, leaning forward. 'I look forward to it.' His hands rested on the desk, only a few centimetres from my thighs. 'I'm glad you want to spend more time with me.' His voice softened. I felt his fingers slowly trace my outer thigh. 'I was worried that we cut it short.' Jimmy glanced up at me, his eyes locking with mine.

'I was worried about that too,' I admitted. Truthfully, I hadn't stopped thinking about winching him in the lift and feeling his giant dick press hard against me.

'I thought about getting the footage from the elevator from the security guys.' Jimmy smirked, like he was reading my mind.

I blushed, peering down at him, then giggled.

'I'm serious, Ella. That was some hardcore sexy shit in there!'

I burst out laughing, pushing his shoulders away playfully. Jimmy grinned and stood up. He moved his hands through my hair, and suddenly we were kissing – first slowly, then deeper. His arms and hands caressed my head and body. He pulled me in and positioned himself between my legs. Fucking hell, I'd never felt so much desire in my life. His lips felt soft, his tongue swept around mine and I could hear myself moaning, craving his touch. Every inch of me wanted this. Wanted him.

Jimmy ran his hands down my body, squeezing my breasts and moaning in my mouth as he did. I drew him in as close as I could, dying to be near him.

'Ella,' he gasped, shaking his head. 'We should stop.' He managed to pull away, his eyes sparkling. 'Jesus,' he panted. 'We've been on one date. I don't want you to think less of me. I like you,' he said, looking almost annoyed at himself for admitting it.

'I like you too.' I smiled, composing myself.

'And anyone could walk by. I wouldn't do that to you.' I could see that his mind was in overdrive.

'Jimmy,' I said softly, snapping him back to me. I leaned over and pressed the privacy button on the blinds, allowing the morning sunshine to fade us slowly into darkness.

'I might only be here a few more weeks. I need this. I want this. You.' I gulped, having never felt so brave in my entire life. Maybe it was all the shit with Philip, knowing that I deserved this, deserved so much more than how he'd treated me. Maybe it was fear of the stalker. But I needed this, needed to do something I wouldn't regret later.

His dark eyes fell on mine. 'Fuck, so do I, Ella.'

He lunged back on top of me on the desk, kissing and biting my neck. I fell back, hearing things scatter off the desk, but I didn't care. Jimmy pushed up my dress, then pulled my lacy black thong down to my feet. I kicked it off completely as he ran his fingers down my pussy and I felt my body contract.

Please touch me, I begged silently. He pushed one of his fingers into my mouth, then leaned over the top of me, kissing me. His hand began rubbing my clit, pushing in and out of me – teasing, fast then slow. My back arched against the desk.

I was so close to climax already. I began to moan. 'Yes, yes, I'm going to . . .'

Then – just as I came – Jimmy slid his dick inside me, making me scream with satisfaction. Fucking hell, I was shaking. He felt huge. Jimmy was moving his arse on top of me, grinding into me, and I wrapped my legs tight around his waist.

'Do you love my big dick, Ella?' he asked, grinning down at me like he knew exactly how much I loved it.

Fucking hell, I didn't expect this chat. I was surprised, but weirdly his words and the look in his eyes were making me even hornier.

'I love it. It's the biggest dick I've ever seen,' I just about managed to say back.

'Good. You'd better get used to it, girl. You're about to be seeing and feeling it a whole lot more.' Jimmy thrust in and out. I could hear the desk pounding the floor, and the heavy rhythm of it made me feel alive. His gorgeous face on top of me, his muscles visible through his jogging suit – everything was perfect.

'Jesus, I'm gonna . . .' Jimmy came, pushing his tongue down my throat, his body shaking as he squeezed every last drop out inside of me.

'Wow,' I said, flopping my head down. I was sprawled across the desk, staring at the ceiling. 'That was . . .'

'Unbelievable,' he concluded, pulling out of me and throwing himself back on his chair.

He was still fully dressed, with his boxers and trousers at his knees. I sat up, tugging down my dress to hide myself. He sat there, cock still semi, looking like a baton ready to be gripped.

'Your dick is . . .' I found I was at a loss for words on how to compliment such a mythical creature.

Jimmy laughed, glancing down proudly at himself, then leaned his face close to mine. 'Wait till you see what my tongue can do.' He gently kissed my lips, and I froze with pure delight. *Yass, a licker as well. How did I get so fucking lucky?*

After ten minutes of heavy petting and random kisses, I headed out of Jimmy's office with a giant smile on my face and a fanny full of his sweet American candy. I wasn't sure this day could get any better.

*

I was showering when I heard Zola and Katy enter the apartment. When I was dried and dressed, I went through to the living room, where they were sipping coffee on the sofa like zombies, trying to re-energise before work. So, I filled them in on my morning desk-based session with Jimmy.

Zola's mouth gaped wide. 'OK, who are you and what have you done with my friend?' she asked.

'Ella!' Katy squeaked. 'I'm sorry, but I can't deal.' She was shaking her head so rapidly that I started to worry she was having a seizure. 'We've both had sex in the office with two men who are basically brothers! We could be sisters!'

'Oh, dear God,' Zola moaned under her breath.

'I know,' I admitted. 'This really isn't like me, but I felt so amazing doing it. He's the first guy I've ever met that I've had that immediate spark with.'

Zola hummed. 'And what first attracted you to Jimmy Link, the multi-billionaire, Ella?'

I squinted my eyes at her.

'I'm sorry, I'm just saying, but you clearly do have a type.' She was reminding me of Philip, but I shook my head.

'No, this is different. This feels so different. Philip chased me down. I was sceptical, and clearly quite rightly so. We were too different. But Jimmy and I are much more similar. He likes the same things, he goes running, he's laid-back . . .'

Zola threw a pillow over, whacking me. 'You're the most uptight person I know!'

'But that's why it's good!' I explained. 'And, Jeez, his dick . . .' I rolled my eyes, thinking of it again.

'Tell us now!' Katy was bouncing up and down on the sofa. 'What was it like?'

I paused, trying to find the words. 'Put it this way – if that bridge,' I pointed out the window at the stunning view of the Brooklyn Bridge we had, 'if that ever went down, he could swing his big old beefer out and we'd all be able to reach Brooklyn no bother.'

Zola and I burst out laughing, but Katy looked confused.

'You wouldn't want people walking on your man's dick, though, would you?' she said.

Zola and I doubled over in hysterics.

'Were you careful at least?' Zola asked.

'I'm still on the pill with Philip, so don't worry about any bratty baby Ellas!' I laughed.

'Really, the pill turns me psycho,' Katy chipped in. 'I just get them to jump off the train before it gets to the station!'

Zola and I turned, shocked, to Katy.

'You could be riddled, Katy! For fuck's sake, you need to use condoms from now on, you have no idea how risky that is! Especially the rate you're pumping and dumping!' Zola shook her head in genuine horror.

'Really?' She seemed surprised, innocent even, as if years of sexual ed hadn't been drummed into us. 'Fine, I'll go to Walmart on the way home tonight, stock up for all of us.'

'Good! Come on, we need to get ready for today – it's a big day for the app. A lot of changes,' I said, smiling.

'You smashed this revamp,' Katy said, high-fiving me with real energy.

Zola nodded. 'Yeah, I'm dead proud of you, Ella. I think this idea is fair, genius and it helps to make things safe.'

'Thanks, guys.' A wide grin spread across my face and I reached over to hug my two best friends. But just as I did, Katy's phone pinged.

'Oh no,' she moaned, having not even checked the screen yet.

'Is it . . .?' Zola asked, watching Katy pull out her phone.

'Yep.' She glanced up at us, fear taking over her face.

We huddled together, reading the message.

Unknown: *OK, time's up, bitches. I warned you – vanish. No more switching the app, no more fucking other people's husbands. Stay? Then I'll bulldoze you – and his empire. With a smile X*

'Zola!' Katy was panicking. 'Zola, what does that mean?'

Zola turned to me. 'It means Jimmy *is* the problem. Whoever this is plans on taking him down, and we're collateral.' She gulped. Zola was never scared, but I could see this latest missive had shaken her.

'We have to tell him,' I said decisively, panic rising inside me too. 'Someone is planning on ruining his company, his life!'

Katy shook her head, her eyes desperate. 'You can't! You'd have to tell him about me, Ella. That would ruin our lives! We need this contract. We need the money, the boost to our careers.'

I buried my face in my hands. 'I have no idea what to do.'

Eventually, Zola spoke, steady and calm. 'Here's what we do. We continue what we're doing. We pretend this isn't happening. Ella, you fish for as much information on Jimmy's enemies as you can, and in the meantime, we make the best app that's ever hit America. We distance ourselves from Britney – we know she's involved. But we can play dirty too. I'll hack her server and see who she's been emailing.'

A wave of defeat washed over me. For the first time, I'd found someone, someone special, who I liked immediately. There was no second-guessing his intentions. I knew it was early days, and I knew it was more than likely a holiday fling, but I respected Jimmy. I admired him. I didn't want to lie to him.

'I'm so tired of drama,' I said.

I rested my head against Zola's, and she gently kissed my forehead. 'C'mon, babe, it's game time.'

Chapter Thirty

Ella

Over a week had passed since the announcement that Stars and Swipes was being revamped into a much friendlier, safer spot for dating, and the team at Flirtify was delivering outstanding results. The tech department had downloaded data from a wide range of dating apps. Jimmy and Katy had scored a coup of a meeting with the police commissioner for real-life NYPD tips on the safest ways to date, then added the information on to the app. I felt like we were really breaking through. I also got the go-ahead to put together my own PR campaign involving one of the most iconic venues in New York, the Met. I planned to host an investor media night there the week before the app launched – a romance-themed event. Then, for the official launch party the night before Thanksgiving, we'd head to the Four Seasons, throw a lavish black-tie event and incorporate the holiday as much as possible, with a gratitude tree in the lobby showcasing the relationships we were thankful for.

We hadn't received any new messages from the stalker, which was the longest we'd gone without communication. Zola's plan of continuing to knock it out the park with our jobs and not feed into an ever-darkening paranoia spiral seemed to be working.

Jimmy and I were also progressing well following our office romp. We'd instigated a continuous flow of flirty messages. He'd sent the most stunning red roses to the apartment, and we'd had a romantic dinner at his favourite restaurant in Little Italy. I tried to gather as much information as I could about scorned exes or unhappy employees or disgruntled competitors whenever I was with him, but every time I fished, he seemed utterly oblivious to any beef. His attitude was that if there were ever a problem at his company, he'd simply handle it head-on. The problem was he didn't know he had a problem in the first place.

Today, I was getting ready for work, having completed my usual morning run and finished finger-twining my hair into loose waves, when I heard a deep voice enter the apartment.

'Good morning, ladies!'

I immediately recognised Jimmy's sexy tones and came scurrying out of my room like a child on Christmas Day.

'Well, this is a nice surprise!' I called out, wanting to hug him as he came closer. Jimmy's snow-white shirt and black suit looked fresh out of the wrapper. I felt almost afraid to touch him.

'I thought I'd surprise my girl.' Jimmy leaned in, kissing my neck while I giggled, feeling that immediate rush of pleasure from his touch.

'Can you two get a room, please!' Zola moaned, joining us in the living room, fully dressed for work.

'Hey, Zo. Coffee's on the countertop,' Jimmy said, his eyes diverting to three takeaway cups waiting for us. 'There's sugar at the side. I wasn't sure of your orders.'

'You're the best boss ever, do you realise that?' She bulldozed towards the coffee, just as Katy stumbled out to the living room, completely engrossed in her phone, not noticing any of us.

'Good morning?' Zola called out extra loud, forcing Katy to lift her head. 'Coffee, babes?'

'Oh, morning.' She grinned. 'Oh, hey, Jimmy! Didn't see you there.' She headed to the kitchen counter, lifting a cup. 'Is this for me?'

'Sure is,' Jimmy replied, still struggling – to my intense gratification – to keep his eyes off me.

'So, are we heading into work together?' I asked, curious as to why he'd shown up so early.

Jimmy pulled my hands in. 'I thought the girls could head in and we could catch up a bit first, if that's all right with you?'

'Sure.' I grinned, wondering if I was finally getting a chance at round two of his Loch Ness Monster. We'd been dating properly since our office romp, and as respectful as I found that, I was craving his dick more than I'd have ever thought possible.

'Fine with us. You ready, Katy?' Zola said, walking to the elevator. 'Katy! Are you ready?'

'Yeah, sorry.' Katy laughed, a little flushed as she broke eye contact with her phone screen once more. 'I think I might have a visitor over tonight, so I don't know if you guys have plans, or . . .'

'Who?' Zola halted, glancing between Katy and me. Zola had been on the highest alert since the stalker – she didn't want to go out or talk too loudly in the office. I was sort of glad, as this drama had been keeping her focus away from Curtis. Zola had said he'd stopped texting her apology messages now, and I knew it bothered her. I'd walked past her on the sofa and seen her reading, then rereading the old WhatsApp messages. I felt terrible for her and was glad that work and the stalker at least gave her a distraction from her life back home.

'His name is Cobi, and it'll be purely for sex,' Katy stated, sniggering at her phone. 'We met on Tinder.'

'Fuckin' hell!' Zola shook back her hair while Jimmy nearly choked on his coffee.

Katy held her head up high. 'There's no point in looking for Mr Right, so I'll go looking for fun instead. And you should see the messages this cunt's sending me – whoa, am I gonna have a whole lot of fun!' She laughed – and the sound was pure filth.

'Tell Zola in the car, please. Jimmy does not want to hear this.' I placed my hands over his ears.

Katy rolled her eyes as she and Zola headed for the elevator, both of them turning to give us a cheeky wave as they left.

'So.' I smiled at Jimmy once we were alone. His dark eyes stared up at me. 'Did you really want to "catch up" or . . .' I leaned in to him but drew back a little at the lightness of his kiss.

'Something has been on my mind, Ella,' he said, and my stomach dropped. *Does he know?*

'I've wanted to tell you this for a while now, and the longer this has gone on, the harder it is, because I really like how well things are going here. Between us, I mean.'

I felt nervous. Fuck, he seemed so serious. He drew me to the sofa, and we sat down side by side. I wasn't about to get my hole, after all.

I gulped. 'You can tell me anything, Jimmy,' I reassured him, wondering if this was maybe the moment the entire mystery was about to be solved.

He sighed a little before starting. 'I know I mentioned before about being in the foster system, yeah?' His eyes looked heavy, and he sat with his hands interwoven, focusing on them.

'Yes, I remember.' I nodded.

'Well, the truth is . . .' He glanced up from his hands, and there was a long moment of silence between us. 'Look, Ella, when I was younger, I was wild. I did some bad shit, which I went to juvie for. I was taken away from my mom and Fee, and ended up in the system, but when I got out, I never did that shit again.' I could hear the determination – and the truthfulness – in his voice.

'OK. Erm . . . What . . . what did you do?' I asked. He'd hinted at this before, but still my heart raced, wondering what type of man I'd been falling for.

'My friends robbed a liquor store, and I was there. One of them punched the old guy in the face, knocked him out, then we ran off.' He shrugged, and I thought I'd never seen him look so defeated. 'That was the final straw. I was always in and out of trouble, hustling away, but charges were brought against us and I got sent to juvie for six months.'

I breathed, taking it in. I almost felt bad for him. I could see how ashamed he was, telling me his darkest secret – he looked vulnerable, clearly wondering if this was a dealbreaker.

'When I got out, I vowed never to be that man again, and I'm not.' He cleared his throat. 'But I thought you should know the truth of who you're getting involved with. You have a right to know, and you're so inquisitive – every time you asked me something, I felt like I was lying to you.'

I shook my head and held out my arms, reaching for him. 'Jimmy, that was a long time ago. You're not the same person you were. You were a child,' I reassured him as I cradled his head in my arms. 'I don't care about who you were then, just who you are now.' I felt his body relax in my arms as he finally got this huge fucking secret off his chest. But I couldn't help wondering if any of his past friends or acquaintances held a grudge against him. Maybe they were jealous of the man he was today? Of what he'd achieved? Maybe they wanted to bring him down?

'What happened to the old man who was hurt during the robbery?' I asked, running my hands through his short, close-shaved hair. 'Was he OK after the incident?'

Jimmy sat up. 'He's good. He's keeping an eye on you.' When I gave him a puzzled look, he smiled. 'He's your doorman, Otis. I reached out when the block his shop was on got bought up a few years ago and brought him and his family out to the city, set them up. It was the least I could do.'

I couldn't hold back the smile that spread across my face then. Yes, he was precisely the man I knew him to be, if not better. Using his wealth for good, treating people right, making amends for past mistakes.

'Ella?' he asked.

'Yeah?'

'I haven't scared you off, have I?' His voice was full of worry. 'Or given you the ick, as Katy would say?'

'No ick here,' I replied. 'I don't think there's anything that could scare me off you, Jimmy Link.'

He stared up at me for a few more seconds, gratitude pulling at the corners of his mouth. Then he leaned in for a kiss. I pushed my body against his, feeling things instantly steam up between us. I stood up, took hold of his hand, then led him through to my bedroom.

Chapter Thirty-One

Zola

Zola entered the tech suite and forced a smile as she noticed Ethan already sitting at his desk.

'Morning, Ethan,' she said cheerily. He glanced towards her, then back at his screen.

Great, she thought – another morning of not entirely comfortable silence. She pulled out her phone and opened her archived messages. Still nothing from Curtis. She then scrolled through his Instagram to check his uploads and number of followers – still the same as yesterday. She sighed, feeling sickly and troubled. She hated what Curtis had done, but she also wondered if she could have done more to save their relationship. Curtis wasn't a horrible person, Zola knew that. But he had no ambition, no motivation, and as the years passed, they grew into entirely different people.

'So, how are things progressing with the app? Did we get the final candidates downloaded?' Zola asked, finally pulling out her seat and sitting.

Ethan grunted back, and Zola felt herself getting more irritated. Ever since she'd arrived, he'd only offered one-word answers or shot her daggers when she entered the room like she was an intruder, an inconvenience. Today, she'd had enough. She'd just endured a thirty-minute car ride listening to Katy read out every increasingly explicit message from her Tinder porn star who was promising to rearrange her ovaries. She was on high alert with the stalker, and Curtis was AWOL. She was craving a normal, polite conversation. Darren was on his paternity leave, and with only Ethan as backup conversation, Zola flipped.

'Look, Ethan,' she began, putting her coffee down on the desk with a decisive *thunk*. 'I get that my being here is a new thing for you, and you don't like change. But I am here, whether you like it or not. So maybe if we worked together, we'd get this project finished a lot quicker, then I'd be out of your hair, back to Scotland, and you'd be happy!'

In the wake of her outburst, she closed her eyes briefly, then leaned forward to switch on her laptop. In the process, however, she knocked her coffee off balance and watched in horror as the hot black liquid cascaded over her laptop.

'Fuck!' she shouted, jumping up, making sure she didn't spill anything on her new cream playsuit.

'And that is exactly why no liquids are to be consumed in the tech suite,' Ethan replied as smug as ever, pointing to a sign that clearly stated the drinks ban.

Zola reached for a bundle of tissues, frantically patting her keyboard dry. 'Yeah, yeah. You're right,' she agreed sarcastically. 'As ever.'

'Look, Zola. It's not that I don't want you here. I don't care. But I like to know who I'm working with and what their capabilities are. Then I can work out what I can talk to them about.'

Zola turned to Ethan, utterly confused, holding up the soggy, coffee-drenched tissues. 'What?'

'I asked for your IQ, but you still haven't given it. I want to know on what level I can discuss things with you. Until I know what you can understand, how am I supposed to know what to talk about?' He was fully serious, not a smirk or glimmer of humour in sight.

'It's a hundred and twenty-nine,' Zola mumbled under her breath. 'I did do it when you asked, but I didn't send it over because I didn't quite reach Mensa level.'

Ethan stood up, his chair scraping across the floor. 'You're the fifth highest in the company, Zola,' he said, looking impressed.

'I am?' She let out a confused laugh, sussing out his change in energy. 'Fifth highest, though – that doesn't seem too impressive.'

'That's four higher than Darren.' He rolled his eyes. 'And, now that I know who I'm dealing with, I can show you real coding and how it performs at a much higher level than what you're doing now.'

Zola laughed, nodding, but feeling completely confused by the shift. She didn't trust easily, but there was an innocence and straightforwardness in Ethan that she felt she could believe in. 'That all sounds great, but . . . I don't suppose you know anything about hacking?' she asked. 'It's always interested me. I just can't seem to get past the firewall.'

Ethan's eyes squinted mischievously. 'Because I built it.' He grinned. 'You know, a straightforward hack is pretty insulting. I'm capable of a lot more.'

Zola tilted her head. 'Oh yeah? Prove it.'

'Who do you want to hack and why?' Ethan was curious, and quite rightly so.

Zola felt her cheeks go warm as she tried to think on the spot. 'There's a woman in PR, who Katy heard on the phone; she seemed suss. Katy thought she might be sabotaging the app. Maybe working with another app company or something?' Zola could hear her voice squeak at the end, which made her wonder if she was trying to convince herself or Ethan of the fake reasoning.

'Britney!' He scurried back to his desk, looking pleased to be joining forces. By his quick actions, Zola knew he had no alliances with her.

'And you're really not going to say it's breaching the policies or breaking the rules?' Zola turned to him, watching him hit the keys like Elton John at his Glastonbury appearance.

'As if those dumbasses will know a thing about it,' he said, his brain almost beaming with sheer logical intelligence. 'That's why your friend Katy came here the other week?' he asked, surprising her.

'Yeah,' she said, remembering that Ethan had left the tech room for them to speak. Zola pushed her chair up beside him.

'Watch it,' Ethan warned as she came closer. 'Physical touch is a major no-go for me.'

'Of course,' Zola agreed, shuffling her chair back. 'Got it.'

Chapter Thirty-Two

Ella

After a morning of serious shagging, Jimmy eventually left to attend a meeting with his investors. I decided to take a walk along the Hudson with my laptop under my arm, heading to a local coffee shop to get some work done. We had been in New York for just over a month now, and the weather had shifted from late summer into fall, which was always my favourite time of year, with fashion at its peak. Today I opted for a long trench coat, leggings, and a long-sleeved plain top, paired with my UGG Mini Classics.

Since pushing Britney as far away from the PR side of Stars and Swipes as possible, I had been handling the launch events on my own, spending most of my time chasing or enquiring about vendors. As I entered the bustling open-plan coffee shop, I set down my laptop, then ordered a latte at the counter, constantly checking that my computer hadn't been lifted before returning to the table with my drink.

Ahead of me was a morning of back-and-forth emails with companies about potential set-ups for the investor party. I needed it to be perfect – to match that classy, sophisticated New York vibe I was going for. Back in Glasgow, I had endless connections for events of every kind, but over here, I knew no one. I wasn't going to ask Britney for any of her contacts and risk possible sabotage from that fucking crank, so I checked every review on each retailer, making sure they were not only reliable and available, but also the best in the city.

It was just past noon when a text from Zola popped up in the group chat on my laptop. I lifted my phone to read along.

Zola: *I hacked Britney's emails, nothing incriminating.*

Katy: *Nothing? What's she emailing about?*

Ella: *That's annoying!*

Katy: *Where are you, Ella? Just stopped by the office x*

Ella: *Came to the wee coffee shop beside the apartment to work on the events x*

Zola: *Well, while you're doing Britney's job, she's spent the morning sending Fee details of new office furniture she wants x*

I shook my head as I scrolled through the chat, feeling exasperated that we were getting no closer to the truth.

Ella: *Hopefully she won't have an office at all when we get to the bottom of this shit x*

Katy: *Or a home!!*

I felt my face drop. *Wow, that was a bit harsh, Katy*. But I suppose Britney *was* involved in blackmailing the life out of the poor girl. Maybe it was deserved, just a little.

'I'll have a black coffee, please. Thank you.'

I glanced up as I heard a soft Scottish accent cut through the crowd and smiled at its familiarity. I had gotten so used to hearing New Yorkers speak in that rat-a-tat self-assured way of theirs; it felt homey and welcoming to catch a glimmer of Scotland. I wondered when I'd be heading back home and what the weather would be like when I got there. God, I missed my own bed. My own well-ordered space away from Zola and Katy and their constant mess.

'Ella?' the Scottish accent called out, and I sat up, peering through the crowd. It did sound very familiar.

'No way! Ella, is that you?' the voice said again.

I stood up, my eyes scanning the lunchtime rush queue, then landing on a tall, jaw-droppingly handsome man.

It was him – it was Philip.

My face fell, my heart dropped and my legs gave way, causing me to drop back down heavily onto the padded seat beneath me with a thud. What the fuck?

'Wow! I thought that was you!'

He sounded excited, like the last time he'd seen me he hadn't dumped me or left me with a two-hundred-quid bill for steak and champagne. Before I knew it, he was rushing over to me, his coffee sloshing over the rim of his mug.

'How are you?' He put his drink down on my table and held his arms out for a hug. I remained rigid, completely gobsmacked. Still, his smart navy jacket clung to me as he bent down. I could smell him; that deep, musky, fanny-tingling aftershave that I loved so much, now it was making my stomach turn.

'I'm fine . . . yeah, fine. I'm surprised to see you,' I admitted, still pulsing with shock.

'Just flew in. A few meetings. How's it been?' He slid into the booth beside me like we were old friends and this was a beautiful impromptu encounter. Like nothing was wrong. Like we hadn't not long split up and never spoken since.

'Yeah . . . erm . . . yeah . . . it's going well,' I stammered.

He sipped his coffee, then said, 'I considered calling, but . . .'

'But you were busy.' I managed a somewhat sarcastic laugh through my pounding heart. 'Saw it in the papers.'

Philip seemed slightly uncomfortable at that, gently tugging his shirt at the collar for more room. 'And you've been a busy girl, I heard.' He raised a brow.

Fuck. I could feel my pulse soar, my Apple watch vibrating – *Warning: heart rate excessively high*. I pulled at my top, trying to disguise my impending heart attack. *How the fuck does he know what I've been up to?*

'Yeah, big shot. Actually, landing that deal with Jimmy Link? Impressive work, Ella!' He took another sip of his coffee and looked up towards me. His face, his eyes, his lips – everything was so perfect. I'd built him up in my head to be a complete wanker, yet somehow, right now, he seemed as charming and attractive as ever. 'What's he like then?' Philip asked.

'Who?' I asked, still reeling from shock.

'Jimmy!' he said. 'Who else? And how are the girls settling in?' He had so many questions that my head felt like it was on the waltzers.

Suddenly, my phone began ringing and I jumped up. 'Oh, sorry, this is a vendor . . . I . . . I have to take it. You know how it is, duty calls.'

I felt a punch in the gut using his catchphrase – the one with which he'd continuously disrupt our date nights. I pointed towards the coffee shop's door and headed outside, legs trembling, hands sweating, walking out of sight of the large glass windows. I felt my body arch over, hoping to feel better, but nausea took over me. What the fuck was happening? Why was he acting like nothing had happened?

When my phone stopped ringing, I picked it back up and called Zola.

'Hey, you OK? We're just at lunch,' she replied casually. Meanwhile, I felt like my arsehole had been ripped out, run over by a yellow cab, then volleyed straight into the Hudson.

'Zola,' I hissed, 'Philip is here!' I fought to stay calm as people passed me in the street. 'He's here in the fucking coffee shop!'

'What? What are you on about, girl?' she replied, and I heard how there was now a combination of awkward laughter and panic echoing through her voice.

I repeated, 'I am at a fuckin' coffee shop, and Philip fuckin' Khan has just walked in and sat beside me!'

I heard a huge gasp, then silence.

'Zola!' I snapped, panic running rampant through me. 'Say something!' I wanted to cry. I could feel my face scrunch up to an even more unflattering, distorted angle than Kim Kardashian's when she breaks down in tears.

'Shut the fuck up!' she eventually mustered.

'What do I do? He's acting like we're pals,' I said, running my hands through my hair, which was now damp with sweat.

'OK, settle, petal. Why is he in New York? For you?' I could hear a crunch as she went back to her lunch.

'Are you seriously eating right now?' I snapped.

'Ella, focus.' I heard her swallow. 'Why is that cunt here?'

'Meetings. He said meetings,' I replied, trying hard to remember the twisted chain of events from two minutes earlier.

'OK, well fuck him, then. He's moved on, so have you. Don't overthink this. Play it cool, wish him well with the meetings, finish your coffee and leave.'

She was right. This didn't need to be complicated. I had moved on – Jimmy made me happy and I wanted to see where it could go with him. I owed Philip nothing. My back straightened. *I can do this.*

'Yeah?' Zola continued.

'Yeah. I can do that,' I said, believing it even as I was trying to sound more confident.

'Yes, you can. Now go back in, make an excuse to leave and phone me back when you can,' she said. 'Got it?'

'Uh-huh. Got it.' I hung up and closed my eyes, feeling the cool autumn breeze hit my face.

I steadied myself, reminded myself that I could be assertive and leave. I was allowed to do that. Re-entering the coffee shop, I saw Philip scanning my notes on the laptop. As he looked up and grinned, I walked back to the table and carefully resumed my seat beside him.

Philip pointed to my screen. 'I see you're still doing PR work for your campaign?'

I see you're still a nosy bastard, I wanted to reply, but instead I sipped my coffee with a dignified nod, angling the laptop away from him.

'And you've changed it up quite a bit from The Dicktionary Club.' He glanced down at the floor, looking sombre. 'Perhaps I reacted too hastily to you coming here. I thought you'd be out here, slating men and getting on your high horse about all the horrible things they do, but this seems different. It's . . . it's . . .'

'It's fair,' I said quickly. *And none of your business*, I wanted to add.

'Wonderful,' he said. 'The app idea is wonderful, Ella. Congratulations.' A soft, contented look washed over his face and I smiled nervously. I sipped more of my coffee and noticed his eyes were still fixed on me.

'What is it?' I asked.

'Do you know, I wondered if I'd bump into you over here and what I'd feel, but it feels like us still, it feels like how we were before.' He leaned his head against the back of the cream leather booth and sighed. 'I was wrong to try to hold you back from coming to the States.'

'Yeah, you were. I had to do this for me,' I said, swallowing. 'The girls needed it too.'

I felt his hand squeeze my leg. My body froze. *What the fuck?* Is he getting the idea that I'm still keen on him? This felt wrong. Did he think one squeeze of my leg and a half-arsed apology was going to get my drawers off? I shimmied up slightly, freeing my leg. He was the problem, and even if I got over him taking the huff about

New York, I was hardly going to see past the fact that he was shagging hot young influencers the minute I was out of his bed. I could feel my blood begin to simmer. *Who the fuck does this cunt think he is?*

'I saw that you've moved on,' I said, managing to remain calm. 'And I'm happy for you, genuinely. I suppose it was hard to watch it play out in the media like that, but at the same time, it made me realise how wrong we were together.'

Philip leaned both elbows on the table and covered his face with his hands.

'No. Ella . . . I'm so sorry that—'

'No need to apologise. God, I'm over it.' I laughed softly.

He turned to me, his eyes glossy with tears. I had never seen this much emotion come out of him before. 'You do deserve an apology, Ella. I was messed up. My ego was hurting that you just walked away when I'd asked you not to.'

I felt my face twist. 'I was working, Philip.'

His hands shot into fists. 'For God knows how long!' His voice raised, then he let out a tired sigh, realising he had almost lost it. 'Look, I acted out. Erin and I are over; we never really began. I was handling your rejection poorly, instead of handling it like a man. I invited in a young, fame-loving, money-grabbing woman who idolised me. She was an ego boost. Nothing more. And, I suppose, deep down, at the time I wanted you to see it. I wanted you to hurt. I had her out in the press, attending idiotic events that I didn't even want to go to, wondering if you'd see us together and reach out.'

'Right . . .' I managed, totally taken aback, feeling like I had no more words. I felt hurt ache in my stomach, even as he said her name. Pain stabbed me in the chest. He did this for a reaction from me? What kind of schoolboy bullshit was he spinning?

'I need someone straightforward, supportive,' he said, more animated. 'You're the real deal, Ella.'

'I need that too, Philip. And you didn't give me those things. You took over.' My voice was low. Admitting it out loud made me feel ashamed of myself and how I'd let it happen. 'You wanted me to follow your schedules, fit into your life, but you shut me off as soon as you disagreed about me coming to New York.'

He rubbed his eyes and spoke quietly. 'I can if you . . .'

'I've met someone else,' I cut over him. 'I'm happy with where it's going and—'

'Pardon? Ella?' He shook his head like I'd just stunned him with a frying pan. 'Someone from New York?' he questioned, seeming much more tense all of a sudden.

'Yeah. He's kind, supportive and—'

'And from New York?' Philip laughed, holding out his hands as if it was the dumbest thing he'd ever heard. I didn't know if I felt sorry for him or wanted to jab him straight in the jaw.

'I'm not doing this with you.' I stood up. 'I appreciate the apology. I hope your meetings go well and I'll maybe see you around.'

'Ella, sit down,' he moaned. 'Come on, I haven't seen you for a month!'

I continued to squeeze around the table, the coffee cups swaying back and forth. 'And whose fucking fault is that?' I could feel the anger finally seething out of me.

'I waited. I waited in that restaurant, and you never came back!' My voice was getting louder. I could feel my entire body tremble. 'I waited in the house, making sure my fucking TV volume was below ten just in case you rang the buzzer and I missed it. Do you know how pathetic that made me feel?' I let out a gasp of air, trying to push back the wave of emotion and steady myself. 'Then you fuck around with some new piece, getting papped all about town, only to show up here and question me about my new relationship that has just fucking started?' I sighed. I had no energy left. I picked up my laptop and placed it under my arm. 'Let me move on, let me be happy. Please.' I inhaled a long breath, determined not to cry over this fuckboy man again.

'OK.' He looked as if I'd just shot him. Completely stunned. 'If you change your mind, I'm here for the next few weeks.' His eyes blurred, like he was holding back just as much as I was.

'I won't.' I managed a smile, grabbing hold of my trench coat and snatching up my bag.

I had taken a few more steps when I heard him call out, 'Pilates!'

I felt my eyes shut at our private nickname, the one I'd made up the day I met him. There were so many good memories; I hated that he had to ruin them in the end. Eventually, I turned back.

'Who's the guy?' he asked. 'Do I know him?'

I nodded. 'Yeah, it's Jimmy Link,' I said and turned out onto the street.

Chapter Thirty-Three

Katy

Later that night, Katy had finally tidied up the apartment and lit some candles, ready for a night of passion with Cobi, the six-foot-six basketball player who'd promised to have her walking like John Wayne and screeching like Mariah Carey by the end of the night. Ella was spending an overnight at Jimmy's after her traumatic, unexpected encounter with Philip, and Zola was pottering around the apartment, looking lost. Katy had noticed she was far more subdued than usual and wondered if the whole Curtis saga was finally taking its toll on her friend.

'How's it looking?' Katy asked Zola, who was slipping on her trainers.

Zola glanced around, smiling. 'First time you've tidied, I'm impressed!'

'I don't have to tidy normally, not when Ella lives here.' Katy shrugged. 'OK, so I've shaved, tanned, moisturised and stretched. This man is filthy, Zola!' A wide, overhyped grin spread across Katy's face as she pulled out her phone. 'I asked him what he wanted to do with me. You wanna hear it?'

Zola turned in disgust, her face screwed up. After Curtis, the absolute last thing she was thinking about was sex.

'And he said, when he turns up, he wants me to answer the door completely naked. I'm not to say a word, just let him fuck me up.' Katy was covering her mouth like this was the sort of romantic fantasy she'd always dreamed of.

'You're not going to, are you?' Zola asked. 'What if Ella forgets something and walks in with Jimmy and you have the beef curtains out?'

'Ew.' Now Katy screwed up her face, but it was fleeting as a dirty smile soon returned. 'I think I am, Zo. It feels liberating, you know. Out here in New York, in a stunning apartment. Look at that view . . .'

'Exactly, that view is enough, babe. You don't know this guy. What if you don't fancy him and you've already shown him your goods?'

Katy huffed and returned to reading her messages. '"My big dick is so hard for you right now, baby. Are you sure you have what it takes to let twelve inches inside of your cute little pussy?"' Her grin looked almost evil, like it had been carved up to her eyebrows. 'Of course, I'll fancy him. He has a twelve-inch cock, Zo! What's not to fuckin' fancy? I'd open the door nude to Boris Johnson *and* shag him if he had a twelve-incher, for fuck's sake.'

'Right, whatevs. When is Mr Twelve Inches arriving?' Zola asked, pulling on her coat. 'I'm going back to the office to help Ethan with the last part of the app.'

Katy looked at her watch. 'He's en route – to,' she held out her fingers, quoting him once more, '"fuck me right up."' She let out a screech of happiness.

'Oh, God.' Zola rolled her eyes. 'I don't think I ever want a man near me again.'

'Have you heard anything from Curtis?' Katy asked, tugging off her top and admiring her naked torso in the reflection of the glass windows.

'Not for three days, and I'm cool with that.' She shrugged. 'It's done.'

But Katy knew her friend was still hurting. What he'd done was awful; there was no going back for Zola. She was strong, independent and deep. Now she just had to find herself again.

'You are dealing with it so well, Zo. Like so well. He's a fucking useless prick.' Katy was hobbling, pulling off her leggings while still standing up. Zola watched on, shaking her head as Katy stood there with only her thong on.

'You're really answering the elevator to him naked?' she asked.

'Yup.' Katy grinned. 'And I have extra-large johnnies at the ready,' she said, gesturing to the stack of rubbers piled up on the sideboard.

Zola giggled at the sight, shaking her head. 'Well, at least you're being safe! But I'm going before the flaps come out. Let me know you're OK, yeah?' she warned, pointing a finger towards her friend as she left the apartment.

Katy stepped out of her thong and stood entirely stark-bollock naked in the centre of the living room. She paced a few steps back and forth, wafting her hand from her fanny up to her nose, ensuring there were no unpleasant odours. She rocked back and forward on her feet, feeling a tingle of nerves and sheer sexual excitement, then picked up her phone.

> **COBI TINDER:** *That pussy better be waiting to be ripped apart! I've not stopped thinking of fuckin' you hard all day!*

Jesus, how explicit, she thought. What if she couldn't handle it? What if he was too big and she had to tap out? *OK, calm*, she ordered herself, breathing deeply. She wanted this – she wanted thrilling, no-strings-attached, amazing sex.

> **COBI TINDER:** *Walking into the elevator now. Be ready.*

Fuck. She could feel her heart pick up. Her eyes focused on the numbers above the elevator counting their way up to thirty-one. *Jesus, how should I stand?* She lay with her legs wide open on the couch – *fuck, too dirty*, she thought, jumping up. The numbers had stopped moving. Fuck. She scrambled onto the wooden floor in the centre of the room, bent over, arse out in his direct view.

'Katy?' His accent seemed a lot softer than the bulldozing sex fiend she'd anticipated.

'Yeah?' she replied, looking over her shoulder and catching a glimpse of the tall, skinny man who seemed entirely shocked by her chocolate starfish greeting. 'I'm ready for you, big boy! There's plenty of rubbers for you to use!' she moaned as sexily as she could.

'Yeah, sweet.' He stumbled across the room, pulling off his denim jacket, then kicking off his Jordans. Katy could hear his steps as he circled the place.

'Cobi, get over here!' she called, feeling the hard wooden floor begin to hurt her wrists and knees.

'Yeah, yeah. I'm here, girl.'

She heard him walk up behind her and glanced at his naked body. He was tapping his limp dick up and down on her arse, as if praying it would spring into action. She sat back on her bottom and faced him.

'Do you want this dirty wee bitch to suck him good?' She bit her lip, feeling sexy. Cobi was an average-looking guy, tall but more like six foot. There was no way he was six foot six without his Jordans. She leaned in, moaning as she held his dick; it flopped to the side of her hand like an uninspired slug. *Maybe he's a grower*, she thought. After all, Cobi had promised she wouldn't be able to sit down for a week once he had his way with her.

She began sucking him, managing to get to his stomach without a gag in sight. 'Mmm . . .' she moaned, breaking the quietness of the room. 'Do you like that?' she asked, running her tongue up his ever-so-slightly aroused penis. 'Do you like me tongue fucking your big – emmm . . . your cock?' She realised how very far from big it actually was at present.

Cobi seemed distracted; he was clearly trying hard to concentrate and didn't seem to like the dirty talk despite being full of that patter all afternoon.

'One second, I got to take my time, let me pace, girl.' He stepped back, turned his body from her and started violently wanking in the middle of the room.

Katy watched on, sitting cross-legged on the floor. Jesus, he was breathing through his teeth, baring them like some crazed animal, hoping his dick would rise. Slowly, very slowly, his slug's body was growing thicker and beginning to take shape. Katy was twisting her neck, watching on at every tug, wondering when she'd be able to join in.

'Cobi?' Katy eventually said, feeling that the quiet chugging and panting noises echoing around the apartment were rather awkward when she wasn't involved. She was wondering if he had completely forgotten about her and was now simply enjoying his wank alone. 'Where do you want me?' She stretched out her body like a gymnast, hoping that some weird, creative position would be on offer.

He didn't say a word, just ripped open the extra-large condom that, once in situ, made his dick look like a chipolata in a pop sock, hobbled on top of her missionary-style and started thrusting.

She lay there, feeling her body move up and down the floor, which was now sticking to her back, watching him sweat as he pounded in complete silence. As his face scrunched up, she examined the clothes on the floor. *Maybe I should have offered him a drink?* she thought. *Or played music. I wonder what music he likes? It does seem awfully quiet in here.*

After a few more minutes, Katy started making some seriously sexy noises.

'Oh yeah, yeah,' she panted. 'That feels so good!' She was straight-up faking, hoping maybe all he needed was some encouragement to get filthy.

'Mmmmm . . . Do you like how wet I am?' she continued, not even sure if she was. 'Cobi, aghhh,' she called out. 'Your dick is so big, I love it.'

Still no reply.

'Does my pussy feel good?' she asked, squinting her eyes up to him.

He seemed distracted, like he was shagging a rubber doll; evidently, he wanted zero interaction.

So, like a true sport, she stopped trying. She lay back for a few more minutes, only feeling the weight of him on top of her, before she'd finally had enough.

'OK, Cobi, stop, stop.' She shook her head and sat herself up, forcing him to fall to the side. 'You promised me this big bad night of filth, and you can't even make eye contact!' She covered her breasts up with her hands as if he hadn't been welcomed by her arsehole instead of her face ten minutes earlier.

'Huh?' Cobi mumbled, seemingly completely confused.

'Huh?' Katy spat back. 'Get your stuff, please.' She pointed to the lift and sighed.

'What are you doing? You wanted this!' he said, pulling on his jeans and slipping his feet back inside his trainers.

'I wanted to be fucked!' she shouted.

'I was fucking you!' he hissed back. 'You're fucking crazy, girl.' He headed to the lift, looking over his shoulder in case she turned completely psycho.

'Call that fucking?' she snapped. 'Well, you're a fucking fraud! Did you AI those texts? Because you've shown up here with a Temu dick!'

He slipped into the elevator without another word, the door closing behind him. Katy let out a huge groan, flopping back onto the cold floor.

'Why, God? Why?' she called out. 'Why can't I even get a decent no-strings-attached shag?'

Chapter Thirty-Four

Ella

That night, I stayed over at Jimmy's – which meant it was our first morning waking up together, entangled in one another's arms. Slowly, I opened my eyes and turned to face the alarm clock. Jimmy pulled me in tighter.

'Mmmm . . . too early,' he moaned. I giggled and let myself be hugged. His chest was warm against my back; his arms close against my skin. I had never been much of a cuddler. I didn't mind a small hug, then I liked to move on. But Jimmy was so kind and caring, there was something about his touch that made me feel peaceful, like I could trust him. I wanted to stay here all day.

I hadn't dozed off again for long before his alarm went off, and I felt him kiss my forehead.

'Good morning, beautiful,' he whispered as he shut the alarm off, then headed into the en suite and turned on the shower. I lay there for a moment, marvelling at how ginormous his bed was, its feather-grey silk bedding cool beneath my naked body.

I sat up, glancing around as he hummed to himself in the shower.

Jimmy's apartment reminded me of our Hudson Yards apartment, but his had an incredible view of Central Park and was spotless. I inhaled deeply – jasmine and elderflower. *I could get used to this*, I thought, letting the sense of comfort settle over me. I switched on the seventy-inch TV and flicked through the apps till I settled on Netflix, almost automatically landing on *Gossip Girl*, my go-to distraction.

I picked up my phone and skimmed the group chat, smiling at Katy's rants about her date. *When would that girl ever find the man of her dreams?* Then, noticing an archived notification, an unsettled feeling stirred in my stomach before I clicked it.

Philip: *It was great seeing you yesterday. I'll be here for a few more weeks, if you fancy catching up at some point. Or we can wait till you're home. I'm sorry, Ella, I do know I fucked up this time x*

'Everything OK?' Jimmy's voice called out, and I felt my heart jump. I forced a smile as he stood before me with a towel tucked in around his waist.

'Uh-huh, just watching *Gossip Girl*.'

'You love that show, right?' Jimmy laughed, walking around the bed and into his gorgeous walk-in wardrobe. 'Are you hungry? Pancakes will be on the table in twenty.'

'Of course, I am! I'm getting totally spoiled here!' I laughed, bumming my way to the edge of the bed, dodging the silvery stains from our night of passion, then heading into the wardrobe behind him. I wrapped my arms around his chest, which still felt damp. 'I'm going to shower and then I'll get organised,' I said, resting my head against his back.

Jimmy turned to face me, kissed me and smiled. 'Take your time, your boss said you can be as late as you wish today.'

As I left the wardrobe and headed towards the bathroom, I passed by the bed and noticed my phone sitting there. Not wanting Jimmy to know Philip was here or that we'd chatted, I picked it up and kept it close. I wasn't sure why, but it felt uncomfortable – like I'd done something wrong – and I didn't want Jimmy to think badly of me. I clicked off Philip's message without replying.

After showering, I got dressed in a pre-planned outfit I'd taken to Jimmy's the night before: cream trousers, a brown booby strapless top, with an oversized white shirt to sit over it. I brushed my hair out and applied some concealer. With those finishing touches, I felt fresh and ready for another day of chasing down companies and planning the launch events.

As I walked through his hallway to the open-plan kitchen, I heard voices. I paused in my tracks, not knowing whether I should continue.

'We're on thin ice with the investors, they don't love the idea, and with the extra money you're spending on the Met? Like seriously, you authorised the Met?'

My stomach flipped, knowing that I'd suggested that venue. I had no idea Jimmy would get a hard time about blowing the budget. It was his company, after all.

'Morning,' I said, noticing Travis and Fee cornering Jimmy in the kitchen.

Fee looked in complete shock. 'Good morning, girl.' She turned to Jimmy and pushed back his shoulder. 'You didn't say you had company, brother!'

Jimmy raised an eyebrow. 'I didn't get a word in edgeways, sister! Come sit down, Ella.'

Travis seemed edgy, barely meeting my eyes or saying hello. Maybe he knew I was aware of his secret and feared I'd tell Fee or Jimmy.

I walked over and took a seat at the breakfast bar, where a massive pile of pancakes waited.

'Peanut butter?' Jimmy smiled.

'Nutella?' I laughed. 'If you have any.'

Fee let out a laugh. 'Oh, he's got some, it's the only thing I have on mine.' She opened the cupboard door and passed me a large jar of Nutella. 'Come on, Travis, we'll let these two lovebirds get their breakfast, but think about a plan, Jimmy. I mean it. We need to have legitimate answers for the board,' Fee said assertively.

'See you in there,' Travis mumbled, keeping his head low and heading towards the door.

'Bye, guys!' Fee giggled, following him out.

When they were gone, I took a few mouthfuls of pancake and turned to Jimmy, who seemed lost in thought.

'Are you OK?' I asked. 'Like, is everything OK with the business?'

Jimmy shook off his distraction and smiled. 'Yeah, yeah.' He grinned. 'How are the pancakes?'

I put down my cutlery and sighed. He was always so happy; I didn't like seeing him stressed. 'You know, a problem shared and all that . . .' I rolled my eyes, remembering that's what he'd said to help me when we were at

Summit One. 'Just saying!' I held up my hands. 'But I'd like to help if I can.'

Jimmy managed a small laugh, then sighed and sat down next to me at the breakfast bar, leaning his elbows on the polished granite worktop and interlacing his fingers.

'The investors are stressing over the app launching,' he said slowly. 'For the past eighteen months or so, we have made some silly decisions on apps launching that haven't paid off.'

'Shit,' I said.

'And the investors have, of course, picked up on the misfires. They can pull the plug on all our deals if we don't keep up with downloads and sales. So, the board is giving me one last chance to get the money back. I suppose it's all down to Stars and Swipes – it's the next big app we're launching.'

I tried to grasp what Jimmy was saying. *One last chance?* But it was *his* company. Shouldn't he be in control? I realised I didn't know. Business at this level was beyond me, but I wanted to help, even if I had no clue how.

'I founded the company, but the board runs it,' he sighed, as if sensing my confusion. 'I have a seat, but if they feel I'm running it poorly, like losing money hand over fist or making bad decisions with deals – as some of them have insinuated – then they can pull me out.'

'And how badly have the other deals gone?' I asked, feeling sick for him, while not wanting him to think I pitied him.

Jimmy's eyes looked sad, hurt, and I sensed he'd been dealing with all this stress alone. 'Well, they've lost the investors millions, put it that way. But I hadn't signed off on the other apps, Ella. It was the other members of the team, they were their projects, but when you sit at the top, then you become the one who's ultimately responsible.' He placed his hands on his heart. 'I know I'll fix this. This company is all I have.' His voice was shaking.

'So, what do you need from Stars and Swipes?' I asked, seeing that I needed to be blunt with him.

'It has to be such a success that the board is willing to overlook the previous losses and that the investors will feel inspired enough to agree to keep backing my company,' he said, closing his eyes and sinking his head onto my shoulder.

'It will be,' I promised, squeezing his hand. 'We'll make sure it is, OK?' I felt motivated and determined to help him. Jimmy had worked so hard on turning his life around but I wondered if the board held his less-than-squeaky-clean past against him, regardless.

I couldn't help but think: what part did the stalker play in all of this? What part did Britney play? I knew she was involved. Maybe she deliberately sabotaged his deals. Britney and her cronies must want the app to fail so that Jimmy loses his company. But why?

A stabbing pain struck my stomach. The world was growing darker and more twisted. Someone out there wanted him to lose everything.

Chapter Thirty-Five

Ella

I left Jimmy's alone and headed straight to Times Square to get to the office, as he was on a pretty intense call about the board with one of the accountants. I had already texted the girls to meet me there, and both Zola and Katy were sitting at their desks when I walked in.

'What's going on?' Katy asked, looking worried. 'Please tell me you haven't got a text!'

'Got a text,' Zola cackled, impersonating *Love Island* from her desk. 'Too soon? Not funny?'

I turned, making sure the door had shut completely behind me before I started talking. 'No,' I replied to Zola, then I began. 'OK, so Travis and Fee stopped by Jimmy's this morning and didn't realise I was there. They were grilling him about investors and talking about fixing it with the board and some heavy stuff like that.' I took a breath, trying hard to cover ground before we were disturbed, while at the same time getting to the critical points. 'So, when they left, I asked Jimmy what was going on.'

Confusion flickered in their eyes, their furrowed brows betraying how quickly I'd lost them.

'Uh-huh?' Zola questioned.

'Basically, Jimmy is at risk of losing his whole company. There have been dodgy deals with app launches and the investors have lost so much money . . . And they are blaming . . .'

'Daddy Warbucks,' Katy interjected.

'Yeah, so TLDR the investors who invest in all the apps Flirtify develops are threatening to pull out of other big deals too if ours isn't a massive – like world domination standard – success.'

'And you think this has to do with the stalker?' Zola asked, biting her fingernails.

'Oh, come on, is the Pope a Catholic?' I sighed.

'Yeah,' Katy nodded. 'Obviously. What, he is?'

Zola darted Katy a look, then came back at me. 'It must be,' she sighed. 'But why pester us to go home?'

'If Stars and Swipes flops, the investors and the board will turn on Jimmy, blaming him, which will possibly allow them to justify taking over the company.' I peered through the glass, which gave me a view of the office. I watched everyone working away, struck by the horrible knowledge that one of them was plotting Jimmy's downfall.

'Well, we can't let it fail,' Katy said quietly. 'No more distractions. We only have a couple of weeks left before Thanksgiving.'

Zola sniggered. 'Babe, you're the one getting distracted all the time!'

I bit my lip so as not to smile. Zola was right, but her shagging antics had come to be an expected quirk of Katy's personality.

'Yeah, yeah, but not anymore, OK? I deleted Tinder after that fucking twelve-inches-my-arse fraud last night. No more dates, no more sex. We need to get to the bottom of this shit.' She sounded motivated.

'OK,' I agreed, convinced.

'Wait, Ella, sorry.' Zola held up her hand to me and swivelled back to Katy. 'No more sex? Really?' she asked. 'So, I can actually get a decent night's sleep again?'

'Really.' Katy held out a pinkie towards Zola. 'I've decided if I grow the bush, I won't have sex.'

Zola and I burst out laughing together.

'It's true. I'm not going to be tempted to pull with a full-on forest, am I?' She giggled, mischievous as ever, and I shook my head.

'Also,' I added, 'Philip messaged!'

In all the stress of the morning, I'd almost forgotten about that. I watched my friends' faces fall in shock.

'What did he say?!' they screeched in unison.

'He said if I wanted to meet up, he'll be in New York for a few more weeks, or we could catch up when I'm home.'

'As if!' Katy spat.

Zola shook her head in disgust. 'Well, I've had zero communication from Curtis, but his mum posted a picture of them out for a meal in London. I don't know if he's moved back home or if he's just visiting family.'

A silence fell. So much had changed in the past few months that it was hard to comprehend.

'Are you going to reach out?' I asked, knowing she'd have to sort her house and belongings, but also very aware of how stubborn Zola could be. I watched her run her hands through her braids and sigh.

'Are you going to reach out to Philip?' she asked.

I almost gagged. 'No way!'

'Same.' She managed a smirk.

'Does Jimmy know Philip's here, Ella?' Katy asked. 'Does he know who Philip even is?'

I shook my head guiltily. I was about to ask their opinions on my quandary when a knock sounded at the glass door behind us. Fee stood there, waving cheerily. I gestured her in, and she entered, all excitement.

'Hey, I was planning on a quick catch-up debrief in the conference room if y'all can spare a few moments? Just to see where everyone is at with the app design?'

I grinned. 'Sure!'

'Yeah, right now?' Zola stood up. 'We were just having our own little debrief of last night.'

Fee's face fell, then she burst out laughing. 'Ew! You mean of my brother! God, I'm glad I missed that,' she teased.

'Oh, and Katy!' Zola added. 'She's bringing back the bush!'

Fee gasped, a little uncomfortable at the overshare, then nodded. 'Yeah? Good for you, girl!'

I laughed, blushing slightly. 'We'll be one minute, Fee. And please? Don't listen to her!' I shoved Zola's shoulder as Fee turned and headed back to the conference room.

'Did you see that reaction?' Katy whispered. 'When you said about my bush?'

I nodded. 'I did. It was weird.'

'That bitch definitely has one!' Zola cackled and we joined in, heading out the door.

We moved to the conference room, taking a seat beside Ethan from the tech suite just as Jimmy, Travis, Fee and Britney walked in. Jimmy waved for Fee to chair. She rolled her eyes, drawing smiles from the room. Jimmy was too fixated on his phone, hardly noticing.

'OK, everyone, I'll keep it short. We'd love to know where everyone is with Stars and Swipes. We have a crucial meeting with the board today, and we need to assure them we're on track for launch.' She was smiling and confident, but her tone seemed panicked. I knew, of course, how important this meeting was. 'Ethan, Zola . . .' Fee turned to the pair. 'I suppose we should start with you guys.'

Both Ethan and Zola opened their mouths to speak, then smiled at one another. 'You go,' Zola said.

'We have the software and linked the relevant dating apps,' Ethan said. 'Zola is editing the layout, but we'll have a useable app by the end of the day.'

I grinned, knowing how much work the pair had put into it.

'Zola? Does that sound about right?' Fee seemed surprised at how far advanced their work was.

She smiled. 'Yeah, the features are all there. I'm basically tweaking the user interface based on feedback from your testing team. We should be able to send out a link tonight for everyone to see and have a play around with.'

Jimmy looked up from his phone. 'Damn, that was fast work.'

'We've been working fifteen to twenty hours a day on this,' Ethan stated bluntly.

'Thank you.' Jimmy shook his head in awe. 'And your dedication doesn't go unnoticed.'

My phone lit up in front of me.

Jimmy: *You look so beautiful today x*

I was smiling at the screen when Fee called on Katy.

'Yeah, we have over ten thousand reviews in at present from the university students who have rated their dates so far. But since we changed the app a little, we've also used the Flirtify social media channels to recruit different demographics, asking them to review in exchange for a free subscription. We want a broader age range, so it's not an app only accessible to Gen Z.'

Fee nodded. 'And how many people do we think will have submitted reviews by the time we launch?'

Katy glanced through her phone, checking her notes. 'We're estimating fifty thousand.'

Jimmy hummed. 'Let's put out paid ads on socials and get that number up. People are sick of how toxic and unsatisfying the dating app culture has become. We can get more people to do the reviews.'

Katy grinned. 'I can do that.'

'And PR,' Fee said finally. 'How are you getting on, Britney?'

There was a silent tension in the room. Surely, Fee was aware I was doing that now? I thought everyone was. Britney's face was thunder, her brows stuck to her hairline as she opened her mouth to speak.

'Ella's on the PR for this one, right?' Jimmy cut in, his voice neutral.

'Yeah, so it's all going well,' I said carefully. 'I've planned the investor party one week from today, and I've organised the launch party too, which will take place the following week, on the night before Thanksgiving as planned.'

Fee glanced at Jimmy like she wanted to say something.

'It'll be a great night. I can send the plans out to everyone when I'm back at my desk,' I added, keen to reassure Fee I had it all under control.

'I'm sure it will be, but do you mind me asking why Britney isn't taking the lead on this one?' Fee said.

Great.

'Difference in opinion.' I managed a smile.

Britney let out a laugh without a shred of humour in it. 'Yeah, call it that.'

What a Class A cunt, I thought.

Zola and Katy were nudging me from either side so much that it was beginning to hurt.

'Look, Ella's sorted it, and it looks perfect,' Jimmy piped up, shrugging.

Fee held a hand to her head. 'We need this launch to be more than perfect, Jimmy. Absolutely no dramas, especially when the investors are there.' She pulled a face at him as if to say, *or you could be out*. Her worry was clear – she knew the investors' reactions would determine Jimmy's future and didn't want any mistakes jeopardising him, and by extension, her and Travis. 'Britney is more experienced,' she continued, pressing her point.

Katy scrunched up her face. 'Than Ella? Ella's knockout at events.'

I nudged her back to keep quiet.

'But not in New York. Britney knows the investors. She knows what they like. She's done this a million times before.' Fee sounded stressed, concerned that my inexperience in the city and with their individual network could risk the launch's success. 'Look, I know you did PR in Glasgow, but this is different, Ella. I don't mean any disrespect, and I know your plans are advanced by now, but we use specific vendors, we use particular caterers, and Britney is right here. She knows this . . .'

'Enough!' Jimmy called out, almost making me jump. 'Ella, Zola and Katy created this app. They know how they want investors and the public to perceive it. If Britney's plan didn't fit their expectation . . .' He paused and hummed. 'Their vision, even . . . then they can change it.' Jimmy sounded angry. I had never seen him lose his shit like this before, but I knew how much was at stake for him and how pointed this questioning must seem just now.

I glanced towards Zola and Katy, who looked as awkward as I felt.

'Fee,' I said softly, trying to calm the tension. 'I know how vital this pitch is, and I'm happy for any suggestions on my PR plan. In fact, I'd welcome them. But at least let me send over the details.' I managed a smile. 'The investor launch is only a week away. I have it handled.'

'I've worked in PR for years,' Zola added. 'And Ella is outstanding at her job. This project means everything to us, too. The events will run perfectly. I do not doubt it.'

I glanced at my friend, my emotions stirring at her words, but doubt lingered. Fee was right: I hadn't worked in New York or met the investors. But I knew

Britney was shady and somehow involved in some of the weirdness that was happening to us. I couldn't let her near this project.

'Send over the plan,' Fee said with a deep sigh.

'Copy me in, will you?' Britney added smugly.

Ethan let out an uncomfortable laugh at the tension, then stood up. 'I need to go somewhere quiet now.' He headed towards the door but then turned back to the table: 'Zola, are you coming?'

Zola turned to me, and I offered her a reassuring smile. She stood. 'Yeah, we'd better get on this. Lots of work to do.'

Jimmy agreed. 'Yeah, let's all crack on. You've done great work so far. Let's keep up the momentum.'

His inspirational words seemed to get lost in the awkwardness of the room, and I hurried towards the door.

'Ella,' Fee called out.

I paused, letting everyone else leave first until it was just the two of us.

'That was nothing personal, OK?' She rubbed my shoulder. 'I know Jimmy isn't going to see it like that, but I'm his sister and this app rollout has to be perfect.' I could see the concern on her face, but at the same time, I felt pissed at her gunning for me in front of the staff.

I gently shrugged off her touch. 'Look, I get it, but give me a chance, Fee. I changed Britney's plan because it was tacky and outdated. Mine is classy, and it'll tie in with the app like a dream. Plus, I've shown Jimmy and he likes it.'

Fee laughed. 'C'mon, Ella,' she sighed. 'Jimmy would like your plan regardless. He's head over heels for you, and I love that for him, for both of you. I really do, but this is work. Important work.'

I felt my cheeks flush.

'You know, I've never seen him like this before, and I hope for both your sakes it works out. But I can't sit back and let him jeopardise this company because he's too trusting of a girl he's only met a hot minute ago.'

I shrugged. I felt unsettled by a strange feeling of happiness at his sister's blessing, yet disappointment that she thought I was part of the problem. I didn't know what to say.

'I'm sorry you have doubts,' I said at last, 'but I'm not part of the problem here, Fee. I'm trying to help fix it.'

She paused, then opened the door. 'It's been a stressful few days. Please let Britney help. That's what she gets paid for, Ella. Yeah, she can be a bit of an ass, but she's damn good at her job, too.'

I managed a smile, but I knew deep down that bitch wasn't getting anywhere near my project. She was trying to bring it down.

I just had to prove it.

Chapter Thirty-Six

Ella

Another week passed, and I spent most of my time reaching out to the investors' and board members' secretaries and ensuring the catering staff noted any dietary requirements for the launch party, which was scheduled – already! – for the following day. I had sent my launch night plan to most of the office, but intentionally left out Britney and Fee. I couldn't risk Fee sharing it with Britney until I had hard evidence that she was somehow involved in Jimmy's take-down. The strength of that suspicion drove my caution.

Late at night, after work, Jimmy and I explored New York, had dinners from every corner of the world in every district, and afterwards we mainly stayed at his. It felt like my dream life. I was finally living. I loved having someone not only to date, but to talk to – someone who didn't judge me, someone who made me laugh, feel sexy, someone who pushed me to be the best version of myself. My connection with Jimmy made me realise how superficial and one-sided my relationship with Philip had been. I felt lucky to have him. Even with Philip lurking in New York, probably partying with strippers or chatting up young women in trendy bars, I didn't care. For the first time in forever, I felt secure enough to let someone else into my life. I pushed away the reality that I would be heading home soon whenever it entered my head, knowing how unintentionally attached I had become to Jimmy.

Zola was working hard behind the scenes, too. Now, the investor/media party was only one day away, she seemed to be pouring all her energy into the app to distract herself from the chaos of her relationship breakup at home.

Zola and Ethan had sent us the link to the app. It was finally up and running! It looked amazing, packed with all the extra safety info I loved – tips on checking in with friends, spotting a narcissist and escaping a bad date. It was better than I could ever have imagined, and I was so excited to share it with the world. This was something I could be proud of.

Katy was also working hard – finally focused and producing results. She was uploading feedback and gathering recruits. Altogether, things seemed to be coming together. Still, a dark cloud hung over us as we wondered if the stalker would strike again. They'd been quiet for weeks, and I wasn't sure if that was a good sign or bad.

I was sending the final timeline for tomorrow's event to Brooke from the Met, who had been my right-hand woman while planning this event, when there was a light knock at my office door and Britney stood there, her hair scraped back into a seriously tight bun. *Ouch*, I thought. *That bobble head is going to be killing her when she takes that out.*

'Ella,' she said in her usual condescending tone.

'Britney.' I matched her tone, adding a polite smile.

She tilted her head, and I noticed how my demeanour had unsettled her. 'I understand you like to work alone. You seem a bit of a control freak, and that's not a criticism.' She laughed, a sharp, high-pitched noise barking out of her.

'Go on.' I crossed my legs and arms, wondering what she had planned for us now.

'So, I've compiled a list of the board members' dietary preferences for tomorrow night. Some have serious allergies you need to be aware of,' she said, passing me her clipboard. 'Trust me, we do not want Russell Todd anywhere near shellfish.' She smirked as if we were gossiping together. But I knew Russell was, in fact, a lover of shellfish, and it was Noah Banks who had the allergy.

'Oh, this is so useful.' I scanned the clipboard, noting how she'd mixed up likes and dislikes. This was childish sabotage, but if that was her best shot, I'd play along. 'I'll call the caterers right now. Thanks, Britney.'

'Who are you using? For catering?' she asked.

I paused, not wanting to reveal my secrets. 'It's a sushi place in Chinatown. I've heard people raving about it.'

She looked unimpressed.

'Do you like sushi?' I asked.

'No,' she replied, her face turning red. 'Not a fan. But anyway, I'll leave you to it.' She paused. 'Just thought I'd help.'

I grinned as pleasantly as I could. 'No, thank you, seriously.' I nodded. But as soon as she exited, I chucked the entire clipboard into the bin. *What a fucking fanny.*

Moments later, my office phone rang and I lifted it to the crook of my shoulder. 'Hello, Ella speaking.' I was still typing up emails to vendors for the launch night, feeling a little distracted and under a serious amount of pressure.

'Hello, miss. We have a gentleman down in the lobby looking for you. He has a delivery.'

I paused, wondering what was due. I'd ordered so many boxes – merchandise, influencer walls, decorations – it could be anything.

'Can't you sign for it, and I'll head down?' I asked.

'No, ma'am. It has to be you,' the voice said.

'OK, then I guess I'll head down now.' I sighed, standing up from my desk, heading towards the lift. I intentionally walked past Jimmy's office and glanced in. He was in a meeting but still managed to check me out as I passed.

I smiled as a message came through while the lift descended.

Jimmy: *Dat ass, wow xxxx*

The lift doors opened to the lobby, and I headed towards the security guard. He pointed at a tall man dressed in a smart jacket and dark jeans. I felt my heart fall to the floor.

It was Philip.

I waited until I got close enough and muttered through my teeth, 'What the fuck are you doing here? I'm working!'

He arched an eyebrow. 'Can I have my nose back now? Jesus! I forgot how crabbit you get when you have a deadline approaching. Next week, isn't it?'

I was seething; I could feel the anger rise from my toes to my face. 'I am not crabbit! And yeah, but I have an investors' launch tomorrow to get through first.'

'Clearly,' he pointed at my face, 'you are supremely crabbit.' Then he laughed casually, as if we were two old friends catching up. 'Look, I wanted to see you. I was in the building and . . .'

'You were in the building? *What?*' I ran my hands through my hair.

'Well, I wanted to get into the building, but the place is like fucking Barlinnie.' He laughed. 'I wanted to see you! And you haven't replied to my messages.'

'Because we're not pals, and I have a boyfriend, Philip.' I glanced at the people coming in and out, hoping they wouldn't catch any of this unsightly domestic.

He laughed lightly again. 'And you can't have a chat with an old friend because you have a boyfriend? Hmmm . . .' He held his finger up to his face. 'What would The Dicktionary Club say about that, I wonder? Controlling or . . .'

'They would say you're being a manipulative prick, actually!' I spat.

Philip's shoulders drooped and he smiled sadly. 'I only want a chat, Ella. Five minutes of your time, that's it. I've had a thought . . .'

I glanced around again, making sure I hadn't been spotted.

'Please,' he added.

'Five minutes, then I have to go back to work,' I agreed. 'But not here. Let's head outside.' I made my way towards the exit, with Philip a few feet behind me.

We stepped out into the bustling streets. The noise of tourists and busy New Yorkers chatting on their phones and out for the day's work and pleasure surrounded us. I continued walking, away from the Times Square madness, up a small street, turning to see Philip behind me. I kind of hoped he'd gotten lost in the chaos.

'What is it then?' I asked, finally able to hear myself think.

'When you get home, back to Glasgow, after the app's launched, I was thinking . . .' He paused, a glint of excitement in his eye. 'I was thinking you should work for me.'

I felt my jaw drop, utterly confused. '*What?* Why would I do that, Philip?'

'At my company's PR division. You could help plan events, do what you're good at, and have a steady income so you wouldn't be worrying about finances and—'

'Philip, I *have* a job. I have my own company with Zola and Katy.' I managed a laugh, utterly perplexed by his offer. 'We have a great income coming in with this app about to launch, then who knows what's next.'

Philip became worried all of a sudden, pacing the street. 'But what if it all falls through? What if the app doesn't do as well as you hoped? You need to be smart, and a permanent position at a company that's thriving is maybe what you should consider. Be sensible, Ella!'

I couldn't decide what bothered me more: his lack of trust in the app or his lack of confidence in me. Philip was only offering me work now that I was succeeding, as if he wanted me dependent on him. Before, when we were totally skint, I hinted at a possible collaboration for one of his events, but he ignored it. But now he suddenly wanted me to work with him, to work for him!

'Why would the app not be successful?' I challenged him. 'You know nothing about the app or the people who work day and night on it, Philip. When I struggled before, you didn't offer me work, but now that things are going well, you want me to pull back? Are you afraid of my success? Is that what it is?' Suddenly, it all made sense. I used to rely on him and admire his business sense. Now I was finally managing on my own, he seemed to resent it.

'You think I'm jealous?' Philip snarled. 'Of you?' he added, as if nothing could be more absurd.

I was so lost for words. The wind was blowing behind me, and I was cold. I didn't have time for this. I turned to walk away from him and this ridiculous conversation.

'I'm not jealous of you, Ella,' Philip called out.

I held my hand out, brushing off his words as I continued to trek back to the office.

'I'm jealous of him!' he said.

I turned back. Philip stood there looking beaten down, glued to the spot where I had left him.

'I'm jealous of Jimmy fucking Link, OK? I'm jealous he gets to work with you every day. He gets to see you, laugh with you, debate with you even.' He stepped closer towards me. 'Look, I know I fucked us up, and I'll regret that forever. But I miss you. I miss having you in my life, and if you ever need the work, I honestly believe you'd be a great asset to my company. I shouldn't have left you that night. I should have appreciated you more.'

He breathed out a steady breath. 'That was all I wanted to say. No malice, no bitterness. I just miss you.'

I felt the cool wind sweep past my face, and I wasn't sure if that was making my eyes water or if it was all the things Philip had said.

I managed a slight nod. 'I missed you too, Philip. For a while, it consumed me – how it felt, missing you. But, I promise, you'll get over it. I definitely did.' I turned back around, and this time I knew the tears that were falling were all on me.

Chapter Thirty-Seven

Ella

It was the afternoon of the investor launch and I was packing up the last load of boxes from the office to take to the venue. I had lived and breathed every aspect of this night a million times over in my head, so much so that I felt confident contentment rest on my shoulders. I was excited to meet the investors and showcase Stars and Swipes to the American media and influencer scene.

The night would take place at the gorgeous Metropolitan Museum of Art, smack bang in the centre of New York. It was an exquisite venue, with that famous stone staircase leading up to the museum beyond, which was every fashion girl's dream. I had booked a space inside the Met at the Charles Engelhard Court. It was an open courtyard-style gallery space with statues that rose from the floor. Tables would be placed between these. I had assembled a dress-up team to transform the glass-roofed space with red velvet curtains and lighting, and to create influencer and media walls for the perfect selfie stations. A stage would be set up in the courtyard, where Zola, Katy and I would talk to the crowd, introducing the app and everything it offered. I'd also hired a jazz singer who would weave between the tables, wooing everyone with classic love ballads. I had it all arranged, from timings to table settings, and every preparation was checked, double-checked and thoroughly rehearsed in my head, leaving absolutely no room for disruption.

I headed to the Met in a yellow cab, and as it pulled up, I noticed a familiar black sports car parked directly in front of us. I grinned, immediately recognising the registration plate – Jimmy. I paid the cab and shuffled up to its kerbside door, taking hold of my box of QR cards, which would enable easy Stars and Swipes downloads for the guests. As I stepped onto the street, I felt a hand on my back.

'Let me get that for you,' Jimmy said, taking hold of the box.

'Did you miss me that much from this morning?' I laughed, having only left him a few hours ago.

'I always miss you, Ella. Every day, every minute.' I felt his lips graze my cheek, making me blush. I knew if a Scottish guy said that to me, it would give me the immediate ick and my fanny would turn as dry as Mother Teresa's, but there was just something about Jimmy, something about that confidence and honesty and accent, that was making me fall in love with all that soppy shit.

'Same.' I scrunched up my nose at him.

He laughed at my expression and shook his head, then we both turned to take in the grandeur of the Metropolitan Museum of Art before us. Although I had always wanted to visit the Met as a guest, I'd never imagined I'd be hosting an event *inside it*. The iconic red banners hung from the classic limestone building, reflecting the sunlight and making the entire structure look like a palace set in the middle of Fifth Avenue.

'First big event, and you've chosen the Met to host it.' I could feel Jimmy's eyes on me, watching me, but I couldn't pull my gaze away from the gallery. People were gathered outside, having lunch and chatting with friends. I literally felt like I was in an episode of *Gossip Girl*.

'Go big or go home, right?' I said, feeling the autumn breeze blow through my hair.

'Let's not talk about you going home,' Jimmy joked.

I giggled, but a strange, uncomfortable realisation came over me that I'd have to leave this place soon. That I'd have to leave Jimmy. Glasgow was my life, where I was from, what I knew. I loved being in New York. I was determined to make this life last for as long as I possibly could, but unlimited credit cards, stunning apartments on the Hudson, and feeling truly happy with the best guy in the world weren't sustainable – not for me, not for anyone. I knew that, in my heart.

We headed up the vast expanse of steps, and I couldn't help but want to race to the top in sheer excitement. Jimmy was casually carrying the box as I soaked in the atmosphere. I dodged out of the way as people posed and laughed on the legendary stairs, taking photos. My heart swelled. I loved this place. When we reached the top, I took a few moments to catch my breath and admired the view. I was overlooking the fast, chaotic city, knowing that tonight hundreds of influential New Yorkers would be here to see what my friends and I had created. I started to feel a knot of nerves gather inside my stomach. I hoped and prayed we could pull it off and save Jimmy's company in the process.

When Jimmy caught up, we headed inside and were greeted by Brooke, who had so efficiently helped me organise the whole evening over the past few weeks. I stepped in behind them, immediately noticing the world turn quiet.

'Brooke.' I grinned as I saw her.

'Ella, it's wonderful to meet you in person,' she said. I noticed the echo in her voice travel across the vast space. Brooke was an older lady, dressed in a classically cut emerald green suit. 'The setup is looking awesome already.' She winked, walking through a grand arch leading us upstairs to the courtyard. We followed her, Jimmy pointing out different passageways to the exhibits the Met was hosting, from ancient Egyptian artefacts to European oil paintings. We giggled like teenagers at the nudes, Jimmy pulling faces at the unfortunately sized cocks most of the men were sporting. I knew that if Picasso were still around to capture Jimmy in paint, he'd need at least three canvases for the giant schlong he was packing.

When we reached the Charles Engelhard Court, I watched the activity flow in and out as designers styled the venue. I felt my hands shake, hoping they were as good as reviews had promised, but I knew I had really gone out on a limb by booking different suppliers than the ones Britney usually hired. We stepped through the door and light hit us immediately. The roof was glass, like a grand conservatory, and small pools of water reflected the light streaming in from above. The courtyard stood so grand and magical, looking straight out of the set of *Bridgerton*.

'Wow.' Jimmy's eyes opened wide, taking it all in.

I turned to Brooke and squeezed her arm. 'This is truly perfect, thank you.'

'It's one of my favourite spots in the museum,' she said with a nod of appreciation.

I watched the team add our own Stars and Swipes touches to the decorations. Charging stations sat beside elegant stone statues of naked women and men, mixing modern and classic. Red velvets were draped, creating a more romantic look, and roses floated in the water.

'I'll let you take a walk around.' Brooke smiled, noticing my jaw still on the floor. 'And I'll see you tonight.'

'I can't believe I have lived in New York all my life and I've never seen this place before,' Jimmy said softly as Brooke left us.

'It's incredible.' I gulped, feeling pride burn inside. I'd done it. I had done all this alone.

'Ella,' Jimmy said. I felt him looking at me. I turned to him and smiled.

'Yeah?'

'I think you should know, I've fallen in love with you.' His voice was soft. It hit something inside of me. I hadn't heard those words for so long. Philip and I never said them after months of being together, although I'd felt like I loved him. But it wasn't like this. This, right now, felt so simple and uncomplicated. So pure.

'I . . . I love you too,' I replied.

He kissed me then, and I felt my eyes fill. Everything about this day was going to be perfect.

*

After making sure everything was going smoothly with the venue preparations, I headed home to the apartment to get ready for the night ahead. I felt giddy, with the biggest, cheesiest declaration of love building me up, making me feel like fucking Wonder Woman. Zola and Katy were almost ready, with their makeup and hair done, and now they seemed more interested in necking back champagne and listening to Olivia Dean on full volume as I hopped in the shower. As the water cascaded over me, I thought about how lucky I was. How lucky we all were to be here. I thought about how many second thoughts I'd had about coming to New York, when really it had been the best decision I'd ever made. But something stirred within me, thinking of Philip, hoping he was OK. He'd hurt me so much by moving on so quickly, I didn't want him to hurt the same way now. Philip was kind, and I knew he regretted what he'd done with Erin. It felt messy, unfinished, maybe, and as much as I tried to oust him from my mind, I found him popping back in unexpectedly.

I got out of the shower, moisturised, then began styling my hair into a sleek French roll. To keep the elegant vibe going, I went for a bronzed, minimalist makeup look. I opened my wardrobe and pulled out the sleek silky red dress I'd chosen, and smiled. This was it. It was absolutely right. I pulled it over my head and admired the backless detail, then slipped into a pointed classic heel – but not too high. I didn't fancy heading up the stairs at the Met in my favourite pair of hooker heels and risking a tumble.

When I was dressed, I walked through to the living room and joined Katy and Zola. Both of them gasped when they saw me, and I giggled, giving them a twirl. Katy was wearing a sky-blue halterneck dress that fell just above her knees, while Zola had gone for a brown and white cow-print leather boob tube minidress.

'We're going to the fucking Met!' Zola screamed and passed me a glass of champagne.

'Oh my God, I can't wait for you to see the place! The venue is the wildest, most stunning thing I've ever seen!' I said, laughing excitedly to my friends. 'I can see the investors loving it so much they dive even deeper into their pockets!'

Zola scoffed. 'They better! I could live this lifestyle for a whole lot longer!'

'So, guys, when I was there . . .' I began, biting my lip, about to explain the mutual declaration of love between Jimmy and me.

At that exact moment, Katy's phone pinged.

I watched the smile drain from her face in an instant.

'Oh, fuck. It's them.' She turned the screen, showing:

Unknown: one new message.

We huddled together to read.

Unknown: *Hey, girl, miss me? I can't wait to watch the mess from the Met. It's not too late to run home*

> *to Scotland. Cinderellas who leave early avoid the messy midnight meltdown. Clock is seriously ticking, bitches. X*

'So, they are planning a mess?' Katy trembled, still trying to understand who this could be.

'It's a bluff.' Zola shook her head. 'They won't risk anything, not with the investors there. Whoever this is knows we're onto them.'

'Are we?' I asked. 'It doesn't feel like we are, and we even had some peace for a while there. I thought all of this was over.'

Suddenly, the buzzer went off, making us all jump.

I pressed my hand on my heart. 'It's fine, the taxi must be here.' I breathed deeply, trying to steady myself.

'Do you think they're going to sabotage the night, Ella?' Katy's voice trembled with her terror at the unknown, and I felt my own fear, too. But I had worked so hard on this night. I wasn't letting anyone get anywhere near that stage except the three of us. I wasn't risking another art museum fuck-up like the one I'd had back in Scotland.

'No.' I shook my head. 'No one is fucking anything up, babe. This is our night. We've earned it. They're just trying to scare us.' I started to wonder about the wording – mess from the Met? Britney did try to mess up the information about the guests' allergies. Was she thinking of a vomiting and diarrhoea mess? Surely even she wouldn't be so disgusting as to sabotage us with literal shit.

Zola agreed, necking back the last of her bubbles. 'All they have are empty threats. Whoever this is has never actually done anything. They're a keyboard gangster, and we can't let them get into our heads. Especially not tonight.'

'Yeah, exactly!' I pulled back my shoulders, determined to brush off my nerves. 'Grab your bag, let's fucking go!'

Chapter Thirty-Eight

Ella

Zola, Katy and I held hands anxiously as we headed up the iconic Met steps in complete silence. I knew the stalker's message had affected us all, despite our best attempts at a pep talk. The Met had put down a red carpet and hired security, while photographers lined the staircase, snapping away as we headed into the building and made our way towards the courtyard. Violin music played elegantly as we entered, and I turned to my friends to watch their reactions as we stepped into the courtyard. It had been transformed. The night sky made the glass roof even more beautiful, and the small pools of water rippled with the sound of laughter and music.

'Wow,' Katy gasped.

'You seriously outdid yourself, girl,' Zola said, hugging me tightly.

'It's amazing,' I agreed, my eyes skimming the crowd until I spotted Jimmy in his tux, entertaining guests. 'You two good?' I asked, wanting to see Jimmy and show off my new dress.

Katy looked nervous, but Zola rolled her eyes and put a hand on Katy's back. 'She'll be fine. Go mingle with your man!'

I smiled at my friends, then darted across the floor, weaving between the tall pop-up cocktail tables intertwined with elegant statues until I found Jimmy. I tapped him lightly on the shoulder as he was mid-sentence, and he turned.

'Wow, Ella!' He kissed my cheek, then stood back to take me in. 'You look sensational.'

I grinned, watching his eyes dart up and down my body like he couldn't wait to undress me.

'So do you, Mr Link.' I leaned forward and kissed his cheek, smelling his deep Tom Ford cologne that immediately caused my clit to double in size.

'Uh-hum.' One of the gentlemen Jimmy was standing with cleared his throat and side-eyed the pair of us.

Jimmy laughed, and I felt his warm hand touch my lower back.

'Lucas, this is Ella. She's one of the creators of Stars and Swipes, and she's the person who has arranged this whole evening, in fact. Ella, this is Lucas, one of our biggest investors at the company.'

'It's so nice to meet you, Lucas.'

I held out my hand to shake his. He was a plump man in his sixties with a grey beard and expensively cut suit. He held my hand and kissed it firmly, taking a second to pause as it touched his lips.

'Welcome to the city that never sleeps,' he said.

I felt my creepy radar hit one hundred, so I pulled my hand away as politely as possible and rested it on Jimmy's.

'I must say, this venue, this evening, it's quite the thing,' Lucas said.

I smiled, knowing he was probably paying for most of it.

'This app deserves a big bash. It's a belter.' I grinned, feeling Jimmy's hand gently rub my back again.

Lucas and Jimmy exchanged a few more words before the older man drifted away to another cluster of people. We stood gazing around the room, watching as guests socialised and the champagne flowed.

'This is perfect. You are perfect.' Jimmy kissed my cheek again.

'Thank you,' I said, looking into his eyes.

'Ella!' Fee's high-pitched voice echoed through the room, as she came charging towards me. 'OK, you have *killed* this. This party is insane!'

'And?' Jimmy prompted.

She took hold of my hands. 'And I'm sorry I doubted you. I just . . .' She shrugged. 'I was nervous that you'd pull it off, but this is absolutely incredible.'

'Thank you!' I laughed, knowing I had smashed it out of the park. 'I'd have been nervous too if I were you. But I always keep my promises and we all know that this app deserves the very best parties!'

Travis strolled up to join us, and I managed a fleeting smile towards him.

'The media are heading in just now,' he said.

I scanned my eyes across the venue, watching Katy and Zola chat with Ethan. 'I'm gonna go get the girls. We'll do our first speech in a few minutes.' I squeezed Jimmy's hand and walked across the floor towards my friends.

'Hey.' I smiled at them as they laughed with Ethan.

'Party looks cool,' Ethan said.

Zola grinned. 'You hate parties!' she teased him, then she and Ethan laughed together. She'd actually made Ethan *laugh*. I noticed a twinkle in her eye that I hadn't seen in a long time. Was she flirting with the techiest tech dude ever? I wondered.

'He hates socialising but can obviously spot a well-run event, right?' Katy chimed in.

'Exactly,' Ethan said stiffly. 'If I weren't on the board, I wouldn't be here, put it that way.'

I turned to Zola, and our faces both wore the same expression. 'I didn't know you were on the board!'

'Me neither!' Zola said, sounding more shocked, as if it were something he should have brought up.

Ethan nodded. 'Yeah. Department heads all get a seat. It's pretty boring, honestly.'

'So, wait. Is Britney on it too?' I asked, scanning the room again. I hadn't seen that traitorous bitch yet.

Ethan sipped his champagne. 'Britney, Fee, Travis, Jimmy, me, and a few finance guys too.'

I wondered if he knew about the company's financial troubles. Surely he had to, if he was on the board . . .

'I only attend the meetings when it's absolutely compulsory,' he said. 'You know how those situations make me feel,' he said, turning to Zola.

I felt a tight grip on my arm, as Katy gasped loudly. 'Ella, isn't that . . . the guy . . . the weird Texas guy from . . .' She lowered her voice to a whisper. 'From that crazy speed dating.'

I swivelled my head and immediately recognised the cream suit. My eyes dropped – Jesus, that extra-large bulge was impossible to forget. I felt my chest tighten and my face flush.

'Fuck, that's Leo!' I gasped the words so loudly that my exclamation drew stares from the guests nearby.

'Yeah, Leo's a major investor in the city,' Ethan said. 'How do you know him?'

The three of us – Katy, Zola and I – shared an awkward glance and, acting in silent agreement, each chugged down another glass of champagne. We stood watching Leo swagger around like John Wayne at the party. *What a small fucking world*, I thought.

A moment later, I felt a light tap on the shoulder.

'The mics are set up for you all.' Brooke smiled, edging us towards the front.

'Great.' I nodded, looking at Katy and Zola. 'You ready for this?' I asked, suddenly feeling a ball of nerves fly around my stomach.

'Of course!' Zola added. 'C'mon, we've worked so hard on this. Own the moment, ladies.'

'OK, let's go.' I led my friends towards the front of the stage. 'We need to speak slowly, remember?'

Zola laughed. 'You're the one with the accent, babe. I got this.'

The three of us stood centre stage overlooking the courtyard packed full of investors, press and influencers, who all seemed to have their cameras at the ready.

We waited until the music naturally ended to begin. I could see Jimmy front and centre, beaming up at me encouragingly, alongside Fee and Travis.

Zola lifted her mic and, as confident as ever, she began.

'Welcome, everyone, to the pre-launch party of the world's latest way of dating. My name is Zola and joining me on stage this evening are my two best friends and colleagues, Katy and Ella. Tonight we are going to introduce you all to our innovative and unique new dating app – Stars and Swipes.'

A polite round of applause filled the space, and I felt myself grin widely. I couldn't believe we had actually pulled this app off in such a short space of time. I stepped forward to continue my part of the introduction speech.

'I'm sure many of us in the room have had the unfortunate experience of using dating apps, which come with so many obstacles. Does the person you're meeting look like their photographs? Is this stranger safe to spend time with? Does anything they say on their profile have even a passing acquaintance with the truth? The problem is – we simply don't know. It's all down to chance. It can be downright scary to open yourself up to the possibilities of heartbreak without all of these unknowns muddying the waters even further.' I paused for a second, glancing down at Jimmy, who was nodding after every word I said. 'But what if we could have a way of answering our most important questions up front? Stars and Swipes is a brand-new app built on an AI tool that enables users to research each date before meeting them in person and, what's more, to access crucial feedback on the past experiences of others. With this app, we've formulated a safe way to date, opt out of time-wasters and avoid dangerous individuals.'

Katy stepped up beside me for her part. 'Not only does Stars and Swipes expose the untrustworthy men and women of the dating scene, it also offers users far more information than the generic dating apps out there. We've done our research, extensive research, and included the vital data points that are important to all Americans, like religion, goals, political affiliation, right down to favourite basketball team – or whatever sport you guys like to watch.' A few bursts of genuine laughter filled the space, and Katy's face lit up. I watched Travis grin as she spoke. 'If you would all take out your phones and scan the QR codes set out on each table, we'd love to give you a demo on how easy and accessible Stars and Swipes really is.'

People began rustling in their pockets and handbags, pulling out their smartphones.

'Smashing it,' Zola muttered under her breath, noticing how engaged and receptive the audience was.

I nodded happily, agreeing with her and giving Katy a nudge of encouragement too.

Suddenly, a swarm of message notifications fell over the phones in the room. A cacophony of beeping and vibrating filled the packed space. I watched guests nudge one another, pointing and tipping their heads in our direction. Some gasping, some giggling. I looked at Jimmy as he glanced around, attempting to shush the rapidly rising noise level.

'Sorry, guys. It's probably best if you put the phones on silent for this,' Katy said. 'I know you're all really important and have a lot of people wanting to contact you, but if you could please give us a few more minutes.'

A flash of cameras blinded me. I held my hands over my eyes. What the fuck was going on?

'Hey!' Jimmy called out to the press. 'Enough!'

'Mr Link, do you have anything to say on the *DeuxMoi* headline about your new app?' a reporter called out.

'What? What headline?' He seemed frustrated and on the edge of anger as the crowd surged around him, shoving mics and cameras in his face. 'Can we let the demo continue?'

'Are these allegations true?' another reporter asked.

'Mr Link, were you aware of any of this?'

'What are you talking about?'

'Guys, what's going on?' Katy whispered as I watched Jimmy pull his phone from his pocket. Immediately, his expression changed.

'I have no idea,' Zola mumbled. 'Ella?'

I could feel myself shaking with worry. 'I don't know.'

Jimmy's eyes were on his phone, skimming whatever story had been published, then he glanced up at the three of us on stage.

'Is this true?' he asked. I could barely hear him over the noise of the crowd.

'Is what true?' I called back, but I couldn't hear anything over the intense din. I felt Katy cling to my arm. 'Jimmy? What is it?' I said, stepping towards the edge of the stage to be near him.

'Jimmy?' Fee insisted.

I watched his hands flop to his side. She grabbed hold of his phone and lifted it, her eyes scanning the article.

'Did you know?' he repeated to me.

I reached the edge of the stage, the light blinding me.

'Know what?' I cried, panic building up. What was going on?

'Did you know Katy was sleeping with my best friend? My brother-in-law?'

Absolute darkness slammed into me.

How the fuck did he know?

Next to Jimmy, Travis stared at his phone, looking like the world was crashing down upon his head.

'Did you know, Ella?' he asked me again.

I nodded. 'I knew.' It was all I could say. I couldn't lie. But I wanted to tell him that it was much more complicated than he might be thinking right now.

'Jimmy, we need to talk.' Travis tugged at his arm.

Fee was surrounded by people rushing to her side, shielding her from the press, who had suddenly turned full-on paparazzi. I noticed Britney clinging to her, drawing her beady eyes off us like we were the fucking issue. Everything had happened so quickly. We were stuck.

'Jimmy, it was a mistake,' Travis called out, forcing Jimmy's shoulders around to look at him. 'She was just a silly girl. I got carried away . . .'

Then – punch. Jimmy struck Travis straight in the face. Someone screamed. Shit, I could feel my heart race.

'Stop it!' I called out. 'Jimmy, no!' I dived off stage and pushed my way over to him. His breathing was frantic. Travis lay flat out on his back, blood streaming from his nose.

Jimmy turned to me, his eyes glossy with tears. 'Is this article true? You girls sleep your way to the top? Is that what this is?' His head was darting between Travis and Fee and the press pack, who were lapping up the drama. Security was scrambling through the crowd. Phone screens darted in our direction, soaking up the scandal playing out in front of their eyes.

'Of course not! Why would you say that?' I felt a combination of anger and sadness fall over me. 'Someone has planned this to take us all down.' I knew as I said it that I sounded insane. 'Jimmy . . .' I clung to his arm.

He shrugged me off. 'Don't fucking touch me, Ella.'

I felt my knees wobble. Around me, the influencers were TikToking the whole ordeal. A flood of New York accents surrounded me, making me feel like I was stuck in the middle of a teenage rom-com gone very, very wrong.

I turned to Katy and Zola, who were being grabbed and heckled as they came off stage, and I raced back over to them to try and protect them from the press.

'How long has your affair been going on with Travis Mason?' one man asked.

'Are you two in love?' another called out.

'Move!' I shouted. 'Fucking leave her alone!' I pushed my way towards my friend. Then, like an angel appearing by my side, I felt a tap on the shoulder.

'This way,' Brooke said calmly. 'Follow me.'

The three of us were escorted under a small archway into another room. We closed the courtyard door, pushing out the pack of journalists desperate for the tea. As soon as we were alone, Katy crumbled, sobbing on our shoulders.

'Stay here for as long as you have to,' Brooke offered, giving us a reassuring smile.

'Thank you,' I replied, hugging my two best friends.

*

We sat in a numb silence, questions swirling in our minds. Who did this? How did they know? Was this the work of the stalker? Had they planned this all along?

'Can someone read the article?' Katy eventually mumbled. By now, the chaos from the courtyard had quietened.

I glared at Zola, who shook her head, then passed me her phone so I could read it aloud. I cleared my throat and began.

'*Dating Shame!*' I huffed at the headline as my two friends kept their eyes on the floor. '*The Scottish trio's mission to change America's dating game with their multi-million-dollar app, Stars and Swipes, which is due to launch next week just before Thanksgiving, has been exposed as a con. The Glasgow-born girls, who have promised to help Americans find true love, have been exposed as adulterers and money-obsessed playgirls, storming up steamy affairs and connections with married millionaires and extorting them for a lavish lifestyle since they first set foot in New York. Katy McIntyre, one of the app's founders, was spotted late-night romping in Central Park with Travis Mason, board member and head of finance at Jimmy Link's Flirtify. Travis is married to Link's sister. At the same time, Mr Link himself has been duped into dating another Scottish founder, Ella, in a twisted love affair. Ella Banks has had a string of affluent partners in the past and a source close to the trio described her as "fame-hungry, power-obsessed and someone who is more than willing to sleep her way to the top"*.'

I felt like the air had been sucked out of my lungs.

'They still think I'm Scottish,' Zola eventually said.

'At least you're not a fame-hungry, power-obsessed whore,' I managed, feeling an acrid burning in my stomach. I thought about Jimmy pulling a Will Smith punch in front of all those people. It would ruin him. What about the app? The investors? Too much was going on for me to focus. I needed to get out of this room. I needed to explain myself.

'I want to go home now,' Katy said, breaking down again.

Zola and I cooried in, silence again between us, knowing that in this moment we all felt exactly the same way.

Chapter Thirty-Nine

Ella

After an hour in that tiny room, Brooke ushered us out to a waiting car and drove us home. Katy sniffled quietly, hugging herself, her eyes red and distant. I sat beside her, useless. My thoughts spun: had we ruined everything? Was there a way to fix this, or had the worst already happened? The drive passed in a blur, every second weighed down by dread. No messages from Jimmy. Panic crept in again with the memory of his punch, him telling me not to touch him, the press capturing everything. My chest tightened. Fuck. Fuck. *Fuck*.

We got out of the car and walked up to the apartment block foyer together. The doorman opened the door with a smile.

'Good evening, ladies,' he said, but his tone seemed reserved, as if he already knew not to start a conversation.

'Hi, thank you,' I said, passing through.

As we headed up in the elevator, I watched Katy's distraught face, her cheeks still damp with tears.

'Are you OK, Katy?' I asked, hating how pointless the question sounded, but my brain felt so foggy I had nothing else.

She stared at me for a few seconds, her eyes shining with unshed tears, then lowered her head in defeat.

Zola let out a long exhale and rubbed my shoulder just as we walked into the apartment together. I let my two friends enter first, following closely behind.

'Ella,' Zola whispered as she turned her head, gesturing towards the sofa. 'Look.'

The man sitting sombrely on the couch, a cloth wrapped around his knuckles, was Jimmy. I wasn't sure if I should run up and hug him. I wanted to feel better, but at the same time, I knew things between us had changed.

'We'll be in my room,' Zola said. She placed her hands on Katy's shoulders and gently guided her into the bedroom, leaving Jimmy and me alone in the living room.

When they left, I stepped towards the sofa. I looked at him. His suit was unbuttoned at the neck, his face puffy from tears. I took a seat beside him.

'Jimmy, look, I'm sorry I didn't tell you . . .' I began.

He shook his head. 'No, Ella. You don't get off that easily.'

I paused, my mouth dry and heart pounding, not knowing what to say.

Finally, he looked at me. 'How could you keep this from me? Katy and Travis? How could you be in my company every day and not say a word? How could you be around Fee? You came and ate pancakes with my sister, knowing that her fucking husband was sleeping with your best friend?'

Shit. I wanted to clarify that Fee didn't actually eat any pancakes that day – it was only me – but I knew now wasn't the time to get into nitpicking details.

'Katy slept with Travis, yes. It was our first day in New York, and she met him randomly on Tinder. She had no idea he worked for you or that he was married. He lied to all of us, Jimmy!' I pleaded my friend's case, knowing now was certainly not the time to reveal that they'd also shagged in the snack cupboard.

'When did you know?' he asked, leaning forward. My nerves buzzed. Jesus, this would go down like a fart in a spacesuit. There was no good answer.

'The day we had our interview,' I admitted, feeling completely ashamed. 'But you have to realise this was the chance of a lifetime for us. We didn't think it was fair that Travis not being able to keep his dick in his pants should be the reason we miss an opportunity like this!'

Jimmy looked too exhausted to reply, rubbing his eyes and sighing as he tried to process everything.

'Then the messages started,' I said.

'What messages?' Jimmy said, a little more sternly. 'Ella?'

I paused, realising how much I'd kept from him – feeling a sharp ache of regret for leaving him in the dark, wanting to shield him from the mess. I didn't want him to judge or think we brought drama. I thought I could fix it alone, without him ever knowing.

'Katy started getting messages, threatening us to stop working on the app and telling us to go back to Glasgow. They knew about Travis and her, so they tried to blackmail her with it.' I turned to him, more animated now. 'We've been trying to figure out who it is, Jimmy! I think they have something to do with your previous apps failing.'

He slowly gazed up from the floor, his eyes glassy with hurt. 'What? So, hold up, you figured all of this out, and still you kept it from me?'

I gulped, knowing how wrong it sounded. But at the time, I was focused on protecting my friend.

'Yeah, but . . .'

'But nothing, Ella.' He stood up, looking disgusted. 'I've shared the worst things about me with you. I told you I was in juvie as a kid.' He laughed as if the whole notion of confiding in me was now ridiculous to him. 'But someone has been threatening you, trying to destroy my company, my career, and you didn't think to give me a heads-up? Did you not think to trust me enough to know how to handle that?'

Fuck. I knew he was right, and shame burned inside me.

'I . . . I . . . Look, there was so much going on, Jimmy. You don't get the pressure I've been under. I was starting this with you, trying to get over my ex. Then he turns up and . . .'

'What?' He covered his face, the white cloth on his hand gently unfolding.

'Nothing happened. I told him about you! I told him how happy I was! But—'

Jimmy chuckled, but it wasn't a cheering noise. I felt like I was spiralling. 'Glad you told him something, Ella.'

There was a pause. I was utterly drained, a heavy numbness settling in. Even trying to explain seemed to make it far worse.

Eventually, I said in a soft voice, 'Look, someone has a vendetta against you. We have to find out who it is before it's too late. The app is ready, it's not going anywhere. But we have to find out who this stalker is and why they're—'

'It's already too late, Ella.' His voice was low. He took a few steps towards the kitchen and placed his hands on the worktop, his back to me. 'I'm losing the company. There's a meeting set for Monday morning, at which the board will appoint a new CEO. Hopefully Fee will get it, but I don't know for sure.' He shrugged.

'No, Jimmy!' I stood up and walked towards him, reaching out to comfort him.

'Don't touch me, Ella,' he said, standing, his whole body rigid.

'For fuck's sake. I'm trying to help, can't you see that?' I called out, my voice echoing through the apartment louder than I'd meant.

'You could have helped if you'd told me before the shitshow that was tonight. Why didn't you tell me all of this?'

His voice was raised, louder than mine, and I stepped back.

'You know the papers are saying you and your little friends are money grabbers, and I didn't want to believe it. But maybe they're right?' he snarled. 'You came here, fucked me as well as fucked me over. Ha, you even fucked my sister over, and now . . .' He held his hands up in the air. 'What now? What's next?'

'What's next is you should fight for your company instead of moping around and blaming me! You should get ready for this app to launch! You know the papers print a load of bullshit! Don't you dare tell me you think that shit is real!'

Jimmy rubbed his face in frustration and something close to despair. 'The biggest investor pulled out after I punched Travis. The app is gone, Ella. I'm done, you're done. We're all fucking done!'

I felt the wind knocked out of me – all the work, all the planning, all of it for nothing.

'Can we not find a new investor?' I asked naively.

Jimmy uttered a laugh under his breath. 'Do you know someone willing to invest two million in a company that doesn't even have a CEO?'

Everything drained from me. My legs shook, my arms felt as if they were holding twenty-kilo dumbbells. I stared at nothing, frozen as the silence settled in.

'You told me you loved me.' Jimmy's voice broke as he spoke, grief etched into his face. His eyes finally allowed tears to fall, and I immediately felt my bottom lip quiver, my heart breaking at the sight.

'I do.' I ran over to him and grabbed his jacket. I'd never met someone as amazing as him, and I knew I'd meant those precious words.

'You don't. You would have been honest with me if you had,' he said, his hand trembling as he lifted it and ran it down my makeup-stained face. I could sense this was coming to an end and a wave of panic rose inside me – I didn't want him to let go, to give up, not yet. Not like this.

I shook my head, tears streaming down my cheeks. I was gasping for breath as I tried to explain. 'I just had to protect Katy,' I cried, my voice shaking under the pressure that was now too much to withstand. 'Please, understand that, Jimmy.'

There was a long silence as he leaned in and hugged me tightly. Relief and dread collided inside me. I didn't want to let him go. I took a breath, inhaling his scent, clinging desperately to his warmth and solidity.

'I gotta go, Ella. I'm sorry, but too much has happened now,' Jimmy said as he gently raised my chin to look at him and managed a small, sad smile.

'Jimmy, wait. Don't go, not like this,' I pleaded.

He kissed my forehead and pulled himself free from my grip. 'Goodbye, Ella. I know you'll have an unbelievable life.' He took a few steps towards the elevator, his footsteps growing fainter.

'Jimmy, wait. I love you! Please,' I called out, not caring if I lost what little dignity I had left. I was prepared to beg for forgiveness.

There was silence, and I paused, hoping he'd turn back. Then I heard the lift door shut.

'I guess I just love my friends more,' I whispered before collapsing onto the floor.

I broke down in wails, my chest heaving with sobs, knowing I'd truly fucked everything up.

I wasn't sure how much time passed before Zola picked me up and helped guide me to her room. I lowered myself down onto the mattress beside Katy, who'd fallen fast asleep. We didn't say another word until morning.

*

I woke at six, numb and woolly-headed and praying that last night had all been a nightmare. I sat up. Both Zola and Katy were already awake and cuddling one another.

'Hey,' Zola said, her voice croaky.

'Tell me this is a bad dream,' I said, shaking my head.

'I wish,' Katy said, turning her phone screen towards me. She was on TikTok, scanning the Stars and Swipes feed. 'We even made it to the For You page.'

She tossed me the phone, looking completely fed up. Videos of how the night had unfolded flooded the screen. From the glitzy Met to a knockout finish, it was all on camera. It felt like The Dicktionary Club all over again, only on a much grander scale.

'And look at the video with Leo, the big sleazy creep,' Katy said.

I felt nausea hit my stomach as I scrolled down to see the big Texas cowboy speaking to the media about having previously met us on the dating scene and how we'd told him we'd love a rich man to take care of us.

'What a lying piece of shit!' I shouted at the phone.

'Exactly!' Katy hummed.

'I wouldn't give that cunt a nod in the desert,' Zola spat, 'and he's making out as if we were the ones all over him.'

'Is Jimmy raging at me?' Katy said, and I could hear the worry in her voice. I shook my head.

'He's raging at me, babe. He's fuming because I kept it all from him: Travis and the stalker. He said we're done, that there's no going back. He's going to lose the company.' As I said it, I felt a piercing pain stab me in the heart.

'We heard,' Zola admitted. 'Ethan called us about an hour ago. We told him all about the stalker. He promised he's going to go digging.'

I sighed, running my hand through my hair, which was now in some form of crazy beehive. 'There's no point.

Jimmy has to go to work on Monday. The board has called a meeting and that's when he'll be officially fired.'

Zola swung her legs out of bed. 'Well, give him two days then. He might come up with something.'

Katy sat up, turning to Zola. 'No, I want to go home, Zola. I can't stay here two more days.'

Zola glanced at me, then back at Katy. 'We can't leave it like this. It feels wrong.'

I understood where she was coming from, but part of me wondered if Zola was delaying heading home as a way of putting off dealing with her own shit with Curtis. She hadn't heard from him in weeks, and it didn't seem like she wanted to. But she had her house and breakup to sort through.

I passed Katy her phone and reached for mine on the bedside table – nothing from Jimmy, but four missed calls from Philip.

I dismissed them and clicked on WhatsApp, noticing my archived chats.

Three unread messages from Philip.

Philip: *You OK?*
Philip: *Ella? Let me know you're OK?*
Philip: *Call me.*

I locked my phone and stood up, not knowing how the day would pan out, but hoping to keep as low a profile as possible.

Chapter Forty

Ella

It was past two in the afternoon, and I was still lying in bed, although I'd moved from Zola's to my own. Every glimmer of light from my phone sent my head and heart into a frenzy. Jimmy hadn't reached out since leaving the night before, and I lay in bed contemplating every decision I'd made since arriving in America. I had no idea why I'd thought I could keep this under wraps. There was so much pressure, and I'd been determined to live an unrealistic fairytale life as far as I could. I'd wanted to protect Jimmy and handle this on my own. I didn't want to puncture the fantasy we'd built between us.

I heard Zola's voice chatting on the phone most of the day to Ethan, and as much as I admired her for trying, I knew she was fighting a losing battle trying to sort out the shitshow we'd created.

I was doomscrolling down my TikTok feed, watching endless videos from different angles of the catastrophic night, when Zola came to the door.

'You have a visitor,' she said. Her voice was low, as she nudged her head towards the living room.

I sat up so quickly I felt the room spin, realising I hadn't eaten or drunk anything for almost twenty-four hours. 'Jimmy?' I felt my blood warm. *Maybe he's come to sort all of this. Maybe he's found a way to fix us.*

'Philip,' she whispered, making sure he couldn't hear us. 'I can tell him to leave if you want . . .'

I shook my head. 'No, it's fine.' I glanced at my pale face in the mirror and untangled my hair, brushing it abruptly to get the tugs out.

Zola watched me with concern on her face, entering my room and closing the door for more privacy. 'Look, Ella, remember what he did, OK? He's floating around here for some reason, we've no idea what, and you're vulnerable right now. I don't like it.'

I stopped brushing and faced her. 'He just wants to make sure I'm all right – it's not like that anymore,' I assured her, reaching for a wipe and cleansing my patchy skin.

Zola continued watching me in silence for a few more seconds.

'What?' I said, reaching for a chewing gum, knowing my breath must smell like a bag of dicks, but having no energy for a full dental hygiene session.

'Be careful, yeah?' she said, her voice tight with concern as she opened my door and let me walk through to the living room. 'I made you a coffee, you'll need it.'

I could feel her hover in the hallway behind me, tense and wary, like a stray cat waiting to attack.

I headed through to the sitting room where Philip was standing, his eyes fixed on the gorgeous afternoon view of the Hudson. I cleared my throat and he turned to me.

'Ella.' His voice sounded panicked, like he'd been genuinely worried about me. 'You didn't answer my texts!'

He walked over to me, arms out, and wrapped them tightly around me. I felt rigid, like I was doing something wrong by embracing him. But it also felt nice – safe and familiar.

'I've been spiralling,' I managed to say, with a slight laugh.

Philip pulled back, still gripping my shoulders. 'I bet you have! I saw the newspapers and the TikToks.' He pulled a face at how ugly everything was. 'The things they've said about you, about Katy, it's awful.'

I nodded, agreeing, but I had no energy to go over it all again with him. I pulled away from his grasp and sat on the sofa, clasping my hands round the coffee Zola had made me.

'You should try telling Jimmy that,' I managed, reliving the moment from the night before when he was questioning my intentions.

Philip bristled slightly, uncomfortable when I said Jimmy's name. He sat beside me. 'So, what's the plan?' he asked. 'I want to help if I can – could I talk to the media on your behalf? Maybe they'd listen if it came from me?'

I shook my head, knowing no one could do a thing, but grateful for his offer. They were only interested in ruining people's lives, not printing a story on how they got me all wrong.

'It's pointless.' I shrugged. 'This entire trip has been pointless.' I felt my voice crack. 'I've lost everything in the process, and it's all been for nothing.' My eyes glazed over, and I scrunched my face up, determined not to cry in front of him.

'Hey, come on! I'm sure it hasn't been pointless. You had a little drama at a party, Ella. You still have the app launching next week! Remember the last gallery drama you had? You basically put that Italian guy on the map.'

I covered my face. 'The app isn't launching. A major investor has pulled out . . . so . . .'

Philip went quiet, clearly out of ideas for pep talks. Silence settled between us.

'I've ruined my entire career. If someone sticks my name into Google for recommendations, all they're going to find out is that I'm a fucking money grabber.'

Philip moved closer. 'Well, the offer at my company's PR firm still stands,' he said softly, likely thinking about how I'd reacted the last time he'd mentioned it. 'But I can also help you if you want to try it on your own for a bit longer. I know a lot of people back home, Ella.'

I forced a smile as I watched him genuinely try to help me. As much as his recent actions infuriated me, he had always been kind. I could see he was trying. Philip's eyes locked with mine and he matched my smile.

'Thank you,' I said quietly, feeling drained of pretty much everything I had.

'Come here!' he said, stretching out his arms for a hug. I dragged myself up the sofa and leaned into him, properly this time. His body felt warm, strong, protective. I closed my eyes and inhaled a long, deep breath.

'I know things aren't great between us, Ella. And I know I hurt you, but I'm going to do everything in my power to fix this. I'm sorry,' he said, his voice still soft.

My thoughts ricocheted in my skull. I felt lost, uncertain, raw. But it felt nice to have someone on our side. Someone who knew me, who knew my friends and knew we weren't any of the awful things the media had made us out to be.

We sat in complete silence for a while. Philip ran his fingers through my hair. I had missed this for so long, I'd dreamed about his touch, his comfort, his warmth, but now it felt strange, like nothing. After my time with Jimmy, it all felt entirely different.

Then I heard a voice call out from behind me.

'Zola! It's me!'

I turned to see Ethan standing beside the elevator, his eyes fixed on me, cuddling Philip. He looked a little more uneasy than usual.

'Hey!' Zola called out, looking happy to see him as she came out from her room. Then her gaze fell on me. Her smile dropped as quickly as Katy's knickers when she caught wind of a twelve-inch cock. She placed one hand on her hip and paused, biting her lip.

'You have got to be fucking kidding me,' she muttered under her breath. 'Ella, a word!' She pointed to the hallway, summoning me. I stood up like a naughty schoolgirl and dragged my feet through. 'One second, guys,' Zola said to Ethan and Philip, then stormed behind me into the hallway.

When she reached me, I could see the fury blazing in her eyes.

'What the fuck was that, Ella?' Venom seethed through her teeth.

I took a step back, wondering who the fuck she was talking to, because there was no way it could be me.

'Excuse me?'

'He fucking cheated on you!' she continued.

I felt my face radiate enough heat to warm the city with anger. 'What are you on about? I know exactly what he's done! And just for the record, we'd finished!'

If I were being honest with myself, I wasn't sure whether we had or not, but it had been a grey area when Philip and I broke up. I didn't have the mental strength to dive into the finer details of that right now.

'What is your fucking problem anyway, Zo?' I spat back. 'Philip and I have history, and he's trying to make amends. He's shown up to help me, to help all of us! It's not like that anymore. He's a friend!'

Zola laughed, her body swaying from side to side. 'Oh, yeah? And how's he going to help? Eh? By snuggling up in Jimmy's house with Jimmy's girlfriend. You're pathetic!'

'*What?*' I was furious now. I had no idea why she was gunning for me. 'No, actually, he's offered us jobs at his company for a start.' I shook my head, not knowing why I was under attack for a stupid hug from my ex.

'And why do you think he's done that, babe?' she continued. 'He's controlling you, Ella.' She slowed her voice, as if I were the thickest person in the world. 'He wants to keep you down here in a little box where you'll stay forever. He doesn't want you to become successful, to grow! Because then you won't need him anymore!'

I laughed. 'You're acting like a lunatic. He's just trying to fucking help, Zola. He's being kind!' I tried my hardest to keep my voice low, but I knew the men in the living room would spot a domestic. 'And if he was controlling me, why would he offer you and Katy a job too?'

Zola was rocking on her feet, like she was about to explode with rage. 'Because he's trying to win you back!' Then she turned her head towards the living room and called out, 'But you can tell Mr Khan I'd rather shovel shit all day than work for him!' She turned back to face me with a wide grin.

'You are fucking out of order, Zo!' I barged past her towards my room, noticing from the corner of my eye that Philip had left the apartment.

'Yeah, well, I'd rather be out of order than be treated like a total fucking sap!' she called back.

I turned, feeling it hit me all at once.

'This is what it's all about, isn't it?' I snarled, realising why she was being so bitter. 'You're jealous.' I shrugged. 'You're jealous that Philip came to New York after he fucked up, and Curtis didn't. You're raging because he's willing to change, when you haven't heard jack shit from Curtis for weeks. That's why you're so angry, that's why you don't want to go home. You're scared.'

Zola stood in a daze, as if I'd taken a steamy piss in her cornflakes. She was motionless, speechless.

A jolt of adrenaline made my hands tremble. 'You're scared to make a decision. You act tough, Zola. But honestly, you're probably the most pathetic out of us all.'

I turned around, charged into my room and slammed the door shut. I felt sick and crouched down to my knees.

My heart was racing, my hands were shaking. *Why did I say that? Why was she so horrible?*

A few moments passed. Out in the hallway, there was silence. I stood back up, opened the wardrobe and pulled on my long coat and UGGs.

I had to get out of this apartment.

Chapter Forty-One

Ella

I stormed through the living room and slammed my hand on the lift door to open it. In the background, Katy called my name faintly, but I ignored her. I ignored Ethan, too – he was still awkwardly pacing with his backpack at his side. Furious and hurt, I stepped into the elevator. I wanted out. I wanted away – away from New York, from Jimmy, from my friends, from all the mess happening around us.

As I stepped out into the autumn air, my shoulders dropped. The breeze whizzed by my face and hair, making me shiver. I started walking with no sense of direction, no place I had to be. I walked, with every conversation with those close to me from the past few days bouncing around in my head. I thought about Fee and Travis, my heart aching for her. What must she think about me, knowing all this time? I thought about Jimmy, who had lost his company and reputation – something he had built with such determination from the ground up. I let out a huge scream and noticed people staring at me like I was insane.

Eventually, I reached a rubbish-littered alleyway, buildings surrounding me, but I couldn't see any landmarks to figure out where I was. The sun had set, and I realised I must have been walking for hours. My stomach ached with hunger. I turned around, noticing graffiti on the walls and a group of sketchy teenagers staring and whistling towards me. This place, wherever it was, felt dodgy and really unsafe. I pulled out my phone and walked back the way I'd come, wondering who I would call.

I found myself dialling Philip; the only person who seemed to care about me right now.

'Hey,' he said, sounding tired, but surprised to hear my voice.

'Philip, I'm lost and I didn't know who to call,' I whimpered, peeking over my shoulder, making sure I wasn't being followed by the hooded teens.

'Lost? Ella, where are you?' he asked, sounding more concerned.

'If I knew that I wouldn't be fucking lost,' I snapped, but felt immediate regret. 'Sorry!' I added.

'OK, just think, is there anywhere you recognise? Or . . .'

My phone was beeping and I looked at the screen. **Low battery, 1%.**

'Fuck, my phone's about to die!' I panicked.

'It's fine, I've got you!' Philip insisted. 'I have your location, stay where you are and I'll be there in twenty minutes. You've walked for miles, Ella!'

I was confused. How did he know where I was? But at the same time, relief washed through me.

'OK, right. I won't move.'

'See you soon,' he said.

'Philip,' I said. 'Thank you.'

My phone went dead, but I pretended to chat on it regardless. 'Yeah, oh my God, New York. It's pretty cool. I'm just waiting on my boyfriend, he was at an advanced jiu-jitsu class there.' I spoke as loud as I could as the hooded teens passed. 'He's just around the corner. Maybe he stopped off at the gun shop,' I added for good measure.

Twenty agonising minutes later, a yellow cab finally slid to the kerb beside me. I stood rooted – exhausted, trembling, every muscle tight with fear and relief. I had never felt so vulnerable, so utterly desperate to see Philip. He lowered the window and smiled.

'Get in,' he said, looking relieved I was still in one piece.

I made my way into the car and looked at him, his tanned skin, his gorgeous eyes. This man could get anyone he wanted, yet somehow he was here with me.

'Thanks for coming,' I said, letting out a puff of breath as my legs finally began to rest.

'Who were you talking to?' Philip asked with a slight smirk, noticing my dead phone screen as the taxi set off.

'No one, I was using it as a deterrent.'

Philip let out a huge laugh and I gasped in shock.

'What? I said my boyfriend's just at the gun shop.' I giggled as I realised how far-fetched I sounded. 'Listen, it worked.'

'It did, it did.' He chuckled. 'I do like you calling me "boyfriend", though.' He raised his brows cheekily, and

I hit his arm and shook my head. 'Do you want to be dropped off at the apartment?' he asked.

I hesitated, anxiety twisting in my chest. Zola hadn't called. The memory of our fight stung, every harsh word echoing, and I pictured her still furious, still hurting from what I'd said.

'Or you could come back to mine? Chill out for a bit,' he offered, sensing my reluctance to go home.

'Would that be OK?' I asked. 'I had major beef with Zola, and I don't fancy stepping back into that right now.'

Philip smiled, looking relieved. 'Whatever you want, Pilates.'

The rest of the taxi ride slipped by with Philip sharing stories about New York, his conversation lightening my mood. Soon, we pulled up outside the Ritz-Carlton, and I side-eyed him.

'Canny hide money, can you?' I sniggered as the doorman opened my door.

'Can't take it with you either,' he laughed, paying the cab and stepping out.

We headed through the grand foyer and Philip steered us towards the elevators. We stepped inside, and he pressed for the second floor. I smiled, remembering his fear of heights, and knew he must have requested a lower-level room for a reason.

When the elevator reached the second floor, Philip allowed me to step out first and pointed to the room directly across from us.

He took the key card from his pocket and swiped it down, then opened the door. As I stepped inside, the lights turned on, detecting my movement. His room was a grand suite with a large living area and a bedroom off to the side. Everything was a pinkish cream with pale gold accessories, elegant and pristine. I walked over to the wide window, which gave a view of Central Park. Almost by reflex, I tried to work out where Jimmy's apartment was. I knew it was close by.

'What are you looking for?' Philip asked, creeping up beside me as if he'd read my mind.

'I'm not looking at anything, just the view!' I forced a smile, but inside I felt pain. So much had happened with Jimmy, and I knew he was probably in an apartment around the corner, feeling like shit, while I was in the Ritz with my ex.

'Would you like me to run you a bath?' Philip asked. 'You look cold, Ella.' He walked around to face me, placed his warm hands over my cool ones, and grinned.

'No.' I pulled them away and took a seat. 'I'll be fine in a few seconds, thanks.'

Philip sat down beside me and reached for the TV remote. An F1 race came on the widescreen. Instantly, I flashed back to life with him before, watching all the things that he liked. Although he was being kind and caring now, something felt off.

I stood up. 'Do you have a charger I could plug into?' I asked, scanning the suite.

'It's just over there.' He pointed to a small table. I spotted the cable hanging off it, plugged in my phone, then took a seat back on the sofa.

'Are you OK, Ella? You seem . . .'

'I'm fine,' I breathed, knowing myself I was being awkward, but something didn't feel right here. 'I hope you don't get the wrong idea because I'm in your hotel room.'

Philip laughed and rolled his eyes. 'I do not think we are going to have sex, Ella, OK?'

I managed a smirk at his bluntness. 'OK, I just had to check.'

'But . . . if you wanted to, then of course . . .'

'Philip!' I slapped his arm and he laughed. 'You haven't changed one bit!'

'My feelings haven't changed either.' His voice was suddenly softer, and I closed my eyes for a second. This was too much of a head fuck to deal with.

'Please, don't start this. I'm tired and all over the place. My head is too busy as it is.' I rubbed my temples, feeling a headache coming on. I wondered if I could ask him to order me some food, a drink.

'OK, I'm sorry.' He cleared his throat. 'Again.' He took a deep breath as if he had no idea how to kill the time if he had to behave himself.

'Look, Philip, last night was one of the worst nights of my life. I still have to process it. I've lost so much. I need support from a friendly face. That's all I want, OK?'

'OK,' he said. 'You've got it.'

He opened his arms to me, and slowly I let myself lie down, curled up against his chest.

'The things that have been said, in the press and on socials, have been so awful. I can tell Katy is terrified,' I said.

'No wonder.' He tutted at the drama. He began stroking my hair, allowing me to talk.

'I watched a TikTok today, and someone actually said I had made a pass at her rich grampa one night in Tennessee. I've never even been to Tennessee!'

'You're the only ten I see,' Philip joked. I turned to face him, hoping he'd be serious. I wanted to vent, to be understood properly, to moan to someone and even try to work things out. 'I'm sorry, that one was too easy! Back to being serious. Ella, you have to stop watching TikTok. Especially right now – just stay off social media. It's not going to do you any good.'

I agreed, but I knew there was no way I'd resist.

'I think coming back to Glasgow, or a nice holiday somewhere, a reset, is honestly what you need.' He was playing with my hair again, and I could feel myself relax into his body.

'A holiday would be amazing,' I admitted. I couldn't remember the last time I'd had time off in the sun. 'Zola wants to stay a bit longer, to try to fix things more, but maybe I'll suggest it to the girls when this blows over.'

He paused, and I sensed I'd not quite said what he expected me to. 'I just don't like you girls getting hounded by this stalker. Look what they've done, Ella. Someone is going to serious lengths to get you out of the country. Maybe you should listen.'

I held my breath.

Panic crashed over me. I couldn't move. My heart hammered, icy fear surging through every vein.

'What is it? What's wrong?' Philip said as I sat up.

'It's you,' I gasped, scrambling to my feet.

'What? What's me?' He stood up and stepped towards me, a slight laugh in his voice.

'Don't you dare touch me!' I said quietly but seething with rage. 'I'll . . . I'll . . .' I pushed myself against the wall. 'I'll fuckin' deck you if you come closer!'

Philip put his hand on his hip and laughed. 'Deck me? Jesus, Ella!' He shrugged off my behaviour, but I could see he was panicked. His skin had turned blotchy and red, and his hands were trembling.

'I never told you about the stalker, Philip,' I said, feeling the air being pushed out of my lungs. 'I never said a word to anyone, but somehow you know.'

I watched his face collapse at his fuck-up.

'It's you,' I choked, my voice shaking uncontrollably. Terror and disbelief warred inside me. 'It's been you this whole time. You've been tormenting Katy with those texts!'

'No, NO!' he shouted, holding out his hands, stepping forward.

'Don't come near me, Philip! I swear to God,' I screamed. 'How did you know then? Fuck, you've done all of this to get us back to Scotland. Really? We've been paranoid, jumpy, scared out of our fucking minds!'

'Ella, it wasn't me.' His complexion had turned grey.

I leaned down to the table, turning on my phone, still keeping eye contact, making sure he didn't come towards me.

'Who are you calling? Ella, stop it. What are you doing?' he demanded, still edging forward.

'The police, I'm phoning the police. You are a psychopath, Philip, and I'm going to tell the fucking world!'

'No, stop! Ella, put down your phone, and I'll tell you calmly how I know. It's not me! I could never, I would never—'

'Look at you, look at the way you're acting!' I laughed out of blind fury at the state of him. 'You've done this! How could you do this to me!'

Philip eventually stepped back and sat down on the sofa, leaning forward in thought.

'I did something awful, something you'll never forgive me for, but I did not send Katy those texts,' he said, wiping sweat from his forehead. 'Will you sit down? Please!' He gestured to the chair, but there was no way I was getting any nearer to him.

'Keep talking,' I shouted, hearing my voice hit off the hotel room's tranquil walls.

'When I met you in that café on the first day I arrived in New York, it wasn't by coincidence.' He paused, sighing heavily and pushing his hands through his hair. 'I still had you on my tracking app, from when you went on that hill walk in Glencoe and got scared in case you got lost?' He grinned at the memory.

I thought back; it was months before. I had been in my hill-climbing phase, all Glaswegians go through one, and I'd got lost and Philip had to guide me down, tapping into my location from work.

'So, you did stalk me?' I said bluntly.

Philip almost laughed under his breath. 'I'm not a stalker, Ella. I found you, the same way I found you tonight in that dodgy neighbourhood.'

I could feel my hands begin to shake with the weight, the tangle of it all.

'When I met you in the café, you ran off outside, can you remember?' He glanced over to me, his eyes bloodshot and his handsome face haggard.

I nodded back.

'And I presumed it would be to text or call the girls, but your laptop was open and I read the messages on the group chat. At first, I thought it would be your reaction to meeting me, but I soon realised that you girls had a stalker. I read what Katy did with Travis, and I took pictures of your chat on the laptop.'

I shook my head, trying to make sense of it all. 'You were reading my messages when I walked back in?' I said, briefly remembering.

He nodded, looking ashamed.

'Then you told me about Jimmy, and I got mad. I was so angry with myself, Ella, that I blamed you. I had flown over here to win you back, and you had moved on. You seemed . . .' He thought about his words and shrugged. 'Different, happy. Like the old you again.'

I felt my lips tremble from the betrayal, how he'd invaded my privacy without a second thought, and at the mention of Jimmy. 'I was fucking happy, you idiot!' I cried. 'Then what? Eh? Then what happened?'

'Then I told the *DeuxMoi* site about Katy and Travis, I told them you were money grabbers.' He hung his head in shame.

'What?' I called out.

'I stopped by your office, tried to win you back, but you completely rejected me. I got so angry that I sent the screenshots to the gossip sites. I caused this, Ella. I'm . . .' His voice cracked. 'I'm so, so sorry.'

Numb. I was utterly paralysed that someone who I cared about, someone I'd shared a bed with, had done this to me, had done this to my best friends.

'I tried to fix it,' he said.

I began to edge away from the table and towards the door. I needed air, I needed to get out.

'Ella, please. I'd do anything to take it back,' Philip cried, standing up from the couch.

I shook my head at the pathetic man in front of me.

'You've ruined my life, Philip.' I was trembling. Tears, snotters and pure, intense hurt traumatised my body.

'Please don't go,' he sobbed, standing up as I got closer to the door.

'Don't go? Don't go! Are you fucking serious? You have made me fall out with my friends and lose the man I love. You have destroyed my reputation and my business. The app was my one unbelievable chance to be successful, Philip, and it's gone now. I've lost *everything*.'

He glared at me, his eyes red and watery. 'Look, I can help fix it, Ella. I promise I will do whatever you want.' His voice was croaky, but there was determination behind it.

'I want you to stay the fuck away from my friends and me! I never want to see your face again!'

I opened the door and slammed it shut behind me, crying as my shaky legs reached the stairwell. I wanted to pause and take a breath, but I didn't want to risk him coming after me. *How could this happen? How could he do this to me?* I reached the reception, pale and trembling, and headed out to the street, hailing down the first yellow cab I saw.

'To Hudson Yards, please.'

Chapter Forty-Two

Ella

I headed up in the lift, still in a daze, with tears flooding my face. Guilt and disbelief crashed over me – I couldn't believe what just happened with Philip. How could he do this to me? To someone he was trying to win back. He was making me smaller, ruining my dreams and opportunities, just like Zola had said. Shit, why did I say those awful things to her? My stomach churned, knowing she was right all along, hoping she still wasn't reeling from our gloves-off argument. I mean, I knew Philip wasn't over the moon I was dating Jimmy, but his decision to involve the media and jeopardise our app, forcing us to return to Glasgow, was nothing short of fucking psychotic. My head was in overload, bouncing between everything that had happened.

The lift door pinged open, and I paused, taking a second to think.

'Ella?' Katy called from the living room. 'Is that you?'

'Ella?' Zola called, more sharply.

I cleared my throat and stepped out. 'Yeah, it's me,' I said, heading to the living room where they sat with Ethan, typing. Had he been here since I left all those hours ago?

'Are you OK?' Katy fussed, heading over to me with her arms wide. 'You look like shit and we've been so worried. Where did you go?'

I shook my head at Katy, unable to speak for a moment. Zola saw my distress and stood, her expression turning concerned as she came towards me.

'I'm sorry,' I said, 'For everything I said, I was bang out . . .'

'Ella,' she cut in. '*I'm* sorry. You were probably right. I've been a dick since Curtis, and if you want to be with Philip then . . .'

I blew out a gasp. 'I do not want to be anywhere near that fuckin' prick ever again!'

Zola and Katy shared a look, curious to see what had gone down.

'So, Philip has been tracking my phone – that's how he "bumped" into me at the coffee shop on the first day he arrived,' I began, my voice trembling. Both my friends leaned against the sofa, bracing for more drama. 'He also tipped off the press about Katy and Travis.' I gulped, anxious that Katy might blame me for letting Philip near our chat.

'What?' Katy exclaimed in pure disbelief.

'He read our chats, they pop up on my laptop. The day I met him in the coffee shop, and I went outside to call Zo, he read all our chats, took pictures as well. Can you believe that douche! I'm so sorry, Katy. I had no idea he'd do that.'

Zola sank back on the sofa, as her head flopped down between her knees. 'I'll kill him!'

Katy was still processing. 'But why, Ella?'

I breathed slowly, my exhaustion weighing on every word as I walked around and took a seat on the sofa. 'Because he was jealous of Jimmy and me. He wanted the app to fail and thought if I moved back to Glasgow, he'd have a better chance, I guess.'

Zola put her arm around Katy, who had fallen unusually quiet. 'But he has no beef with Katy? And she's got the brunt of this whole thing!'

'Collateral damage,' Ethan chipped in, his eyes still glued to his laptop.

I began to explain exactly how I caught Philip out while my friends hummed and hawed at the tea.

'So, he claims he's not the stalker.' I rounded up my ordeal. 'But who knows what that posh prick is capable of?'

At the same time, the three of them replied, 'He's not.'

I sat up, wondering what they had uncovered.

'It's someone from the company, someone who has high-level clearance. I managed to track down who authorised the apps that failed in the past. Looking at their business plans, they would never have worked and should never have launched. Someone at the company has put these apps out there, then tampered with the marketing at the last minute to ensure they fail and so turn the investors on Jimmy. It's been the same person at Flirtify every time. I'm trying to hack the server just now to see who the authorisation code belongs to, but it's going to take some time,' Ethan added casually.

I glanced at Zola, and she smiled, impressed at Ethan's work.

'Will we have answers by Monday morning?' Katy asked, knowing Jimmy's meeting with the board was approaching in only a couple of days.

Ethan shrugged, finally looking up from the screen. 'I sure hope so.'

I breathed a sigh of relief, a tiny glimmer of hope returning that I might be able to fix some of this mess, if not for me, then for Jimmy.

I walked towards the kitchen, opening the fridge for a bottle of water. It had been the worst couple of days of my life, but the idea of leaving New York with some clarity and even a little bit of dignity might make this trip more worthwhile. I took a sip, noticing Zola had wandered up beside me. Katy and Ethan were gazing at the computer screen together.

'You OK, babe?' Zola asked, rubbing my arm.

I was drained and riddled with guilt, but I replied with a smile.

'Look, you were right,' she said. 'I'm running from anything to do with Curtis because I don't know how to face it.'

I set down my water to listen to my friend.

'And I know he's a fucking arsehole, right? He's lazy, he's selfish and he fuckin' cheated on me.' She pointed to her chest and pouted. 'Like seriously, imagine cheating on me.' Then she flicked back her hair, and I laughed at her sexy sassiness.

'But he's always been there. He's like your oldest pair of knickers you hold on to because they are comfy even though the crotch is stained with period blood and the elastic is gone. It's hard, man.' She leaned on the counter. 'It's so sad and disappointing that he did this. And there's this part of me that can't help thinking, maybe I caused it . . .'

'No!' I cut in. 'No one makes you cheat, Zo. That's on him!'

'But I did it to him last year too!' She covered her face. 'OK, I might not have slept with the guy, but I was unfaithful. What if I deserve this, Ella? What if this is *my* karma?'

I shook my head. 'It's not. And again, you did that because you were unhappy, he was being so distant, and you worked through it!'

She sighed, deep down knowing I was right, but I could tell excuses and doubts were flying through her head. 'What if I never meet anyone? I'm not in my twenties anymore! What if I'm alone forever?'

I laughed, knowing the minute she wanted a man, he'd be there.

'What if you meet someone who isn't lazy, who isn't selfish, who treats you well, oh, and who doesn't fucking cheat?' I shook my head, brushing off her negativity. 'You deserve to find love. Real love, Zola. And if you don't, then surely a life of true happiness with your friends is better than a life of misery with that big pussy back home!'

Zola glanced across at Katy and Ethan.

'You don't have to rush anything. I was mad before.' I smiled, placing my hand on top of hers. 'I know this is a big decision, and I was out of order earlier. I should never have said those things to you.'

Zola was zoned out, still observing Ethan and Katy's interactions. 'Maybe I should rush,' she mumbled. 'What am I waiting for?' Then she headed to her bedroom, grabbing her phone off the counter.

Chapter Forty-Three

Zola

Zola paced her room, lifting her phone and hovering over Curtis's name. She heard it ring the international dial code, then hung up immediately. 'Fuck,' she hummed.

Suddenly, her phone began buzzing in her hand and she saw that Curtis was calling back. Nerves piled up inside her as she answered, bracing herself. Her anxiety shifted into a tense anticipation.

'Zo? You good?' Curtis's voice came through. 'Zo?'

'Yeah. I'm here.' She cleared her throat, steadying her tone. 'Are you free to talk?' Zola asked, checking her watch and remembering it was dinner time back home.

'Yeah, sweet,' he said. She could hear his background noise fading and knew he must have paused his game. 'Was starting to wonder if you'd ever speak to me again.' Hearing his anxious tone, Zola sat on her bed.

'So was I,' she admitted, her voice softer with resignation. 'But we need to sort a few things out, and I needed space after what you did, Curtis.' As she spoke, sadness began mixing with her resolve while she listened to his heavy breaths, unsure if he was getting upset or angry.

'I've thought about everything and I think it's best . . .'

'Zola, look, don't do this . . .' he said. 'You have no idea how sorry I am. You have no idea how much I regret everything that happened. That's why I told you. That's why I called . . .'

'Curtis,' Zola interrupted. 'It's not about the girl at the gym. Yeah, she upset me, she bruised my ego, I suppose, and she probably sped this up, but we haven't been great for a long time.' Zola felt her voice croak. She knew what she was saying was the truth, but even so, she didn't want Curtis to be hurt. 'I don't want to be together anymore. I want to take my name off the lease, you can have the flat or whatever, but I'm not going to live there when I come home.'

'Please, Zo. No. I'm sorry, look, I'll do whatever you want,' Curtis begged. 'I'll change, babes, truly I will.'

Holding the phone away, Zola took a breath, then spoke steadily. 'I know you would. But I deserve better. You do too. Fuck, we need to go and be happy, Curtis. We've had our shot at this, but we're different people now.'

She thought back to them as teenagers, hopelessly in love. He was cool, stylish, laid-back, and she loved how close they were. But slowly, as the years progressed, he seemed to stay in the same place, with no get-up-and-go, while she soared into an ambitious woman who wanted to build a great life.

'Can I change your mind?' he asked. 'Because I was happy, Zo. With you.'

Zola puffed. 'You maybe thought you were, Curtis. But you wouldn't have done that to me if you were, babe.'

She continued the call for another twenty minutes. Curtis sobbed, full of regret and emotion, but eventually accepted Zola's decision, although he was still promising to one day win her back. Eventually, she hung up and flopped back on her bed, sobbing into the duvet. She felt a weight being lifted from her shoulders that she hadn't known she was carrying, but also an overwhelming sadness for Curtis, knowing he'd never find anyone else like her.

After an hour of getting herself together, Zola walked into the living room wearing pyjamas and her hair scraped back from her face. She spotted Katy and Ethan, who were still working hard on the laptop.

'Are you OK? Ella's just gone for a shower,' Katy asked, having only just realised how long Zola had been missing for.

She smiled, not wanting to chat about her messed-up life in front of Ethan. 'Yeah, just got a bit of a headache. How's it going?'

'Still the same,' Katy shrugged. 'We're completely clueless.'

'I've hacked into the bank account, but there is no name on the account, just a bunch of codes,' Ethan said, still firing away on the laptop.

'That's something,' Zola said positively.

Katy grinned. 'You're amazing at this, Ethan, you should work for the FBI or something.'

Ethan tilted his head. 'They did ask, but I said no. They didn't pay enough.'

Katy erupted into laughter, clapping her hands as if he was joking. She turned her head and whispered to Zola, 'Fuck, I think I love him.'

Zola's brows raised as she watched the pair interact. Ethan was always kind to Katy, as if he saw how innocent she was. He'd never said a bad word about her involvement in the Travis Mason scandal; he just showed up to help. Was this a mutual connection? Zola wondered. But sadness swelled inside her. Was it the call with Curtis, or something else? Her brain was a scramble. It had been a tough twenty-four hours.

Zola opened the fridge and lifted out a carton of orange juice. 'I'm going to try and get a few hours' sleep, wake me up if you find anything,' she said.

'We will!' Katy bopped happily on the sofa at the side of Ethan. 'Night!'

Chapter Forty-Four

Ella

It was Sunday afternoon. I was pacing the living room while Ethan worked on taking down the snake at Flirtify. I didn't know how long he'd slept, if at all. He was working when I went to sleep and was still hard at it when I woke up at seven. Katy was zonked beside him on the sofa when I got up, a fleecy blanket draped over her. Maybe he'd gotten up early for some peace from Katy's endless questions. I wouldn't blame him. When she had a man in her sights, that girl would stop at nothing to impress him. But now, we were all up, anxiety thick in the air. It was less than twenty-four hours until Jimmy was set to be fired from Flirtify. Philip had tried to call several times and sent a simple *I'm sorry* text, which made my bones rage. I still couldn't believe he'd done this to me, to my friends. There was no way I'd ever speak to that disgusting dickhead of a man again.

*

Around two, Katy's phone beeped from the side of her; she was with Ethan, who remained stern-faced and slightly sweaty at the laptop. She lifted her phone, then turned to Zola and me, and her contented expression completely disappeared.

'The stalker?' Zola asked, suddenly tense.

Katy shook her head, eyes flicking to Ethan as he worked. She nudged her head towards the breakfast bar and slowly got up to meet us there.

'Travis Mason has just messaged,' she gulped, keeping her voice low.

I let out a huge sigh, honestly having no time for any more drama.

'Saying what?' Zola asked, pointing to Katy's phone in her hand.

Katy's eyes lowered and she read the message aloud: '*Hey, just checking in and making sure you are all good? I'm sorry you were a part of that, Katy. Are you at home?*' Katy's colour drained from her panicked face. 'What do I fucking say?'

Zola glanced at me, then back at Katy. 'OK, breathe,' she instructed her. 'Why is he asking if you're home? He must want to visit, but why?'

I huffed. 'Probably to make sure his wife hasn't contacted her about the affair!'

Zola raised her shoulders. 'Fair. It is a bit strange that Fee hasn't reached out.'

'You didn't reach out to Curtis's gym girl,' Katy interrupted, and I watched Zola look like she'd been slapped right across the dish.

'Katy!' I said under my breath.

Zola regained composure. 'She's right, but ouch, girl!'

'Sorry.' Katy shrugged. 'Different circumstances, I know.'

Zola took a second. 'OK, well, why don't we invite him up? Ask him what he knows, but don't tell him we're onto the snake! Or even searching for them! We could probably get great intel from him.'

Katy looked terrified, as if we had asked her to have a coffee with Ed Gein, 'I don't want to! I'm a terrible liar and I'll forget all the details. Plus, what if he tries to kill me?'

'There's more chance he'll try to shag you,' I replied bluntly.

Zola and Katy both smirked, and Katy's face changed; the idea clearly appealed to her for a fleeting moment.

'Err . . . No. No, I can't. I'm sorry, but I can't,' she said, crossing over her arms like a child and raising up her chin.

Zola sighed. 'OK, we can't force you, babe. But you did get us into this mess in the first place, just saying,' she added.

I giggled at how ruthless and stubborn my friends were being.

'I don't want to be alone with that man,' Katy moaned.

I turned to Zola, completely understanding Katy's point. Although Travis had always seemed harmless, we had no idea who he was or what he was capable of. Especially now that he was exposed and set to lose everything. What if he did try to silence her? There was a stalker out there, and we still had no idea who it could be.

'We could be in my room?' I suggested. 'Yeah, so we could stay quiet and camp out in my room, and you could just tell him to be quick because we're on our way back or something?'

Katy chewed her bottom lip, going over her options. After a moment of Zola's impatient toe tapping on the wooden floor, she caved.

'Oh, for fuck's sake, fine!'

She grabbed her phone, and the three of us came up with a reply to Travis together.

> **Katy:** *Hey, yeah, didn't expect any of that, to be honest, but I'm getting there. Hope things haven't been too tough on you. I'm home. Zola and Ella are just grabbing a pizza, is everything OK?*

We hovered over the phone, nervously watching his WhatsApp status change to 'typing'.

> **Travis:** *I'll be up in ten mins if that's OK? Can't get you out of my head. And I'm really sorry again.*

Katy's eyes were filling up, and I was almost speechless. This man had put her through complete and utter hell and here she was, nearly falling for the same shite all over again.

'Dry your eyes, mate!' Zola nudged her, shaking her head at the sudden emotion.

'No bother, Mike Skinner!' she spat back, angrily.

I burst out laughing, both of them joining in. 'Katy, remember all the shitty things he's done to you, babe. It's your turn to use him and get any information you can to fix this.' I smiled.

'OK, yeah. I mean, it's only Travis. I got this,' Katy agreed, looking a bit more confident. 'I'd better go get ready!' She scurried out of the kitchen in a flash towards her room.

I turned to Zola, who seemed worried. Noticing her anxious glance, I tried to reassure her. 'She'll be fine!' I said.

Zola tutted. 'She better be.' Then she called out to Ethan, who seemed oblivious to our conversation. 'Please, dude. We need you and your laptop in Ella's room, now.'

Ethan cautiously glanced up. 'Excuse me?' he said.

I laughed and said, 'Katy's doing some intel on a guest, so we have to be hidden for a wee while.'

Ethan nodded, stood up and lifted the laptop. I actually had no idea how someone could have the patience or intelligence to do what he was doing, but I was so grateful that he was. After all, this was a guy who was good enough to say no to the FBI.

I turned the side light on in my room and let Zola and Ethan get settled. Ethan pulled out the desk chair and sat down, while Zola stood just behind him, leaning forward slightly as she watched him work on the coded messages in fascination.

'I'll check on Katy,' I told Zola and Ethan. I walked to Katy's bedroom, planning to see if she was ready, but she wasn't in her room. So I pushed the bathroom door open and there she was, standing bollock naked in the bath, one foot up on the edge, beef curtains and clit staring straight at me like a fucking Demogorgon.

'Aggghhh!' I screamed.

'Jesus! Fuck!' she called out, jumping up to protect her modesty. She shoved one hand behind her back and one over her tits, completely startled, then breathed a sigh of relief, pointing for me to close the door.

'What the actual fuck are you doing?' I asked, trying not to stare, but completely baffled by the scene in front of me.

'Well,' she puffed, out of breath from the total jump scare, 'I was trying to shave when you walked in. But I got a fright, thinking it might have been Travis, and I've . . . I've . . .'

'What? What are you talking about?' There was so much information to process, so much on display, I didn't have a clue where to look.

Katy turned her body slowly, revealing her naked back. My eyes skimmed down a little further.

'You shoved the razor up your arse?' I gasped, noticing a pink tail dangling out of the centre of her crack. She skimmed her hand over her bum cheeks, feeling for the thing. 'I thought you were Travis,' she said as if that justified any of this commotion. 'And obviously it would be a pure riddie if he saw me shaving for him, so I hid it!' With a slight tug, she pulled the handle out. 'I panicked, Ella, OK?'

I could feel my face squirm in pain for her. 'It's a good job you didn't go in with the blade side, there would be a fucking blood bath.' My jaw was still gaping open, knowing I'd never get this vision out of my head. 'Why are you shaving anyway?' I asked, realising the possibility of sex must have been on her mind.

'Because my fanny is like Grizzly Adams' fuckin' beard, why do you think?' she snapped, turning to me and, after a cursory rinse of her Gillette Venus, continued to shave frantically. I looked at the patchy pussy. She was right; it was far too long and she was getting nowhere. That bad boy needed a short back and sides at the Turkish barber's before even attempting to get a cheap razor through it. She threw her hands up, still hacking away at random sections of the foliage of pubes.

'It looks like cow print now,' I said, biting my lip, desperate not to laugh.

Katy bent over and burst into giggles. 'It's too long to shave with one razor, it's clogged up like an old hoover! Ella, what am I going to do?'

I shook my head, handing her the towel, noticing the bathtub was now clogging up, too. 'You're not going to have sex with him, so you don't need to worry, Katy,' I said, smiling. 'C'mon, he'll be here soon, you don't have time for this pube sesh!'

She huffed, reaching up to switch the shower off and grabbing hold of the towel.

'What's up with you shoving things up your arse since we got to New York, by the way?' I said, remembering the butt plug from the month before.

'Literally!' Katy laughed. 'Well, look, at least if I have to pump him for info, I'm clean!'

I screwed my face up, hating the idea of Travis ever touching my friend again. 'I'd have built up all the fanny plaque I could manage for that cunt!'

She giggled, stepping out. 'Oh, and by the way, don't tell Zola about her razor.' She pulled a face, as if to say *Whoops*, then skipped through to her bedroom and quickly pulled on her jogging suit.

Chapter Forty-Five

Katy

Katy heard the lift door ping open. She braced herself for another encounter with Travis Mason, the guy who fucked her then chucked her, returning to his wife, who she'd never even known about. She tried to remind herself of how easily he unsettled her, how much of a hold he had over her, even though she was wary of it now; there was always something about him that reeled her in. Katy wasn't sure what he wanted from her this time – maybe comfort or distraction, or simply answers, given the recent scandal.

Travis walked into the living area towards her. It was a large space, and it seemed to take forever for him to reach her. Katy could feel her heart rate pick up as he came closer. He wore casual jeans and a hooded black jumper, with Nike trainers.

Katy stepped nearer to him. 'Hey.'

The silence in the apartment seemed to grow as his footsteps echoed, bouncing off every wall.

'Hey,' he said softly.

Katy grinned, relieved he wasn't coming in all Stormin' Norman at the drama unfolding in the media. 'Do you want a drink or something?' She glanced at the kitchen, eye contact feeling too much. He looked good, his eye darkened as a result of Jimmy's punch, but somehow he almost suited it, she thought.

'No,' Travis said. 'I just wanted to see you, I'm not sure why,' he admitted.

Katy's heart thundered. This was the sentimental shite that always seemed to get her into trouble. 'Well, come and sit down,' she said, walking around the sofa and taking a few short, sharp breaths to regain composure. 'How are things with Fee after . . .' She didn't want to repeat what had happened; it was still far too raw.

Travis lowered his head into his hands, then sat up, the bruising on his face more apparent the closer he was to her. 'You can imagine,' he breathed. 'I stayed at the house last night, while she stayed out. She says she can't be near me, and I don't blame her.'

Katy was fidgeting with her hands, realising the intensity of what she'd done. Even if she was initially duped into believing he was single, she knowingly pumped him in the snack cupboard afterwards, fully aware of Fee. Fully aware that Fee was in the same fucking building at the time. She cringed. Guilt pressed down on her heart and shoulders.

'I'm sorry about the app,' Travis continued. 'It was a great idea, and now it's such a waste,' he said, tutting and sitting back.

'Yeah, shame,' Katy said, too tense to risk saying more.

'So, I take it you girls will be heading home soon?' Travis asked, his eyes flickering upwards. Katy noticed he seemed more curious than casual, almost as if he needed to know their plans for personal reasons.

'Erm . . . Yeah, right. I suppose that's the plan. Woo-hoo!' She fist pumped the air. 'Better look out my fur-lined leggings for the trip back to Scotland.' She laughed, cringing at herself.

Travis let out a slight chuckle. 'So, eh . . . when? When are you thinking about going?'

Katy felt her face twist. He was seriously acting very oddly. She knew heading home was on the agenda, but the girls wanted to tie up the mystery of the stalker before they left, so they hadn't actually booked flights. 'Erm . . . Was it tomorrow?' Katy bluffed, feeling like Travis was pressing her for info. 'I'm sure it is. Yeah, like tomorrow, in the morning. Or the afternoon. Ella has organised it all, of course, I just . . .' her voice suddenly became high-pitched, 'go with da flooow!' She felt like whatever he was planning involved them leaving the States, so she rolled with it, lying without compunction.

Travis breathed out slowly. Katy wondered if it was relief that left his lungs.

'I'll really miss you.' She smiled. 'I know it didn't go to plan, and I know it got really messy, but that first date of ours was probably the best anyone has ever treated me, like ever. I'll always remember it.'

Travis looked like he was in a daze. 'Me too. In another life, maybe,' he eventually replied.

Katy agreed, fidgeting with the cuffs of her sleeves. 'So, are you going to try to fix things with Fee and Jimmy?'

He stood up and started pacing the floor, suddenly looking uncomfortable. 'Fee – *yes*. She is my wife after all, but after tomorrow's board meeting, I'm not sure Jimmy will ever want to reconcile.' He walked to the back of the sofa, deep in thought, as if the weight of the world was on his shoulders.

'Will the board really take over his company?' Katy asked, knowing the answer already, but noticing how it was affecting Travis.

He shrugged. 'It seems that way,' he replied simply. 'But with any luck, Fee will take over and keep Jimmy's name on it.'

Katy got to her feet and walked towards him. 'That's so sad, though. He's built the company up from nothing, you all have, and for it to be just taken away from him. Who would do something like that?'

'It's not that simple, Katy.' Travis's tone grew sharp, making her step back. 'There have been discrepancies happening for years that the board are aware of.'

Katy was desperate to reply that it was his division's job to keep the money in check, but he seemed pissed and she didn't want to make him angrier.

'Right. I just mean, it's a shame. Jimmy's a great guy,' she replied innocently.

Travis glanced over to her with glazed eyes. She wondered when the last time he slept was; his eyes were puffy and exhausted, not only from the punch. 'He can be, but business is business,' he grunted. 'You don't get it.'

Suddenly, there was a screech of cheering and hollering from the bedroom.

'YES!' Zola's voice called out, followed by cackles of laughter.

Travis stood completely rigid. 'Who is that?' he demanded, pointing towards the hall.

Katy panicked; her arms hugged herself tight. Her mind raced – *should she accuse him of hearing things?* But she pictured him walking in, uncovering Ethan at a laptop in their apartment, and dread twisted in her chest.

'It's just the girls,' she said, shrugging it off, unfazed.

Travis looked horrified. 'You told me you were alone,' he muttered under his breath.

'Duh, I was?' Katy managed a laugh, her heart beating against her chest. 'But they came in just before you arrived, and I said I needed the room. It's fine! It's only Ella and Zo.' She shrugged again, rolling her eyes at him, but wondered why he was suddenly acting so sketchy and suspicious. This was not the smooth, confident man she met on that first date.

'Well, why are they screaming like that?' Travis pushed, stalking in restless circles. Katy could feel her stomach churning; anxiety flickering through her as her body tightened in response. She could feel the urgent beginning of nervous diarrhoea, especially after the razor incident. Her discomfort seemed to intensify with each of his probing questions; she could feel sweat trickling down her clammy back.

'I don't know,' she said with an idiotic giggle. 'Will I ask them? Oh, yeah! Maybe they've managed to add on a bag for the flight cheaper than they expected.' She shrugged. 'Have you seen the price they charge for extra luggage these days? It's fucking ridiculous. You know I booked a trip on Ryanair once, have you heard of them?' She was waffling, using any absurd thought for a distraction, 'Anyway, the fucking luggage ended up costing more than the flight itself!'

Travis was studying Katy, glancing down the hallway, then eventually resting back on her far-too-innocent face.

'Do you have the same problem with budget flights in the States?' she asked.

Travis relaxed slightly, smirked, then placed his hand on her face. 'I don't do budget flights, babe.' His mood shifted; his arrogance returned. 'I just wanted to say goodbye.' He tapped her cheek. 'Safe flight. It's been fun.' He winked.

Katy stood in complete disbelief. What was happening? Did he know? Was he double bluffing?

'Thank you,' she said, clearing her throat. 'Fun, such fun.'

Travis stepped towards the lift and pressed the button, facing the door.

'Travis?'

He turned back, raising his head slightly.

'Did you really mean in another lifetime?' she said, knowing he was a total dick but still craving his affection.

He sighed, gazing at Katy, now with no interest in her whatsoever. 'Sure, maybe.' The door opened. 'Say hi to Nessie for me.'

Katy stood bewildered, shaken and glued to the spot. *Why did he turn so cold? Did I lie so much that he eventually believed me and understood that I wasn't going to be an issue? But what happened to Mr Nice Guy?* Replaying him looking down on her. There was something off, completely off. She turned on her heels and thundered to Ella's bedroom, pushing open the door.

'He's in on this!' She felt weak, totally disorientated, like she had been lied to and manipulated all this time.

'What?' Ella jumped off the bed and came over to Katy, rubbing her arms, 'How do you know?'

Katy glanced at Ethan, who was writing on a piece of paper now. 'He changed, so suddenly. He was caring at the start, sweet, then I realised he was just trying to get answers out of me. He started asking when we were going home, and all of this – so I lied and told him tomorrow. Then he heard you guys and seemed panicked – as if our presence threatened whatever he was planning – so I made up some story about how you must have got cheaper luggage allowance.'

'Did he believe you?' Ella said.

'Yeah, I mean, I was talking sense, the luggage pricing is ridiculous.' Katy's face twisted, reliving the moment, trying to make sense of it. 'But then he turned into a complete, uncaring prick. Like he had the answers to the questions he wanted and realised I wasn't a threat, maybe? Everything changed in an instant, and he looked at me like I was dog shit on his shoe!'

Zola walked a few steps towards Katy. 'You bluffed him, babe!'

Katy shook her head. 'I didn't, I just . . .'

Ella giggled. 'You totally did, Katy! You won, you told him we were going home, and we're not. He won't expect what's next now, thanks to you,' she said with a huge smile towards Zola and Ethan.

Katy was confused. 'Help me out here. I have no idea what's going on.'

'We have a code that's linked to a member's ID at Flirtify.' Ethan's voice was as deadpan as usual, but his grin was wide.

Katy's jaw hung open, not entirely sure what that meant, but she could only assume it was positive.

'Tomorrow morning, before the board meeting, we're going to sneak into the IT department and run the code against the list of employee names. Then the snake will be exposed!' Zola clapped and let out a huge whoop of relief.

'Then we'll find out the stalker?' Katy said, her weeks of torment showing.

Ella wrapped her arm around her. 'Yeah. It must all be related. Katy, we've almost got them!'

Katy felt her legs grow wobbly and she crouched to the ground, covering her mouth in disbelief. She then bolted up, ran towards Ethan, flinging her arms around him.

'Oh, he doesn't like physical . . .' Zola began.

But Ethan held his hand up and embraced Katy. 'It's fine. I have a sister just like her,' he said, patting Katy's back until she was ready to let go.

'So, wait, how are we going to get into the building?' Zola asked. 'They've probably revoked our access cards after the Met debacle, and that place is harder to get past the front desk than into my local GP's surgery!'

The four of them thought for a few moments.

'There's a lift in the basement,' Ella said. 'Jimmy and I used it one night. Would you have access to it?' she asked Ethan.

He hummed. 'Sure. All board members have access to that parking lot, but I prefer to ride my bike to work.'

Zola shot him a stare, as if to say, *dude, you can break your routine this one time*.

'But tomorrow I will borrow my mum's car,' he conceded, his eyes rolling slightly at the inconvenience.

The three of us smiled at his reaction, and Katy pushed back her shoulders. 'So, we finally get to the bottom of this tomorrow then?' she asked.

'Too right.' Ella smiled. 'Yep!'

Zola grinned, striding towards Ella's bedroom door. 'So, let's get the heads down, guys, and finally catch this bastard!'

Chapter Forty-Six

Ella

The following morning, Katy, Zola and I were huddled together, standing outside the apartment, trying to avoid the coolness of the fresh New York day as we waited for Ethan to arrive. I had spent most of the night awake with nerves, wondering who the culprit was, or even if we'd know them. The possibility that it could be anyone at Flirtify, from a cleaner to Jimmy's best friend, kept me on edge. Katy, however, was now convinced that it was Travis after his shifty behaviour the previous evening. Zola didn't have a specific suspect but was eager for justice. All three of us waited in the cold car park, at close to 8 a.m., each of us unintentionally dressed in black. Katy wore a black woolly beanie, black leggings and a black sweatshirt. Zola had on a black Calvin Klein lounge suit, and I wore a pair of Skims leggings and a matching top. We looked like we were about to rob a bank, which made me worry whether our clothing choices would actually attract more attention.

Ethan eventually pulled up in a Prius, and we all squeezed into the back. He was wearing the smallest pair of glasses I'd ever seen and a pair of leather gloves.

'What's with the gloves, MJ?' Zola asked as the three of us shuffled in, trying to find extra room.

'They are driving gloves,' he stated bluntly. 'They allow a better grip of the wheel.'

We giggled slightly at his attention to detail with absolutely everything he did. There was such straightforward directness radiating from Ethan, and I was so grateful we'd managed to recruit him to help us out.

'Are we organised then?' I asked.

'Yes.' He swallowed, not taking his eyes off the windscreen. 'We will arrive just before nine and the board meeting is at ten, so that will give the system more than enough time to detect the employee number.'

I felt a shaky breath leave my body. This felt even worse than the long-ago Who Shot Phil Mitchell saga. Someone had it in for Jimmy, for us, but maybe if I somehow managed to save his company from being taken away from him, I could leave New York with my head held high.

We all gazed out at the passing city as Ethan drove, then he turned into the parking lot. Zola, Katy and I immediately ducked our heads in the back and Ethan threw an old blanket over us. Pressed up against Katy's mouth, I pinched my nose. 'Have you brushed your teeth?' I whispered.

Katy's eyes pinged open in anger. 'Yes, actually,' she hissed back. 'Have you?'

But I pulled my face back. 'What with? A fucking jobby stick?'

Zola began to laugh hard, just as Ethan pulled down the window, and she slapped her hand across her mouth to stop.

'No bike today, Ethan?' we heard a security man ask.

'No,' he replied as bluntly as ever.

We sat tight as the car paused for a few seconds, the barrier lifted and then I felt us tilt down slightly as we drove into the underground car park.

Zola sat up first, adjusting her braids, and then Katy and I joined her. I noticed the lift just to the left of Ethan's car and smiled at the memory of Jimmy and me dry humping inside it after our first date. Now, we glanced around, making sure no one was about.

'Ready?' Ethan said. 'Go!'

Together we all raced out of the car. Zola led the way, heading towards the lift with Katy and me right behind her. We squeezed inside, in a mad panic, budging past one another. Ethan followed behind, pressed the button and we felt the lift begin to rise.

'That felt very straightforward,' Katy breathed. All our adrenaline levels had been spiking since last night. A few moments later, the lift stopped and the doors opened.

Ethan popped his head out and stared from left to right, 'OK, move!' he ordered. The three of us walked so quickly that we were almost jogging around the corner towards the IT department.

When we arrived, we started clapping with relief.

Ethan headed straight to the monitor and began typing. Zola stood behind him in complete awe.

'This is the program here. If you read out the sixteen-digit code, then it will search the database. It takes around ten to fifteen minutes.'

Her voice steady, Zola read the code; it was a combination of numbers and letters. Ethan focused on typing each character as she spoke. Meanwhile, Katy and I stood a few steps back, hands at our sides, careful not to touch anything.

'Ethan, are you down here?' a voice called out. I recognised it instantly: Britney.

Instant fear and panic flooded through me, and I raised my hands in the air to my friends, not wanting to move or speak. I pointed towards the security cameras he'd set up outside and the female figure poking her face up at the door we were behind.

'I'm here,' Ethan called out, walking towards the door. 'Don't come in,' he said abruptly. 'I don't like anyone in my work . . .'

'Blah blah blah, I know. The board meeting has been moved up, it's starting now,' Britney said.

I made eye contact with Zola, who looked like someone had stopped the music in a game of musical statues, one hand reaching out to the keyboard, the other in her pocket.

'No, it's at ten,' Ethan replied.

Britney let out a nasty laugh. 'No, it was at ten, but we wanted to get it over with. No point in delaying the inevitable. Come, or don't come, your choice. I'm not sure your vote will matter anyway.'

She sounded so smug, so dismissive towards Ethan that I wanted to open that door and kick her straight in the flaps.

'Ten would suit me better. I was told ten, and I don't like . . .'

'You don't like change, don't we just know it! As I said, you don't have to come. I'm heading there now.'

Britney's footsteps echoed down the corridor until they faded completely.

'What now?' I panicked. 'We don't have time!' My voice was low, my eyes were pinned to the cameras, worried she could return at any time. 'They must have changed the time deliberately, hoping people couldn't make it.'

Ethan turned to Zola. 'You know what to do. I will stall the board as much as possible, and if you get an answer, then come straight into the meeting.' He grinned at her, clearly believing she was more than capable of this, then nodded slightly to Katy and me.

'I'll stall as much as I can,' he repeated, then walked out of the department.

'Fuck,' Katy whimpered.

Zola was already sitting at the desk. 'Never mind fuck, girl, read that code out to me.' She snapped her fingers. 'Let's get a move on here, people!'

Katy held the paper up to her face. 'OK, first we have capital K for Kevin.' Zola pressed the key. 'Then small b for boobs, as in small boobs, like mine.' She giggled a bit. 'Then W for wanker, sorry capital W for massive wanker.'

'Ella?' Zola hummed, sounding frustrated.

I grabbed the paper from Katy's grip and finished the code using the correct phonetic alphabet like I was Juliet Bravo herself. When she was happy, it was checked and double-checked. Then Zola pressed enter, and a search bar with a small timer appeared on screen.

'What now?' I asked, feeling my arsehole twitch with nerves.

'Now, we wait.' Zola puffed.

I gulped; the countdown was happening. We stared at the screen as the search bar slowly moved along. I wondered what was happening in that boardroom and how Jimmy was doing with his stalling. If Fee was holding it all together; after all, she'd not only found out her husband was a cheat, but her brother was about to lose everything. My eyes stared back at the screen, hoping I could perform some Matilda badass shit to make it go faster. I could hear Zola's foot tapping nervously on the floor.

'Look!' Zola pointed, making us all jump.

One match found.

I turned to Katy, who leapt for me, hugging me tightly. 'Who?' she said. 'Who is it?'

Zola's glare remained on the monitor. 'It will tell us when the search is complete, I think.'

It was all too much. My chest tightened as I imagined Jimmy signing away his company in defeat. Was he fighting for himself, or letting it all slip away? Waiting felt like torture – ten minutes stretched into an eternity.

Then the timer stopped and a new window appeared.

Employee number: one match.

I gasped, Zola held her hand over her mouth in shock, while Katy covered her face.

Finally, we had our answer.

Chapter Forty-Seven

Ella

We raced out of the IT suite and headed towards the main offices. People stared as we rushed past, but I barely noticed them. All I could think was: *Don't let them make a final decision, not until we show the facts.* Then I spotted the boardroom and I felt a slight simmer of relief that we were so close, staring at the boxed-off room. Through the glass walls, I saw Jimmy at the table in his black suit, black shirt and tie. He looked defeated, exhausted, as if he'd already decided to give up. I hoped that it wasn't too late. Sitting at his side were Fee, then Travis, about five men I had never seen before, followed by Britney and Ethan.

'Come on.' Zola bolted even quicker, dashing over the last few metres and swinging open the door. I was next, then Katy came panting behind.

'What the fuck are they doing here?' Fee shouted, turning to Jimmy, then squinting her eyes towards her husband, who didn't know where to look.

'Sorry . . . please excuse me—' Katy grabbed the jug of water from the centre of the table and poured herself a glass, completely breathless.

'We have some evidence we'd like to share. Some that we think will make you reconsider whatever decision you are going to make today,' Zola began.

Britney stood up. 'I'm sorry, but you have to leave. This is a board meeting, and after your stunt at the Met, I think—'

'I think you should shut your mouth,' Ethan cut in.

Jimmy was glancing around in complete confusion, his eyes sad. 'Ella, what is going on?' he asked. 'This isn't the time or the place for more drama!'

'We know who has been sabotaging the company,' I said. 'It's been the same person signing off on a bad investment every time. They are trying to ruin your business, Jimmy!'

The board members sat up, suddenly very interested in our presence.

'These girls have done nothing but lie since they arrived,' Travis scoffed. 'Why would we believe anything they said?'

'The only lie we were forced to tell was because you decided to shag us!' Katy spat.

I turned to Zola and back to the room, packed with board members. 'Not all of us,' I felt the need to explain, 'just her.'

One of the older gentlemen sighed, clearly having no time for any of this. 'What is the evidence? Of the sabotage, I mean.'

'No, I refuse even to countenance it! I want them out, Jimmy! Now!' Fee held her hand up, palm facing Katy's face as if she couldn't stomach us even a second longer.

'We are going back to Scotland after this, I promise,' Zola said. 'Just let us tell you. We've figured it all out – and you do need to know.'

Jimmy turned to the boardroom and shrugged.

'Be quick,' another of the older men replied.

I turned to Jimmy and quietly mouthed, 'I'm sorry.' Then, I looked at the board members and delivered my answer: 'It's Fee Link.'

I said it without any preamble in case they changed their minds and called for security. My hands were shaking, but I felt brave, determined to stand up for Jimmy.

'What the fuck?' Fee twisted her face up, looking as if I'd just made the most ridiculous statement she'd ever heard.

Jimmy glanced at Fee, watching her reaction, then back at us. He slowly shook his head in disbelief.

'I don't know why, but Fee is behind all of this,' I added, feeling every inch of his pain. It was his sister who I was accusing, and I knew how much he loved her.

There were gasps, then mumbles of confusion.

'You don't believe this shit, do you?' Fee laughed, shaking her head. 'It's not true! Why are y'all trying to ruin my life? First, Travis and now this?' She covered her face and pretended to sob. 'I can't take any more of this!'

Ethan pulled back his chair. 'It is true. I ran every poor investment and it always came back to the same employee. The evidence is there in black and white.'

Gasps and groans came over the board as they dissected this development among themselves.

Britney was staying extremely quiet in her chair, and so I turned to her. 'And the lovely Britney was in on it too.'

'What?' Jimmy pushed back his chair; his hands squeezed into fists. I wasn't sure if he was angry at them or us.

'I . . . I . . .' Britney's face had turned purple with nerves and indignation. 'I only did it because she promised me VP!' She whimpered guiltily. 'Fee said I'd get a bigger office and a rise, I just had to sway the votes to get her brother out! It wasn't my idea, Jimmy, it was—'

'Enough!' Jimmy shouted, and I could see from his face that he was finding it hard to accept all of this. 'Why would you do this, Fee?' he asked, turning to his sister. She was stone-faced.

'Jimmy, what are you talking about?' she said. 'I had nothing to do with those investments.'

'They have the fucking evidence, Fee!' There was a pause. 'Look, I can call the investors in here and go through the business plans and the accounts if you . . .'

The entire room was weighed down by the heaviest silence imaginable.

'No,' she muttered.

Jimmy's shoulders dropped at the realisation of what she'd done. His breathing was far too rapid, like he couldn't find the words or the oxygen in his lungs to quiz her. 'Did you do this deliberately?' he finally gasped. 'Did you try to turn my company against me?'

Her face was stern, impassive; she showed no emotion whatsoever.

'But why, Fee? I'd have given you any money you needed. Any job.' His face contorted in utter devastation.

'Job?' She seemed enraged. 'I didn't want any other job, I wanted yours. Hell, I've earned it.' She slammed her hands on the desk, making me step back. 'I work harder than anybody else at this company, and who gets the legacy? Who do the press remember? YOU!' she almost snarled, looking down on her brother. 'Even after all the shit you put Ma through as a kid, in and out of juvie, while I looked after her. But still, she obsesses over you, the golden boy!' She put on a high-pitched voice, imitating her mother: 'When is Jimmy coming over? Why can't you make my dinner the way Jimmy does? Why can't you be more like your brother?' She rolled her eyes. 'I am done living in your shadow, Jimmy Link. I deserve this fucking company!'

My jaw was hanging open, and not just at the spite in her voice. I couldn't believe she was spilling the tea so easily.

'Then perfect little Ella snapped you up and I must admit, it was great for me – you were so off your game, brother. But then my PI mentions that my deadbeat husband,' she rolled her eyes, glaring in Travis's direction, 'was cheating on me again – only this time it was with Katy, our newest employee.'

Katy pulled back her shoulders, furious. 'So, you stalked me!'

Fee laughed. 'I sent a few messages, that's all. Get over yourself, girl. I didn't want the app to launch, I wanted more heat on you, Jimmy, for the board, but someone tipped the media off and ruined the app better than I ever could!' She laughed, and I flinched at how evil the sound was. To think I was sucked in by this woman's blueberry muffins!

Zola rolled up her sleeves in disbelief. 'You're one sick, twisted bitch!'

Fee shrugged. 'I shot my shot, girl. You shot yours with the app, and we both lost. No investor will touch you now.'

I couldn't believe how crazy this psycho woman was. I had no idea it was her all this time. Fuck, I'd even felt sorry for her.

'And no company will touch you with a ten-foot barge pole, hen!' I replied sharply.

Fee sniggered. 'That's where you're wrong, though, *hen*. The board won't fire me, will you? Because you'd have to announce publicly what I'd done and, God knows, that would be bad press! Come on, you know I'm right. Give me a slap on the wrists and be done with it already.'

Jimmy had had enough. He walked past me and opened the conference room door. 'Get security up here now!' Then he looked at his sister. 'That's where you're wrong, Fee. Actions have consequences, and I'm not afraid of publicly shaming my sister when she's behaved this appallingly.'

Four security guards marched into the room.

'Remove my sister, Travis and Britney from the building, please, seize their laptops and revoke access to all areas of Flirtify. From immediate effect.'

'No, Jimmy. Wait. You can't do this!' Fee screamed. 'I'm your sister!'

He shook his head, turning the other way, while the three of them were physically escorted from the room.

Silence fell once more, and my friends and I glanced towards one another – our job was completed. We had done everything we'd set out to do, and so we, too, headed for the door. As I walked out, I turned back and locked eyes with Jimmy. He gave me a slight nod of appreciation, but I wondered if finding out the truth would actually end up hurting him more in the long run. We wandered back through the building at a much slower pace than we'd entered, in complete, crushing silence.

Chapter Forty-Eight

Ella

We found ourselves sitting in the Tick Tock diner a few blocks down from the office, and within twenty minutes, we were surrounded by cookies & cream milkshakes and a giant plate of fluffy buttermilk pancakes. The food looked amazing, but I wasn't even sure I could eat. I couldn't believe what had just happened, what Fee had admitted to. Zola was texting Ethan, trying to gauge the aftermath of it all, while Katy sat shovelling warm pancakes loaded with strawberries and Nutella down her gob.

'How could Fee do that to her own family?' Katy said as the pancake pile diminished, shaking her head.

Zola agreed, taking a long slurp of her milkshake. 'She's one crazy ass bitch.'

I nodded. 'Did you see his face? Jimmy was devastated.'

'She really thought she'd get away with it,' Zola said.

I scooped a chunk of ice cream out my milkshake. 'She almost did!'

Zola sniggered. 'Yeah, thank God for Ethan! He's the best.'

Katy agreed, still munching. 'Oh my God, literally. He's got this whole hyper clever, obnoxious thing going on, but it's like so fucking hot.'

I screwed my face up at the thought of Katy being attracted to him, noticing Zola's cheeks flush.

'I just wish we could launch the app.' Katy had moved on again, as a new thought crossed her mind. 'We're not going to get paid now, which means we're going to head back to Glasgow completely fucking skint. Do we even have enough in the business account for flights?'

I felt my head fall onto my hands. Not having to worry about money for so long with the Flirtify company credit card had allowed me to avoid reality. Now it was crashing back as I realised my own financial vulnerability. Since launching our own business, our income had never been dependable, and we were only scraping by before.

'Probably, just enough for flights.' I sighed. 'We should start advertising for jobs on our socials again.'

Zola shook her head. 'It's so shit how it's all turned out. So unfair. We have been wrongly accused of so much because of Philip fucking Khan. People are slating us, when in fact we have been the ones who have saved an international company from collapse.'

I nodded, frustration and sadness warring inside me. As unfair as it all was, I took comfort in the memories – at least we'd lived the most exhilarating, wild few months of our lives together in New York, side by side.

Katy was still munching through her pancakes. 'We should make a TikTok about it. Make a plea to investors?' She shrugged.

I glanced up at Zola, knowing her idea wasn't a bad plan.

Zola was swaying. 'But what would we say, if we were to do the TikTok? There is so much shit that's happened here,' she replied.

I sat up, feeling my brain firing into action. 'Well, we can't mention that Fee was the stalker; she could sue us, and we all know how Americans love to go to court. But we could say we've created this great dating app to make dating safe again and the media has spread untrue stories about us . . . That . . . I don't know . . .'

'That have made investors pull out. We play it like a conspiracy,' Zola added. 'Americans love to go to court and they love a conspiracy theory. We play it off like, *Why are they trying to stop this app from launching?*'

Katy was grinning, Nutella covering the sides of her mouth. 'Then we make a plea for investors!' She clapped her hands. 'It's worth a shot? I mean, Flirtify own the rights to the app? So, we can't sell it.' She shrugged.

I smiled, knowing that it was probably our only shot, but I hoped Jimmy wouldn't mind. I hoped it wouldn't paint his company in an even worse light.

We finished off our meal and headed back to the apartment to set up and rehearse our TikTok.

We dressed in plain, modest clothing, keen to rebrand our image from the money-grabbing whores that the media had painted us as, and I set up my phone on a tripod facing the sofa.

The three of us sat close, ready. We'd thoroughly gone through who would say what, careful not to blame anyone outright, but to be suggestive enough that it wasn't our fault.

My phone pinged from the tripod, and I stood up, wondering if Jimmy might be reaching out.

Philip: *Can we talk? I know I fucked up. X*

I screwed my face up, ignoring the message, and pressed record, running back to the sofa.

Katy began, 'My name is Katy, and these are my friends, Ella and Zola, and we want to tell you our side of the story.'

I jumped in next. 'We were brought over to New York to develop and create a dating app that would help Americans really find true love. And we put together a way to finally eliminate time-wasters and spot abusers or narcissists before having to meet them. We had the privilege of working with Flirtify, one of the largest technology companies in the United States, and together we created something magnificent.'

Zola tilted her head dramatically, then faced the camera. 'Unfortunately things turned sour. We held a pre-launch party with investors, influencers and the media to reveal how our app, Stars and Swipes, would change the way dating works today. However, during the pre-launch, the media launched a bitter attack on us, on the integrity of our characters, and they didn't hold back in spreading untrue stories.'

Katy rubbed her eyes as if she were in tears. 'We will attach some of the awful headlines below,' she said with a demure sob. *Jesus*, I thought, *give this gal an Oscar*. 'And this caused two major investors to pull out, making our app unable to launch this Thanksgiving.'

I rubbed Zola's shoulder, then returned to the camera. 'Stars and Swipes is an app for safeguarding both women and men, and we don't understand who has leaked false information, but someone out there is trying hard *not* to protect the American people. Last year alone, thirty-one per cent of women were assaulted by someone they met on a dating app. Thirty-one per cent!'

Katy shook her head, sorrowfully. 'And Stars and Swipes, the app for the people, for you, hasn't been allowed to launch. So, I ask why? Who doesn't want to protect you? Why have they spread such horrible rumours about us?'

'We have been stalked, threatened and humiliated, all while someone out there has tried to force us to leave this app alone. But we will not stand down, we are determined to share our story.'

I stood up and paused the recording. 'We smashed that.' I grinned proudly to my friends. 'And amazing emotion from both of you!'

Zola smirked, flicking back her hair. 'It is true, though, even if all we do is clear our names, then it's got to be worth a shot.'

Once it was uploaded, I sat back on the sofa with my friends, scrolling through photos of Jimmy and me in my camera roll. I wondered how he was holding up and whether I should reach out. But I understood that he needed space. So much had happened between us that was unfixable now, especially as the reality of returning home to Glasgow loomed closer, but I cared for him and wanted to make sure he was OK, regardless of how things had unravelled between us.

My phone pinged again.

Philip: *Are you home? Or still in NYC?*

'Ewww! Leave me alone!' I screamed at my device.

Zola laughed, lifting her head. She had been playing the video we just made on repeat, commenting back to everyone to help the algorithm prioritise us. 'Philip?'

I nodded. 'Yep!'

Zola returned to her screen, then sat bolt upright. 'No way! Flirtify have reposted our video!' She gasped. 'They have two million followers!'

Katy lunged over our laps. 'Shut up!'

I grinned, grateful for the repost. I wasn't sure if Jimmy would have been pissed about the video, especially since it heightened the drama around his company. But I was glad he reposted it, and relief washed through me, knowing his anger wasn't directed at us anymore.

I snuck off into my bedroom, took out my phone and messaged him.

Ella: *I know how difficult that must have been today. Thinking of you x*

I hovered, staring at my message as he read it almost instantly, but nothing came back. My breath caught – what was he thinking? I sat frozen, hope and dread battling inside me, desperate for even a single word to confirm he was all right.

After a while Zola and Katy drifted in, both still staring at their phones.

Zola laughed. 'The comments are gold!'

Katy grinned. 'It's been shared three thousand times.'

They dived into my bed, cuddling up with me, as we watched the number of views climb, knowing we were slowly clearing our name.

'Guys,' Zola said eventually, popping down her phone. 'We do have to think about going home,' she said. 'Our work is done, and we can't stay here forever.'

I shimmied down the bed, knowing she was right but feeling a pang of sadness at the reality of leaving. Returning home meant facing uncertainty, facing a small apartment. It meant facing a city where Jimmy Link was thousands of miles away.

Katy sighed. 'Let's look at flights tomorrow. Today, let's just enjoy going viral.'

Zola giggled, picking up her phone again. 'Deal! Ella, you good with that?'

I nodded, the ache in my chest flaring up. 'Back to reality,' I said with a wobbly smile, grief threatening to leak from my voice at the thought of leaving all the mess and magic of New York behind.

Chapter Forty-Nine

Ella

The following morning, I woke up at five, keen to get a run in before finally heading back to Glasgow. After mentally mapping my route and setting my watch, I aimed to reach the Brooklyn Bridge at sunrise. I stretched quickly, pulled on my favourite Gym Shark beige set, then added a body warmer for the chilly New York air. When I was ready, I slipped out of the apartment and started running. The cool wind felt fresh against my skin; almost no one was out yet as I followed the river and soaked in my surroundings. A ferry passed and I smiled, watching it drift along the calm water before settling into a steady pace. I passed through the towering buildings that seemed to soar from the sky, each one bigger and shinier than the next, then I smiled as I saw the Statue of Liberty standing proudly across the water. Soon, I rounded the curve of Lower Manhattan and the Brooklyn Bridge appeared, more iconic and impressive than ever. I picked up speed, catching the first rays of sunrise glinting off the buildings. Reaching the bridge, I couldn't stop grinning as my footsteps echoed on the wooden planks of the walkway. The sky shifted to a glowing orangey rose, and at the midpoint, I paused – taking in every inch of the city. The water below seemed silver, night melting into day. I held the bridge's rails, knowing I'd remember this moment forever.

'Ella?' I heard someone call out my name.

I turned, almost dazzled by the rising sun. I could see a man in an all-black jogging suit, a North Face hat pulled down to keep his ears warm.

My eyes widened in surprise; I could hardly believe it.

'Jimmy,' I gasped. 'You're here.'

He grinned, breathless from his run, then walked towards me, pausing his Apple watch. 'Yeah, I changed up my route today. Decided to watch the sunrise,' he said, gesturing towards the sky, now brighter than only a minute earlier. 'Couldn't really sleep . . . so . . .'

He joined me at the rail, still panting, and together we gazed out at the morning unfolding.

'Are you OK?' I asked, knowing there was no way anyone could be OK after the fucking madness that went down yesterday. Everything had changed between us, and I could feel it. It was strange being beside him and not touching, not flirting, but too much had happened now for it ever to go back to like it was.

'I'll get there. Now that I know, it's easier, I guess,' he said.

I hummed, torn. There was so much I wanted to say, but nothing felt right. Only a few days ago, he was my boyfriend, then he left me in my apartment begging for his love. I got it, I totally did. I'd fucked up, and I knew that helping him keep his company was the least I could do, but I really didn't deserve any more from him after what I did.

'Jimmy I . . .'

'I saw your TikTok,' he said. We both smiled as we spoke at the same time. 'I thought it was great, but kinda timid for what you could have said. It kept a lot of the team up all night,' he added, laughing.

I felt my stomach pang again, hoping it didn't cause him more grief. 'Fielding the media?' I asked.

'Uh-huh.' He turned his body round to face me, his elbow leaning on the bridge. 'And a pretty wealthy European company have seen it. They have offered to invest the rest of the money,' he said.

I nearly choked.

'They have only one condition,' he said, shrugging as if it might be a problem, 'that it must launch during Thanksgiving week, as planned.'

'That's this week!' I laughed. 'We can't make that happen in that time . . . I guess?' I asked.

He placed a hand on his hat, rubbing it. 'Technically, it could. But there's a lot of heat on the app, on my company, Ella. Maybe keeping quiet for a bit, and launching it next year, would work best for all of us.' He was still undecided. 'I was going to swing by today and discuss it with you.'

I gazed at the sky, now brilliant with light. 'A lot of heat on the app – good and bad press – with all eyes on you, Jimmy. Maybe act while everyone's paying attention,' I quipped. 'I think you should go for it.' Knowing it would benefit me just as much than returning home to an empty fridge and a debt letter for not paying my gym membership for months.

He laughed, acknowledging my influence over him.

'I knew you'd say that, Ella.' He chuckled under his breath. 'I'll be honest with you, I'm just so tired – exhausted by the drama and the infighting and now the fallout. I don't know if I have a big launch left in me.'

I placed my hand on top of his, immediately feeling his breath pick up from my touch. 'I'm sorry I wasn't honest with you, Jimmy. I thought I could fix it all, but you deserved better than that.'

'Ella, no, I get it,' he said. 'You were protecting Katy, protecting yourself. I was just mad as hell.' He breathed out a puff of frustration. 'I should have replied last night. I didn't know what to say,' he admitted softly.

I smiled. 'No, no, I get it. It was mental. I didn't know if I should have come round to check on you or . . .'

Jimmy stood up straighter and side-eyed me. A tiny cheeky smile appeared on his face.

'Well, that would have been nice,' he admitted softly, suggestively, then he reached out his hand and held my chin.

I closed my eyes, not wanting to see the pain I was about to cause him. 'Jimmy, you should know, I'm leaving New York,' I admitted. 'Zola is looking at flights, probably as we speak, and we are planning to head home in the next day or two.'

When I finally opened my eyes, his face still mirrored disappointment.

'It's been amazing, and yes, fucking insane at times, but this isn't my life. It's just not.' I shook my head and his hand fell by his side.

'Because of Fee?' he asked, and I could see his embarrassment at his sister's actions.

I shook my head. 'No, because Glasgow's my home. We have created the app. Our job is done.' I smiled. I knew he was wondering where he fitted into all of this, but truthfully, I wasn't sure. I loved my flat back home, even if it was small, and my life with my friends. I wasn't about to risk all of that for a fantasy.

'Well, what about the launch? Will you wait till Thanksgiving?' he asked, his eyes focusing on the sky, on the bridge, anywhere but my face.

I laughed, confused. 'What do you mean? You said you didn't want to launch this week.'

Jimmy sighed, forcing himself to make eye contact. 'And you said you did. Look, we have an investor; we could wrap up this whole deal for you. If you're in?'

I grinned. 'It's two days away! You said . . .'

'The work has all been done, Ella. You planned it all! Remember? Show up and enjoy the launch you deserve. And I promise to keep my sister more than a ten-block radius from all of us. She won't get anywhere near us.' He paused, and I saw the sadness in his eyes. 'I've stepped up my security too.'

'What's happening then? Will you get the money back?'

'Hopefully.' Jimmy hummed. 'I have a good lawyer. Hey, I'll tell you about it at the launch. How about that?' He smirked, hoping some juicy gossip would be enough to persuade me.

I hesitated, unsure if this launch had simply become a way to keep me here longer, knowing it made letting go harder.

'But you know I'll have to leave afterwards. I have to get back to living my life, to working,' I said.

He grinned. 'I do understand, Ella.'

'OK, well, I guess we're giving the app the launch it deserves,' I finally agreed.

We stood together, watching as the city came alive. Jimmy lifted his arm and tightened it around my shoulder as we took everything in together.

It felt like a fresh start was on the way. My New York chapter was closing, and soon I'd be heading home changed, confident, but with a piece of my heart always belonging to this city, and to Jimmy Link.

Chapter Fifty

Ella

I entered the apartment to Zola screeching and jumping, while Katy stumbled down the hallway at her noise. Ethan stood nearby, grinning at Zola's excitement.

'What is it?' Katy moaned. 'It's too early, Zola! Sssshhh!'

Zola screamed again, jumping up and down. 'We have an investor! The launch is back on!'

I smiled, knowing Jimmy must have emailed the board.

'Shut up!' Katy bellowed, but still joining Zola in a dance party. 'Ella?' Katy beckoned me. 'This is good news, we'll get paid!' She screamed again, in joyful realisation of how much this would benefit us financially too.

I laughed. 'I know. I know! I met Jimmy this morning,' I admitted, noticing their jumps had suddenly halted.

'You met Jimmy?' Zola looked shocked, as if I had been keeping it a secret.

'Did you meet him for breakfast?' Katy asked, still giggling, completely hyper from the news. 'Did he give you Jimmy's special link sausage?' She began thrusting up and down, while Ethan stood rigid as fuck.

I walked over to the sofa and sat down. 'No, I met him by chance, while I was out for my run. It was nice. He told me about the investors, and I said we should go for it.'

Ethan nodded. 'He's called a meeting; the investor is joining us today to sign the paperwork.'

I beamed, overwhelmed – happy and ecstatic that we made it, but also sad it was ending.

'I should go,' Ethan said, lifting his bicycle helmet from the countertop and strapping it on. 'I just wanted to deliver the news.'

Zola blushed as he passed her. 'See you,' he called out. She waved back.

My two friends sat down beside me, ready to hear the Jimmy chat. I called out, 'Ethan, who is the investor anyway?'

He turned his head. 'Khan Enterprise.'

My heart froze. I felt dizzy.

I heard the lift doors close, and I looked to my friends, who seemed even more gobsmacked than I was.

'He doesn't mean Philip Khan, does he?' Katy asked.

I pulled out my phone and began frantically texting Philip.

Ella: *TELL ME YOU ARE NOT THE INVESTOR!!!!!*

Philip: *You're welcome?*

Ella: *No, you're not welcome, Philip! This has fuck all to do with you??*

I paused, waiting for a reply, but nothing.

Zola pulled my phone from my hand. 'OK, think for a second, yeah? He is doing us a favour.'

I shook my head, feeling all my emotions build. 'He has to involve himself again, though. He will take credit for this brilliant app we've created, Zo. I know he will. I wanted this for me! I had to do this for me, for us! Not for fucking Philip Khan.'

I felt Katy's hand rub my back. 'Maybe he is doing it because he feels bad he ruined it in the first place?'

I sank my head in my hands, worrying about having both Philip and Jimmy in the same meeting room together. Would they swap stories? *Jimmy will think I'm bat shit crazy when he finds out about this one*, I thought. My heart raced. I wanted the app to launch, but really wished it could be done without Philip's help.

'This isn't the end of the world, Ella,' Zola said, keeping me calm.

I paced, debating whether to call Philip or Jimmy, weighing the pros and cons.

At once, our three phones pinged and we leapt towards them. It was an email from Flirtify.

We can confirm that the launch of Stars and Swipes will go ahead on Thursday, with grateful thanks to Khan Enterprise for investing in our product. We look forward to seeing you all at the Four Seasons, ready to celebrate. Congratulations to all involved in this project, especially the creators, Zola, Ella and Katy.

All at Flirtify have enjoyed working alongside these three Glaswegian ladies and hope to collaborate again.

Sincerely yours,
Jimmy Link.

My shoulders slumped. Philip was involved, but our app would launch, and I really hoped it could change the American dating scene. But the launch was now tarnished with Philip Khan's unasked-for investment.

Jimmy: *The deal is done! I have so much paperwork to read over, but I'm glad I got to see you this morning. You will always be my first thought as the sun breaks x*

I read his message over and over, clutching my phone. This cunt was smoother than Rabbie Burns. He did something to me anytime I thought about him, and it scared me. I didn't want to lead him on or complicate things.

Ella: *Glad I saw you too x*

It was simple – maybe too simple. My mind was a blur, my heart heavy with confusion and longing.

By one, I got productive – chasing vendor emails and ensuring our launch stayed on track. I couldn't handle another setback, so I got to work properly, while Zola searched Skyscanner for the cheapest way home.

Around five, the lift door pinged open, and I stretched my neck out to see a huge bunch of flowers arrive, swamping Otis, the doorman.

'Jesus!' I laughed. 'Who are they for?' I sat up, placing the laptop to the side.

'Miss Ella,' he raised a brow, with a kind smirk. 'My shift just ended, so I thought I'd pop up with them.' He passed me the flowers and grinned.

'That was kind of you,' I said, sniffing the vast array of flowers. 'Want a drink or something to eat? You must be cold at that door all day.' I put the flowers on the table and stood.

Otis leaned forward. 'No, ma'am. It's an honour.' He smiled. 'I was brought up in the roughest neighbourhood in this city. I feel grateful every damn day standing at that door. Hell, I hadn't even seen a building this grand till I got here.' He pointed to the floor and laughed.

'Do you miss it?' I asked. 'Your old neighbourhood?'

Otis looked shocked, as if I'd asked a trick question. 'Every damn day, but it ain't like this. My life is better here, but you can never take away your past; you feel it in your soul. When someone asks me where I'm from, I say the Bronx, as proudly as I can. It shaped me, Miss Ella, you know?'

I grinned. 'I get it,' I said, thinking how much I missed home – the fresh cold air, the banter, the nightlife, the accents.

'I'll go now, but you enjoy those gorgeous flowers, now. There's a message inside too.' He waved and entered the lift.

I leaned over the flowers again, lifting the card-sized envelope, wondering if Jimmy had sent them after our early morning run. There was so much tension which remained between us, so much love. I knew I could feel it.

I ripped open the envelope and unfolded a letter. As my eyes scanned down the writing, my heart picked up the pace.

Dear Pilates,

I know you are probably reading this, wondering why I haven't come up and said what I'm about to say to your face, but the truth is – you won't allow me to! That's not a criticism, it's one of the things I adore about you. I know you're already aware that I invested in the app, and it's not by any means a play on you, but perhaps an apology for destroying something you worked so hard on. I also know this doesn't make what I did any better, but I am trying. I'm sorry that I have hurt you, Ella. I moved on far too quickly, my ego was hurt, and I acted out of character.

But I know I want you, no one else, ever. We have enjoyed so many amazing memories together, so many inside jokes, and I can't let any of that go. You opened up to me, let your guard down – finally – and I didn't appreciate that. But now I do.

Please don't be angry at the investment. I am trying to make things right. (And hopefully make some money out of it, if it's as good as you promised.)

I'll look forward to seeing you at the launch.

Always yours,

Philip

I scrunched up the letter, then let it drop to the floor. I felt my face grow warm as I tried to hold back the tears. I wasn't sure why he kept pushing this. I let out a sob, remembering how we met, those first meetings, the first time we had sex; he was practically removing dust from my vagina, it had been so long. He made me glow again, made me feel sexy, until he didn't. Slowly but surely, everything else piled up and I became less of a priority for Philip. I seemed to be the only one pouring everything into our relationship at the end, and he would simply waltz in when he felt like it and control exactly what we did and when we did it. But I didn't feel like that with Jimmy. He pushed me to be better, encouraged me to grow. He asked me things, remembered what I liked and what I didn't. I couldn't help but think that maybe I was destined to meet Jimmy, just for a short time, to remind myself of the good men out there, to show me how love is supposed to feel. I curled up on the sofa and sobbed, full of sadness, for the two men I had to lose to get myself back.

Chapter Fifty-One

Zola

It was the evening of the launch party, and Zola, Katy and Ella had gotten ready in their most elegant dresses. Ella practically shone in a silver floor-length dress encrusted with tiny jewels and crystals, while Katy kept it more classic in a black floor-length number with a huge split up the leg. Zola had more trouble deciding, always keen to make a trend statement, and in the end, she opted for a puffy, Cinderella-style navy-blue gown with white gloves that came up to her elbows. The three friends sipped champagne, waiting for the car to arrive. Zola noticed Ella being particularly quiet, and she wasn't sure if it was because Philip would be at the ball, or Jimmy would. The girls had booked their flights home to Glasgow the day before and had only twenty-four hours left in New York.

Zola raised her glass. 'To New York. It's been tough, full of tears, but it's brought us closer.'

The three of them clinked their glasses together.

'To Stars and Swipes,' Katy added. 'The app that's going to change the world.'

They toasted again.

The intercom buzzed. Zola grinned. 'This is it! Ready?'

Ella nodded, slightly zoned out.

'Ethan's going to be at the party!' Katy said, suddenly energetic.

Zola swung her head around. 'How do you know?' she said, watching Katy reply.

'He's texted me, obvs!' she said, still typing. 'He's picked out a nice suit for tonight too.'

Zola's face fell into a smile. 'He looks good in anything.'

The three friends left the apartment and headed into the sleek black limo Jimmy had arranged for them to travel in style. As Zola stepped in, she noticed how silent Ella was and gently rubbed her arm to comfort her.

'It's going to be fine,' she said reassuringly, as the car began moving. Katy was so busy texting on her phone that she didn't even notice.

'My head's just fucked, Zola,' Ella admitted as the car sped through the glittering city lights.

'Why? What's going on?'

Ella's lip trembled. 'I loved Philip, but he hurt me so much. Now he wants me back, but I don't want to be hurt again.' She sighed. 'And I have to say goodbye to Jimmy, the only genuinely nice guy I've ever met.'

She turned to the window, thinking.

'Philip's maybe got in my head a little,' she said at last. 'He said he got me to open up, stopped me from being uptight and lonely like I was before, and he's sort of right.'

Zola squeezed her hand. 'So what? Curtis taught me how to cook spaghetti – doesn't mean I stick around for him.'

'What if he has changed, and I'm just too scared to try again?' Ella said. 'I was happy at the start with Philip in Glasgow. And what if I'm only clinging onto Jimmy because I know it's ending. Fuck, I feel like I did when I was fourteen and had to leave my Turkish boyfriend, Usif, after a two-week Marmaris trip.' She almost smiled. 'Jeez, it was awful.'

Zola pushed Ella's head onto her shoulder. 'Do you know what I think? I think you meet some people in life who teach you things, yeah? Particularly about yourself. So, imagine, life is this one big journey, in this big fancy limo, OK?'

Ella smiled. 'OK . . .'

'And some people in life jump in your limo for a ride, they sometimes teach you great things, then have to get off, because it's your fucking limo, babe. Some people's journeys will last longer than others, too; all the while, you're learning, you're changing.'

'So . . .' Ella shrugged. 'You think Philip should get out of my limo?'

Zola giggled. 'Babe, he was out of your limo a long time ago! Thatt cunt's trying to catch back up, but you're going way too fucking fast!' She winked.

'And Jimmy?' Even saying his name hurt.

'Jimmy might just be one of the awesome people who come in for a short time and make the drive incredible, but that's up to you, I guess.'

Ella agreed, taking a deep breath as the car slowed down, pulling up at the Four Seasons.

'You do realise she heard that whole limo analogy thing on TikTok?' Katy said. 'I saw it too!'

'And you do realise you'd need a fucking double-decker bus for the number of cunts you have let ride your limo!' Zola pushed her on the shoulder, and we all began laughing.

The driver opened the car door and allowed Katy to step out on to the red carpet, then Zola. Zola turned back and watched Ella hover, 'Come on, babe. We got you,' she said.

But Ella looked terrified. 'I can't. I don't want to,' she admitted.

Katy lowered her head. 'Ella, it's our night! What are you doing? Come on.'

Zola crouched down, too. 'You've worked so hard on this, Ella. You deserve to celebrate.'

Ella managed a smile. 'I know I have, but I'm going to enjoy it more alone, somewhere I can actually hear myself think, somewhere it is my achievement and not Philip's. You two can handle the speeches, right?'

Zola grinned, feeling proud of her friend's decision but also gutted she was missing out. 'Absolutely. Unless you want us to come with you? We could patch this full night, really leave New York in style?'

Ella shook her head, laughing. 'No, I think I'd rather be alone. I'm sorry. I just really need to do this.'

The driver closed the door and headed back inside the car. Zola and Katy stepped out to the bright lights of the gorgeous hotel and walked up the steps, waving to the assembled photographers.

'Where is she going?' Katy whispered, posing for the pictures. 'Do you think she's OK?'

Zola nodded. 'She's strong as hell. She'll be fine.'

They entered the grand hall, where groups of stunningly dressed people surrounded them as a beautiful singer sang on stage. Katy pointed, noticing the gratitude tree that Ella had spoken about. People surrounded it, writing little notes of what they were grateful for, before hanging them on the tree. Exquisite round tables were set out perfectly with candelabras decorating the centre. Zola spotted Ethan writing and tapped him on the shoulder.

'What are you grateful for then?' she asked. 'Working with me?'

'Yes. And meeting you. All of you,' he said as Katy joined them.

'Great venue,' Katy said. 'You look so handsome, Ethan,' she added with a giggle like a crazed teenager.

'Thanks.'

Zola lowered her head as Katy complimented him. She knew she had feelings for Ethan, but she wasn't entirely sure what they were yet.

'Er . . . Zola, would you perhaps like to dance when the band plays?'

Zola glanced at Katy, who went from smiling to glaring.

'I like to dance too!' Katy butted in.

But Ethan seemed to ignore Katy and stood awkwardly, as if he had to get something off his chest and now was the only time he could do it. 'I wasn't sure if I should ask you, but now you're leaving and—'

'Yes,' Zola cut him off, thankful for the gesture. She turned to Katy, 'If you don't mind? I mean . . .'

She shrugged. 'Sure, I don't care.'

'I won't dance with him if you don't want me to, Katy. I just . . .'

'See that bouncer guy who follows Jimmy about? He has been seriously checking me out since we arrived. I'm going to find out his name and check his Insta!' Katy flicked back her hair, then wandered up to stand beside her latest love interest.

Zola turned back to Ethan. 'I sort of thought you and Katy maybe had a thing going on?' she said, curious, and needing to be honest, but not wanting to seem insecure.

Ethan laughed. 'No, she's sweet, but too much like my sister.'

Zola shook her head, smiling as she took in Ethan. He was helpful, kind, honest and incredibly smart. She knew she was beginning to like him more than as friends. 'Well, I would love to dance when the band plays.' She leaned forward and kissed him on the cheek. He stood up straight and grinned. 'In America, we kiss more like this.' Ethan placed his hand on Zola's lower back, pulling her close to him. He grinned and then pushed his lips against hers. Instantly, she felt a rush of adrenaline and desire, opening her mouth and snogging him. She felt his hands move up and down her back.

'Wow!' She laughed as they eventually broke away. 'I think I prefer the American way.'

'Mmm . . . me too.' Ethan smiled. He seemed relaxed, happy. Zola blushed.

'I should make sure Katy's OK.' Zola's eyes skimmed the room, trying to track her friend.

'I'll get us drinks and come find you.'

As Zola headed back into the crowd in search of Katy, she noticed Philip and Jimmy were cornering her. Zola picked up the pace and pushed them back a little.

'Hey! What's going on?' Zola hissed.

Katy popped her hand on her hip, turning slightly to face the others. 'These two want to know where Ella is. I said I don't know.' She pushed Philip's shoulder back as he towered over her, asserting some space between them.

'And she's right,' Zola concluded. 'In the car, she said she needed space and didn't want to come in.'

Jimmy rubbed his forehead. 'I didn't realise the investor was her ex! Is that why she's gone?' He seemed panicked, as if he'd only just found out.

'Yip, he's her ex, all right,' Zola said as she ran her eyes up and down Philip.

'Do you know where she'd go? I do need to talk to her,' Jimmy continued.

'And so do I!' Philip nudged Jimmy with his shoulder. 'Did she get my letter?'

'She got it and read it. She still needs space,' Zola said, holding her hands up.

Jimmy leaned in. 'Zola, what did she say, exactly? Please. Think.'

'She said she needed a place to think, somewhere quiet, away from it all.' Zola shrugged. 'I have no idea where she's gone, all right!'

Philip sneered. 'So, she's hitting the fucking library, then?'

Jimmy, on the other hand, smiled, his face lifting into a grin. 'Thank you, thank you, both!' Then he bolted towards the exit.

Philip turned to Zola and then to Katy, confused about what had just happened. 'If he worked that out from that description, he fucking deserves her,' Philip muttered, pacing the floor anxiously.

Chapter Fifty-Two

Ella

I finally stood at the top of the Empire State Building, gazing out at the twinkling lights of New York City; it was everything I had dreamed of. Crowds gathered around me, nudging their loved ones at my ridiculous dress and skyscraper heels, but I didn't care, because finally I could breathe again. I closed my eyes, inhaling the deepest, coolest breath, feeling it travel down my body. This city made me find myself again, it made me come alive again, and, OK, our visit had been packed with drama, stalkers and crazy men trouble, but we did make a difference here. We left our mark. I leaned my hands against the railing, looking down at the people who passed in the street below, wondering how many of them would one day find love because of the app we'd created. It felt rewarding, like I could finally let go of New York; I could say goodbye to the city now I had found myself again.

'I thought I might find you here!' I heard a deep American voice and turned in surprise. Jimmy stood there in his tuxedo, looking as handsome as ever, carrying a cute bunch of pink peonies.

I gasped, noticing people gawk at us. 'You're here! How?' I laughed, completely confused.

'I knew you had a thing for tall buildings,' he said softly, letting out a small laugh.

'Well, at least I'm not the only one totally overdressed now.' I smiled, glancing at my dress. As he got closer, he stood beside me.

'We missed you tonight,' Jimmy said, glancing out at the city.

My face twisted. 'I'm sorry, I just couldn't do it . . .' I admitted, knowing it sounded like a poor excuse.

Jimmy remained calm, his eyes still on the view. 'That's OK,' he replied coolly. 'Because of the last one? Were you worried or . . .'

I felt my chest tighten. 'I wasn't worried that anything would happen. I suppose I was scared to see you, if I'm being completely honest.' My vulnerability made me feel exposed, but I was done with lying to this man, lying to myself.

Jimmy turned to face me, a smile on his lips. 'OK, you gotta explain that one to me.'

I walked a few steps around the circular balcony, struggling to steady my voice. 'It's hard to see you when I know I'm going home. This is all about to end.' I rested my head against the railing, caught between frustration and sadness. 'I love my life in Scotland; that's my home. But then I met you and everything was great – until it wasn't. Now it's starting to feel good again, but I'm going home! Living here in New York isn't real life and I have to get back to reality, Jimmy.'

Jimmy smiled, understanding. 'So, you were scared.' He shrugged. 'That's understandable.'

'I just think that maybe I need to be on my own for a bit. I was with Philip, then I wasn't. Then I met you, and it's been honestly amazing.' I smiled, feeling tears build up, but I was trying hard to hold them in. 'I don't want to chase a man around a city I'm not even from.' I shrugged. 'I want an amazing life, of course! But I want a life that I've made, not one that my boyfriend has.'

Jimmy pushed a strand of hair back from my eyes. 'I understand, Ella.'

I sighed, thankful, grateful for how easily he seemed to get me.

'But us men, we're not all the same,' he said, a small grin edging from his lips. I instantly remembered him saying that on my first day at the office. 'I love you, and I respect you, and if you have to go back to Scotland, then I totally understand. But you do know there's more than one way to make a long-distance relationship work?' He nudged my shoulder playfully to lighten the mood.

'Is there? I asked ChatGPT and the figures are awful. It's basically pointless.' I managed a laugh through the snotters I was producing with those backed-up tears.

Jimmy giggled and said, 'Damn, I should have had Ethan hack that server and tell you there's a high success rate.'

I turned to him, the night sky twinkling around us. Every emotion surged to the surface. 'I will always love you, Jimmy Link, but I have to move on,' I said, feeling a lump in my throat the size of a basketball. I wanted to cry, to wail, to cling to his gorgeously muscled leg. But I steadied myself – I couldn't lose myself again, not now, not when I'd finally begun to like who I was becoming.

'And I will always love you too, every moment, every day,' he promised. We stared at one another for a few seconds. 'Well, I think we have sorted that out. I'm gonna let you enjoy your quiet time up here, Ella,' he said.

I watched him rub his eyes, then he handed me the pink peonies.

'Don't be a stranger, huh?' he called, stepping back a few steps.

I smiled, noticing the flowers he'd chosen, and then my gaze wandered to him. 'How did you know these were my favourites?' I asked, calling out to him.

He held out his arms. '*Gossip Girl*,' he said with a smirk. 'The same reason I knew you were up here!'

I lifted my head, stepping forward. 'Wait! You watched it?'

Jimmy looked at me curiously. 'You told me you loved it, so I thought I'd better catch up. Who would have thought Dan Humphrey, huh? My money was on Dorota!'

I felt my knees go weak. What the fuck was I thinking? My breath escaped my body and I ran up and wrapped my arms tightly around Jimmy and squeezed him. I laughed. I felt free, like I finally had my answer. He knew me, he took time to know everything about me, he had made an effort since the very first moment I met him. I leaned in and kissed him as hard as I could. Jimmy opened his mouth, and I felt his tongue wrap around mine. He pulled me closer, his body pushing into mine. Fuck, I'd missed this.

'Ella?' Jimmy eventually said, his eyes glossy with tears. 'What? What is it?'

I gulped down, still struggling to catch a breath, but for the first time it wasn't fear – just relief and certainty. 'You're not the same as him.'

'No, I'm not,' he muttered under his breath, and I worried that I'd hurt him. 'Of course, I'm not. But you still want to go home?'

I tilted my head, staring into his eyes. 'Well, I heard New York is stunning at Christmas?'

Jimmy kissed me hard again, but his lips felt soft against mine. It was perfect. He was perfect.

'I don't care where the fuck I am,' I said. 'I want you, Jimmy. I want this.'

'We can make it work out, Ella. Whatever we need, we can do it together, OK?' Jimmy promised.

I nodded, grateful and blessed to have *finally* found my happily ever after.

*

Jimmy and I headed to Central Park and sat on a picnic table in the blistering cold. I had messaged the girls to meet us and saw them wander into the park in their cocktail dresses and heels, giggling loudly. We watched Ethan try to steady Zola. She'd probably had way too much to drink, I thought with a smile.

As they approached, they grinned widely, noticing we were cuddled up together.

'So, you found her then?' Zola asked, pointing her tequila bottle towards us as she took a swig.

'I did.' Jimmy laughed, standing up to shake Ethan's hand. Ethan took hold of the tequila, laughing, then stepped away from the table. 'It's against the law to drink alcohol in the park,' he said. The boys walked over to a nearby bin, dumping the booze and allowing my friends and me to chat.

'Well . . . did you pump him in the park?' Katy whispered, leaning close.

Zola burst into a drunken cackle.

'No,' I replied.

'Not even a wee poke?' she moaned, her face falling. She knew she was the only one who'd been poked and dropped in this city.

'No! For fuck's sake!' I screeched, batting off her vodka breath.

Zola hugged me from behind, then slid onto the bench beside me. 'What does all of this mean then?' She raised a brow, drunkenly pointing towards Jimmy, while he chatted to Ethan on the grass a small distance away.

I bit my lip nervously, excitement and concern battling inside me. 'I guess it means we can stay for Christmas, if you guys are up for it?' I really wanted to be in New York with Jimmy, but I knew I'd struggle without my friends here too.

'Ehh . . . duh!' Zola let out a wild screech of excitement, as Katy grinned widely.

'We'll stay for however long you need us to, Ella,' Katy replied. 'But can you ask Jimmy if his bodyguard bouncer guy is single? He's come with us to meet you, but I couldn't get him to chat to me. Not a word!'

I turned my head to the bald, muscular figure standing a few metres away like a brick shit house.

'He's so hot! And he wouldn't talk to me, but I'm sure he was checking me out earlier,' she said, sending a cheeky wave over to Jimmy's head of security.

'Perhaps you need to wait till he's off duty,' I said. 'But, really?' I wasn't quite getting this thug look she seemed to be liking.

'Oh, come on, you know she has a thing for the Grant Mitchell-type, babe! I found out the hard way, remember?' Zola burst out laughing, recalling the time she walked in on Katy strumming herself to his documentary.

We let the laughter simmer and huddled together closely in the moonlit park.

'You know, this feels like the best day in the world,' I admitted. 'Look where we are, and at everything we've achieved.' I glanced over to the sparkling skyline glittering around us.

I felt Zola's drunken head nod in agreement.

Katy's gaze travelled around the glistening buildings. 'And we couldn't have done it without each other.'

I reached out for her hand and clutched it tightly. Because I knew, no matter who came on or off my limo journey in this lifetime, I wouldn't be able to carry on without my two very best friends.

Acknowledgements

I want to start by thanking my publisher, Zaffre, for backing this book and me from the very beginning. A special thank you to Melissa Cox, who has championed both me and this story every step of the way – your belief in it has meant everything.

Thank you to Georgia Marshall for all your hard work and dedication in getting this book out into the world, and to Enisha Samra for the incredible marketing campaign. Seeing these books out there never gets old, and so much of that is down to you.

Beth Whitelaw, thank you for being my right-hand woman – from organising my chaos to keeping everything (and me) on track. Chelsea Graham, thank you for bringing the audiobook to life so brilliantly, and to Lois, Emma and Grace for reading my story so beautifully.

I know there are people I've probably missed (and I'm sorry if I have), but together you are an incredible team. I feel very lucky to be part of Zaffre/Bonnier, and I can't wait for what's next.

To my management team at InterTalent – thank you for your constant support, guidance, and for always going above and beyond. You make this whole journey not only possible, but enjoyable. A special thank you to Milly Lean, Jonathan Shalit and Oscar Janson-Smith. I'm so grateful to have you in my corner.

Rosie McCafferty – thank you for proofreading this book (again), especially when I was deep in my "this is absolute rubbish and I'm quitting" era. You are the best kind of honest, the biggest confidence boost, and an actual lifesaver. I don't know what I'd do without you.

Claire Williams – my sidekick in life and in last-minute panic edits – thank you for stepping in when my eyes stopped working, and my brain followed shortly after. I love having you in our lives, and I am so, so grateful for everything you do for my family and me.

To all the Waterstones staff – especially across Glasgow – thank you for shouting about my books louder than I ever could. Your support genuinely means the world.

A huge thank you to the team at Glasgow Fort, who continue to go above and beyond. Walking past and seeing my books in the window still gives me goosebumps (and yes, I absolutely pretend I'm just casually passing and not staring like a weirdo). And thank you to Smiths Travel, especially Iain Rushworth, for your incredible support. Seeing my books front and centre in Glasgow Airport is one of those "I will never act normal about this" moments.

Mum and Dad – thank you for supporting me in every possible way, and for proudly telling absolutely everyone about your daughter's slightly inappropriate books. Your enthusiasm knows no bounds, and I love you for it. Andy and Les – thank you for everything you do, especially helping with the girls while I disappear into my own little writing world. I couldn't do any of this without you, and I am so lucky to have you both in my life.

To my best friends – Michelle Patterson, Emma McAuley, Lisa Scott, Sarah Scott, Maggie Donnelly, Lisa Murphy and Bianca Rinaldi – thank you for the chats, the chaos, the laughs, and the unconditional support. You are my people, my therapy, and occasionally my bad influence.

Christopher Williams – my favourite person. You came into my life and somehow made everything brighter, lighter, and a lot more fun. Thank you for holding everything together when I'm stressed, overwhelmed, and running on Monster Munch and Irn Bru. You make me laugh every single day, you support me without question, and you never let me forget who I am when I start doubting it. I see everything you do for our team, and I'm so grateful, even if I don't always say it enough. I am deeply thankful to have Kai, Claire, Albie, Uncle Jord, and Joe in our lives, too, all thanks to you. I love you – always. Sneaky creeps forever!

I also want to take a moment to remember Lynne Stewart, Chris's lovely mum, who we lost while I was writing this book. Lynne, you were so warm, kind, and full of life. You raised the most incredible son, and I see so much of you in him every single day. I know how proud you would be of him – and of all of us. You are so deeply missed and never far from our thoughts and daily conversation.

And to Joyce Anson, who also passed while writing this – the girls' gran, and such a huge part of my life.

Thank you for helping bring my kids up (and me), for always believing in me, and for championing me long before any of this existed. You made me feel like anything was possible, and that kind of love will stay with me forever. For taking us to New York just before we lost you – a place that means so much to all of us now. We all love and miss you, but I promise to keep our girls happy, and your memory (and your love of leopard print) will always live on in them.

And finally, to my two favourite girls in the world – Olivia and Grace.

You are the reason for everything. On the hardest days, you are the reason I keep going, and on the best days, you make them even brighter. I am so proud of you both, especially after such a difficult year. You are strong, kind, funny, and everything I could ever hope for.

New York will always be ours – and I thought about you every single day while writing this.

This book, and everything I do, is for you.

I love you to infinity and beyond, my gorgeous girls.

With all my love and a very full heart,
Sophie xx